Welcome to Wonderland

A DRAMEDY OF ACCEPTANCE, GROWTH, AND LOVE

BOBBIE CANDAS

WELCOME TO WONDERLAND

A Dramedy of Acceptance, Growth, and Love

Book cover design by Betty Martinez

ISBN: 9798853824324

For Jackie, Jeanne, Susie and Michael
Thanks for shared adventurers in heart, mind, and body

I love spring anywhere, but if I could choose I would always greet it in a garden.

--Ruth Stout

To nurture a garden is to feed not just the body, but the soul.

--Alfred Austin

The violets in the mountains have broken the rocks.

--Tennessee Williams

If a kiss could be seen, I think it would look like a violet.

--Lucy Maud Montgomery

CHAPTER 1

Violet is Blue

VIOLET HILL

Mother considers me awkward, graceless, and socially challenged, but always has hope for improvement. I disagree and think of myself as critically shy. Is there such a diagnosis? I've learned I do best when I can control limited social encounters. That's why I'm better working alone, in a world I'm comfortable and familiar with, the study of soil, seeds, and grasses.

I've been working as a research assistant with Dr. William Hirshfield. After finishing my masters at UT in Austin, I gratefully found my hidey-hole at the UT School of Environmental Sciences. After being hired, I realized it was the perfect job for me. For a year, we've been running experiments and collecting data on soil absorption, attempting to come up with a microbial substance that will turn arid lands into potential blooming fields of agriculture. All well and good for keeping me in my cozy, solitary research lab, but with the added bonus of working toward saving a warm and crowded planet.

Then yesterday happened.

Dr. Hirshfield called me unexpectedly to meet in his office. We normally only met every two weeks for consultations on experiments. I sat down across from his desk, with my sweating palms gripping the arm rests of the chair. The meeting opened with congenial small-talk. I said, "Hello."

As with most people I conversed with, I found it difficult looking at Hirshfield when he spoke. Today I found his floorboards especially interesting. Wide wood panels which had me wondering, were they deliberately distressed or actually marred from age? As he shuffled papers on his desk I reached down and touched the floor. Definitely faux distressed.

He nervously coughed and then continued, "Violet, I must say, your work has been exemplary, but..."

Oh shit... The proverbial *but.* I shuddered slightly.

As I pretended to be intrigued with the floor, Hirshfield said, "I'm afraid I have some bad news to share." He coughed again. "I'll just get right to it. I hate to tell you this, but our next year of NIH funding has been cut. They haven't renewed the terms of our project at the previous level and claim our results are not going as quickly as we initially projected."

He seemed to be talking to himself now, explaining his problems to the ceiling as my eyes nervously flitted up occasionally to watch. "Seems our study is on the low end of their priority scale regarding research grant money. But our idea has so much merit! It dovetails perfectly with climate change issues and food production for overpopulated areas. Anyway...it's probably all politics. Therefore—" He coughed a third time. *Nervous tick or avoidance? Either way, not a good sign*. "I'm having to cut most of my research staff, including your position."

Please no. Had I heard correctly? I was praying he'd single me out as too good to let go. But of course not. My eyes became moist and my body went cold. I had finally found my place in this chaotic world, my comfy, musty den. Where I could reach my fingers deep into sandy soil and disappear into another world within my microscope. I'd clock in for hours of uninterrupted work, eat a sandwich over my work station by myself, needing to only interact with others regarding information I was knowledgeable about.

Now apparently all that was gone.

And what remained? Going home to Mother? I was devastated. I felt like laying down on those faux floorboards and curling up in a ball.

"Dr. Hirshfield, p-perhaps p-part-time. Tw-Twenty-five hours a week?"

In case you missed that, I have a noticeable stutter, which seems to come into full bloom during times of stress.

"I only wish that were possible, Violet. The grant has been downgraded to include lab equipment, supplies, and compensation for only a few key personnel. I'm so sorry. This has all come as quite a surprise. So, we're making adjustments immediately; I can keep you for another two weeks. I wanted you to hear it from me, personally."

I mumbled, "Th-Thank you," then stood up, wrapped my arms across my chest, and meekly asked about a possible reference letter. He went back to shuffling papers and nodded, agreeing to my simple request. I quickly walked out with my head down, making my exit before he had the chance to shake my perspiring palm.

I spent the next few weeks desperately attempting to find a position with another research team within the department. There were several available for volunteer and credit work, but all paid positions were fully staffed. Although my educational credentials were excellent, my interviewing skills were a little shaky. I considered customer service positions, but they never seemed a good match, and I truly wanted to continue within my field of study.

At the end of the two-week period, I decided to call in for financial reinforcement. Via email, I sent my mother news of the change in job status, then requested funds to keep me in Austin while I continued to look for work, but instead of an electronic deposit, she offered this:

Dear Violet,

So sorry to hear about your job loss. I know you've been happy with your little research position. Sometimes these minor hiccups work out for the best. I think you need more stimulation and interaction in your work. When I visited, your lab job seemed so sterile and lonely. I'm sure I can line something up for you through my contacts in Dallas. Come home, darling. The guest house was recently redone and you're welcome to use it. It'll be fun hanging out together again. I believe I'll call Lexy and see if she can revise her schedule and set aside sessions for you. What day should I expect you? Can't wait to catch up! --Mother

She was not going to be sympathetic to my cause. I made a second stab at job hunting, knowing it was only a delay tactic. Was I being an ungrateful little bitch? Sort of. But I knew I'd have to deal with my mother's incessant smiling face, popping in without warning, spewing false cheer, urging me to conform to her standards, and always sending out subliminal messages regarding her underlying sense of disappointment in me.

It had been five years since I'd lived at home. My first year in the dorms had been a disaster. I was happier on my own, renting an apartment for three years while earning my bachelor's and another two for my masters, comfortably surviving in my small, quiet efficiency.

In contrast, Mother's home was palatial, but for me it was a luxurious prison sitting on a green oak-studded hill overlooking White Rock Lake in Dallas.

I dragged out my move. I felt no incentive to rush home knowing what lay ahead; struggling through painful interviews, going through clothing issues and social events with Mother. Yes, still a tender issue at age twenty-four. Then, once again, I'd start sessions with my speech therapist, Lexy.

Unfortunately, research assistant's pay was low, Austin rents were high, and the guest house at Mother's was free. Economically, it made sense. Emotionally, I was an unhappy wreck.

And who could I complain to? *Call 911* -- My mother is inviting me to move into her newly renovated guest quarters. *Put her on trial?* -- She insists on buying me new clothing suggested by her personal shopper at Neiman's. *Lock her up?* -- She's offering me therapy for an affliction which admittedly has recently become worse.

I was a pathetic whiner. Time to get up, pack it in, and get moving.

CHAPTER 2

The Gladiator

TURNER COOPER

The landline was ringing again but I didn't bother to pick up. Letting it go to voicemail, I listened to my wife's warm Texas accent roll softly through the office over the speaker of an antiquated answering machine.

Hi, there. It's Allie. Turner and I aren't here. You know what to do; bye now.

Sighing, I ruffled the soft shiny fur of our Irish Setter, Blaze. Leaning back on my leather sectional, I stretched my legs out over the ottoman, closed my eyes, and wondered how many more hours it would be before I could go back to bed without seeming too pitiful. Perhaps a half-tumbler of Dewar's Scotch and a movie would help pass the time. I silenced my cell and closed the office door so there would be no interruptions. Amazing how many solicitations there were after you signed up for the no-solicitation list. I never realized before... because I rarely was home to hear them. I smiled, recalling a recent conversation with Allie.

'I swear, Turner, we need to get rid of that phone. Unless you're in the market for a time share or extended car warranty, it's useless. No one we know has a landline anymore.'

'But Allie, what about missing out on the all-expense-paid cruise of our dreams, or lending my social security number to a Nigerian prince?'

'Uh, those guys don't call much anymore.'

'I promise, babe... I'll get around to it.' But there it was, still ringing.

Petting Blaze's head again, I said, "Yeah bud, you get what they say about old dogs and new tricks, don't you Blaze?"

Hearing his name, my dog looked over at me expectantly, and then laid his head down on the thick rug. Back to a movie choice. I could punch up something on Netflix, but lately, most of those movies were lame. Either stupid rom-coms or crazy fantasy. How about an old favorite instead?

I got up and perused our shelves of old DVDs on either side of the six-foot screen. "Here's a good one, Blaze. Haven't watched this in years. You'll love it." I popped in *Gladiator,* starring Russell Crowe, sat back down, put my feet up and took a deep sip of Scotch. It was a long film; maybe it would require a full tumbler. Or two.

Three hours later, I'd surprised myself, managing to remain awake through the entire film, and on this viewing I saw the story so differently. That happens sometimes when rewatching a film. My previous memory of it was all about warring strategies, power struggles, and grisly scenes of bodies being torn apart. But this afternoon, I realized the gladiator's greatest desire was to leave all power and politics behind him and return home to his wife and farm. Somehow before I'd totally missed that aspect.

I got up and stretched, checking my watch. "Well, boy...time for that walk now, right? Let's go." Blaze was ready. Hearing the word *walk*, he began looking anxiously about. "Come on, downstairs. She's not here today." I walked through the utility room, switched from bare feet to slip-on tennis shoes, attached his leash, and left through the garage.

The sun was still thirty minutes away from sizzling into the lake, with the air feeling less humid than usual. Even in September, Dallas weather could be brutal. "So, what are you up for? Long one or short one?" I looked at the dog's inquisitive golden-brown eyes. "That's what I thought too."

We headed down our street, turned at the corner and walked down to the bike trail. Under the shade of trees, wearing a loose tee-shirt and shorts, it actually felt good to be out. We walked the half-mile to the large dog park by the lake. I unleashed Blaze, sat down on a bench, and watched him run, dodge, and scamper with joy among the wide range of large breeds released for play by their work-a-day parents.

Eventually, another guy came and sat down next to me and, like a proud papa, pointed. “Mine’s the Goldendoodle. Which one’s yours?”

“The Irish Setter with all the pent-up energy. He’s used to getting out more.”

“Oh, yeah. He’s a beauty. Wait…is that Blaze? Man, I’m so sorry. I didn’t realize…your Allie’s husband, right? She was up here with Blaze all the time. Great lady. I’m so sorry, dude. I’m Kevin. Kevin Wells. My wife and I live nearby.”

I nodded, smiled stiffly, and stood up. “Good to meet you, Kevin. Thanks. I’m heading out now.”

I walked toward my dog, knowing he’d hate being pulled out so soon, but it was time for us to leave. Kevin got up and called out after me, “Hey, if you ever need to talk or anything, I’m here most evenings. Allie, she was awesome. Really gonna miss her around here.”

I nodded, putting the leash back on the setter. “Sure, thanks man.” We weren’t ready for those conversations yet. Blaze and I were damaged goods.

CHAPTER 3

The Winning Ticket

ROSARIO GUZMAN

The alarm went off with news blaring through the radio, jolting me awake from a deep sleep. It was ten PM. I'd showered before bed and rarely bothered with makeup anymore. When your job was washing and folding laundry at a twenty-four-hour *lavanderia*, what was the point? I put on my favorite fitted jeans, a clean white tee shirt, and pulled my shoulder length brown hair into a tidy bun. I forced a smile in the bathroom mirror before brushing my teeth and then repeated my mantra, "It's going to be a great day!" I tried to keep the sound of my voice upbeat, but lately, maintaining positivity was becoming more challenging each day.

My second cousin, Miguel, owned Bright White Laundry, where I'd worked the eleven PM to six AM shift for a year. I was grateful for the work but knew I was capable of so much more. It was boring, repetitious, and surprisingly busy. At eleven PM, Diaz Avenue in East Dallas was dark, but Bright White Laundry sat on the corner of the sketchy business block like a shiny fluorescent-lit beacon for the unwashed.

I walked in waving to co-worker, Enrique, another distant cousin. I hated following Enrique's shift. He was lazy and usually left a string of unfinished tasks in his wake after clocking out.

"¿*Qué pasa*, Enrique? How 's business tonight?"

Seeing me, he'd already grabbed his backpack and was walking to the office to clock out. He stopped and nodded towards the bathroom. "Welcome to Wonderland, Rosario. I just locked the bathroom. Man...you do *not* wanna go in there. That place is nasty. Tonight, if I was you, I'd keep the street people outta there."

I shook my head, once again surprised at his lack of work ethic. "Enrique, you know the person on each shift has to clean the bathroom. That's your job. You expect me to work 'till six tomorrow morning and not use it?"

"Well, I'm not doing it. It's up to you, chica. Gotta fly. Things to do tonight."

"OK, but I'm telling Miguel."

"Do what you have to do, man," he said with a little laugh. "Do you think I give a flying fuck about this job?"

Apparently not. I watched him walk out, while shaking my head. What a jerk! Sad to think I was loosely related to him. Very loosely.

I checked out the place. One lady and two guys were doing laundry after carving out their own personal space amongst the machines. Pretty slow for a Thursday night. I gingerly unlocked the bathroom, needing to see what I was dealing with. Yeah, it was bad. I took a picture to show our boss, pulled up my mask. put on rubber gloves, and got to work.

At six AM, I clocked out and went next door to Daylight Donuts, also owned by Miguel. As usual, I grabbed a chair in the back, craving my morning cup of hot fresh coffee with lots of milk, and then bit into a soft and sweet pineapple empanada. Heaven! The front doorbell began to jingle as I tied on my white apron, ready to face the early risers and day laborers needing their morning sugar rush. I put on my smile and joined the team of two others already manning the front counter.

By eleven AM there were a few late donut-seeking stragglers, but two could easily run the front while I finished clean-up in the back. After clocking out, I walked down the street and boarded DART, eating my lunch from a paper bag as the yellow city bus carried me to the outskirts of Dallas. From there, I walked the remaining few blocks to *Construction Connection.* From noon until four, I worked the final leg of my day in a warehouse cleaning *porta orinales*, or what everyone here calls Port-A-Potties. A place filled with tall, nasty smelling blue boxes that needed a thorough scrubbing and sanitizing before they were sent out for another day of duty at construction sites.

A co-worker, Yolanda, and I punched in at the same time. From our assigned lockers we donned knee-high black, lug-soled rubber boots, elbow length rubber gloves, and tied on long black canvas aprons.

Trudging out to the warehouse, we crossed a road where two guys driving forklifts were moving sanitized port-a-potties onto trucks. As I walked by, they both hooted, whistled, and called out, "Looking good today, Rosario! Your ass, in those jeans... so hot."

I blushed and tried to ignore them, amazed anybody would think me sexy in my rubber encased work clothes.

Yolanda tapped my shoulder. "Hey, don't mind them; they're harmless. Enjoy it while you can. Trust me, nobody's whistled at me in ages."

"How long you worked here, Yolanda?"

"Ten years, girl. Can you believe it?"

"Shit!"

"That's right. Ten years of shit."

I pulled the mask up over my mouth and nose, grabbed a power hose and yelled, "If we're both working here ten years from now, just shoot me. Promise, OK?"

Yolanda laughed and nodded, "Sure, but then who's gonna shoot me?"

At four my shift ended and once home, I had five hours before the whole crazy cycle started again. I knew the schedule was extreme but it was the only way I could maintain an apartment and manage to send a bit of money to my mother in Mexico.

Standing outside my apartment, I pulled a white envelope out of the dented tin mailbox. A thrill momentarily pulsed through me. Carefully opening the white envelope from the U.S. government, I pulled out an unimpressive looking, but oh-so-important, printed paper card qualifying me for legal work in the United States. The coveted *Green Card*. My ticket out of the shadows, away from working lousy jobs that nobody else wanted to do for less than minimum wage.

I'd applied a year ago--scrimping and saving, paying all the filing fees, going to interviews, paying an immigration attorney. And now, here it was; but suddenly my excitement fizzled. Receiving it felt so bittersweet because I had no one here to share my news or happiness with.

I'd purposely tried not to befriend people since coming to Dallas. And I didn't want the people I worked with to know I'd be looking for other work. I wasn't sure who I could trust. Most of my family, the few I cared about, were in Ciudad Juarez in Mexico or dead. That evening, I felt so alone.

I placed the card in a hidden compartment in my wallet, set my alarm for ten PM, removed my clothes, took a shower, and then smiled to myself in the mirror.

CHAPTER 4

Queen of Diamonds

VIOLET

Taking a deep breath and then releasing, I pulled my Subaru into Mother's long circular drive, trailed by a small U-Haul. The four-hour drive from Austin to Dallas, up busy I-35, was stressful. Checking myself in the rear-view mirror, I pulled my long dark mane out of a hair-tie, brushed it, and pushed it off my face with a headband. When I stepped out of the car I shook my hands while attempting to release nervous energy, and told myself all would go smoothly.

Unlocking the front door, I called out into the echoing foyer, "I'm home." No response. I followed chattering voices down a long hallway to the sunroom, calling out again, "M-Mother, I'm here."

"Out here, darling. Come say hi to the girls."

By 'girls' she meant her bridge playing pals of the fifty-and-up club. I stopped near the entrance and saw Mother and her gaggle of girlfriends sitting on cushioned white wicker, amongst the dwarf palms, ferns, and birds-of-paradise. I vaguely recalled these women while I stood there slightly frozen.

Waving me over, she said, "Oh, for heaven's sake, Violet, come over and say hi. You know the girls. Viv, Jan, Chris." She pointed to each one with a playing card in her hand, exposing the queen of diamonds. "Violet's come home for a while, ladies. We're gonna see if she can crack the job market here in Dallas. Give your mom a hug, baby."

I walked over and leaned in, giving her an air pass across her cheek and an awkward pat on the shoulder. "H-hello, ladies. G-Good to see you again."

Mother shook off my attempted embrace, tossing her thick tawny-streaked hair back across her shoulders."Violet, Maria made a batch of pina coladas if you want one."

"No thanks. I sh-sh-should unload."

"In that case, the key to the guest house is on the bar. Go ahead and get yourself settled in. We'll go out for a nice dinner tonight. There's a new place I want to take you to."

"Thanks M-Mother; s-s-see you later."

Of course, I felt their whispers as I exited, sure they were patting Mom's arm in sympathy for her cross-to-bear, the awkward stuttering adult daughter. Screw them. A few sessions with my speech therapist, Lexi, and I would be back in the saddle, speaking with a lighter spraying of word bullets. *M's, P's, S's*--all trouble spots for me. Too bad *Mother* started with that tricky *M.*

I circled the drive and pulled around to the back. On the opposite side of the pool, up the hill from the main house, stood my new home, for now. Both the lower and upper levels of the front walls were glass, offering a perfect vista to the expansive green lawn, a long rectangular turquoise pool, and the lake in the distance.

I unlocked the French doors and was immediately impressed with the update. The walls were painted a clean white and on the left side was a low-slung off-white sofa covered with numerous throw pillows. Above the couch, a large abstract painting pulled out the same soft colors as those of the accent pillows, and a sleek white leather chair and ottoman perched opposite a large bookcase with a flat screen. Note to self: Keep ballpoint pens and markers on the table only.

On the right side of the room was a stone kitchen countertop lining the entire wall with updated appliances and across from the counter was a rough-hewn farm table and chairs. Mom must have given her decorator carte blanche on this one.

I pulled the sheer draperies back and then went to the U-Haul to begin unloading. Within a few hours I had all clothing hung upstairs, bathroom accessories in place, and a small selection of kitchen utensils put away. To hold my vast collection of textbooks and novels on the shelves, I pushed Mother's art objects off to the sides.

As I was emptying my final box, Mother opened the door. "All settled in, darling?"

"Getting there."

She looked quickly around, suddenly appearing agitated. "The shelves. Violet, shouldn't these sculptures stand out more?" She walked over and held a tall swirling hunk of something. "This piece...hand blown glass, by the way, is a beauty. It's a Hughes Lamont. You're totally hiding it like this, Violet."

"J-J-Just had to find a place for everything." I was immediately reminded of the white quilted comforter and canopy bed I had as a child—the bed I could never sit or play on.

She went across the shelves, shaking her head, pulling out her collected art pieces, adjusting their positions, showing them off to their advantage. Sighing with relief, she said, "Much better now, see?"

"Sure. Looks good." I had no energy for an argument within her perfect world.

"So, dinner tonight. Let's try Turkish--Cafe Izmir? She looked at the jeans and faded tee I was wearing. "The place is casual but not *that* casual. I think a change of clothes is required. Six o'clock? So glad you're home, Violet."

I robotically nodded yes to all comments and finished with, "Yeah, m-me too."

I braced myself and thought, take the bad with the good. Dinner with Mom--pros and cons: good food filled with a minefield of conversation. I breathed in and out slowly, calming myself. I'd eaten little in the last few weeks. I needed to have a healthy appetite or she'd think I was having eating disorders again. Checking my watch, I decided there was time for a short nap before hunting down an outfit that wouldn't have me put under house arrest for a fashion faux pas.

At six sharp, she swung her Range Rover in front of my door, just as I tied a scarf around my neck that would hopefully help disguise the black *Target* t-shirt and basic black trousers I'd put on.

I stepped out and told her, "P-Prompt as always." I had to laugh. "Th-thanks for the lift."

"Well, I know that driveway is so steep. So, in the mood for Turkish?"

I stepped up into the seat. "I g-g-guess...don't know if I've had it before, but I'm game. I'm actually r-really hungry."

"I'm so glad you mentioned that. You're looking unnaturally thin. You've got to try the *Iskender*. I'll order for you. It's to die for, with lots of butter. Perfect if you're needing to gain weight."

I shook my head. *Here we go.* "I'm f-fine. Just a few pounds under. The move has kept me b-b-busy." *Just drive, Mother.*

Soon we were seated at a small round table, lit by candle light, drinking a deep red Cabernet. It perfectly complemented my enormous plate of grilled beef and lamb, served over soft pita bread, topped with a tomato sauce and searing liquid butter. Exquisite and packed with calories. Chalk one up for Mother.

As we finished dinner and contemplated dessert, she jumped into it. "Now, baby, let's talk jobs. By the way, that scarf looks good on you. The blue plays up your eyes. You should do that more often, play up the eyes. They're beautiful, you know. You favor me in that regard."

"Thanks."

"Back to jobs."

I was about to take a gulp of wine, but stopped. "Actually, if you don't m-mind, I'd like to do m-my own job search first."

"Well, a little headstart and a push certainly never hurt. Remember, in job hunts it's *who* you know, not necessarily *what* you know."

"That's unfortunate. I appreciate it, but g-give me some time to check around." *Good job, Violet...Assertive but not ungrateful.*

Later that evening, I plugged in my laptop and did some searches at UT-Dallas, UT Health Science Center, Southern Methodist University, and some local commercial labs. There were a few promising openings, so I excitedly filled in online applications, attached my CV and personal statement, and pressed send. This was all followed by a bout of stomach cramps. Nerves or rich food? I was never sure.

After giving my new spotless bathroom a full workout, I stood in front of the mirror practicing casual interview banter. But I sounded worse than usual. Who could listen to that voice? I was seeing eye rolls and embarrassment looking right back at me.

Perhaps Mother was right. A friendly reference with a personal introduction would make everything go smoother. Reconsidering her offer, I typed out an email request to Mother for her help. But wasn't I taking the easy way out? Was my stutter and anxiety *that* bad? I had strong academic credentials and a great ability at retention. Didn't that count for something?

With determination, I went back to the mirror and practiced additional interview conversations. But I sounded even worse. "M-M-Mrs. Jones, happy to m-meet you." I watched my contorted face struggling over numerous consonants. I returned to my laptop, read through my email to Mother and pressed send.

CHAPTER 5

Dead Wife, Messy Life

TURNER

The first thing I spotted was the empty Dewars bottle on the nightstand. Not surprising, considering my head felt like oddly shaped Legos rattling around when I attempted movement. Crap, eleven AM. Way late for work. Then I remembered; I was in mourning. Sleeping late was perfectly acceptable behavior. I rolled back over, my arm reaching out to pat the space next to me. Still empty. I closed my eyes again.

Now someone was knocking. On my upstairs bedroom door? Weird. I squinted toward the clock on my nightstand. High noon. I sat up, shook my head, knocked the cobwebs and Legos around, followed by yelling out a raspy, "Hello?"

Through the door I heard a muffled voice. "Mr. Turner, it's Sally. Your maid. Allie always had me come Wednesdays. You want me to clean up here?"

"Sally?" *Our maid was named Sally?* "Uh, hold on, please." I stretched out my shaking legs on the side of the bed, threw on yesterday's t-shirt and shorts, finger combed through my mess of bed-head, and opened the door. Sally looked like she was ready for business. Hands on her hips, a stout, fortyish-looking woman with short graying hair, khaki shorts, and a tucked-in Izod polo. "Hey,

Sally...we ever met before? Seems like we should have, since you obviously have a key to my house."

"Briefly...maybe once in passing? So sorry about Allie and your recent loss, sir; she was one of my favorite clients. I've been cleaning your home for--wow, three years now? I guess it's time we officially met. I put off coming by for over two weeks." She held out her hand, and offered an engaging smile.

"Good to meet you. Call me Turner." I coughed, clearing the rust from my voice. "So...what's the procedure here?" I stepped out into the hallway, looking at her armory of cleaning tools next to my bedroom door.

"Well sir, first I should ask if you want to continue Allie's arrangement. Once-a-week cleaning, bottom to top, full day service, off two-weeks a year with dates to be decided by me. I come nine-to-five every Wednesday. She gave me the house keys a while back; with all those meetings she had on Wednesdays."

"Meetings, huh? Glancing at my watch, I said, "So, you've already been here over three hours? You're either a very quiet cleaner or I'm a heavy sleeper."

"I'd say the latter, sir." She patted the top of her vacuum. "Little Betsy here is effective but makes a racket. Actually, I tried your door earlier. Thought I'd let you sleep it off."

"Alright, heavy sleeper, obviously. Uh, considering it's only me living here now, maybe once every two weeks would do it?"

Sally squinted and shook her head. "Turner, I hate to say it, but this week has to be the worst condition I've ever seen this house. I think you may actually need me twice a week. Unfortunately, I have no openings in my schedule, so it'll have to be once a week, every Wednesday. Lots of dog hair, man hair, rings on the tables, crumbs in the kitchen, garbage and laundry piling up. Hate to say it, but you *really* need me, sir."

"Damn, Sally, sounds like I do. OK, for now, *mi casa es tu casa*. Go forth and vacuum. I'll be downstairs if you need me."

"Thank you, sir. Just keep it clean down there."

"Yes, Captain." I saluted and smiled thinking I *did* need a Sally in this new solo life. I turned toward the stairs as she spoke up again.

"Oh, sir. Blaze was fed and walked this morning."

"Bless you, Sally."

Coffee. I followed the scent of freshly brewed aroma to the kitchen and poured myself a cup. Blaze got up from his bed in the utility room and padded over for a head rub. "Sorry I'm so late today, buddy. Rough night."

Deep in the recesses of my cargo shorts pocket, I heard my cell buzzing. My company, *Rapid Logistics,* flashed across the screen as I picked up. "Hey Fern."

"Hi, Mr. Cooper. So very sorry to bother you. We miss you. Your father's on the other line. Hold please."

I knew I needed to take a seat to get through this call. I grabbed a stool next to the kitchen island.

"Turner...we need you, boy. When you coming in? It's over two weeks now."

I sat at the counter, sipping from my cup, with my banging forehead resting in my hand. "Not sure, Dad."

"You need to come in, son. Everyone has questions and it seems you're the only one that has answers. It's time to get your head back in the game."

"Sorry Dad, can't say I feel quite right in the head or the heart right now. Like someone siphoned all the gas in my tank and let the air outta the tires."

"Maybe the work will get your mind off Allie."

"It's not just Allie, Dad. It's everything I've been doing. I need time to think."

"Well, *think* up here at the office, and get yourself a shrink to talk about the rest. I've got all the department managers meeting me here at three today. We need your leadership, son."

Every bit of my body ached, from hair to toe nails. I had no desire to hear about all the multiplying supply chain problems. I paid managers a lot of money to figure all this shit out. Surely, I wasn't the only person with solutions. Business was a mess, I felt like a mess, my life was a mess. But glancing around the kitchen, I had to admit, my house was now quite ship-shape. It was a start.

I sighed, pounding my fist on the counter. *Fuck it*. "OK, Dad. See you at three."

Down the hall from the kitchen, I headed to a guest room to shower, knowing when I tried, I could clean up pretty good. But there were some messes a hot shower just couldn't solve.

CHAPTER 6

Nightmares and Daydreams

ROSARIO

I'd crawled beneath my iron bed, but even with a pillow pulled over my ears, I could hear the rumbling of yells and threats outside. I couldn't make out the words but I knew *La Linea* was doing the threatening. Along with voices, I heard the pop of gunshots, or was it the backfire of a car? Neither were uncommon in our Juarez neighborhood. And then...a chilling thump against the door, followed by two heavy whacks.

I waited under the bed for silence to surround our small house. The quiet came over like a slow dark fog, only interrupted by the barking of a few backyard dogs. I finally scooted myself out across the linoleum floor and stood up. I didn't want to open the door. Those final noises had set my teeth on edge. I peeked out the windows. All neighbors' lights were off.

I turned on the phone's light and slowly undid the latch and pulled. The rough-planked door felt heavy and weighted. The hinges squeaked in a slow eerie pitch as I yanked harder, watching it swing in. Then I gasped and fell to my knees, keening over in agony and terror, vomiting at the threshold. I forced myself to look up again, letting out a howl like a crazed animal as I wiped my mouth with a pajama sleeve.

Hanging from the door, by the serrated blades of two large knives slicing through each hand, was the body of my twin brother, Roberto. Blood was everywhere, now coagulating on his body, clothing, and the door. I recognized the splattered white Puma jacket he was so proud of and a silver belt buckle my father had given him. A scribbled note was pinned to the jacket, but I lacked the courage to yank it off to read it.

My brother's head was missing.

I finally stood, pushed the door closed, and bolted it, although I knew the lock offered little security. They would be back. I sat down on the sofa and called the police. Someone official would show up eventually, but there was no guarantee they could be trusted.

My noisy alarm jolted me awake, tearing my brain away from the grisly scene. The recurring nightmare of Roberto's murder always woke me with bone-chilling fear and disorientation, forcing me to touch things that I knew to be real. My hand on the warm plastic radio--real. My feet sliding inside fuzzy pink slippers--real. I was drenched in sweat and turned on the chrome faucet of the shower--real.

That horrific dream, revisiting the worst night of my life, continued to plague me every few weeks. It used to be almost every night, so, at least there was that improvement.

La Linea was part of the reason I'd remained so solitary since coming to the U.S. As the enforcement gang of the Juarez drug Cartel, *La Linea*, was also known to have branches outside of Mexico in several cities in Texas, Arizona, and New Mexico. They weren't as open and ruthless as the police allowed them to be in Mexico, but they were definitely a presence in the underbelly of some US cities, protecting their turf.

Remaining vigilant, I lived as anonymously as possible. Whenever I began to feel safe or complacent, I'd pull out the ripped paper which had hung precariously on Roberto's jacket. In a jagged scrawl in Spanish, it read: *We're coming for you next.* I kept it folded at the bottom of a little jewelry box; one of the few things I'd brought with me from Juarez.

Roberto had been both a brother and best friend. Always looking out for me and wanting to do right by our parents. That's what brought both of us to Juarez; a place where we found decent factory jobs and earned enough monthly to send extra home.

U.S. owned factories along the border, the maquiladoras, attracted a lot of the new, green graduates from the countryside. We were eager to learn a trade and bring home a steady paycheck. Speaking passable English was a plus. But the cartels weren't stupid. That's where they found their best recruits. As we left work each day, they kept their eye out for fresh-faced, bright kids ready to make serious money. They preyed upon new arrivals, recruiting the men for trafficking, sales, and enforcement, and women too, often used as drug mules.

Within a few months of arriving in Juarez someone noticed my twin, Roberto. He wanted nothing to do with *La Linea*, but they wouldn't leave him alone. When they started harassing me, making me offers, that's when he got really angry.

Now horrific dreams were all I had left. I came to Dallas hoping for escape, but also to honor his sacrifice, to show him I would do better for the both of us. Momma, a widow for the last seven months, was still back home and received an extra hundred dollars a month from me. It wasn't much, but it kept food on her table.

With documented police reports of Roberto's assassination, gruesome police photos, and the threatening note from his jacket, my immigration lawyer presented a strong case for my asylum and eventual US citizenship. But for now, I had my green card and would soon have a social security card. I couldn't wait to apply for an honest-to-God competitive job with a decent wage.

But tonight, Bright White Laundry was still my destination. I showered again, dressed, and brushed out my shoulder length brown hair, taking a little extra time to add eyeliner and lipstick, just enough to admire my own reflection for a change. At the laundry, I had a lot of regulars. Truckers, hospital employees, shift workers, who all dropped off laundry to be picked up the next day. They liked that I remembered their names, and asked about special instructions. I took an interest and they seemed to appreciate it.

"Rosario, *mi novia*."

I looked up from sweeping, knowing it was smiling Carl, one of my few Anglo customers. His Spanish accent was terrible, but then again, so was my American accent.

"*Hola* Carl. So, what kind of messes you have for me today?" He was a butcher who worked late hours at a small meat packing plant.

"Oh, the usual, blood and guts all over my whites. Give 'em your deluxe bleach treatment. Nobody gets 'em clean like you."

"Yes, it's my top-secret formula, Carl. Then I whispered, "I presoak and wash them twice."

"Well, whatever you do, it does the trick and my wife loves you for it. Hey, brought you some extras."

Carl handed me a couple small packages of frozen meat. I never knew if he bought them for me or if they just conveniently fell off a shelf, but I never asked and was very grateful.

"*Gracias*! Looks like burgers this weekend. Everything will be ready by noon tomorrow. Your wife picking up?"

"Yeah, I'll let her know. You're awesome Rosie! Catch you next time."

Although I appreciated customers like Carl, I daydreamed about being able to get up at a normal hour. Then I'd eat breakfast at home, drink a slow cup of coffee while discussing my day across a kitchen table with someone I loved. I'd be happy working my eight or nine hours, then come home and live like the real people did.

I felt like my customers and I were part of a separate underworld, the ones most people never realized were there, toiling away all night so the *normal* people's worlds were never disrupted. Maybe, once I had the magic social security card, I'd become one of them.

But where could I work? All I knew was what I *didn't* want to do. No more scrubbing port-a-potties, no more washing blood stains in the middle of the night, no more glazing donuts at six AM. I was thankful for the jobs, but currently my days consisted of hard work and little sleep, with time for almost nothing else.

Hopefully now, an opportunity was waiting around some corner. As I dropped Carl's whites into a bleach-heavy pre-soak, I began to daydream about life on the other side. What would it look like?

CHAPTER 7

Learning to Talk the Walk

VIOLET

I'd been acclimating for several days. In other words, doing nothing. I stretched and flexed in my deep-dish bed, swaddled in silky high-thread-count sheets. I raised my head up, looked down at a glistening pool and thought, this was all *way* too easy. Get your ass up and start preparing for whatever the hell you plan on doing. You tell yourself you don't want Mother's help, but what are you doing about it? Although...a morning swim would be invigorating about now.

I was on lap fifty-two, when I took a side breath and saw Mother's gold-heeled mules approaching pool-side. "Vi...Vi!" She clapped thinking I hadn't heard.

In mid-flip, I stopped and turned. "Yes?"

"Pulled a few strings, got you in for a one o'clock with Lexi today. I know it'll be great for the two of you to connect again." She said it as if my speech therapist and I were besties from junior-high. Although, it was almost true. I'd been seeing Lexi since fifth grade. Probably now in her mid-fifties, she had been a listener, teacher, mentor, and doctor to me for years. At one point, I considered myself done with her services; thought I'd gleaned all I possibly could from her. But right now I honestly welcomed the sessions.

I shook the water off my face. "G-Good. Thanks for arranging."

"Well, I know how you procrastinate. I thought you'd appreciate it if I got the ball rolling. Oh, and I haven't forgotten about that email you sent the other night. Give me a week or so and we'll discuss some job options. Some of us have things to do. I'm running late, Vi. Dinner maybe?"

"Sure." Forty-eight laps to go and then perhaps a three-mile run at the lake. Plenty of time.

~

Showered, with my damp hair pulled back in a headband, I sat in the waiting room of Lexi's new and impressive looking offices. Appointments must be booming. Perhaps speech impediments were all the rage right now? Within a few minutes, her receptionist ushered me in.

Lexi sat in a soothing-blue upholstered dome-like chair that seemed to cocoon her petite body. Her friendly brown eyes looked out through large black framed glasses as she stood up to greet me, while I quickly scoped out the soft impressionist paintings of children playing on grassy fields. I felt calm now that I was back in her safe, comfortable world.

She stood up and gave me a brief hug. Lexi knew I wasn't a hugger and kept it short. "Violet, so good to see you. Truly. When your mother called, I told Ellen to clear the decks for an hour or two. Have a seat. Let's get to it."

"Thanks, Lexi. G-G-Great to s-s-see you as well."

"So, tell me what brings you in?"

I told her about my recent job loss and explained how that job had been vital for me in so many ways. "I wanted to find something else in Austin, but M-M-Mother insisted I come back home, and now I'm incredibly anxious about g-going through a round of interviews."

"So Violet, while doing research work, were you still practicing your word re-directs, switching out the trouble consonants? How about doing your elocution drills from time to time?"

"Honestly, no. I thought it was all b-b-behind me, but maybe I got too com-pl-pl-placent. I wasn't talking to people much. Kept to my-myself mostly."

"Hmm," she said, pursing her lips together. "I see you've regressed. I can tell we've got lots of work to do. I want you strong and confident for those interviews and what lies beyond. Tell me honestly. In Austin, was it the work you loved so much or the comfort of working so often in solitude?"

I took a minute to reflect. "P-p-probably a little of b-both."

She nodded. "Hiding from people won't really solve our problems. But, let's get started, shall we?"

After a few days of Lexi sessions, and several one-on-ones between myself and a mirror, I felt a tad more confident. But I now realized it was an affliction that might never be fully cured. Instead, it was something I could make better through practice. Lexi suggested embracing it, avoiding the trouble areas, and making people aware of my stutter when the situation called for it.

At our most recent session, she explained, "While interviewing, take the elephant out of the room. Tell them about your impediment at the get-go. That way, you've put your interviewer more at ease if a stammer bubbles up. They're not caught off-guard wondering what's happening or feeling uncomfortable for you. I'm not sugar-coating it, Violet. Some people will still discriminate; it happens. Many don't even realize they're doing it. But most HR associates will appreciate your honesty."

After a thorough role-playing module, I felt ready to see what Mother's career connections might have in store for me. I laughed, conjuring up what Mother might come up with. Possibly working as a low-budget event coordinator in charge of balloons and crepe paper? Or, maybe a science advisor for high-society women needing socially-correct green topics of conversation? It was bound to be an interesting list. I sent Mother an email letting her know I was ready for a meet and greet.

I was still in bed checking my email and dejectedly threw my phone down. Once again, I'd had zero responses from the university labs I'd sent my resume to. I'd waited eagerly for two weeks and no one was taking the bait. Then I heard a text ding. Ruffling through my sheets, I pulled out my phone. It was Magna Temple, my mother's personal assistant, up to her normal early-morning efficiency.

Good morning, Violet. Your mother is ready to discuss a few Dallas career options with you at 10:45 this morning. Does that time slot work? Let me know. –M.T.

Bless Magna Temple! The woman was a God-send to my mother who retained her services as secretary, financial advisor, personal assistant, and occasional lunch and bridge partner when mother fell short on friends for the day.

Anyway, about my schedule...I saw no obstacles in the way of a morning chat about jobs. There was certainly no clamor of interest through my own efforts. I texted a reply: *Morning Magna. 10:45 is fine. See you in a bit. How's the temperature in there?*

She replied: *Pleasant so far, but you never know after our Monday morning financial strategy meeting. See you later.*

When it came to Mother, Magna had always been my secret co-conspirator. Originally, Magna had served as my father's administrative assistant for years until he died ten years ago. Then Mother acquired her capable services, working together five days a week. But last year, at the age of seventy, Magna announced her semi-retirement and began coming in only three days a week. A year later, Mother was still having trouble adjusting to Magna's act of disloyalty.

I attempted a bit of makeup and nervously dressed. Viewing this as an interview rehearsal, I decided my standard suit was required. I donned my classic pin-stripe shirt and dark-navy Brooks Brothers pants and jacket. I thought it a safe choice, showing Mother I was serious about finding a good position. I walked down the steep, long drive in my flip-flops and went through the glass doors of the sunroom in the back. Approaching the office, I took a deep breath and then exhaled, saying to myself: *I am calm. I am good. I am smart.*

I walked through a set of slightly open walnut-paneled doors.

"Good m-m-morning ladies!" I decided to open with enthusiasm. Both Magna and Mother, sitting at opposing double desks, looked up.

Magna smiled. "Look at you, Ms. Executive!"

Mother gave me a two-second appraisal. "Attractive suit Violet, but is it too, I don't know, too suit-y? There are so many ways to girl-up a suit now-a-days; aren't there Magna?"

"I suppose. But I like it. Simple, professional. Nothing wrong with a classic."

Then Mother stood up and peeked over her desk. "God forbid... what do you have on your feet? Those rubber things need to be outlawed."

I intervened. "Thank you b-b-both, but the flip-flops will be replaced and the suit isn't the issue here. The job's the issue."

Mother smiled and said, "So true. Have a seat darling."

I sat down in one of the two floral-print upholstered wing chairs in front of their matching desks.

"So, M-Mother, I'm ready to hear a few options."

"Aren't you the eager-beaver? OK, Magna, my files please." Magna handed them to her. Mother opened the first manilla file folder with a flourish and seemed to be digesting the information for the first time, nodding her head at the details inside.

"Here we go. This one was an easy ask. The Perot Museum needs a coordinator and tour guide for their student tours. You recall that museum, dear... it's all about natural science, rocks, dinosaurs and such. So exciting! And I've been a big contributor for years. Think about it, Violet. This is a perfect fit for you! Answering questions from school children. You're so clever about all this science info. And, no need to be on edge regarding public speaking. By that I mean...you'd only be speaking to children."

My eyes bugged out at her remark, but I ignored it. Considering the position, I shook my head, thinking the idea sounded absurd. "Sorry, I can't think of anything I'd r-r-rather *not* do. You do know I'm a m-m-molecular b-biologist, correct? And children make me nervous." I was certainly over-qualified, and I cringed at speaking in front of large groups of children, especially ones that were certain to mimic me, like eleven-year-old assholes. To my recollection, children were like parrots, shouting out and repeating awkward phrases that I'd certainly be spewing.

Magna stood up, stepping out of the firing zone. "Who's ready for coffee? I'm getting a cup."

Mother and I ignored her hasty retreat. "Violet, so negative already? And sadly typical. You haven't even given it a chance to sink in. Keep an open mind, dear. Let's move on."

I calmed down. *One down, two to go. Hit me.* "OK M-Mother. Let's continue."

"Alright then, this next one has excellent merit. And they're willing to train, given your scientific background *and* my position on the board. It would be as Head of Food Services for North East Center Hospital. Apparently, they normally hire only registered dieticians for this, but again, I told them you were a quick study and I'm sure you learned a lot about food in your biology studies. Down side...I believe there is a hair net involved. But, it's a minor obstacle." With that mention, she flicked her hand as if swatting an imaginary fly.

I looked down at my tightly clenched hands. "That sounds like a d-damn big learning curve. I appreciate your confidence in m-my abilities but it sounds almost dangerous to put m-me in that spot." I briefly flashed on my nervous stomach disorder. Was I a wise choice in overseeing the healthy nutritional menus for sick patients? "Uh, OK. Number three?"

"Now Violet, I pulled some strings here, but I think this last one would be absolutely lovely. Just imagine...working as a head gardener at Botanicals United of Dallas, designing a new xeriscape garden featuring plants of the Southwest. I've told them about your research work at UT with that *stuff* you were conjuring up for dry soil and they had a huge interest in that. Again, you'd have to study up a bit, but maybe my new gardener could teach you a thing or two."

I had never even taken care of a house plant. Never mowed a lawn or planted a flower. I was sure Mother's lawn guy would come up woefully short on teaching me the level of garden design that

Botanicals United was known for. Nodding, trying to appear positive, I asked, "So, that's it then? Thank you. I'll give those files a thorough read-through, M-M-Mother." *Thanks for not really knowing me at all.*

At that point, Magna walked in with a tray containing three cups of coffee. She stopped, leaned over with her beverage tray and said, "Everything good, Violet?"

I reached up, taking a cup and saucer. "Make mine an Irish coffee please," and gave her a smirk.

Mother stood up, clutching the strap of her nude-leather Birkin bag. "No coffee for me, thanks. Now Vi, I know it's not *exactly* what you were doing previously, but that's what makes job searches so exciting. I'm leaving now for an appointment. I want you and Magna to go over these in detail together. She knows more about the nuances of the positions than I do. We'll talk later. And keep an open mind!"

After she left, we sipped coffee in silence for a minute. "Magna... I'm serious about that whiskey in my cup. You have to know, I'm not remotely qualified for any of those po-po-posi—jobs.

Magna smiled, as gentle creases formed around her mouth and she patted the back of her heavily-sprayed perfect platinum up-do. "So, none of these three jobs sound slightly feasible to you?"

"All three are absolutely ri-ridiculous. I have no expertise in any of those areas."

Magna took another sip. "I understand you feel that way. Violet, you were lucky in Austin, being able to find a job that perfectly matched your skills. But think about it this way...A lot of people feel unsure, like a fish out of water, when they first take a job. And you're right; in some ways, you don't have detailed knowledge of these three positions."

Magna folded her hands on the desk and continued. "But one thing I *do* know is that you're at your best studying up on a subject, behind the scenes. Take cues from those around you and ask questions. I know it's scary working in new surroundings. But you are a clever woman. It wouldn't hurt to at least *apply* and find out more about the responsibilities. People are hired for their potential, their education, their intelligence, and most importantly, their ability to adapt. Be more malleable."

My eyes were directed at shoe level below her desk. Her pumps were interesting. Chunky, but not too matronly. "I don't know, Magna. I'm not a very b-b-bendy person."

"Violet, none of these jobs are a done deal. We only procured the interviews. Now, I'm sure the people conducting the interviews might be aware of your mother's influence, but you actually have to sell yourself to get hired for the position, just like anybody else applying."

I sighed loudly, sitting with my arms crossed against my chest. "M-M-Maybe you're right. Perhaps I should apply at the gardening one? At least I wouldn't be sp-speaking to a crowd of rugrats. And I'd only be killing p-plants instead of human p-patients."

Magna nodded. "Excellent points. Yes! Let's start with that and we'll do some mock interviews."

She stood up from her desk, leaned over as if to shake my hand and said, "I must say Ms. Violet Hill, you look lovely today, great suit. Have a seat. Now tell me a little about yourself."

With my eyes still glued to the floor, I responded, "Sure, but f-first tell me, where'd you get those p-pumps?"

CHAPTER 8

Break the Chain

TURNER

The hot shower helped tamp down the fugue and fog created by the contents of my previously full bottle of Scotch. But it would be a monumental lie to say I was feeling tip-top about addressing the biggest problem to hit the supply chain industry in decades. I was drinking way too much, feeling way too guilty, and way too uninformed on current business to offer much in the way of solutions.

I sucked it up, combing back the hair sticking up all over my head and continued to dress for the office, replacing unlaundered cargo shorts with khaki trousers and a clean white polo.

I drove the seven miles downtown to Rapid Logistics. It was a company I'd created and spun off from my father's small trucking business about twelve years ago. A little past three, I walked into the conference room. I saw Dad seated at the end of the sleek Scandinavian table surrounded by matching beech-wood chairs. I hated this room. It looked good but those chairs were so darn uncomfortable. I cursed the decorator every time I had to spend a few hours there making nice with clients. The table was surrounded by my top people. Sam in shipping, Helene, who oversaw trucking, Ed on rail, and Melissa, who headed up short-term delivery systems. All experts in their fields.

But today, they seemed to be lacking the ability to communicate with each other. I was pissed I'd been called in; so, not in the best of moods. As I entered, all went quiet. I stopped, with hands in my pockets. "So, tell me, what are the biggest problems you five clever people aren't able to solve?" Not the most positive opening line I'd ever used when greeting associates.

Dad spoke up first. "Now, son, it's a clusterfuck out there. Customers are having conniption fits, calling every few minutes wondering where their damn stuff is."

I tried to remain calm. "Yes, I understand. It's happening all over the country. Actually, all over the world. It's almost October now, folks. We started hearing rumbles about this back in July and August. And it's going to get worse. So, the question should be--how can we get ahead of this and what are we doing about it for *our* customers?"

Sam-in-shipping spoke up. "Turner, some of our containers are now in range or waiting at the LA port, but things are really backed up and neither of our contracted trucking lines are fully staffed. They can't keep up and aren't hiring drivers fast enough."

I nodded and looked at Helene who was busy tapping away on her laptop. "Helene, what 'cha got? Any breakthroughs?"

She shook her head. "Not really. A couple loads got out on trucks yesterday. But it's gonna take weeks to catch things up."

Everyone began mumbling again.

Leaning over the back of a chair at the table, I turned up the volume. "OK look, I know right now everything is a mess with delays. Who could foresee huge layoffs, hiring shortages, raw material shortages, and then every American with a laptop deciding to order shit-loads of stuff?"

Everybody's eyes were on me again. "We're one small company with contracts to get this stuff delivered and keep our clients' flow of goods moving. Let's put our heads together and get these current delivery challenges worked out. Dad...Helene? What are we gonna do about trucking?

Helene raised her hand timidly. "Independents? I can call around the southern Cal area. See who we can scrounge up."

"Perfect! Let's do it. And Dad?

"I still got all my old contacts. Let me make some calls." He nodded over to Helene and said, "Let's also check independents in Arizona and Nevada."

I did a thumbs up. "Exactly! Offer them twenty percent over normal rates until all this calms down. All the big boys will soon start paying extra. We need to get ahead of the curve."

I punched up the receptionist's line. "Fern? Please locate Sarah-from-sales and have her join us...and you better order some pizzas to be delivered. I explained to the team, "We need sales input. I want us to focus *only* on top clients today. They bring in sixty percent of our revenue and we can't have any of them jumping ship. Melissa, if we can't get enough trucks, do you think you can get some short-term delivery systems to haul some of the freight from the shipping containers over to the rail lines?"

She glanced up from her laptop, looking over her glasses at me. "That might work. Let me get on it. Ed, you'll have to get me up to speed on the rail connections.

Ed loosened his tie, pulled it off and nodded. "Sure thing."

Sarah-from-sales walked in looking frazzled, with her blonde hair pulled up in a bun held together with a pencil. "Sorry, boss. It's tough being on the other end of those customer calls. Nobody wants to hear *I'm not sure*, or *maybe another six weeks*."

I pulled out a seat for her. Still standing in front of the group, I said, "I know it's tough being on the receiving end. Sarah, let's take a look at our top client list. These other sharp people are going to work hard at getting you *real* delivery dates to give our clients.

And remember guys, most other supply chain companies are in the same crappy, convoluted spot we're in. But we're small and nimble. Let's cut through the red tape and get on top of things. *Now* is the time to use your charm and rapport. Pull out some favors."

I walked over to a white board behind the table and wrote up all backed-up orders from Sarah's list of top clients. "I need everyone on this list to have an accurate delivery date next to it by tomorrow morning so that Sarah can call all of them ASAP. Sarah, I'll coach you on the best way to deliver the message. Trust me, they're going to appreciate the truth, even if it's a delay. At least when you give them a definite date, they can make plans around it.

Sarah nodded. "Thanks Turner, that'll definitely help."

Laptops were clicking, everybody's cells were lighting up, a slightly more positive buzz started to fill the room instead of grumbles.

After coaching Sarah and seeing some results from each department manager, I cleared my throat and called out, "Everything gets documented. Get my dad to sign off on every discount or delivery bonus we're honoring. I have to leave now. But my cell will be open to you for any questions or problems. You may not see me for a while; need to make some decisions. But you're exceptionally smart and capable people who can be problem solvers when you work together. That's why you're here."

They were silent for a second, offered nods and small waves, and then went quickly back to their screens or phones.

I walked down the hallway, my heels echoing against the tile floor. The elevator couldn't come fast enough. I didn't want to spend another minute at the job which I had allowed to gobble up years of personal time. Precious time I could now never give back to Allie.

The ding of the elevator door startled me. The doors swished open and I was grateful it was empty. I leaned my head forward on the cold metal panel. How could I have *not ever* met a maid Allie had employed for three years? How did I *not know* that Allie always spent Wednesdays in meetings? How could I have been so oblivious to my selfishness?

Allie went through weeks of chemotherapy with her breast cancer but came back strong. *Of course* she was immunocompromised. Yet, it had still come as a shock to me. I was guilty of so many self-absorbed atrocities as a husband. I needed time away for some serious self-reflection.

I'd given *Rapid Logistics* all my time and energy. It was time for me to give something back for Allie. Maybe some type of memorial to her, something she'd been motivated by. It was too late for her, but maybe I could do something for someone else, in memory of Allie.

Was I doing it to assuage my guilt? Yes. But it was something I felt driven to do.

As the doors opened to the parking garage, I told myself, *Good idea...I'll get on it tomorrow.* But right now a bottle of Dewars was calling me home.

CHAPTER 9

The Laundry Prince

ROSARIO

The glass doors to Bright-White swung open with an annoying buzz, knocking me out of my blissful new-career daydream. I immediately became nervous watching hot Victor Morales walk in with his overstuffed bag of laundry. The few times he'd come in, he'd never been anything but polite to me. But was he *too* nice? And wasn't he a little *too* handsome? I reminded myself, calm down Rosario, you're just the laundry girl.

So, it was three AM and he looked as if he was going out, or possibly heading home after a night out. Either way, he looked sharp. Maybe mid-twenties, fitted black jeans, slim-cut sports jacket, flawless white shirt. Dark hair styled to perfection. Never over-the-top. Not too flashy. Just right. But what was he doing at *this* lavandería, in *this* neighborhood?

He walked over to the counter where drop-offs were logged and weighed, looking surprised to see me. "Oh hi… you again? How do you grab all these choice work shifts?"

"*Hola*. Just lucky, I guess. You look very nice this evening."

Our conversations had never gone beyond laundry preferences, so I decided to make a stab at a friendly chat. I was thinking, *My, what perfect white teeth you have*, but instead I said, "So, you going somewhere special at three in the morning?"

"Thanks, actually yes. Have a crack-of-dawn flight at DFW, and I needed this laundry squared away for the week. It's cool I found this place; open all the time, and then there's the added bonus of an attractive uh--washer-folder-person? Sorry, what's your title? Better yet, what's your name?"

I looked down, embarrassed by the almost-complement. "Rosario, and I guess I'm the night manager."

"Night manager. Impressive."

"Oh yes, that's why they pay me the big money. So, Mr. Morales, what can I do for you this morning?"

"Impressed again... you remembered my name, Ms. Rosario.

"I try. I get a lot of regulars here but you've stood out."

He looked confused. "I just come in, drop my bag, and go."

"But you look different. So nicely dressed, stylish, clean. You should see what I see! My last customer, Carl, a very nice man. But his drop-offs—covered in blood." I stopped to laugh as Victor's mouth fell open. "Don't worry. He's only a butcher, not a criminal."

"Yeah...this crazy shift you work, I bet you see a little of everything. Hey, what do you do during normal hours? We should go for coffee sometime. Maybe find mutual interests other than laundry. When's your day off?"

"I only have Sundays off."

"Sundays are good. What's your number?"

That question immediately made me feel cautious. I rarely gave my number to anyone. But I was intrigued. "I tell you what. You give me your number and I'll call you next Sunday. I could meet you somewhere."

"Sounds good. I'm happy to pick you up though."

"No... It's best if I meet you. So, you live around here?"

"Not too far; this place is along my route. Hand me your phone and I'll put in my number."

"I have to fill out your information on the laundry form. I'll get it from that." I pulled out my pad, filled out his name and number, and asked about special instructions.

He stood there and watched me carefully, making me nervous.

"You know Rosario, I've never asked anyone out that already knew whether I wore boxers or briefs."

"Or the color of your sheets," I said, pulling out a wrinkled set of navy pillowcases from the bottom of his bag. "Guess I know all your intimate secrets now," I said with a laugh.

His face actually blushed in a charming way, "I'll keep a few things under wraps. So, what do you enjoy doing? Any special requests for Sunday?"

I looked up and thought for a second. "Anything outdoors is good for me. After working all week, I love sitting outside for coffee when the weather is nice."

He snapped his fingers, and nodded. "Know the perfect place." Then he glanced at his watch. "Call me around ten, Sunday morning? But right now, I have a plane to catch. See you then, Rosario."

As the doors shut behind him, I melted in place, stuck to my office chair. Had that really happened? I had a date with an attractive, interesting man. My first date since I'd moved here, excluding hanging out with a few cousins and those weren't worth counting. Victor appeared to be friendly and successful. Then doubts immediately crept in.

If he was so successful, why was he asking *me* out? I worked at an all-night lavanderia. Wait until he heard about my other job, cleaning port-a-potties. Maybe I wouldn't mention that. Perhaps it was like the Cinderella story, and he enjoyed playing the handsome prince swooping in to put low-skilled working girls on a pedestal?

What would I wear? What did we have in common? Would it be safe? What would Roberto tell me to do? I thought about it, picturing my twin's smirking face. He would say, *Jesus, Rosario. Just go get a free coffee, and don't worry so much. Not everyone is a reject, maniac, or gangster.*

Roberto was probably looking down and laughing at me right now. Maybe it was time to have a little fun. It was only coffee. Let's see...It was already Monday morning. Only six days to go!

~

I was staring at my phone while holding it in my palm; it screamed out *ten-fifteen, Sunday*. My finger had been perched over Victor Morales' number since ten. What if he'd forgotten? He had asked me so casually, perhaps it was all a big joke?

I'd washed and straightened my hair, tried a new coral lipstick, and put on a pair of tight turquoise jeans and a print top. The weather outside was perfect. Just do it. Press the call button--now! It was ringing...once...twice. I'd give it four rings and then hang up. On the fourth, I heard:

"So, this is either *Scam Likely*, or this is Rosario."

Relief flooded my voice. "*Hola* Victor. Yes, it 's Rosario. *¿Qué pasa*?"

"I've been waiting for your call. I'm hungry."

"Yes, where should I meet you? The address please."

"Uh, how about the main entrance of Botanicals United of Dallas. Most people just call it BUD. Best outdoor patio in the city. You know it?"

"Sorry, never heard of that place."

"I'll tell you what. Why don't I pick you up in front of the laundry? Might be easier. Can you be there in thirty minutes?"

"Yes, I can do that. See you soon." At night I took the bus to Bright White, but today I'd walk. By ten-thirty-three, I was leaning against the window of the donut shop next door, considering grabbing a jelly donut to tide me over, but maybe I should wait. Had Victor mentioned food? I went in and got four donuts. They were always free for me; my one employee perk. When I came out there was a small black SUV waiting near the curb. I peeked inside, but it was empty.

From behind, I heard his voice and turned. "There you are; had me worried for a minute. I went inside the lavenderia to look for you. Only saw one person inside talking to his stolen shopping cart."

I glanced over at the laundry windows. "Oh, that has to be Charlie. Every morning, he goes to the donut shop, buys coffee, then goes to the lavenderia and sorts through all his stuff in the cart and pretends he's doing laundry. An hour later, he wanders out.

Victor smiled, clicked his lock and opened my door. "Hop in."

"Thanks."As he got behind the wheel, I held up my white bag. "I stopped and got donuts. Super fresh. I work there too."

"Wait, what? You worked this morning? At that donut place?"

"No, not today. Sunday is my one day off. No matter what."

"OK, so BUD's not too far from here. A few miles. It's cool...a cafe located within the gardens. If you like being outdoors, I think you'll love it."

We drove into a busy parking lot and walked to an entrance line. While walking through, Victor explained, "There's several different gardens inside. Uh... *jardins muy grandes*."

"Victor, I wondered if you spoke Spanish. You have no accent."

"I *barely* speak Spanish. Just trying out what I remember from high school. Your English seems pretty good though. Did you grow up here?"

"No. Near Jaurez, but I learned in school too. My brother and I would practice every day together and we watched lots of American movies."

We walked into an open flag-stoned piazza and I was immediately intrigued. "Victor, this is so incredibly beautiful."

Guarding the borders of the walk-ways were thousands of orange pumpkins, surrounded by gorgeous explosions of fall colors from flowers draping over their pots in shades of gold, orange, and purple, and overhead there were broad shady trees covered with deep red leaves. Walking further within was a large sparkling fountain within a pond. I'd never seen such natural beauty layered together in my life. I breathed in all the scents, closing my eyes for a second. Fresh cool air, damp leaves, rich moist earth. Everywhere I glanced there was another unique plant, a winding path, a romantic stone bridge, and this was only near the entrance.

Victor directed me over to tables with umbrellas near the service counter. "I'll get the coffee. Let's sit here."

He pulled out a chair for me. But I wasn't really ready to sit down. I would have rather run through the place, touching the velvety petals, or try laying down on the spongy green grass. "Thank you. *Café a leche*, please."

Ten minutes later he came back with coffee, salad options, and two sandwiches. "I should have asked. Hope you're not vegetarian. These turkey paninis are the best."

"This looks wonderful. You're making my bag of jelly donuts look very sad right now."

He sat down, touching my hand on the small table. "So, Rosario, I've been waiting for a week to look into this beautiful face and those huge brown eyes of yours. Tell me about yourself."

"Well, I have some excellent news to share." I pulled out my new social security card that I'd recently received. "I'm so happy about this and you're the first person I've shown it to. Maybe my time at Bright-White will be coming to an end. With this, I hope to start looking for better work."

"Hey, congratulations! What do you have in mind?"

I told Victor a little about my past and my vague hopes for the future, but stayed away from the dark episode of Roberto's murder. I didn't want that clouding this perfect morning. The food was delicious, the air felt cool but the sun had come out, and Victor was so handsome. It was as if our eyes had locked onto each other and we couldn't look away. As we were finishing our meal, Victor offered to walk me through the gardens. As we both stood up, his phone buzzed.

He looked down at the screen and said. "Excuse me; I need to take this." Victor walked to the patio's edge and looked concerned, talking briefly into the phone. He came back to the table shaking his head. "I'm so sorry. Bad news from work. Something has come up and I'm going to have to catch an afternoon flight to LA. I apologize for having to cut this short."

"Really? We haven't even looked around yet." *And just like that... the carriage turns back into the pumpkin.*

"Look...Rosario, you should stay... as long as you want. Just take your time and wander through. I know you'll love it." He pulled out his phone and started tapping. "I'm scheduling an Uber to take you home. Is that OK? Let's say one-thirty? That should give you plenty of time to wander. Uber will charge my account, but the driver will have your contact number. He handed me his phone. "Here, put it in for me. Have you used Uber before?"

I nodded my head, a bit upset. "Yes, I have. Thank you."

He took both of my hands. "I promise. We'll try this again. It's been a real pleasure." Before he turned for the exit, he gave me a brief hug and then quickly walked out.

I looked around. Suddenly, everything looked less vibrant as I tried to decide which garden path to take.

Of course. My first real date in Dallas would end early with him walking out. Why should I ever expect something good? He'd seen a pretty girl in a laundry, but then reality hit after we'd spent an hour talking. We were from two different worlds.

But I repeated my daily refrain to myself and thought about it. I was in a beautiful place. I had the day to myself and would make the most of it. Besides, Victor now had my number if he wanted to see me again. I hoped he would call.

CHAPTER 10

Sowing Seeds of Doubt

VIOLET

My interview with the Botanicals United's master gardener was scheduled for this afternoon. Ms. Molly Hayes, head horticulturist, would be determining my immediate future. But Magna and I had prepared for all possible questions with three interview practices. Whatever I lacked in experience, which was vast, I would cover with good bullshit and quick-study abilities. And hopefully, after my recent sessions with Lexi, I was ready to dodge the difficult consonants and troubling word combinations.

Once again, I donned my navy Brooks Brothers suit, and popped into the main house to borrow Magna's semi-stylish pumps and grab some afternoon coffee. Mother and Magna were enjoying a cup at the kitchen coffee bar. As I walked in, Mother squinted at me, leaned back for the full view, and said, "We still need to *girl* you up."

"M-mother, it's a gardening position. I don't think fashion plays m-m-much of a part in the p-process."

"Well, never underestimate the power of good fashion sense. Let's start by opening up your shirt collar." She got up and fussed with my three top buttons, opening and lifting the collar in the back a bit. "See, Magna. Better already, don't you agree?"

Magna gave me a nod. "I like it. Here are the shoes, Violet," she said, handing me the pumps I'd admired the other day.

I stepped out of my flip-flops and slipped them on, growing taller by three inches, topping out at six-feet. Mother snapped her fingers and said, "Don't move. I have the perfect accessory." She came back with a two-strand choker of pearls and attached them at the back of my neck. "Violet, if I teach you only one thing—remember this. You can never go wrong with pearls."

I rolled my eyes and nodded. "Certainly words to live by, M-Mother."

She stood back, tossing her streaked hair back behind her shoulders, admiring her handiwork. Both Mother and Magna mirrored my reflection, looking pleased with the effect. I grabbed my coffee and a piece of Melba toast. "You're certain this isn't all too m-much? Maybe too pro-professional?"

Mother dismissed me and went back to reading her newspaper, but Magna assured me enthusiastically, "You look lovely, Violet. Now go get that job!"

Once at BUD, I was directed to the HR office and filled out an application while waiting in an area with a few other job seekers. Everyone, except me, was dressed casually, in knit tops or tee-shirts with jeans. Wearing my suit, with the neck-clutching pearls and old-lady heels, I felt like I should be applying for cemetery-plot sales.

The HR coordinator walked over. "Violet, Molly is ready for you. Just go down that hall to the left." She had called my interviewer Molly. I was planning on using her last name, Ms. Hayes, to avoid the pesky *M-L* combo, but maybe calling her by her last name would sound too formal?

I walked down the hall while reviewing all of Magna's instructions. Don't forget eye contact. Every four seconds, make sure you're looking the interviewer in the eye. Don't stare at the floor. Smile. Don't be too serious. It's Ok to have a fun conversation, even in an interview. I started to panic. There was so much to remember. I wiped my sweating palms on my jacket, and opened the office door.

"Violet, so good to meet you. I've been hearing good things." Standing up, she reached over to shake my hand. "I'm Molly Hayes, have a seat." She sat back down and offered a tepid smile. I nodded, stared at her desk, and didn't attempt her name. "So, as head horticulturist here, I coordinate all the gardens and their associates. Then, under me, each garden has a lead gardener."

Stop staring at the desk. Head up, eyes forward, nod. Molly had a pleasant middle-aged face. Rosy cheeks, with an auburn wedge haircut and an ample body. Must not have been doing much digging and shoveling lately.

"Violet, as you may have heard, we are creating a new area dedicated for xeriscape gardening. With emphasis on matching our soil and climate with more drought resistant plants, and encouraging guests to find beauty in more typical Southwestern flora. With your biology background and recent research, we thought you might be able to offer a unique perspective."

She looked at me expectantly. This wasn't really a question and Magna had not covered this. I'd have to wing it.

"Uh, Ms. Hayes..."

"Oh, call me Molly, please. We're all family here."

"OK, thanks." I'd ignore that request. "F-First. I sh-should tell you; I have a slight st-stam-m-mer. Didn't want you to think I was ch-choking or anything." I forced a laugh and looked up immediately. *Were we having fun yet?*

"Not a problem, Violet. Thanks for letting me know. Go ahead."

"Well, I was certainly excited to hear about your p-plans for the new garden. I th-th-thi...believe it's wonderful and certainly time for s-s-something like this in Dallas, with our m-mild winters and hot summers. It's really not feasible to maintain these big lawns requiring so m-mu... a lot of water." *Yes! Three trouble-spot pivots. Lexi would be pleased.*

Molly nodded, looking back up from my resume. "Right, well we're certainly not suggesting we do away with our existing gardens, but yes, it'll be a nod to an alternative. But we need to make it look inviting, with perhaps an interesting, sparser look but with its own individual beauty. What did you have in mind? Did you happen to bring in a mock-up rendering?'

What? No one suggested that! "No...I didn't, but I'd be happy to create one for you s-soon. Today, I can explain what I envisioned." I had looked up numerous drought tolerant plants over the last few days and memorized the list. "I'd suggest incorporating s-salvia greggii, lantana for b-b-butterflies, and kaleidoscope b-blo...flowering abelia shrubs would be so nice for color. A section for bl-blooming cacti would be great. Their red and yellow blooms are fantastic. Then for height, I'd add V-Vitex trees. They smell great, and there are also desert willows with their nice p-purple flowers.

"Yes. All good suggestions. But as you may know, here at BUD, it's all about presenting these plants in a unique design, creating a feast for the eyes, an explosion of color, or an interesting turn in the path. That's part of what your job would entail. Are you up for that, Violet?"

Positive smile, eyes up, nodding affirmation. Check. "I believe so. I'd be excited to sh-show you some xeriscape garden plans soon."

"And your leadership skills? You'd be overseeing a small group of gardeners for the project."

Leadership? Was fabricating a story appropriate? "Well, let's see; while at my lab position I c-collaborated with other researchers and my pr-professor. But I often took the lead with ideas and suggestions. And there's always leadership in sp-sports! I was a captain in team s-s-soccer. I would also add that I work well within a team." *Soccer captain? Yeah, my elementary school team, Pink Lightning, where they rotated the captain's title every week.*

"I see. Well, you're young. These skills can be honed. Lots of books on that. And, of course, I can initially offer more direction for your team. Yes Violet, I'd love to see your creative ideas on paper. And we *so* appreciate your family's support! Apparently, your mother is a pillar of strength to the gardening community. I'm certain the BUD director is excited to see what you can do."

"G-Great. When would you like to see those drawings?"

"Let's get you started next Monday. You can bring them with you." Again, she was checking my resume and application. "It looks like your salary here would be a little over what you were making in Austin. The position starts at forty-five thousand. She stood up holding a bundle of papers. "Here are booklets on policies, procedures from HR and garden brochures. Familiarize yourself with all of this and if you have questions don't hesitate to call. Just ask Nina in HR about your uniform shirts. You'll need those right away."

That was it? I had the job?

I was still sitting, as I reached over and took her paperwork. "S-So, I'm hired before you see my ideas?"

"Looks like it." Molly was waiting for me to leave, and honestly not looking too thrilled about it.

I realized this all came a little *too* easily. The interview was over. The job was mine. But... designing something for a world-class garden, and instructing others to follow my feeble lead? Highly questionable. I was certainly in way over my head and surely Ms. Molly Hayes knew it. But it was a starting point and if she was willing, so was I.

Outside the offices, I looked around the gardens at BUD, wanting to visualize possible expectations for a new garden. I nervously rubbed at the choker on my neck, hoping little pearls of wisdom might inspire me. A bunch of oysters had spent a lot of time on this hunk of jewelry; surely it held some special knowledge. After fifteen minutes of garden observation, future expectations felt overwhelming, making me sick to my stomach, as I dashed into the closest restroom.

Heading to the exit, reality hit me. I was a scientist, and donning a monogramed green shirt would not turn me into a gardener. But then again, maybe with time, study, and inspiration, all things were possible. Perhaps designing a garden could be like a trial and error science experiment?

Later, as I pulled into our driveway, I saw Mother's gardener raking leaves from the beds surrounding the house. I stopped before pulling up to my place, and got out. We hadn't officially met, but we'd been waving and nodding to each other for the past few weeks. I took several deep breaths. Eyes forward, walk, and smile.

"Hello, it's M-Mark, isn't it? Good to officially meet you. I'm Violet Hill, S-Suzanne's daughter." He was tall with a lanky physique. His face was slightly sunburned with deep crinkling around his light blue eyes, with his hair tied back in a short ponytail. Actually, not unattractive, for a fifty-something guy.

"Yeah, seen you around; good to meet you."

"S-So, I understand you haven't been here too long. W-What days do you work?"

"Been here, what, three months now? Part-time, Mondays and Fridays. I deal with Magna primarily. Only talked to your mom once or twice."

"B-B-Been doing gardening for a while?"

"Yeah, the last ten, fifteen years or so I've done the landscaping thing." At this point he stopped raking and turned to face me. "Honestly, I'm an artist. A painter really. But turned to lawn care to keep gas in the tank. I live in the neighborhood, a garage apartment, in exchange for maintaining their lawn. You know... I get by."

"Actually, that's quite interesting. I have s-s-so many questions for you. I know this sounds st-strange, but I just got a job as a g-gardener and have very little pr-practicle experience. It'll be primarily xeriscape. Know much about that?"

He studied me quizzically, looking down at my suit, pearls, and pumps. "You sure about that? You don't strike me as the gardener type. But, yeah, I've done a few lawns in that style. Good for people who like low maintenance."

"W-wonderful. So, I'd love to ask you some questions. I think I may be a little in over my head with this job. Any ch-chance we can talk over dinner? My treat, of course. Any pl-place you like."

"Today? I'm kinda busy. Had some plans."

I looked down at the ground, frowning. I'd impulsively put myself out there and rejection was about to smack me in the face.

He shrugged his shoulders. "Fuck it, Violet. Throw in a few extra beers with some bar-b-que and you got yourself a deal."

Relief flooded through me. "Perfect." *Yes, an ally!*

CHAPTER 11

Mail Call

TURNER

There was knocking on my bedroom door...again. I rolled over; eyes glued shut. Synapses beginning to charge...now firing on partial cylinders. I pried my eyes open, cleared my throat, and would have killed for a glass of water. A raspy noise emerged from the deep. "Yes?"

"It's Sally out here, sir. Just ready to get a move-on upstairs. That's Sally, *the maid,* sir."

"Hold on." *Sally?* As bad as I felt when I stood up, I was pleasantly surprised to find I still had on yesterday's clothes. Good, no need to get dressed. I opened the door, rubbing my crusty eyes.

"Hey Sally, I'm confused. I thought we'd agreed on Wednesdays."

"Yes, sir."

"So...?"

"It's Wednesday sir. Again. We met last week."

"Really?" I looked around the hallway, embarrassed by my stupidity. "Wow...been so busy. Guess I lost track, sorry."

"Uh, Turner, before I get started, feel free to shower. Take your time. I'll just grab some lunch downstairs." She turned and quickly skedaddled.

I nodded, closed the door, yanked off my tee-shirt giving it a sniff, and almost gave myself whiplash. How long since I'd showered? No idea. I shuffled to the attached bathroom and couldn't avoid the double mirrors on both walls reflecting my image under multiple light fixtures. I looked worse than I smelled, and seemed to have taken on a grayish hue, appearing closer to fifty than my spry thirty-five years. I guess that's what a daily diet of Dewars, stale chips, and picante sauce will do for you.

I pressed in the puffy bags under my eyes, hoping they'd deflate like blow-up pillows. They didn't. My hair was dirty and matted, my cheeks hollow, my sexy, scruffy look had shifted to full, fuzzy beard. I stepped into a steaming shower hoping all the bad stuff would simply flow down the drain.

Afterward, I noticed my hands were shaking as I tried to hold my razor. This drinking thing was out of control. I swatted my face with aromatic aftershave and band-aids, and went on a closet hunt for clean clothes. Feeling half-alive I headed downstairs, ready for my public shaming from Sally. I was sure her subtle recriminations were about to spew forth.

I went into the kitchen, sniffing around for a fresh batch of the good coffee like she'd made before. "Sally, I'm finished upstairs. It's all yours."

She was sitting on the last stool at the island, scanning her phone, while eating a salad. Without looking up she said, "Well, you certainly have taken on a fresh new scent; I'll give you that. Turner, hate to ask, but that trash bag is so loaded down with your empties, I can't lift it. Mind taking it to the recycle bin for me? Thank you."

"Message received, Sally. Got any more of that salad? I could use some greens."

"Sorry, brought it from home. It's all but gone. Have a seat though. I noticed a few eggs left in the refrigerator. I'll rustle you up an omelet and coffee."

"You are my angel."

Sally got up, pulled a few basics out of the fridge and whipped me up a quick breakfast, while I sat silent with my face in my hands waiting for the fog to lift.

After placing the eggs in front of me, I said, "Smells wonderful.

Sally? Last week you mentioned Allie had meetings on Wednesdays. What kind of meetings? Did you know where she went?"

"Not really sir; seems like you should know though."

"You got me there. It's just that Tuesdays through Thursdays were my travel days. I was always out of town mid-week. Seems like she and I would have talked about it though, right?"

"Well, I do know she kept a calendar at the kitchen desk. I'd start by checking there. Oh, I fed Blaze, but he needs a walk."

"I thought you took him out when you worked, like last week."

"That's when I still felt sorry for you. Now, you're just wallowing in the mire, sir. A walk will do you good." She gathered her cleaning tools and said, "I'll be upstairs."

Speaking to the trailing vacuum hose, I said, "Yeah, I'll check that calendar. Makes sense." God, she must think I'm a total idiot.

I went over to the area in the kitchen we'd always called *command-central.* It was a corner alcove with a built-in desk with three deep drawers and a bulletin board on the wall above. Anytime I'd leave random things laying around--sunglasses, keys, baseball caps--Allie would stuff them in one of those drawers. Then, when I couldn't find something, she'd ask, 'Well, did you check command-central?' And there it would be.

In the corner of the desk, standing upright, were four cookbooks and her spiral calendar stacked beside them. For some reason, I'd rarely bothered to check it. I leafed back through her final weeks, starting with the week before she went back into the hospital. These were appointments she may not have kept because of illness.

Wednesday: *8:30 check-up Dr. Shumach*--That was her oncologist.

10:45 Nature's Kitchen -- No clue on that.

12:30 Mesquite Mike's with K --This one I knew; bar-b-que joint across from Botanicals United of Dallas. Allie loved her BBQ.

2:00 Willis and Brown --Again, no idea.

Wait...Willis and Brown...actually, that name rang a bell. I went to the office and fast-forwarded through a few weeks' worth of messages on the answering machine. Yes, there'd been two calls from the offices of Willis and Brown encouraging Allie to call them back for payment. I had ignored the calls thinking it was a scammer. I dialed the call-back number.

"Willis and Brown law offices. How may we help you?"

"Uh, not sure. I'm Turner Cooper. My wife, Allie Cooper, received a few messages requesting a call-back." The receptionist asked me to hold. After a few moments I was put on the line with Arnold Brown, attorney at law.

"Brown here. How may I help you?"

"Not really sure. I'm Turner Cooper. Apparently, my wife, Allie, had an appointment with you. She was probably unable to make it, uh, September fifth? And we've received a few messages from your firm. Just curious, can you tell me what this appointment was all about?"

"Well, we were calling about the matter of an unpaid bill and future services. She initially gave us a small retainer, but the work was completed and we sent you the papers."

"Mr. Brown, I'm sorry to tell you but Allie passed away. September tenth."

"Oh...I see. I'm stunned and so very sorry for your loss, Mr. Turner. She seemed like a very nice person. So then, as her husband, I assume you're responsible for her remaining debts?"

"What's all this about? What papers?"

"It's awkward sir; an unusual situation. I'm not at liberty to discuss them, but the papers appear to be signed for. You should have received them."

I responded with a lazy sigh. "I probably did. Have at least four weeks of mail stacked on my desk. Hold on a sec." I rummaged through a menagerie of mail, finding a fat manilla envelope from Willis and Brown. I picked back up the receiver. "OK, got it. Let's see." I tore open the envelope and read the opening sentences. Then I reread them. I was blown away, yelling into the phone. "Fucking divorce papers? What the hell is this?"

"Sorry you're receiving this at such a *delicate* time, Mr. Turner. Your wife started this procedure back in midsummer. It dragged on a while. So, shall I send the final statement---"

I slammed down the receiver. *Hate that land line! Nothing but trou-*

ble. My dear, sweet, loving wife had all but divorced me? And I'd never had a clue. How was that possible?

I briskly headed down the hilly street with Blaze leading the way on a long leash, as the two of us began a desperately needed conversation. As usual, he let me do most of the talking.

"Divorce? Can you believe it! She always seemed so happy and upbeat. I gave her everything she needed; didn't I, boy? She no longer had to work that marketing job, had time for all her hobbies and interests. Yes, I'd been preoccupied--a lot, but come on! She could have at least talked to me about it, right Blaze?"

When I said his name, he turned his eyes up at me and barked. "That's what I was thinking, dude. Divorce! What got into her? Was she that miserable?"

We walked quickly, Blaze setting the pace. "Hey, bud. What do you think? We'll create a special memorial for her. Think she would like that?" Allie had been a loving, dependable partner. I knew, for the last several years I'd been consumed with building the company. I'd been gone *a lot,* chasing down new accounts. But divorce? And then to get hit with the lawyer's bill? I didn't understand any of this.

My monologue was broken up by Blaze's barking while he went ballistic running toward a tall, young brunette woman. She was jogging in skimpy running shorts and a sports bra, and charging up the hill in a full-on run, wearing ear buds. She appeared not to notice Blaze until he rapidly leapt toward her. She screamed loudly in fear, while I grasped the leash, yanking him back toward me.

"I apologize. He never does this. Maybe he thought you were my wife. They used to run together down this street."

She just stared at the dog in fear and then turned her eyes to the ground, not looking at me. "No harm d-d-done."

"Sure you're OK?"

"Yes, th-thank you." Then she abruptly turned, and continued dashing up the hill.

I petted Blaze's head and scratched behind his ears, trying to calm him down, still holding tight to the leash as his eyes followed the woman, giving little whimpers. "It's not her boy. Sorry, pal. That's not Allie. You only get my sorry ass."

By the time we returned home, I'd walked off some of the shock of the law office call. Instead, I convinced myself I was on a discovery mission. Maybe there was a side to Allie that I had no idea about... or, I was just a lousy husband and deserved her divorce papers. I had to find out. What were her Wednesday meetings about? What was Nature's Kitchen? She had lunch with *K*. Who was *K*? Perhaps a close girlfriend who might have answers?

I rifled through all the drawers of command-central and found two more calendars from the previous two years. I took all three and sat down in my office and started flipping through the oldest first, looking for clues and information, an elusive paper trail of dates and phone numbers. Perhaps I'd get the closure I needed. I had to find out.

CHAPTER 12

Carpe Diem, Baby!

ROSARIO

I took my time walking through the gardens of Botanicals United. My head was full of self-doubt following Victor's quick exit after only an hour. I was confused and hurt. I'd felt like we were making a connection; with light and breezy conversation. He'd definitely seemed interested, then poof! He was gone.

Coming down a small hill, there was a slight ravine and a small Japanese garden caught my eye. The ground was covered in delicate green ferns and decorative rocks, with a small creek bed bubbling through it and a mist rising above the plants. The atmosphere felt so transformative and calming. I sat down on a shaded wooden bench next to the stream and considered Victor.

Maybe I shouldn't really be angry with him or myself. Yes, he ran out a little too quickly, but perhaps it had nothing to do with me. It was probably a real business trip. He said he traveled with his job all the time. What was it he said he did? Johnson and Johnson something? We didn't get into details, but it sounded like a big-deal for a young guy. Maybe I'd get another chance, but if not... his loss.

I had to remind myself; I was lucky to be here. It was my day off, so I shouldn't waste it. With my mind more settled, I got up and followed a path through a wide expanse of lawn surrounded by rich blooming beds. I wasn't familiar with several of the flowers, but I knew mums. As far as I could see, there were round, heavy nodding heads of rust, orange, burgundy, and bright golden hues; mums of different sizes and heights, buttressed up against hundreds of tall, wispy brown cattails.

Behind these, there was a backdrop of trees with their leaves in transition, dropping down in bright splashes of red and gold across the walking trail, looking like a messy artist's palette. I decided to collect several of the brightest ones to book-press later for a memory. Stopping to pick up a few, I heard a little beep. Behind me was a small electric vehicle carrying two women in BUD uniforms.

They gave me a friendly wave as they passed, while I eyed the open back of the cart filled with hoses, tools, and flats of pansies. Each turn of my walk revealed a new vista of blooms, shimmering koi ponds, and dancing fountains. While walking, my thoughts kept returning to those workers in their green shirts and khaki pants. Were they trying to tell me something? Wouldn't this be the most perfect world to work in? How could I not be happy coming to this place every day?

I passed joyful kids rolling their bodies down the sloping lawn of an outdoor theater. Then, I spotted a quinceanera princess in a billowing turquoise dress being photographed on a bridge, in preparation for her big fifteenth birthday. I was reminded of my quinceanera back in Mexico. So much fun! Ahead of me walked smiling mothers pushing strollers, and couples walking hand-in-hand.

If I was around all this color and happiness each day, I'm sure I could find joy; something I'd been missing for quite a while.

Sure, working here would involve a lot of grunt work and it would get crazy-hot in the summer. Probably a lot of digging, watering, fertilizing, nurturing new young plants into soft soil, but I was used to hard work. And didn't I always love being outdoors, even when the weather turned cold? I remember helping my mom at home, with her flowering bushes and citrus trees. I'd enjoyed assisting her when they needed pruning and watering.

A job here would certainly be an upgrade from my current positions. You couldn't get much lower than laundry and cleaning port-a-potties. As I wound my way back to the exit, I proudly felt the weight of the new employment documents in my wallet, making me feel more confident that I might be able to snag a new job, perhaps even here.

You know that saying--*everything happens for a reason*? Perhaps this was why I had the unexpected date with my elegant laundry prince? Maybe this was where I was meant to be? A safe place to work, forge new friendships, and cultivate happiness.

I walked quickly to the exit gate, after receiving a text that my Uber was minutes away. *White Toyota Corolla, Driver: Nico*. I saw the car drive up, waved, and the driver unrolled his window and asked, "Rosario Guzman?"

I responded, "Hello, Mr. White Corolla." Cute driver! Loose, brown curly hair, big eyes, with a handsome face that needed a shave. While I settled in the backseat, he asked how my day was going.

"Nico, I'd say I'm seventy-five percent along the way to perfection. It's been a pretty good day for me."

"Alright! That's what I like to hear." He pulled out of the parking lot and then adjusted his rear-view mirror. "Liking your attitude. You wouldn't believe the number of people I pick up that never say anything beyond hello, and if they do speak, they complain about how bad their day is going."

"Don't worry. No complaining from me today. Have you been inside the gardens? *Tan bonita*! You should go."

"Too busy trying to make ends meet. But you're right, I need to check it out. You mind me asking where you're from?"

"Juarez, Mexico. Been here a little over a year. Trust me, I know what you mean about making ends meet. Back in Mexico, everyone thinks it's like Candyland once you get a job here. Not for me! But I always take Sunday off. Everyone needs at least one day off to play and dream."

Nico stopped at a light and turned slightly to face me. "Cool. Like a mental health day, right? Yeah, if I'm not working, I'm usually studying. Still trying to get my associates' degree; I started a little late.

"So, what do you study?"

"Almost finished my associates in computer science and then I hope to get my bachelors at UT Dallas—but those courses are high-dollar! That's why I work so much."

I leaned up to the front seat and said, "You'll get there, and I don't think it's ever too late."

"By the way, I'm from Greece. Been here five years. My cousin talked me into coming."

I laughed thinking about my cousins. "Cousins...what would we do without them? I actually work for mine right now. But hopefully, not much longer."

"Yeah man, I don't know where I'd be without Gus. We're really more like brothers."

"Lucky you...my cousin's more like a controlling mafia boss. But at least he gave me a place to work. I'm grateful for that." Looking out the window, I was beginning to recognize my neighborhood. After hearing a little about his immigration story, I immediately felt a connection with Nico, thinking we'd be able to relate.

A buzz came through on his phone, offering a pick-up on Jefferson Avenue. He turned the corner and swerved to a stop in front of my apartment building.

"That was quick. I didn't realize I was so close to the gardens." I smiled, said goodbye, and reached for the car's door handle.

He turned to the back seat as I was getting out. "Hey, Rosario, maybe you're right about taking a day off. I know a great little Greek place close by here. Why don't you let me treat you to a glass of Ouzo?"

I sat back, considering the offer for a second. "What-zo? Probably, I shouldn't."

Nico shrugged his shoulders. "Too bad. What about this? I'm gonna text you my number. Anytime you need a ride, you call me. We'll become real friends and then we'll clink some glasses together."

I laughed at his persistence. "*Bueno.*" As I was about to get out again, it hit me. Why waste another week? I should start researching and applying for new positions today. Perhaps even the gardens had openings. "Actually, Nico...do you know the public library on Worth Street? I need to do some research there. Instead of drinking, could we study together this afternoon? I could use a little help with the library computer."

He pulled up his backpack from the floor, and yanked out two text books, smiling. "I'm always reading my school stuff between pickups. I know that library. Lakewood area, right?"

He picked up his phone and said, "Let me cancel this pick up and I'll cut out for the afternoon." Then he started the car and took a deep sigh. "So, studying, Rosario? Not usually my idea for a day off. But for you, I'll sacrifice."

"I really appreciate it. I think I'd love to start college too...someday. You know, Nico, we may have arrived in this country a little late and a step behind. But if we want to get to someplace better, I think we have to... how do they say it... *carpe diem*? Hey, maybe that's Greek?"

"Hmm, don't think so but yes, absolutely, carpe diem, baby. Let's seize the day!"

CHAPTER 13

A Ham-Fisted Gift

TURNER

With anger and curiosity, I flipped through three years of Allie's life, checking calendar dates and looking for clues of what may have broken our marriage. One glaring observation confirmed what I already knew. I'd not been truly present for many of the activities my wife enjoyed. Sometimes after she'd make a comment, I'd look up, nod and appear interested. But actually my mind was busy with possible clients I was trying to woo or an upcoming business meeting. Had I tried to include myself in her life lately? Not like I used to.

And now it was too late. It would have been easy to correct things. Show more affection. Plan some special date nights. So, in searching for divorce explanations, I'd have to say my abdication of Allie's interests must have topped the list. But why had she never complained to me about it?

I was now half-way through the second calendar, checking notations and dates. I got up and popped open a beer and went back to my desk, then heard a clunking sound in the hallway. Sally poked her head into the office door, "How's it going in here, Turner. That calendar answer any questions for you?"

"Getting there, Sally. Hey, let me ask you...did Allie seem distracted or upset these past several months?"

While putting up her vacuum attachments, she stopped and thought for a second. "No, I don't think so. Honestly...almost the opposite, up until she was hospitalized. Always seemed busy and happy. I know Allie volunteered at Botanicals United a lot. Pretty sure she enjoyed that."

"Yeah, I agree. She seemed to spend a lot of time there."

"Well Turner, time for me to head home. My wife's a stickler for promptness at the dinner table."

I nodded and got up, handing Sally her check. "So you're married? Yeah, gotta keep those home fires burning, right?"

"Sure do. Hey Turner, keep a count on those beers and I'll see you next week." She looked at me skeptically and pushed Betsy, the vacuum, out the door.

I moved back to the office and noticed several BUD notations listed on the calendar. Probably volunteer time slots. I remembered last year when Allie had volunteered as the Easter bunny for their annual egg-hunt. I had gone and taken photos of her in the white furry costume. I think she liked being around kids. At one time we were in the discussion phase regarding a family. But lately she'd seemed to have lost interest.

While at BUD, I'd noticed memorial benches and plaques scattered around the place. Would Allie want that? The perfectly placed bench facing a golden sunset overlooking the lake. That might be a great tribute. It would probably cost a bunch, but I think she would have appreciated that. I pulled up BUD's website, called their contribution coordinator and caught her just as she was leaving for the day. We agreed to meet the following week. I felt good about doing that; taking a step in the right direction for making amends. Maybe I deserved one more beer. Or two.

While pulling the tab on a cold one, I heard the doorbell chime which immediately sent Blaze barking. He followed, as I wandered to the foyer, and checked the peep-hole to decide whether I was ready for a guest. It was a tall lady in jeans with longish blonde hair, who was turning to leave. I decided to engage and opened the door. As she turned back around, I recognized her; a neighborhood friend of Allie's I'd met a few times.

"Hey there, it's Katrina, right? How are you?"

"Oh...Turner, good! Didn't think you were home." She extended her arm, holding a bag. "Here, I brought you a ham."

Odd opening line. "A ham? That's very kind. Thank you."

"I know I'm late in saying this, but I never had a chance to tell you. I'm so sorry about Allie. Her passing came so suddenly. Anyway, Allie had once mentioned to me you're not much of a cook. This is one of those pre-sliced hams. Great for sandwiches."

I nodded and took the wrapped meat, "Good choice. I am a ham man." This was followed by a dead, awkward silence, as she stood there. "Hey, where are my manners? I just opened this beer. Come in and join me. Or perhaps you prefer wine?"

"Sure, wine sounds good." Katrina followed me in.

I led her to the kitchen. "Allie was the wine aficionado. I think there's still an unopened bottle of Chablis in the fridge somewhere. Sound OK?"

"Perfect. Your place looks so tidy. Seems you're managing pretty well."

"Gotta be honest, the maid just left."

Blaze clicked into the kitchen and gave Katrina a sniff followed by a bit of a growl. "Blaze, it's OK. Sorry, I think he's still hoping Allie's going to walk in. They were tight."

"Yes, we walked together occasionally. I have a miniature collie named Sam. Hey Blaze...good boy." She ruffled his neck in an affectionate manner, then looked out the sliding glass doors. "Oh, I love your deck. What a great view. Should we sit outside?"

"Uh, sure. You need a jacket? It's starting to get chilly." She was only wearing a fitted white tee shirt with black jeans, which accentuated her tall, sculpted figure.

"I'm fine for now. I won't stay long. I've just been meaning to drop some food off, but didn't want to bother you too soon. That sounds silly, I guess."

"No, I get it." We both sat down on a pair of wooden Adirondacks separated by a table. "I forget, Katrina. How did you and Allie meet?"

"Let's see. The dog-park? I guess it's been a few years. Yeah, she went pretty often in the early evenings and sometimes we'd walk home together."

"So, you live fairly close?"

"A couple streets over on West Hill. My son and I live there."

Was that code for saying she was divorced? I'd ignore that. "That's cool. I've taken Blaze to the dog-park recently. Loves it; seems like he's in his happy place."

She nodded. "Your view from here is nice. This lot must be higher elevation than mine."

I just stayed quiet for a few minutes, absorbing the last warm rays of the sun, keeping my thoughts on Allie with Blaze, her walks, her friends.

Katrina interrupted my trance. "Well, Turner, I appreciate the wine. I'm going to head home." She reached across the table and touched my arm with her tanned warm hand, making me flinch. "I'll leave you my number if you want someone to walk with. I sure miss my talks with Allie."

"So, you two were pretty close?"

"We were getting to be. You know...girl-talk."

"So, let me ask. Did Allie seem upset about anything to you... before she got sick?"

"Gosh, I don't think so. She seemed involved with Nature's Kitchen and all that stuff."

"Nature's Kitchen? What's that? I noticed it on her calendar."

"From what she told me, at BUD they create recipes from foods grown in the area and let attendees sample the stuff. She seemed quite involved. Surprised you didn't know about it."

We were both standing and headed back through the kitchen. I snapped my fingers. "That's right, she did mention it to me. I forgot. Well, Katrina, thanks so much for the ham and thoughtful visit."

"My pleasure. So, you want my number? Sam misses Blaze. Call me next time you feel like walking."

Opening up my contacts, I handed her my phone, "Sure, just fill in your number."

I closed the door on the attractive woman. All right, that was a little strange. Was this the new grieving widower protocol? Bring over a ham and leave your phone number for a stroll with me and the dog? But maybe I was full of myself and she was simply being a good neighbor.

OK, one last beer and one more calendar to examine.

The following week, I swung into the parking lot of BUD. This was a task I was interested in exploring. Adrianna Wellington greeted me wearing the full regalia of a garden coordinator with a floral print scarf worn with a fall-hued outfit. She then offered me a croissant with rose hips tea.

"I'm a coffee guy; black, would be great."

"So, Mr. Cooper, you briefly mentioned placing something in your wife's name to honor her here at Botanicals United?"

"Yes, I noticed some benches with plaques. I thought that might be nice. Her name was Allie Cooper. She was such a fan of this place. Volunteered here a lot, especially Nature's Kitchen, apparently."

"That's wonderful. We do so love our volunteers. This place could not survive without them. First, let me say, I'm so sorry to hear your wife recently passed. And we hate losing such an avid volunteer."

"Well, it seems it was one of her great pleasures to spend time here so I thought a bench might be an appropriate tribute."

She offered a sympathetic smile. "I have to tell you; we only incorporate benches as we design garden spaces. They have to be a part of the look and feel of each garden. Can you imagine if we dropped in a bench for everyone wanting to purchase a tribute? There probably wouldn't be space for the plants."

"I see. Hadn't really thought about it that way."

"Now, I'm not saying it couldn't happen, but there's some other alternatives you might consider. We do commemorative ten-foot blooming beds for a season, or for a few seasons. Or an honor plaque placed in the sidewalk of a garden. Or perhaps your workplace would like to help sponsor a new garden in her name. What amount of tribute did you have in mind?"

"I'm not sure. Hadn't really thought about it. But that last thing sounded pretty good."

"Excellent. There's a host of benefits that go along with sponsorships and they start at the twenty-five-thousand-dollar level and up. Here, take a look at this brochure."

I glanced through info on the sponsorships which included a tax incentive program, membership, some mention of signage in the gardens and in their marketing. The contribution was high but I wanted something substantial like this for Allie.

I handed the brochure back. "Interesting. I think my company could sign on at the introductory level. Can I choose which garden to sponsor?"

She lightly clapped her hands together hearing my offer. "Actually, we have availability of sponsorships with a *new* garden we'll be breaking ground on shortly. You could be the first! It features xeriscape gardening with drought tolerant plants. An eco-friendly design that uses less water. We're *really* excited about it."

"Yes...I can get on board with that. Allie was all about the environment."

"Wonderful. In fact, the new lead gardener is meeting right now with our head-horticulturist and I think they would be thrilled to hear they already had a sponsor! They're across the hall. Would you like to just peek in, meet them, and hear what it's all about? This is such an amazing opportunity!"

I shrugged, "Why not?"

I followed her across the hall and waited outside while she went in to explain our intrusion.

She opened the door and waved me in. "Come in, Mr. Cooper. They're *so excited* about this. This is Molly Hayes, our horticologist. Meet Turner Cooper. And this is our new lead gardener, Violet Hill. Violet, meet your first sponsor!"

I shook hands with a beaming Molly and turned to the lead gardener, noticing her downcast eyes and awkward attempt at a handshake. Then recognition set in. "Hey, I remember you. My dog almost chased you down on Lawther Road the other day."

She nodded, flicked her eyes up at me and quietly said, "I've been th-thinking about getting a dog...for protection."

Odd response. I followed up with, "Nice." Then there was an uncomfortable pause before I jumped in and added: "Listen ladies, I've been considering what my wife did here; with all her volunteering. Once you get going with this, I'd love to volunteer and help out on this garden I'm sponsoring."

Violet suddenly looked up with relief and said, "T-T-Terrific. We could use a volunteer. S-So you're an avid g-gardener?"

"No. Honestly, I know nothing, but eager to help."

Then she frowned and began studying the floor again. Strange creature, that one.

CHAPTER 14

Careful What You Wish For

ROSARIO

I was eating my morning jelly-donut as my boss, Miguel, walked into the kitchen of Daylight Donuts. He nodded and went into his cramped office. I considered telling him about my new job hunt but knew he wouldn't be too happy about finding my replacement for two positions. Then again, he was my primary work reference. Surely he would understand I couldn't stay here forever at what he paid me.

I got up, washed the sticky sugar from my hands and put on my white apron. Time to face the morning rush. I pulled out a trey of warm, freshly glazed apple-fritters to take out front. As I served the early customers waiting in line, I couldn't stop daydreaming about my previous afternoon with Nico. He'd been so helpful at the library and made job hunting fun...well, as much fun as possible while in a library. He'd helped me write up my resume and fill out an application for BUD. We also went to a site that was loaded with jobs. I filled out applications at a few restaurants and a clothing store near me, but my top choice was still the gardens. Even though I knew it was too soon to get a response, I began checking my texts every hour, hoping for interview requests.

Then I heard the snapping of fingers, followed by "*Café negro y dos empanadas*." My dream time was interrupted as I looked into the eyes of my next impatient customer.

But my mind kept going back to Nico. Yesterday, I caught his large brown eyes glancing at me while he was supposed to be reading. Then his arm brushed against mine as he helped me navigate a website. Just his casual touch sent my heart thrumming. After we left the library, I invited him to my favorite neighborhood taco shop, Teddy's, for a quick dinner. He loved the simple little place, inhaled three corn tortillas filled with spicy meat and picante, and then grinned as if it was the best meal ever.

He was so easy to talk with that I was tempted to invite him to my apartment, but was too embarrassed for him to see it. I had almost no furniture besides a bed, one chair, a turned-over crate I used as a table, and my radio. Even the exterior of the apartment building was depressing, with several broken blinds in the windows, peeling paint on the trim and mold stains on the stucco walls. Besides, Nico was anxious to pick up a few more Uber rides before it got late. But as he left, we made plans to meet up again next Sunday.

Miguel came out as I was wiping down the counters near the end of my shift. He simply said, "Rosario," and tilted his head toward the back. I met him in his cramped office, climbing over a stack of collapsed donut boxes and a case of paper-napkins. He continued looking down as he checked items off his ledger while he asked me, "How was it out there today, Rosario?"

"I haven't checked totals yet, but it's been very steady. Everybody is liking the new jalapeno kolaches."

"*Bien*," he said, finally looking up at me. "Look, I wanted to tell you, I like your work. You been doing real good. I hear things. Customers like you; you keep the place clean, here and at the lavanderia. And I've noticed sales are often better when you're working."

After a full year, I was finally getting a compliment from Miguel. I had to wonder; was he reading my mind? Did he know I was thinking about leaving? I hadn't told anyone at work about my green card yet.

He continued, "So...we're family; not close, but still family. You've shown me I can trust you. I have news. Big plans to expand to two more lavanderias. Just signed the leases...top locations. I can't keep up with everything like before. I want you to manage the lavenderia-end of my business. You're smart, reliable, and don't take crap from people. I like that."

This came as a big surprise. Now I felt conflicted. "Miguel, gracias! Very honored to be considered. I appreciate the offer and I'd like to hear the details, but I have to be honest with you. I recently received my green card. I was planning on looking around for new jobs. There's still more I want to try my hand at."

Miguel's face turned from pleasant to angry. His surly scowl came out, which I'd witnessed several times before. "So, you get the big deal green-card and now you are fancy shit? I gave you jobs when you had nothing but a suitcase."

I didn't blurt it out, but my mind immediately thought about the jobs he'd so *generously* given me. Sure, he hired me right away but everything was under the table and he paid me an illegal wage, *below* the impossible minimum wage of seven dollars an hour. I decided to speak my mind.

"Miguel, I realize you have helped me out this year. A lot. And I'm grateful. But I gave back as well. I never missed a day of work at either place, and never left either place before it was thoroughly cleaned. I also have good customers that come in and ask for me. With the amount you're paying me, I have to work seventeen hours a day, six days a week. I can't keep this up. It's exhausting."

I tried to keep a controlled, firm voice, hoping to sound confident. And I could not show any tears! My firm response seemed to take the edge off his anger.

"You know, Rosario, I must see what kind of worker you are before raises and promotions are given. And you're right; you have given me a year of good service. And I'm picking you out amongst many other employees. This promotion would increase you from six to twelve dollars an hour at forty hours a week. That's doubling your pay with one increase."

I knew that twelve dollars an hour had become almost standard for most starting level employees at many jobs. Quickly calculating the new monthly take-home, at forty hours, I realized it would barely cover rent. I'd still need to work at least one extra job in order to send money back to my mother.

I chewed my lip for a second, deciding if I should try to negotiate. "Honestly Miguel, I think if I'm managing *three* lavanderias, it is not enough. But I will certainly give it some thought and I appreciate you thinking highly of my work."

I could tell, again, Miguel was not pleased with my response and seemed surprised. "I'll look over my operating budget. We can discuss this later. That's all for now."

Sitting on the bus on my way to Construction Connection, I considered Miguel's offer again. A management position might be a good step forward. I would probably set schedules, interview employees, handle maintenance issues, in addition to doing my regular work. I think I'd be good at that job with the right salary. Hopefully, I could switch to working days.

Then my mind went to Nico and I wondered what he might think. I was already excited to see him again. It had been so long since I'd had a friend to talk to. My fear after Roberto's death had kept me from opening up and befriending anyone in Dallas. I knew a few people, but nobody I would consider a true friend. Now that I had opened that door just a little, I was hungry for more.

Three days later, as I left Daylight Donuts, I received a text. I was so excited my hands shook as I tried to reply. Botanicals United had responded to my application and wanted to set up an interview. My dream job! Could it be possible? I scheduled one for four o'clock the following day, their last interview slot. The text had me smiling all the way to the porta-potties, where I asked my manager if I could leave two hours earlier the following afternoon.

That night, I plotted out responses to questions that might be asked. I wasn't sure what was appropriate to wear for the interview, but I decided on a simple white collared shirt and black trousers which I switched into before leaving Construction Connections. At the gardens, I walked through a designated entrance reserved for employees and found the HR office. I couldn't believe I might get to work in such a beautiful place; even the pathway to the office was impressive.

I was in a pleasant, small office sitting in front of an Anglo woman wearing a casual leaf-print skirt and knit top. She welcomed me, introduced herself, shook my hand, and then reviewed my resume. While reading it she asked me, "So Rosario, I see you're currently holding down three jobs since arriving in Dallas. Impressive! Tell me more about what you do... your responsibilities."

I filled her in on the work details and what I liked about each job, always remaining positive. Then she asked why I was interested in working at BUD.

"Honestly, I visited this place recently and saw the prettiest gardens I've ever seen and I thought, if I could work here every day, I would be so happy. Ms. Campbell, I work hard, don't mind getting my hands dirty, and want to move up and build on my job skills. I am very excited for this opportunity."

She smiled and asked about my education, my work history in Mexico, and what my future goals were. We spent over thirty minutes talking and discussed schedules. It was all going better than I ever expected.

"Rosario, I think I've got the perfect spot for you and we have a full-time opening at fourteen-dollars-an hour in our sanitation department. You would oversee all the restrooms and common areas at Botanicals United and have a staff of six other associates working with you. You have the drive and experience. I think you would fit right in."

Blood rushed to my ears, while my face got hot and my heart sank. This was not my dream job at all. "You mean you want me to clean bathrooms?"

CHAPTER 15

A Teachable Moment

VIOLET

Once Turner Cooper said he knew nothing about gardening, my interest in him disappeared. But head-horticulturist, Molly Hayes, appeared thrilled that our xeriscape garden had already acquired a sponsor. Apparently, they were a hot commodity at BUD. And he was a two-fer! A sponsor and volunteer...she could hardly contain herself. In Molly's defense, the guy wasn't bad looking. Tall, nice build, light short hair, handsome face, maybe a little puffy. *But take a step back, Molly, you're practically drooling on him.* I, on the other hand, remained myself; silently aloof and highly professional, keeping my eyes down, focused on my garden drawing.

Right before the benevolent Turner showed up, I'd just rolled out my proposed rendering on Molly's desk, which was drawn up with the help of Mark, mother's gardener, and the bribe of a six pack. I'd come up with a few creative ideas but he helped me flesh it out and put it down on paper. It seemed Mark might be a better artist than landscaper.

The scientist in me came out as I explained to Molly and Turner that I thought our new garden should become more of a teachable experience rather than one with vistas that would blow visitors away.

As the three of us stared down at my garden blue-print, Turner appeared interested, although Molly was yet to be swayed.

I pointed at two round cylinders, representing rain-harvesting water barrels, which were set on either side of a wide stone pathway at the top of an incline. "Here and here we would c-collect the rain-water from the roofs of these s-s-seating areas. The water would then be dispensed as needed down these two rows for hy-hydration of the p-plants."

Turner looked up and smiled. "Brillant; love it. Simple and effective. Why aren't we all doing this already, right?"

Molly interjected, putting her hand on his arm, "It's an old idea obviously, but it might work."

I was grateful for his positive comment and further explained, "Yes, there's a fairly large cottage industry creating these tanks now, so they're p-pretty easy to p-purchase. I also thought we m-might incorporate Dr. Hirshfield's molecular soil substance, blending it into the bedding soil to retain the moisture." I glanced up at both Molly and Turner, explaining, "He was the p-p-professor at UT that I did research for. It would be a great field study for the gardens and for his w-work.

Again, Molly seemed hesitant. "Well, it might not be a good idea if it hasn't been tested before."

"It's been tested, but just not in any co-commercial capacity. Just a suggestion, but again, if it p-proves effective, visitors might be interested in learning more about it."

Turner shrugged, "Don't know anything about that stuff, but it sounds cool. Why not? Ladies, I'm gonna leave you to it. I'm excited about this. Good job, Violet. I know my wife would have enjoyed being a part of this. I'm doing all this for her. So, about the volunteer slots...how does that work?"

Molly responded with enthusiasm, "Let me just say again how pleased I am for you to join us on this little adventure. We have a volunteer coordinator, but I'll make a point of contacting you personally to let you know dates and times once we get the ball rolling."

"Great; I've recently stepped back from some duties with my company so I have a bit more free time. See you both soon."

Hmm. Something about this guy seemed off. I'd always been so shy to speak, so I'd spent a lot more time listening to people than talking. When Turner spoke, I was hearing a little guilt in all his enthusiasm and need to volunteer. Was this friendly, smiling man actually in crisis mode?

As the door closed, Molly's eyes followed him out. She was one eager-beaver when it came to her volunteers. Turning to me with a flushed face, she said, "Well, he's certainly a lucky catch. So, let's discuss plants."

As I went over a list of suggestions, Molly nixed a few but agreed on several others and had good ideas about mixing what worked best for the path-side beds. She opened up her lap top and checked for existing stocks of plants at the Botanicals United nursery. Whatever they didn't have, she would order.

As she made an initial buy for our larger trees and blooming cacti, I asked about my team. "So, Molly, I know a guy who s-s-seems quite knowledgeable and he's interested in working par-par-part time at Botanicals United. Name is M-Mark Hopkins. Any chance we can put him on my team?"

She looked up from her laptop. "Probably. If he has strong landscaping experience, ask him to come by this week. I'll interview him. I do need you to know that our budget on this project is quite tight. It's actually a blessing this garden won't require replanting every season. But these rain tanks of yours? And the solar panels you're suggesting? Just not sure about all that. Sounds unnecessary."

"M-Molly, I understand you want s-something attractive and I think it will be, but this will be d-different. Gardening in the southwest is changing, just like the cli-climate. We'll be advancing ideas of sustainability; that's the whole p-p-point, right?"

She pulled out BUD's newest holiday brochure and opened it, tapping her finger on a photo of a winter wonderland village. "Yes, but look here. Our guests come in expecting to be awed and entertained, to find a bunch of photo-perfect moments, and on occasion, become one with nature. But I don't think they want to be sent to school."

"But learning can be entertaining and we can make it pr-pretty. Shall we visit the gr-grounds together to visualize?"

Her head was down now, tapping on her keyboard, already moving on to another issue. "You go on ahead, Violet. I've got too much on my plate today. And take this list and study up on all these plants. It's important to know all about the product you'll be working with. You can work from home this afternoon." She hit print and then walked over to a large wall calendar. "Let's see, we'll break ground on this maybe next week, Tuesday? For the rest of the week you'll join another team and do some old-fashioned grunt work. Get those soft white hands of yours dirty and calloused. We start at 6:30 sharp. Ask for Bob Rodriguez; he's young but really knows his stuff."

"Sure, thanks." I closed her door behind me and quickly stepped outside. I would call that a less-than-warm welcome from my new boss. For some reason, she wasn't too blown away by my ideas. But she certainly was hot for my volunteer. And what about that early morning start? Nobody had mentioned those hours before; definitely an interruption to my morning swim and run.

But change was good...change was healthy. I kept repeating that thought as I walked over to an area that would soon be the new garden. It was currently separated with a chain-link fence and covered with untended shrubby growth which would all be cut down before the soil was tilled up.

This would be *my* garden. I suddenly felt a sense of pride I hadn't experienced before, and the daunting weight of responsibility.

I looked over the fence at the small scrub trees, and instead saw something else entirely. Delightful seating areas at the top of a crest, a winding rock pathway to the bottom, clusters of purple flowering desert willows, with a breeze blowing the blooms across the reedy stems of lantana tipped with red and yellow, attracting hungry monarch butterflies at sunset. My eyes followed my imaginary path down the hill to clusters of regal Saguaro cactus, surrounded by the smaller golden barrel cactus and mammillaria with their tiny fuchsia flowers.

I was excited to get started, but I knew my limitations and understood I couldn't do this alone. It would definitely require the help and knowledge of others.

As I pulled up the curving drive of Mother's house, I hoped to catch Mark again. I pulled into the carport next to the guest house and wandered the lawn. With my nose on high alert, I quickly caught the scent of pot, not too far away. Next to the pool pump enclosure was a tool shed, the perfect spot for a not-so-hard-working gardener to toke-up.

I called out, "Knock-knock." I heard some banging of equipment, followed by Mark's head poking out of the doors. "Whew, Mark, that's s-some st-strong stuff you got there."

"Violet? What do you want now?"

"I have a w-wonderful opportunity for you."

"What?" Mark stepped out from behind the door, crushing the butt of a joint under his foot.

"How would you like to be a p-part of my gardening team at BUD? Just while we get the new garden set up. It's very exciting."

"Not interested. I'm busy." He tried to close the shed doors as he stepped back in, but I revved up my courage and grabbed the edge of the door.

"B-Busy doing what?"

"My art. I told you. I'm a painter."

"I can tell from your rendering. You're right about being a good artist. That's why I w-w-want you on my team. I'm all about the plants, science, and water conservation. But I need someone that can make it b-b-beautiful. A landscape artist with a vivid imagination. Your drawing was so good. L-L-Let's make it come to life.

"Still not interested." His face looked resolute.

I gave it another stab. "If for no other r-r-reason, do it as a reference. Customers around this neighborhood will pay top dollar to a guy who helped design and p-plant a garden at BUD. They'll be d-dying to hire you. I'll only need you two days a week, maybe three, until the spring."

Mark leaned against the shed and looked up at the sky and shrugged. I don't know...do they drug test there?"

"No idea. They didn't ask me to."

"Yeah...big surprise."

I gave one final push, forcing myself to look him in the eye. "Look, M-Mark, you s-say you love your art. This is your chance to express yourself. Help me create something beautiful and lasting which th-thousands of people will see. I need your creativity. P-Please?"

He gave an extended sigh, "Oh, for Christ's sake. You're not going to cry on me, are you?" We both remained silent for a few seconds, staring at each other. "Damn it. Stop staring at me with those baby blues. I'll do it. Who do I ask for, kid?"

"Ask for M-Molly Hayes. I'll text you her number. Hey, if they hire you, there's no p-pot allowed on the crew."

"Gotcha." Then he stepped back into his dark little shed and slammed the door.

A slight smile crossed my face as I thought about my emerging garden team: a reluctant pot-head artist, a grieving widower with unskilled enthusiasm, and me, initially antagonistic but now willing to learn. Things were looking up.

CHAPTER 16

Man's Best Friend

TURNER

A few days after my visit to BUD, I transferred over a twenty-five-thousand-dollar donation. I felt good about my decision to sponsor and volunteer with the gardens. Allie would have been pleased that I'd followed through.

While patting myself on the back, I was searching the meager contents of my refrigerator, not finding much except beer and out-of-date condiments. Opening the freezer, I spotted one of Allie's frozen low-cal dinners. She used to eat them for lunch, being a stickler for keeping her slim figure. Pasta with chicken in alfredo sauce. I pulled it out with apprehension.

While waiting for the microwave to ding, my father called my cell. "Turner. Whatcha been up to, son?"

"Uh, you know. Walking the dog, cleaning house, life."

"Sounds like you've got too much time on your hands. When you coming back to work? That girl you got in sales hasn't brought in diddly lately. You know that's your strong suit. Never a week went by without you bringing in a fresh new account."

"Dad, that girl-in-sales name is Sarah. She's been with us three months and has brought in six new accounts. Good ones. I bet you didn't think I was keeping up. And the reason I brought Sarah in was to eventually *take over* the sales department."

"Whatever, son. All I know is you are sorely missed around here. You're the life blood of this place. You need to get back in here, Turner."

"You know, Dad...all that time I spent on the road, all those missed nights at home because of meetings and dinners with clients —I don't miss it at all and I can't help but feel that's what killed Allie and destroyed my marriage. Maybe it sounds crazy, but that's how I feel."

"What are you talking about?" He was quiet for a moment, and then responded angrily. "You know damn well cancer and covid took Allie. It had nothing to do with you."

"That may have been what put the nail in the coffin, but stress and mental health has so much to do with one's physical health. I wasn't there for her when she needed me, plain and simple. Our marriage was on the rocks, apparently." I knew I was getting too dark for my father. He wasn't comfortable with touchy-feely things. "Hey Dad, my dinner's getting cold. I'll check back in later."

"If I don't hear from you soon I'm calling back. I'm worried about you, boy."

"I'm OK, Dad. Just trying to make amends and working things out."

I pulled the card-board lid off my frozen dinner and looked down. That was it? Two tiny scoops of pasta and a teaspoon full of chopped chicken floating in a watery sauce. No way. I may have been on a drinking binge for several weeks, but surely, I hadn't sunk so low as to eat this.

I went out to the back deck and called for Blaze. He walked inside, looking at me expectantly. "We're going for a ride boy; your favorite place. It's time for some barbecue."

Mesquite Mike's was a bar-b-que joint with outdoor seating on the other side of the lake. Dogs were welcome and Allie had loved the place. As Blaze and I walked in, it was just shy of four o'clock, too early for the dinner rush and too late for lunch. But a happy-hour crowd would be trickling in within the hour. I had my pick of outdoor tables. I ordered two cold beers, a juicy chopped beef sandwich, a basket of hot fries, with a tart dill pickle on the side. Blaze got the kid's meal. A guy in the corner, on a small platform, plugged in his amp and began tuning his guitar while the strong scent of burning mesquite circled the air. I leaned back into a comfy chair knowing I was going to really enjoy this meal. Then, I closed my eyes for a second, soaking in the relaxing ambiance.

"Look, Sam; it's your buddy Blaze! Turner, I can't believe you're here."

I popped open my eyes and stared up into the ample chest of Katrina, the neighbor who had gifted me with the ham. "Whoa. You caught me napping for a second. How are you?"

"Just swung by to pick up some dinner to-go for me and my son." She pointed to my two beers in the ice bucket. "Is someone joining you?"

I considered lying. "Nope, both for me. Just didn't want to have to get up once I sat down." She continued to stare and smile as her dog tugged on his leash. I reluctantly offered her my second beer. "Uh, join me for a few minutes, if you have the time."

She grabbed the chair next to me and dragged her shaggy mutt over next to Blaze. "I guess one beer couldn't hurt. So, you come here often?"

I responded, forcing a smile. "Every now and then. Good tunes, good food, it's relaxing." *Or it was until a minute ago.* I uncapped the beer for her.

Katrina took a sip. "So, when are we going to meet up for that dog walk we talked about?"

"Uh, did we talk about that? Not sure. I guess when it comes to dog walking, Blaze and I are on a loose schedule."

"But he needs to play. Hey, if you're not busy tomorrow we should meet at the dog park by the lake. These two love running together. Around four or five?"

"Yeah, maybe I'll do that. I'll have to check that schedule."

I was dying to take a big bite out of my chopped beef, but was afraid she'd decide to join me. I never should have offered the beer. After a few minutes of small talk, she said, "I better put my order in. You mind watching Sam for a minute?"

Crap, now I was dog-sitting. With Katrina gone, I went for a bite of my sandwich, as Blaze looked up at me, whining for his. "Just a minute, boy. Gotta wait for your company to leave." I stuffed a few fries into my mouth and his and then took aim at my pickle. What was it about Katrina that bothered me? She was friendly, definitely easy on the eyes, liked dogs. Maybe it was because I presumed she knew more about me and Allie then she let on. Women together... they could talk. Guys on the other hand, never dug too deep. They seemed to stick to the safe topics: sports, work, tools, and cars.

But perhaps Katrina would reveal more if I gave her the time. I was curious if Allie had hinted about divorce plans with her on one of their walks. Maybe I should meet up with her for intel. Just a doggy play-date; what harm could it do?

When she returned she sat down again. I confirmed a time for tomorrow and added, "Hey, don't let me keep you. I know how hungry kids can get."

"That's so true. See you tomorrow then, Turner."

The following afternoon we rendezvoused at four-thirty. Walking into the dog enclosure, I saw Katrina had already scouted out a choice bench with the sun behind us. There was a gentle breeze and perfect fall temps for a light jacket. I joined her on the bench and we released our eager dogs. She'd also brought a picnic basket. Apparently, wine and snacks were requisites for watching dogs romp. I didn't mind. The chilled white wine might loosen up her tongue.

"Well Katrina, this is nice. You've thought of everything. Women are so good at stuff like this."

"Probably just our mothering nature. We can't help ourselves."

"So, tell me a little about yourself. Are you working now?"

"Yeah, luckily I office out of my home. I handle insurance for a large financial group. Insurance snafus, employee disputes, that sort of thing. The best part is, I can start early and quit around three or so which is perfect when raising a son alone. Cal's in sixth grade now and is into so many things. I just dropped him at soccer practice."

I opened the screw-top bottle and poured the wine into our plastic cups. "Cool. Great sport for exercise."

"As a mom, it's fun to watch him. His dad played; still does I think."

Here we go, perfect segue. "If you don't mind talking about it, are you divorced, or does your husband just live somewhere else?"

"Divorced. Almost three years now. He lives in far north Dallas. He's a decent dad, just not a great husband."

"Sorry to hear that. Must be hard. Yeah, I travel a lot for my company. Allie must have complained to you about it. I missed a lot of stuff."

"I don't recall her mentioning that. Honestly, I think she seemed pretty happy."

"Really? That's not the vibe I was getting."

"No,. seriously. She always seemed content and busy; happy even, especially when she was in remission."

"OK. Good to hear that." *She was no help at all.*

While passing me some grapes, Katrina pointed over to our dogs. "Look, they're so cute. Watch how fast they run through those tubes."

Blaze and Sam were racing in a circle through a short metal cylinder installed in the ground. Then a short brown dachshund shot out of nowhere and began chasing the two of them, barking ferociously and growling with teeth bared.

From another bench, I heard a short scream as a tall, thin brunette stood paralyzed as her little dog started a fight with ours. I ran over to the dogs to separate them, followed by Katrina. I grabbed Blaze's collar and immediately pulled him out, while Katrina seemed too intimidated to grab Sam out of the stand-off with the tiny dachshund. I handed off Blaze for her to hold and then grabbed Sam, leaving the weeny dog snarling at no one in particular.

Walking over to the woman still standing frozen with her hands covering her face, I said, "It's OK. No harm done. But I'd keep him on a leash for now. Oh, wow. It's you again. Violet?"

"Mr. Cooper."

"Turner, please. Is this your new dog? You mentioned you were thinking of getting one the other day. Looks like she's going to make a good guard dog. What's her name?"

Finally pulling her hands from her face, she looked down. "C-Cocoa. Got her at the shelter. I wanted a b-big one but Cocoa kept j-jumping up at me when I walked by her cage. I wanted a dog that could run with me, but this is what I brought home." Then she offered up a little smile.

"I'm sure you'll give her a good home. She might be OK for your short runs."

When she finally looked up at me, I couldn't help but notice. Violet's eyes were a stunning light blue. Guess I'd really never looked at her face. She was always looking away.

"She's my first d-dog. I honestly don't know what I'm doing."

"Today, I'd just let her walk around on a leash and sniff things out. The dog park might be overwhelming for her at first since she's used to living in a cage."

"That's true."

I walked over to the snapping Cocoa, attached her leash, and pulled her back to Violet. "Here you go. Any updates on the garden?"

"I'm w-working with a gardener named Mark. We came up with s-some good ideas last night. I think our team will meet s-soon."

"Great. Take my number and text me when it's scheduled. I'd like to come."

Then behind me I heard, "Hey guys, everything calmed down?" Katrina walked up and offered Violet her hand. "I'm Katrina, by the way." And then another guy who seemed to know us came over. This spot was getting crowded. Violet meekly waved goodbye and walked away with Cocoa.

CHAPTER 17

Shitty Shitty Bang Bang

ROSARIO

The lady doing the interviewing sat across from me expectantly. It was a fair offer based on my experience, but all I felt was crushing disappointment. A manager in charge of cleaning toilets? *This* was all I was qualified for? I was silent for a moment. I wanted to work in the gardens, learn new things. Push bulbs full of surprise into the soft earth and watch them slowly turn into stalks of green and blooms of color. I dreamed of starting each morning with the rising sun warming my face and a new set of challenges waiting for me. That's what I wanted to do!

In my mind, I reached over her desk, tore up my resume and stomped out. But in reality, I said, "Ms. Campbell, I appreciate your time and will certainly think about the job, but I must be honest, cleaning is not what I had hoped to do. Thank you very much." I stood up and leaned over to shake her hand as she got up abruptly, looking perplexed at my quick negative response.

"All right then, thanks for coming in. Just to be clear though, where were you seeing yourself working at BUD?"

"In the gardens."

"I see. But according to your resume, you really have no experience with that work."

"Yes, but I helped my mother with her plants. I always enjoyed that."

"Not quite what we're looking for. We prefer people with more landscaping experience who can jump right in, but thanks again for coming. Good luck to you, Rosario."

I walked out hurriedly, my face felt red from a mix between anger and embarrassment. Why did I think a simple green card would open an enchanting door to possibilities? I probably needed to go back to Miguel and accept his offer of running the laundry. The job wasn't that bad, was it? There'd still be a lot of late nights and keeping lazy employees in line, but I knew I could do that. I'd think about it for a couple more days and allow time to hear back from the other places I applied at.

On the bus ride home I forced myself to think about happier things. I pictured Nico's face and thought about the next time I'd see him. That evening, while sleeping before my eleven PM shift began, Nico had called. I always turned my ringer off while I slept. My sleep was too precious. Once I'd arrived at Bright White, I saw his message and returned the call.

"Nico, sorry I'm calling you so late. I'm at work."

"No problem. Actually, I'm in my car waiting for a pick-up near the arena downtown. Concert just let out."

"Oh, so you're working late too?"

"Definitely on weekends. That's when I'm busiest, after everybody's been drinking. Best tips too. That way I can study during the day."

"Ah, makes sense."

"I think I see my people coming this way. Hey, I put a big basket of laundry in my trunk. I thought I'd head your way around three this morning? We can keep each other company for a while."

"Sure! You'd be my first-ever laundry date." I had to laugh. "Sounds so romantic, Nico."

"No kidding...dirty laundry, bright fluorescent lights. The dream scenario. How about I bring you some food?"

"Yes, and I have plenty of detergent to wash it down with."

"See, I knew we were perfect for each other."

The laundry began to get busy right after Nico's call. The bill-changing machine wasn't working so I had to give change from the safe to customers using washers and dryers, and then about six truckers came in with drop-offs that needed to be finished by tomorrow. Between those loads, I was busy sweeping and wiping down all the equipment.

As three AM neared, I was excited about seeing Nico, but after noticing my reflection in the glass of the candy machine, I wished I'd worn something more flattering. I had on an old plaid flannel shirt of Roberto's and some baggy blue jeans. I went into the restroom, and tried tying up the shirt tails in a knot above my waist and rolling the loose jeans up above my ankles.

I kept some high wedges in my backpack, just in case, and put those on in place of old tennis shoes. I was happy I finally had a reason for my just-in-case-shoes. Then I pulled my hair out of its tight ponytail and brushed it out and added bright red lipstick. Standing back, I looked into the wavy bathroom mirror and decided...better. At least, good enough for a laundry date.

I walked out smiling. For the first time that night, the place had emptied. Maybe Nico and I could actually sit in the office and eat together. There was a wide sliding-glass-window in the office, so customers could be observed or helped from the desk. Walking over, I noticed the office door was slightly open. Guess I'd forgotten to close it. Stopping suddenly at the door, I saw a guy wearing low baggy jeans and a tank top, arms covered in tats, with stringy blonde hair, quickly rummaging through the desk drawers making a mess.

I shouted out to him, "Only employees are allowed in here. Get out now!" He immediately wheeled around, slammed me into the door, and put a sharp long blade to my throat. "Bitch, get that safe open, or I'll cut you up real bad. Now!"

With a shaking hand, I pointed to the large sign on the wall posted in English and Spanish:

ATTENDANT DOES NOT HAVE COMBINATION TO SAFE

"Bullshit. Get that safe open. I'm not fucking around." He

gripped my throat with his other hand and pressed the point of the knife further in, as a trickle of blood began to flow, and I was forced to look at his rotten teeth.

I whispered, "I swear. I don't know it. Boss never told me. Try the change machines."

Still pressing me against the door, he glanced out. "Fuck you. I don't want any lousy change. What am I supposed to do with that?"

I softly said a few more words. "There's bills in there too... Lots."

He pulled me away from the door with his hand still on my throat. "Open them...now!"

I shook my head. "No keys. Owner fills it every morning." I could tell he was getting more agitated. I pointed to a tool box in the corner of the office as his hand lifted slightly from my neck. "Bet you could pry one open. There's a hammer... screwdriver. Shouldn't take long."

He inched toward it, while watching me. "Don't you even think about moving."

As he turned to pick up the hammer, I stepped away, slammed the door shut, and pulled my keys out to lock it. He jumped up while grabbing a hammer, and pushed the door back before my shaking hand could fully insert the key.

"Fucking cunt!" In anger, he swung the hammer at me, making contact with the top of my head and knocking me to the floor. Stunned and in immense pain, I saw him jump over me as my vision went dark for a few seconds. Light began to emerge again in bits and pieces. Anxiety and adrenaline were all that kept me conscious.

From the floor, my eyes went to the closest bill-changer and I watched him bang erratically on the metal box with a hammer, while screaming at it. Then he tried prying it open with the other end, while I pulled my phone out from my back pocket, pressed 911, and quickly whispered my location. The thief was distracted by his own noise. He definitely appeared high. Meth was my guess by his manic actions and bad teeth.

I hoped in this neighborhood, on this busy street, next to a donut shop, the police would be quick to respond.

Still dizzy, I slowly pushed myself up, leaning against the door frame for balance, and thought about locking myself in the office, but then realized he could smash the glass window in seconds. I considered limping out the backdoor, but suddenly lights and sirens were blaring. Two police cars pulled up at the curb as the thief quickly abandoned the machine and ran out the door. I actually laughed in pain, watching him trip on his loose-ass pants while stumbling to the sidewalk.

I found great satisfaction watching four policemen jump out of their cars and quickly chase him down. They had him in cuffs, lying face flat on the sidewalk in seconds. Nico walked in carrying his basket of clothes, eyes wide in shock at the outside commotion. He found me leaning over a washing machine exhausted from stress, with my head bleeding.

Nico threw his basket on the floor and rushed over. "Rosario, my God, are you alright? What's going on out there?" He put his strong arms around me and held me close for a few minutes, calming my nerves. I realized then how badly I missed Roberto, my best friend and protector. Then Nico whispered in my ear, "You're safe now. It's gonna be alright."

I slumped into his arms, releasing all my pent-up fear, softly crying into his shoulder.

A few minutes later, after I explained to the police what the thief did, two officers left with him and one remained to take my statement, while a second one checked out my head, asking me if I wanted to go to a hospital. Feeling less dizzy, I declined. It seemed to be a superficial wound which the officer cleaned up with a stinging ointment and a couple of wide Band-Aids. While the officers were still there, I tried to call Miguel about the incident, but he never answered, and I decided not to disturb him further after everything had calmed down.

After the police finished their reports, they said they'd be in touch regarding the guy they'd arrested. Finally alone, Nico and I sat on a couple of the plastic chairs attached to the floor, while he held my hand.

"What the hell, Rosario. Why didn't you just open the safe for the creep? You can't risk your life for a few hundred bucks."

"It may sound stupid but that's how I am. I can't let *anybody* take something from me. Not anymore. They took my brother; the bad guys aren't getting anything else. Besides, I figured those change machines were empty already."

"In that case, it might have been worse once he opened it. You gotta quit this job. It's too dangerous. Working these hours, it makes you so vulnerable. In a way, you got lucky tonight."

"Lucky?"

"Lucky, you weren't killed. I'm staying here with you until your shift ends and I'll drop you at home."

"But I work at the donut shop after this."

"The hell you are! Rosario, you got hit with a hammer and had a knife pushed into your throat. You're going home and getting some rest. Your head is gonna start pounding and you're already getting a big goose egg on your temple.

From his car, Nico brought in two bags holding cold burgers and fries which we decided to toss. I'd lost my appetite. We sat down in the office while I told him all about my earlier disappointing interview with Botanicals United.

He gently caressed my cheekbone with his finger. "So sorry, Rosie. Wow, what a lousy day. Don't worry though. Something's gonna turn up. In my eyes, you should win employee of the year and your cousin should give you a bonus."

"I'm glad you're here, Nico. You're the best part of these last twenty-four hours." I leaned in, our foreheads touching, and held his face in my hands and gave him a deep kiss. His lips were full and felt just right on mine. As I eventually pulled back, he leaned in for more and I ran my fingers through his soft curls, pulling him closer. It was one of those kisses that seeped through my body and could have gone on for hours.

But suddenly, rapid knocking on the office window broke us apart and I looked up to see the angry face of Miguel staring down at me.

CHAPTER 18

Cultivating Conversation

VIOLET

Turner Cooper...why was I continuing to run into this man? Three random times in a couple of weeks. The first, a potential dog attack while running; the second, a weird coincidence at BUD, and the third at the dog park. Maybe fate was speaking? And how did I respond? I barely spoke at all, mumbling out a few sentences.

And just the other day, I thought Turner was masking some guilt about his late wife and now at the dog park he appeared to be with that Katrina woman. After exchanging only a few sentences with him, she was quick to come over to investigate and pee on her turf. Guess the dog park was the perfect place for her. But another guy came over too. Maybe she was with him?

Now secure on her leash, I led Cocoa around the park, allowing her to sniff everything in sight, as I hung on tight. She was my first pet, with the exception of a short stint fifteen years ago with Esther, a spotted bunny. She quickly ran off after I treated her to the last of Mother's tulips in our yard, which Mother later told me were poisonous. Although I was heartbroken and felt terrible, Mother seemed glad to be rid of the dark brown pellets Esther was fond of dropping after I gave her free-range to the hallway outside my bedroom.

After my carelessness with Esther, Mother wouldn't hear of

another pet experiment, although having a dog or cat would probably have been good for me. I have memories of being excruciatingly lonely. As early as pre-school, I recalled young children making fun of my delayed speech, and it was then followed by the stutter which seemed to exacerbate my shyness. My parents assumed it would go away with time, but it got worse.

The grade school I attended was all-girls. I still remember their taunting; the popular girls chasing after me, calling out 'Vi-Vi-Violet.' In the classroom they would sigh loudly or snicker when I begrudgingly stood up to read aloud, giving the dreaded oral report. I became good at avoidance and developed coping skills, hanging out in safe corners reading books and volunteering in the library during lunch. The school librarian and I actually got on quite well. I eventually found a small circle of acquaintances in high school and college that I occasionally befriended.

But after I finished my masters and started working, I resumed old habits. That research job was perfect for maintaining a distance, sometimes I'd go days without speaking to almost anyone.

Now, all that was about to change. I convinced myself I was ready. I was carrying on daily conversations with Magna, and even Mother appeared interested in joining us occasionally. Out of necessity, Molly from BUD, would be talking to me often, and I'd befriended Mark, our gardener. Well, to be honest, he was tolerating me and I'd had to buy his dinner and drinks both times we spoke, but I think he was coming around.

Perhaps Turner Cooper could even become a friend. He obviously must live close by. I'd have to ask about that the next time I saw him. I should practice having that conversation and think about additional subjects we could cover. Maybe another Lexi session was required in preparation for all this talking that was headed my way.

It was about a half-mile walk from the dog park back to the house and most of that distance I ended up carrying the tuckered-out Cocoa. As I walked up the driveway with her under my arm, Mother pulled in, stopped and opened her window while staring at me. Then she finally asked, "Whose animal is that?"

"M-M-Mine. Mother meet Co-Cocoa. She's my new guard dog."

She laughed and then shook her head. "A what? I only hope she lasts longer than poor Esther." After fifteen years, she was still reminding me. "Make sure you tell the gardener about her and *you* will be responsible for all pooper scooping. Will I see you for dinner?"

"Not tonight. I have plans." *Plans with my laptop and a bag of microwave-popcorn.*

"OK, then. And tomorrow you're working, correct?" I nodded back and then she said, "Very good. Make sure that *guard dog* is properly potty trained."

As she eased into her garage, I let out a huge sigh of relief. I had hidden the dog for two days, not wanting to deal with a confrontation. But there was almost none at all. Looks like Mother was becoming more human in her golden years.

~

The other night, while talking with Mark, he described a painting he was currently working on. He painted bands of color on canvas representational of sights he viewed while camping in Big Bend. That got me thinking about the garden. From my laptop, I pulled up photos of rock formations from the Big Bend area out in far West Texas. I stared at the huge multicolored rocks, looking at fifty-million-years of changes in sedimentation. On top, there were blocks of deep red, ribboned with veins of orange, layered over chunks of golden sandstone, built on top of brilliant ocher and then almost black rock; all evidence of movement in tectonics, erosion, volcanism, and fossilization. On some stones, the varying bands of color presented like rolling waves of low mountains across an exotic landscape.

For the xeriscape garden, I thought about creating a stunning rock wall mimicking the bands of color at Big Bend. This could create a perfect backdrop for the plants, blooms, and cacti, bringing in another teachable moment for visitors. A rock wall could be built and then subtly painted much like the photos. To my eye, a wall like this would make our garden so unique from others at BUD, making it stand out as a xeriscape statement.

I couldn't wait to discuss this idea with Mark and Molly. Hopefully she'd hire him this week. He'd be perfect at painting the wall I envisioned. I tried sketching it, but after a few attempts, I knew I needed Mark to flesh out the plan on paper again. I decided to call him.

After a few rings he picked up. "What?" Seemed he was his usual gregarious self.

"Hi M-Mark. How's your evening going?"

"Probably expecting company."

"OK. This won't take long. Are you going in t-t-tomorrow to apply at BUD?"

"I told you I would. Are you checking up on me?"

"No. I got a gr-great idea from the p-painting you told me about... from the Big Bend area?"

"And?"

Mark was sounding impatient. That always made me stutter more; it was as if people just couldn't wait for words to come out of my mouth. I reminded myself--stay calm, be patient. "I think we should create a r-rock wall using those same colors you described. Imagine it as a b-backdrop for all the plants. You would be p-perfect to create that. But I need your help drawing it up on paper to show M-molly, so she can visualize."

"Not a bad idea. I can see what you're describing. Let's see if I get hired first."

Then I forced myself to ask, "Also, I thought maybe you could m-meet me tonight to draw the wall?"

"No. Goodnight Violet." He clicked off immediately.

Well, that could have gone worse. He might have just hung up on me, but instead he said 'Good night.' He was definitely coming around.

The next morning, bright and too early, I dragged myself into BUD, joining the crew of another lead gardener for my continued training. Last week, I worked with Bob Rodriguez, a nice looking, fairly new lead gardener who casually named-dropped often that he'd recently earned his degree in landscape architecture from Texas A&M.

Each lead gardener had a crew of at least five that tended to the needs of the many gardens throughout the property. As a lead gardener, my job was to direct my team on hydration, mulching, weeding, cutting back, and change-of-season replanting.

Bob started me with the basics, replacing beds with pansies, as the mums were dying out. This was a lot of grunt work with hands deep in the dirt, doing the same repetitive job all day. One assistant would dig holes, all at an exact equal distance in formation, while I dropped the small plants in the holes and patted them in. This was followed by a healthy dose of plant food and water. Then we moved on to the next bed.

Although a bit mind-numbing, I did find the repetition and physical exertion therapeutic. And again, I was talking to people. Bob and I seemed to get on well as colleagues. I liked his patience and plant knowledge. I decided to add him to my list of possible new friends.

Later that day, sitting in front of Molly, she asked how my first week had gone.

"Good. Bob seems to be a g-great leader; very inspiring. Apparently having a landscaping degree from A&M is a highly d-desirable quality."

She smiled at this. "He seems to think so. Glad you're getting along. Teamwork is extremely important here. I met with your gardener-friend, Mark, today. He seems to be well informed. I went ahead and hired him, although he didn't come across as all that motivated. He'll do for part-time."

I shrugged, "Should be fine. We have a great relationship."

"Yes, and we're breaking ground tomorrow." She was reading from her daily planner. "We need to finish assembling your crew soon; unfortunately, I haven't had any decent full-time applicants.

While you're here, let me call Nina Campbell in HR. I'll put her on speaker. Maybe she has some resumes I haven't seen."

This part made me nervous. Could I really lead a team of strangers?

"Nina? It's Molly. I'm with Violet Hill, our new lead for the xeriscape garden. Problem here. I haven't had any luck with applicants. I need a couple good full-timers. Got anybody for us?"

"Honestly Molly, I'm short-handed in staffing too. I'll look through the files again and get back with you."

Molly hung up and mumbled, "Well, that's too bad." She got up, and walked to her printer. "Hopefully between now and next week we'll line up a couple more people before our first team meeting. I may have to borrow someone from another team."

She handed me a list from the printer. "Here's some more plant material I ordered. Study up and familiarize yourself with these."

"Sure. I'll read over all this tonight. Uh M-Molly, I had an interesting idea I wanted to sp-speak with you about. Something unique."

"If it involves money and time, it'll probably be a no. Sorry Violet, I'm up to my eyeballs in new projects right now. Let's see if we can get your little team assembled and discuss it then."

"Sure, yes. L-Looking forward to that." I walked away feeling pretty good. Mark was on board, and we had a volunteer, so we only had to hire a couple more people, and Molly had said '*probably* a no' regarding my idea about the painted rock wall. In my book, that wasn't a no. Probably a no, was possibly a yes. A smile crept out across my face as I headed home.

CHAPTER 19

Down the Rabbit Hole

TURNER

I turned back to look at Violet walking away with the ferocious Cocoa. Did she seem a bit off? Then I laughed; she was kind of like her dog, in way over her head, but gutsy. On second thought, looking at her long slender legs in running shorts next to her short stubby wiener dog...the similarity faded pretty quickly.

As I chatted with Violet, a guy walked up to us with a golden doodle who Katrina seemed to know. Then I recalled meeting him too. Kevin--he had introduced himself to me last month at this park. He smiled, letting his dog sniff ours. "Hey there, Katrina. Oh...you're Allie's husband, right? Good to see you again."

"Yeah. Turner Cooper. You have a good-looking dog." I reached over and patted the doodle's curly soft head.

"Yes, she's my baby, 'scuse me a second." Kevin reached down and unleashed the doodle, then he turned and chatted with a few other people he seemed to know.

Katrina was back on her bench and called out to me. "So, Turner, let's finish this." The setting sun back-lit Katrina's long blonde hair as she held up the open bottle of Chablis, pouring herself another glass. She sat back smiling at me and patted the spot next to her. Everything was beginning to feel too comfortable. I needed to avoid this whole scene; way too easy to get caught up in this sticky web.

"You know, I'm good with just the one. I need to start backing off on the alcohol. But those sandwiches look good." Katrina and I chatted a while longer, watching our dogs romp about, as I munched on my turkey and cheese. I tried directing the conversation back to Allie but never got anything from Katrina regarding Allie's divorce request, so I dropped it. The sun had set and I was ready to go.

Just as I came up with an exit excuse, Katrina called out to the Golden-Doodle guy. He smiled and walked over to our bench. Time to bail. "Well guys, sorry to break up the party, but I have lots of work to do this evening. I'm going to collect Blaze and head out. I appreciate the sandwich, Katrina."

"Already? She immediately turned to Kevin. "Maybe you can help me finish this wine and food."

Kevin shrugged, "Sure. I'll take a glass or two. But no food; had a big late lunch at Mesquite Mike's today." He reached over and shook my hand as I stood up. "OK, see you around, dude."

As I left, I figured the two of them would soon be downing their wine while discussing the merits of doggie dates.

At home, I checked in with Dad, got an update from the guys in shipping, and then called Sarah in sales.

"Hey Sarah, sorry to bother you after-hours, but, as you probably know, billing's been down the last few weeks. I really need you to focus on bringing in those two big accounts you've been nibbling at. I realize I haven't met the clients, but if you think it might help, I'm happy to make a few calls on your behalf. Sometimes a personal call from the boss works. Shows full company commitment."

"Appreciate it, Turner, but I think I can close them both by the end of the week. I feel pretty confident, but if not, I'll call in the cavalry."

"Cool, I trust you. I'll be in touch." A decent night's sleep was always better knowing I had the right people working with me.

Skirting the den, I tried to avoid the temptation of the bar and my normal dosage of two shots of Scotch. Passing through the kitchen, the bar continued to call out to me with trumpets blaring, luring me toward the freshly purchased bottles which stood like good soldiers saluting me from the marble countertop.

Evening, sir. We're here to serve. I needed to try harder. I turned quickly, taking the stairs two at a time.

While lying in bed, just as I was about to doze off, something clicked in my brain. My eyes blinked open and my heart stopped for a few seconds as I remembered a notation I'd read earlier in Allie's calendar:

12:30 Lunch, Mesquite Mike's with K.

It was one of Allie's last notations. I reached for my phone, checking the time. Ten-thirty. I pressed in Katrina's number.

"Hello. Turner?" Christ, she probably thought this was a booty call.

"So sorry to bother you this late."

"Never a problem. What 'cha need?"

"Well, I'm just trying to figure out a timeline here. Do you remember scheduling a lunch date with Allie at Mesquite Mike's? Back a few months ago?"

"Uh...no. Actually, I don't think we ever met for lunch. We only did our little neighborhood walks."

"OK, thanks. That's all I needed."

"Oh. You sure?"

"Yup. Apologize for the late call. You have a good night."

I lay there narrowing down options, hating my conclusion. If it wasn't Katrina, it may well have been Kevin. Dog-friendly, sunset loving, wine swilling, good neighbor Kevin, who also seemed to enjoy the food at Mesquite Mike's. And so what? Lunch with a neighbor, was that so incriminating? Kind of. She'd never mentioned Kevin to me. Nothing about him or his wife. Was it odd to go to lunch with a married guy? Perhaps.

All this time I'd been thinking this unexpected divorce was all my fault. I was the one ignoring Allie, letting work be my priority. But now I wasn't quite so sure.

Perhaps Allie welcomed my absence and general fogginess of everything going on in her world. As I was busy building up Rapid

Logistics, maybe she'd spent the last few years building her own separate plans, designing a new life with a new man, while taking half of my company in the divorce settlement. Both Katrina and Sally had mentioned Allie seemed content, even happy, months before her death. If you're miserable in a marriage, why would you be so happy? Unless...you were happy about spending time with someone else. A chill went through my body, as puzzle pieces began to fall into place.

Then I questioned everything. Maybe this was all an irrational leap that my alcohol deprived mind was making? Unable to get the spiraling thoughts out of my mind, I got up and went downstairs to review Allie's calendars one more time.

Damn. I had to pass the bar on my way to command central. I poured a very small amount of Scotch into a crystal tumbler. It was only to get the juices flowing. Just a taste. Now that I knew what I was looking for, I might find a connection to Kevin, or perhaps some other guy, which would indicate my dear, sweet, happy wife was screwing around. At this point, did it really matter? Yes, I had to know.

I was on a mission, anxiously flipping through Allie's calendars, looking for a sign, a trend, a thread that would lead me to a conclusion.

*There...*My finger stopped on a page--July seventh, lingering over a single **K** followed by an exclamation mark. I pulled out my phone, checking my own work schedule. July seventh--Lubbock, Winery Co-op. An overnight stay.

I kept flipping pages. Here was possibly something—June sixteenth, *DaKotas* 7:30—a downtown steak restaurant and a sly use of code, with the K capitalized and bold-faced. *Bitch.* I occasionally met clients there, but the eatery was definitely not a place Allie normally went to. Again, my planner showed I was out of town. Flew home out of LAX a day later.

Here we go—May twelfth, *Farmer's MarKet 10:00,* again with the darkened, capitalized K. I rarely worked Saturdays, but checking my schedule, it was the same weekend I went to the ranch with my parents. Allie said she was busy with a volunteer commitment at the library, but instead, it seemed she was squeezing the eggplant at the farmer's market.

I couldn't believe it. I dropped the datebook like it was on fire, shaking my head. There had to be some kind of explanation. Allie could clear all this up in a quick minute if she were here, but she wasn't, and all I had was this calendar and...

And her phone! I was so stupid. Just check her damn phone. I opened the drawers of command central and found her phone, sitting quietly, dead to the world, next to the charger. I resuscitated it and anxiously started scrolling. It had never occurred to me until tonight to check her phone. I'd never been suspicious; why would I look at her old phone? That was something people did in the movies. I assumed if I wasn't cheating, why would she? I admit, a self-centered perspective.

Opening the text app, I typed in Kevin. Immediately a flurry of texts came up between them. I started with the oldest and worked my way forward. It was incriminating. No dying affirmations of love, but lots of connecting dots and intimate meetings.

Scrolling back, the texting and emails seemed to start about two years ago while planning a Fourth of July pet parade in the neighborhood. I remembered watching that; pets and owners all dressed up, with kids pulling decorated wagons and boom boxes blaring patriotic music. It probably started innocently enough. but it seemed to escalate pretty quickly to evening dinners and planned outings while I was out of town. There were even discussions of a few B-n-Bs booked in rural East Texas. Allie was apparently so confident of my lack of suspicion that she'd never thought to delete these texts. And I'd never had a clue.

The trail went cold about a month before Allie's death. I had to wonder if it was her committing to an actual divorce that scared Kevin off. The secret affair was probably fun and exciting, but dealing with the aftermath of a divorce and a new wife might have been more than easy-going Kevin had bargained for.

That smarmy guy, shaking my hand today, asking me to call if I ever needed to talk...what an asshole. How dare he? And I didn't really care for his curly-haired doodle dog much either.

Thinking about Allie in the hospital during her last two days; she was so quiet, sick, lifeless, and probably heartbroken. But not heart-broken about me.

Was I angry? Sure. And then throw in shocked and numb. I didn't know what to think. The revelation was still too raw. I had to put my head down on the desk. I felt dizzy and nauseous reading intimate words from my wife meant for another man. I knew I'd still been in love with Allie; over twelve years we'd been together. But apparently, she felt differently. Perhaps it was due to my lack of attention, but the distraction and attention of Kevin must have played a part.

I filled my glass again and put the incriminating evidence of her phone back to bed in the drawers of the kitchen desk. I had no further desire to pour over each and every detail. I'd seen enough. Walking back to the bar, I took a sip of Scotch, letting the smooth burn flow down my throat. Then with a gulp, I emptied the glass and poured another, staring at my reflection in the mirrored bar-back. I looked terrible.

What was Allie doing to me? Ruining my life from the grave? No —*I* was ruining my life. Poisoning myself over a woman who had moved on a while ago. Maybe it was time for me to move on too. What the hell! I broke the paper seals on the remaining bottles and watched all that lovely Dewars splash down the drain.

It was time.

CHAPTER 20

Luck Be A Lady

ROSARIO

After the police left the lavenderia, Nico and I had a beautiful time getting to know each other better. There'd been some sweet words between us, with some heart-thumping kisses, and then we had to stop as we looked up at the angry scowl of Miguel.

He pounded on the window, staring at us, immediately making me feel guilty.

Eyes wide, I slid the office window open.

Miguel gave Nico a snarl and said, "Who's this, and why am I here at four-thirty in the morning?"

We stood up and came out of the office. "Miguel, you didn't need to come down. I was calling to tell you about the—"

"You don't call someone at three in the morning unless you're having a big fucking emergency. Then I get here and you're wrapped up with some guy in the office. And I thought you were management material. You really had me fooled."

Then Nico jumped in trying to defend me. "You need to know... you should feel damn proud of Ros – "

"Don't tell me how I should feel! And *you* should not be in that office. Rosario knows the policy."

This argument was escalating too quickly. I shouted back at

Miguel. "We had a robbery attempt! I called to let you know. The police were here and I decided not to bother you with a message after everything calmed down."

Miguel looked around at the empty, well-lit place and lifted his arms. "So? What happened?"

Nervously, I tried to explain to my hot-tempered boss. "I told the thief I couldn't open the safe. He got in the office, threatening me with a knife, so I--I tried to distract him. I told him to open the change machines instead."

"What the hell! Why would you do that?" Miguel walked over to the machine that the guy had attempted to pry open. "Now this thing is bent; might be broken. That'll cost me."

Nico was shaking with rage, pointing at me wildly. "Do you realize you almost lost your employee here? A knife was put to her throat, a hammer to her head, and you're worried that your stupid machine was bent? This is unbelievable!" Nico turned to me and grabbed my hand. "Rosario, no way can you work for this guy."

Miguel yelled back at him, "If she'd followed instructions and kept the office locked, none of this might have happened. Rosario, if you don't think you should work here, you can both get the hell out now. Give me your keys; I'll wait for the morning shift and don't bother coming back to Daylight Donuts either."

I attempted to explain as Nico was urging me toward the door. "But Miguel, he...he hit me. That's how I was able to call the police... when he left for the change machine."

Nico continued to tug at my arm. "He's an asshole, Rosario. Grab your stuff."

Now Miguel was really upset. "You call me that in my own place of business? You're lucky I don't shoot you right here! Both of you... leave now."

I picked up my backpack and walked out filled with emotion, anger, and confusion. How did it all deteriorate so quickly? And to think Nico and I were saying Miguel might even give me a bonus. Some bonus! I sat in Nico's car, feeling so confused, wondering if I could have a do-over of the last twenty-four hours.

It all went south as soon as I turned down the offer of sanitation manager for Botanicals United, when all I wanted to do was work in the gardens. And now, to lose the offer of managing three lavanderias *after* getting hit in the head and threatened with a knife. It was too much.

Nico drove me home and offered to keep me company, but during the drive he was encouraging me to sue for unlawful firing, which I knew I would never follow through on, no matter how unfair Miguel was. All I wanted was to sleep off this bad dream of a day, by myself.

Later in the week, I was on my break at Construction Connections. My boss had given me some extra hours since I'd lost my two other jobs. I was staring at the gray cinder-block wall, still upset about what had gone so wrong last week. Other co-workers were starting to head back to work. I finished my soda and glanced at my watch. As I stood up, my phone lit up with a buzz. It was Botanicals United and a lady named Molly was calling with questions. We spoke for a while and every time I answered a question, I looked at my watch, as the minutes ticked away. I couldn't afford to lose my one remaining job.

Molly said she was the head horticulturist at BUD. I wasn't sure what that was but she asked many similar questions that Ms. Campbell had asked at my first interview; but after a while, she started asking questions about the gardens.

"So, tell me about your gardening experience, Rosario?"

"I will be very honest with you, Ms. Molly. It's not that much. I always helped my mom, near Juarez, with her fruit trees, a few rose bushes, and we have these thick rows of purple Mexican petunias, all summer... so pretty. They don't need much watering. But anyway, this is what I think. I would love to work with you there. From the first day I visited your gardens, I knew I was meant to be there. It's a magical place. I will be punctual, work hard, and learn quickly; that much I can promise you."

"That's exactly what we need. Are you willing to work full-time and study up on some plants on-line?"

I suddenly felt excitement back in my voice. "Yes! I can do it at the library. Whatever you think would be helpful."

After a few more questions, she made me an offer on the spot for fourteen-dollars an hour, forty hours a week, more than twice as much as I'd made with Miguel. There were also chances of earning overtime working special events. I would start at six-thirty AM, but be off by three PM. I couldn't imagine what I would do with all my spare time.

I was hired! I had my dream job! My heart was racing with excitement, as I realized what had just happened.

Today was my first team meeting at BUD. As I prepared to go in, putting on my green uniform shirt with pride, tucking it into a pair of stretch khaki jeans, I knew I had a lot to learn. But wasn't that always the case with a new job? As insurance, I'd kept my position at Construction Connections for one day a week, during one of my days off. I was so used to working, having two full days to myself seemed just too much.

They started my training in the morning with a group of new-hires, teaching us the basics of equipment cleaning and storage, showing us where the foul-smelling chemicals and fertilizers were secured, and then we were told lots of policies and procedures; pretty boring stuff.

At noon I was instructed to gather with my xeriscape garden team for our first meeting. As I headed to the new garden site, I stopped to admire the overlook of the fountains and the glistening pond below. Breathing in the chilly air, I wondered if I could ever tire of this view? I stared out at a stone bridge connecting to another meandering path, beginning to feel a little uneasy about everything that would be expected of me and tried to shake off new job jitters. I walked past an outdoor restaurant where a few people were seated when I suddenly heard my name.

"Rosario?... Rosario!

I turned and saw a table with two men seated and continued to stare as a tall, handsome guy stood up and began walking over. It was my laundry prince!

It had been over three weeks since my abruptly-ended first date with Victor Morales. Should I be angry or dismissive? I didn't know what to think, as he quickly came over and gave me a brief hug.

"So, what are you up to?"

I pointed to the BUD logo on my shirt. "I'm working here now. First day!"

"What? I left you here after coffee and you loved it so much you applied for a job?"

"Actually, yes. That's exactly what happened." I had to smile even though I didn't want to.

"Well, good for you; can't believe you're here!" Victor stood back a step, checking me out. "I gotta say, only you could make that uniform look good."

I remembered. He was big on the compliments, but I was undecided about his honesty. I needed to back away. "Uh, good to see you Victor, but I'm on my way to a work meeting. I can't be late."

He looked down, staring straight into my eyes. "I'm really glad I ran into you. I've been wanting to call but I forgot to add your number to my contacts and later deleted your call without thinking. Actually, I went to the laundry this past weekend looking for you and some guy told me you'd left. I can't believe I'm running into you." He grinned and grabbed my hand. "It has to be a sign."

Why did he have to look so good and have an answer for everything? Should I believe him?

"Hey, let's exchange numbers again. I promise, your number will stay in my phone this time."

"Well, Victor Morales, I don't think I deleted your number. But I'm busy with this new job. I'll give you a call sometime, but I have to go now."

As I walked away he kept talking. "Wait; how about this Sunday? I remember, that was always your day off. I promise; I won't take any business calls this time." Of course, I turned around. He smiled, showing me his perfect white teeth matching his perfect white shirt.

I waved and said, "Maybe. Good to see you, Victor."

Five minutes later, I joined the team. I was staring at the new garden site, but there was no garden. Except for dirt, it was totally empty. Now I suddenly realized all the work we were about to take on. I should have been listening more carefully as Molly spoke to us, but I was too busy being distracted by Victor's face popping into my brain, trying to recall every word he'd said, knowing I would eventually call him.

CHAPTER 21

The Odd Squad

VIOLET

We were having our first team meeting at the new garden space. Molly was leading the discussion of our plans but I felt good about playing a part in the initial design, and today I hoped Molly would incorporate my idea about the rock wall which Mark had drawn up for me. I was relieved Molly was there to do the talking. I still wasn't confident speaking in front of a group.

The weedy, shrub-filled plot of land I'd looked at a few weeks back was now an empty swath of cleared and graded dirt that had a noticeable downward slant, surrounded by a temporary fence to keep visitors out. It was a cold day, with our team members standing around a plywood plank laid across two sawhorses.

Molly stood in the middle of our circle, introduced herself, and rolled out a more detailed rendering of the garden than I'd originally designed. "Ok guys, welcome to the ground floor of a really exciting thing happening. Our first truly xeriscape garden at BUD. We'll be using only plants native to the North Texas and Southwest area, which will require less need for fertilization and water. Truly, a garden for today's time, more environmentally friendly with all the climatic changes taking place."

Everybody leaned over the makeshift table looking at the

drawing and seemed impressed, while Molly continued. "First, let's go round the circle and have you introduce yourselves. I'd like each of you to briefly discuss what you want to get out of this experience and what you bring to the party." She pointed to me and said, "This is Violet Hill, our lead gardener and soon to be your immediate boss. Violet?"

Oh God, I had to talk already? What was it she asked? Experience? Something about a party? I stared down at my white tennis shoes noticing the toes were already covered with dirt. "Well, let's see...looking forward to g-getting to know all of you and lear-learning with you. My background is in the b-bi-ological earth sciences. Recently researched a microbial substance, *Reclamax*, which retains m-moisture in arid soils. It's a polymer based..." I forced myself to look up, realizing everybody's eyes seemed to be glazed over in boredom. I quickly wrapped. "So, M-mark, why don't you go next."

"Will do...uh, name's Mark Hopkins. Art is my passion but gardening is sort of my current thing. Thought it might be cool if we could blend the two and see what kind of wonderland we can conjure up. Got some good ideas."

Molly jumped in, "Very nice Mark. Love to hear about those. Perhaps another time?" She glanced at the attractive young woman next to Mark and asked, "So you must be Rosario? We spoke on the phone last week. Tell us about yourself."

Rosario flashed a big smile at everyone. Maybe I should have tried that too.

"Well, I am new to gardening, but very pleased and excited to be here and ready to work very hard doing anything you need me to do, Miss Molly."

Molly looked pleased and continued, "Perfect Rosario," She looked over at the next victim. "So you must be Jeff Winkleman?"

He was a young gen Z guy, thin, with thick black glasses. "Uh, yeah. Been working in concessions for the last six months. Not crazy about that so I thought I'd give this thing a go."

I was definitely having doubts about Winkleman, but Rosario seemed promising. Next up, a small wispy looking woman that looked to be in her forties. Hard to tell with the wide brimmed canvas hat covering her face. She raised her hand to speak. "Uh, Linda Bell here. I've been working at the Ponds-of-Plenty Garden at BUD for the last few years. I really love it there. So calming. Not sure why I was sent over here."

Molly interrupted. "Actually Linda, we heard what a big help you were at the ponds and thought you'd be a great asset for this new garden."

"OK, but I hope I can get assigned back to the Ponds of Plenty soon."

Molly nodded. "We'll keep that in mind."

Last in the group was Turner, our volunteer. He looked nice today in his jeans, heavy dark-green jacket and baseball cap. "I'm Turner Cooper, good to meet y'all. First-time gardener, first-time volunteer. Guess that's a lot of firsts. Was doing all this for my recently deceased wife; she used to volunteer here a lot. But...the last few days, I gotta say, I'm kind of questioning everything right now?" Then he shrugged and added reluctantly, "Guess I'll give it a shot."

Well, that was certainly *not* a ringing commitment. Disappointing and confusing. He'd seemed so motivated about everything the last few times we'd talked. Maybe this was a good time to roll out my new drawing of the garden featuring the rock wall.

Before I had a chance Molly spoke again. "Team Xeriscape, just so you're aware, we have a four-and-a-half-month deadline to complete this garden. We plan to open the first of March, in conjunction with our largest annual event, *Spring Rejuvenation at BUD*."

Pointing to Molly's rendering, Turner said, "This looks great, but four months? Going from nothing to this? Seems pretty ambitious. Sorry Molly; don't mean to rain on your parade."

"No, you're right, Turner. It is ambitious, but we've worked with tight deadlines before. I think it's do-able." Molly spoke confidently, so I supposed she was right.

While there was a lull, I placed my colored drawing over Molly's and said, "Uh, M-Molly, this was the idea I wanted to discuss with you the other day. M-Mark drew this up for me, and I think it will be a great addition to what you've already pl-planned." It featured a rolling rock wall of various heights and colors, which went down the hill next to the flowering beds. "This wall would be re-re-representative of the rocks in the western region of Texas. I was inspired by photos from Big Bend."

Mark jumped in. "I can paint the wall to resemble the rocks. It's going to look really authentic."

As I glanced at Molly's twitching grimace, I could tell she was not pleased with my timing. I'd just learned my first lesson in management. Don't upstage the boss.

She replied, "As attractive as this might *seem*, time is of the essence as well as budget constraints. For now, we may have to table this idea."

Leaning over the new drawing, Rosario spoke up, "Oh, too bad. That looks so pretty. I like this idea!"

Winkleman, the young concessions retiree said, "I agree. This one looks better. I'd do this version."

Encouraged by their response, I jumped in again. "M-Molly, you were already pl-planning a small wall. This will just be larger, more representative of the area, and will really m-make the garden stand out, but I understand if it's a m-money thing."

Keeping a tight smile, Molly rolled up my rendering, and pointed to the path in her drawing, "If we want to do something fun and different, I had an idea the other night. Picture this...We'll add two topiaries, here and here, shaped like the cartoon characters, Road Runner and Yosemite Sam. We could have them shaped to look as if they're running down the path. Kids love these. Great photo moments, you know? We already have a gifted topiary department that might be able to create them."

The group stood there silently, nodding their heads, then Mark said, "What the hell do two vine covered topiaries have to do with xeriscape gardens of the southwest?"

Rosario looked about for an explanation, asking, "Who is this Yosemite Sam?"

Then Linda Bell, glancing at her watch, asked, "So, are we

breaking for lunch soon? My co-workers from the Ponds of Plenty meet now."

A deafening silence surrounded us for about thirty seconds, before Turner spoke up, trying to ease Molly's frustration. "Actually, Molly, if it's a matter of more money needed, maybe I could bring in a few more donors for the larger wall. And hey, rather than a topiary, why don't we split the difference and buy one of those beautiful sculptures of a longhorn steer to stick right down at the bottom of this hill. Longhorns are representative of the theme--bred for rough grazing and drought tolerance."

Mark nodded, saying "Cool, dude, clever idea."

I kept quiet, but nodded enthusiastically.

Molly shook her head at his suggestion. "Bronze sculptures are a huge investment and might take years to create."

But once again, Mark intercepted her, "Uh, I don't know, man... I'm familiar with a few good sculptors. We could probably make this happen."

Molly began coughing, seeing this whole meeting running away from her and turned on the authority spigot. "OK...for now our task is to get these beds edged off, till the soil, and blend in the bedding mix. And tomorrow, our carpenters will begin constructing the seating areas up here at the top. *Then,* we'll consider the wall."

"Oh, Molly?" I decided to make one more attempt at a suggestion. "I forgot to mention, the solar panels and large rain barrels we discussed before...I have companies agreeing to donate the equipment as long as we pay shipping costs and give them signage of some kind."

"Let's also table that for later discussion. This garden can't be one giant promotional billboard. Now, has anyone here set metal edging along a bed before?" Mark raised his hand. Thank God for Mark.

"Good. After lunch, Mark will lead the team in getting this going. Let's try to have the beds set within a week. I'm going to have another gardener work with me to set the path with white lime marking so you'll know where to begin. I'll see you all in about an hour." The six of us nodded to her and began to wander off, when

Molly called out, "Turner, Violet, if you don't mind, I need to speak with you."

Was I in trouble already? I'd rather go eat lunch with my odd squad.

She looked upset, tapping on her roll of blueprints. "Turner, is this talk about new donors real, or wishful thinking?"

"Depends. How much more is Violet's rock wall gonna cost?"

"Find me ten thousand dollars and we'll do the painted wall instead of the regular one."

Then he asked, "What about the longhorns? Everybody seemed to like that idea."

"Find another five-thousand to ten-thousand."

He sighed, glanced up at the cloudy sky and said, "I'll try. Let me spin the old rolodex a few times and rustle up some donors. Might take a few weeks. Will that work?"

"Yes, three to four weeks should work before we have to make final decisions. At that point, Violet, we'll revisit these ideas of yours, but for now, we'll proceed with the original plans."

"Th-that's fine. So not a definite no, right?"

She turned abruptly. "You both enjoy your lunch."

Turner and I headed up the path for lunch. He seemed lost in his own thoughts. To cheer him up, I said, "Turner, your help m-means a lot. Hope you continue to w-work with us."

"Thanks. But shit...not sure what I'm getting myself into here. It all started with a desire to plant a few bushes and add a bench in memory of my wife, and now I'm not so sure I want to. I'm sensing a bit of a power struggle. Thought this was gonna be a peaceful respite from work, but I've got myself calling in chits from wealthy friends, and finding dang longhorn sculptures at a budget price."

I nodded up at him. "W-We'll get there. And I can just see it. A longhorn headed down the trail, with the blooming cactus at the bottom, and that g-g-gorgeous rockwall.

Turner shook his head and offered a weak smile. "If you say so, boss."

CHAPTER 22

Donation Damnation

TURNER

My shoulders and arms still ached. I'd spent all afternoon hammering in the metal edging along the flower beds at BUD. After turning on the hot tub, I went upstairs to shower, rinsing off the dirt and sweat of the afternoon. Later, with a cold beer in hand, I went out on the deck, dropped my boxers and stepped in. Ahh, perfect. I loved it really hot on a cold evening.

Leaning back and sinking in, I closed my eyes and let the heat and bubbles relax my shoulders and body. It had been a while since I'd done real physical work, and I was feeling so tense; not myself at all. Then I heard a commotion in the kitchen. I opened one eye and looked up through the window. It was Sally.

She poked her head out the back door and started walking toward the tub. "Turner? There you are. Don't you look comfy."

"Yeah, I was. Uh, don't come any closer unless you want to see the full package."

"Oops. Sorry. Had to come back; forgot some cleaning supplies upstairs. I'll need 'em for tomorrow. How you been? Noticed you were up and out early this morning. Good to see you awake before noon."

"Thanks for noting my sleep schedule, Sally."

"You're welcome. I gave Blaze a walk for you. Shouldn't have though."

"Why's that?"

"I dumped some recyclables in your bin and noticed three empty Scotch bottles."

"And?"

"It's a dangerous tightrope you're walking, sir. You need to be careful."

"Appreciate your concern. Sally, are you here to haunt me as the Revenge of AA, or did you really forget your stuff?"

"Forgot my supplies. But you know when it comes to administering advice, I have to step in if circumstances warrant it. But I've said my piece."

"Well, I thank you for walking Blaze and, FYI, I didn't drink that Scotch. I tossed it all out the other night." I took a swig of my beer and set it down. "And Sally, stop giving this beer the evil eye. I had a tough day, I'm thirsty, and I'm only having one."

"And you know what they say about *one*, Turner?" I waited in anticipation of Sally's words of wisdom. "It always comes before two. Have a good evening, sir."

I shouted out, "I appreciate you, Sally."

"You better."

As irritating as she was, I needed a Sally in my life. She had me thinking twice before reaching for that second beer. Instead, I reached for my phone and put on some light jazz, took another gulp, and leaned back again. I was so glad Allie had talked me into putting the hot tub back here. At this moment, it was worth every penny.

While relaxing, I thought about Team Xeriscape and had to laugh. Winkleman seemed pretty useless, but overall, as a group under Mark's tutelage, we had actually completed a fair amount of the edging for the flowerbeds. I was mildly impressed that I had learned a new simple skill. It was a good feeling.

A minute later, my phone began buzzing, cutting out my music. It was...Violet? I considered not answering. I would see her at BUD tomorrow. What could she possibly want? I sighed and picked up.

"Hi there, Vi. What's up?"

"I really don't go by Vi; Violet's fine."

Why did I answer this call? "OK, *Violet*, what can I do for you?"

"Have you called anybody about d-donations yet? I was just w-wondering."

"No. I've showered and I'm in the hot tub. That's as far as I've gotten. I'm beat and won't be doing any phone solicitations tonight. What about you?"

"Took C-Cocoa for a walk and then ran a couple m-miles. Guess I'm r-ready to take a shower too."

"I bet you are. The garden work alone did me in."

"Anyway, I was thinking, b-before you start asking people about donations for the wall, let me ask my m-mother if she has some friends that m-might want to donate. She's p-pretty hooked up in that regard. I'll try to get funding for the wall and you can focus on the longhorn sculptures. That was a g-g-goo-nice idea, by the way. I don't want you feeling like you're responsible for f-finding all the extra funding."

"Thanks Violet. Yeah, cool. That'd be great if you can pull that together. I think the wall idea has real merit."

"Yes, can't wait to see it all f-finished."

"You're sounding pretty confident."

"M-my my dad always told me, if you want to accomplish something, you have to see it all in your head first."

"Smart man."

"Yes, he was the b-best. I miss him every day. You're pr-probably feeling that way about your wife too."

I honestly was feeling conflicted about Allie right now. Betrayed, rejected, and angry about the whole debacle. I didn't bother to respond to Vi's comment. "Well, it was a good day, Violet. I enjoyed working together and meeting the team. I'm gonna say good night now"

"Yes. Me too. And Turner... I guess it's OK if you want to call me Vi."

"Either works for me. Good night, Violet."

As I hung up, my music started up again. Let the relaxation

commence, soothing heat, pulsating jets, and a cold beer. Ten minutes more should do it, as I stared up into a cold starry sky. Then the phone buzzed again. Dammit! It was Katrina. I let that one go to voicemail.

A few evenings later, I pulled open my laptop and made a list of ten guys I knew with enough discretionary income to possibly donate to BUD, specifically for our longhorn statues. I had no problem selling and was comfortable doing it; but asking people to donate was a whole other thing. Looking at the list, I cursed myself for telling Molly I could bring in the extra funds. I suddenly felt very uncomfortable doing this.

First on the list was James, a financial advisor and old college roommate. We went way back and had remained close. James was my top prospect. I reluctantly made the call.

"Hey, buddy, how's the ankle?"

"Turner? Not bad. I should have known better than to go out for fall soccer. I'm getting too old, man. What's up with you?"

"I'm OK...This is gonna sound a little strange, but I've been volunteering at Botanicals United; kind of something I was doing for Allie. She loved that place. Anyway, I'm helping to create a—"

"Hold on a second, Turner. I'm getting Collen out of the tub, hang on." This was followed by splashing, screeching, and then I heard his wife yelling at James for being on the phone while giving his son a bath. Eventually, the noise died down. "OK, sorry. I'm back. A little bath-time crisis. Now, what about Allie?"

"I'll try to keep this short. I'm volunteering at BUD. We're building a very cool xeriscape garden and trying to add a few bronze longhorns along the trail, surrounded by a cactus garden. Anyway, we're looking for donations. It's going to be awesome."

"Oh...a donation." I could hear his tone deflating like a floating bath toy. "How much are you looking for? Although, I gotta tell you, Coop, this isn't a great time. Jen insisted on adding a new guest room and bath six months ago, which I'm still paying off."

"Yeah, I totally get it. We're looking for at least five grand. Now, with the privilege of paying for the statue, your family's name would be on a plaque, you'd get a family membership for a year, free parking and, oh, they have a great kid's garden too. You could bring Collen there to play for hours." I had no idea if BUD offered those options to small donors, but I'd decided to sweeten the deal on my own.

"You're killing me, Coop." He sighed deeply. "Put me down for five-hundred. Sorry, that's all I can swing right now and I'm going to have to slice that off my bar tab at the club."

I was disappointed. I had known James to blow at least a thousand a week on sports bets. "Five hundred it is. I'll swing by your office for a check later this week. Appreciate you, man."

"Hey, it's all for Allie. No problem."

I typed in *five hundred* next to James' name and looked down the list. God, this was painful. It was going to be a long night. Then I was interrupted by an incoming call. It was Violet...again.

"Hi v-v-volunteer. Just wanted you to know. I think I got the cost of the w-wall covered. I'm excited!"

"Seriously? How'd you do it so quickly?"

"I didn't do much. Just gave all the details to my m-mother's assistant. She said she'd ask around and let me know s-s-soon. She didn't think it should be much of a pr-problem. She said the garden ladies love to donate to BUD. It's like home to them."

"Who the hell is your mother?"

"Suzanne Hill. You don't know her. Hangs with a little older crowd."

"Oh...*that* Suzanne Hill? I don't know her, but I know *of* her. She's in the Dallas paper a lot."

"Huh? I w-wouldn't know. I only read the national news on my phone. So, how's m-money for the longhorns coming along?"

"Working on it right now actually. Let's just say... not as good as your project."

"So Turner, you're calling old friends, business contacts, pre-predominantly all men?"

"Yeah, why?"

"I'd try their w-wives instead. They seem to love seeing their names on br-br-brochures and plaques. That's what I'd do. Good luck."

"Yeah, thanks for the tip, Vi." Crap. I crumpled my list and threw it in the trash.

CHAPTER 23

Pole Vaulting

VIOLET

After my second call to Turner, I was pleased. I think he was becoming a friend. Isn't that what friends did; invent nicknames for each other? Actually, I wasn't crazy about being called Vi, but I would tolerate it from Turner. Before phoning him, I'd practiced my conversation topics out loud to keep my stutter to a minimum. Lexi would be pleased with my prep. Maybe I should create a nickname for Turner? Turn, Big-T, T? Guess I'll stick with Turner.

Encouraged by my growing roster of acquaintances, I thought perhaps my next step in building confidence would be to schedule a holiday party for my BUD garden team. Mother always insisted parties were the best social lubricant to gather people toward a common goal. And Suzanne Hill knew a lot about hosting parties. I personally hated them, but perhaps if I controlled my own guest list things would be better. This would be a major step in my socialization skills.

I was hesitant, still recalling Mother organizing a few large, painful birthday parties for me as a child. Highlights involved Shetland pony rides, bounce houses, blow-up slides for the pool, and roving magicians. But each time she attempted a big party in my honor, few of my classmates ever showed up. Instead, the party was filled with Mother's friends and some of their bratty children. I was social suicide in those days. Mother eventually gave up, sensing my growing anxiety.

But I was stronger now. I decided this was a fear I needed to overcome.

If I included my team and the two lead gardeners I'd trained with, Bob and Antoinette, there would be eight. I would not invite Molly. I seriously doubted she would want to come. I could tell I wasn't her favorite person, although I wasn't sure why. Yes, I'd shown her my new plans for the garden in front of the others, but wasn't that my job? Just because she hadn't considered the idea, didn't mean it wasn't a good idea. Anyway...maybe a little holiday party? The weeks were flying by. December would be here soon.

Glancing around the guest quarters, I thought it might be too small for eight attendees. If it was outdoors, the yard and pool were perfect for spill-over, but December weather was never predictable. It could be seventy-five degrees or thirty-five. I'd have to give this party idea some thought.

Rosario, Jeff, Linda and I arrived at the site one morning and stood staring at a six-foot mound of topsoil which had to be shoveled into the beds and then blended with another six-foot pile of sand. The piles looked insurmountable, especially without the help of Mark and Turner. I decided we'd work in two teams, one on each side of the path leading downhill. I assigned Rosario as my partner. I'd noticed she was an incredibly hard worker, while Jeff and Linda enjoyed hanging together to gossip.

As Rosario and I each rolled our full wheelbarrows over to the beds, I began shoveling bedding soil and she followed behind with the sand. I had to laugh, thinking about my mother and the shock she would have seeing me shoveling dirt while working hand and shoulder next to a recent immigrant, sharing the manual labor equally. *Yes Mother, after earning a bachelor's and master's, I was a dirt digger and enjoying it.*

Rosario stopped and asked me, "Violet, what's making you smile today. You always seemed so serious until now."

"Do I? I don't m-mean to be. Guess I've been nervous with the responsibility of completing this g-garden. I just don't want to m-mess anything up."

"You won't. Don't worry so much, *chica*. We got your back. Although... we could do this faster if everyone was here." She whispered to me, pointing to Jeff and Linda, who were still attempting to fill their wheelbarrows. "Poor Jeff. He's not too good. The young ones usually aren't."

"But you're young."

Rosie turned back to shoveling soil. "Yes, but here's the difference. For me, this job is my life right now. I need to hang on to it for a good while. You have no idea how much I like working here compared to what I was doing before."

"Great, gl-glad to hear it. So, Rosario, do you ever go by R-Rosie? I'd like to give you a nick-name."

"Sure, Nico calls me Rosie too."

"Then Rosie it is. Is N-Nico your boyfriend?"

"Hmm, not sure yet. I kind of like another guy too."

I pulled off my baseball cap and tightened my pony tail. "As pretty as you are, that doesn't s-surprise me."

"*Gracias*. What about you? Any sweethearts, Violet?"

"I've *never* had a boyfriend. It's kind of embarrassing but--."

"No way, girl. I can't believe that." Rosie had stopped shoveling and stared at me as if I'd said I'd never eaten before.

"Definitely true, but I'm tr-tr---starting to change things. Pushing myself to get out and m-meet more people." I stopped for a minute, looking back at Jeff and Linda still lagging behind, and shouted up to them. "Hey guys, time to get mo-moving on those beds. First team that reaches the half-way point gets a f-free lunch on me."

~

A few weeks later, I popped into Mother's office. She'd gone out to play bridge but Magna was still busy at her desk. "Hey, Magna. Have a minute?"

She was looking down, typing on her keyboard. "Certainly. Just setting up your mother's holiday calendar. Everything has come up so fast; first events start next weekend. So, what can I do for you?"

"Well, this may sur-surprise you, b-but I was thinking of hosting a small party for my garden team. There w-would be eight, including me, if people actually come."

"This *is* a surprise. Congratulations! I'm sure we can have the cook rustle up some food for your group. Eight shouldn't be a problem. Are you thinking dinner?"

"No. I guess f-finger food, b-b-beer and wine. But do you think eight is too many for the guest house?"

"I always think a tight group works better for a party. Forces everybody to talk to each other. Besides, there's four outdoor propane heaters. I can have Mark set them out on your patio, if anyone wants to sit outside. Let's string some lights up, have the fire pit going, plug in the talking Santa. We'll make it festive!"

"Sounds g-g-great. Maybe we'll leave Santa at the big house though. "

Magna began preparing a list on her laptop, as we spoke. "Of course, I'll need to run everything by your mother first. Now, while I've got the calendar out, let's decide on a date. This is all very short notice; I hope your group of friends aren't booked yet."

I shrugged. "I k-kind of doubt it."

"Let's shoot for Friday, December 17th, although your mother will be gone after eight PM that evening."

"That's a preference, not a problem."

Magna ignored the comment and continued. "And that gives us about three weeks for preparations. As long as your mother is on board with this, everything should be fine. What shall I put on the invitation?"

"I'll do the invites. I was th-thinking...a cactus de-decorated with Christmas lights on the invitation? I can create something on my laptop."

"Yes, perfect for your garden theme, right? Who'd have ever thought...Violet Hill, party planner! I'm proud of you, Violet. I know this is a big step for you."

"Thanks, Magna. It's time I attempted th-this hurdle."

In appreciation, I leaned over to give her a quick hug, which I never did. She wasn't expecting it and the hug became more of an awkward chest bump. First attempts are always difficult.

As I was leaving, I asked, "Magna, how are d-donations coming along for the garden wall?

"Oh, glad you mentioned that, Violet. Your mother is hosting the annual holiday garden club luncheon next Friday. But she *insists* if she is going to solicit donations, *you* have to speak to the group to engage and encourage them.

I sat back down and gripped the arms of my chair as my eyes opened wide. "Why do *I* have to ask them? They're her f-friends. She knows them b-better than me."

"But it's your job and your project. You'll be more successful speaking about the new garden because you're more passionate about it. You understand all the details of xeriscape design. Didn't you tell me your idea was to make it a teaching garden?"

I was looking down, studying Magna's new chocolate-brown ankle boots. "Yes, I s-suggested that."

"Well, Violet, *teach* them about it. If your ideas have merit, I'm sure the ladies will decide to support the project. But you'll need to prepare a special talk for them. Make it fun and interesting. You can do it!"

"I don't know. Those women m-make me so nervous. You know how they can be."

"Well, your mother has been generous enough to offer you the platform. Now it's up to you to make them see something special they want to be a part of." She looked back at her calendar and computer again. "Oh good! We now have thirty confirmed to attend. I need to contact the caterers. Should be a fun group!"

"Th-thirty garden club women? By next F-Friday? What about this... maybe I bring in M-Molly to speak? She's the head horticulturist at BUD."

"I'm sorry, Violet. Your Mother insists. *You* must do the speaking if you want the donations. We're both very confident of your abilities. Now, I've got a slew of confirmations to make and need to get on the phone to the caterers."

"OK." As I left, I attended my own pity party. Why me? All Mother would have to do is ask and most of her friends wouldn't bat an eye writing a check. But no. My stomach was already in knots thinking about standing in front of them as they waited in anticipation for something wonderful spewing from the mouth of Suzanne Hill's daughter.

Sunday morning I woke up early to the sound of rapping at my door. I looked down through my bedroom window and saw Mother zipped up in a gold threaded caftan flapping in the wind like an evil morning angel. She was holding the bribe of a cup of coffee, which meant talking was required. I pulled on my robe and greeted her downstairs.

"How are you, M-Mother?"

"Let's sit and talk. I brought coffee the way you like it. All that frothy milk and stuff."

"Yum. Thanks." We each grabbed a Windsor chair at my table and sat down.

"So...Magna told me the news about your party plans. Just wanted to discuss a few things."

"Sure."

"Top item, Violet. When you want to make plans involving the property, come to *me* first. I always want to be in the know. You're just like your father. He'd make all these big business ventures and never discuss them with me initially. So anyway, who are these eight people? Do I know any of them, or perhaps their parents?"

"V-Very doubtful. It's just my team from BUD. It's not a big deal. Actually though... you do know Mark."

"Mark who?"

"Mark Hopkins, your gardener. He's working with me p-p-part-time."

"Oh, I had no idea. I hope it's not interfering with his work here."

"No. Anyway...I thought a p-party might be a good way to give the group more of a team sp-spirit, using a different setting. I'm taking my cues from you, M-Mother. You always told me that was your strat—strat—plan."

"Yes, I agree. Excellent idea! Guess I'm finally rubbing off on you. A simple little gathering, but let's keep the main house off limits."

"Sure, no p-problem. You think we should set up a chain link fence around the pl-place? Add some security?"

She suddenly looked afraid. "Do you?"

"Kidding. No w-worries. I'll keep everyone on a tight leash."

She reached out and placed her hand over mine. "I'm happy for you, Violet. And I'm also excited to hear your talk at Friday's garden club. I started discussing your project with the girls. Everybody's excited to hear all about it. I do suggest you practice your talk with Lexi first. We all want your little lecture to go off without a hitch. Now, let's talk menus for your gathering. We'll get the cook to bake up a real holiday feast for your group. And, oh... I have some perfect ideas for decorating."

As she discussed bacon-wrapped asparagus spears, I was envisioning myself standing frozen in front of thirty women in blingy holiday garb, all waiting expectantly to be enlightened by me. This was followed by a sudden dread of parties from my past. Tables laden with food, decorations blazing, and nobody showing up.

"Sorry, Mother; keep planning menus." I stood up needing to make a dash to the bathroom. "That coffee must have upset my s-s-stomach." In the bathroom, my heart was racing as my head grew hot and my stomach revolted. I tried to tamp down my nerves, splashing cold water on my face. I had committed to overcoming a small societal hurdle; but now it was feeling more like an Olympic pole vault.

CHAPTER 24
Bad Dreams and Bad Dates

ROSARIO

I was under my bed, huddled next to the wall, listening to the muffled angry voices outside. I knew one of the voices was Roberto's, which had me shaking, curled up in a ball. I could tell he was talking to some very bad guys outside. Then I heard two loud thuds against our wooden door. As I lay there shaking, a tattooed arm suddenly reached under the bed, pulled me out, and yanked at my hands as I struggled against his grip. I was scrambling on the cold floor, trying to get back under the bed, but I quit resisting when a sharp knife was put to my throat, the blade piercing my neck.

The shrill sound of my alarm going off made me seize up, sucking in air as I struggled to figure out where I was. I jerked my bed covers off, breathing rapidly. My hands immediately began touching familiar objects around me as I tried to reassure myself it was just another nightmare. I hit the on-button, letting the noisy radio D.J.'s voice flood my small room. Then, I turned on my light, checking that my small efficiency was empty.

My recurring nightmare about Roberto's murder had suddenly merged with the robbery attempt at the lavenderia. The tattooed arm thrusting under my bed had the same ugly images that the thief had, and the sharp knife at my throat was like his. This new twist made the nightmare even more frightening. How long were these terrifying dreams going to plague me? Perhaps I needed to talk to somebody about this. But those types of doctors were expensive. Maybe later.

I shook off my fear and walked into the bathroom, turning on the shower. The warm water always helped clear my head. I forced myself to think of positive things. Thank God, I didn't have to work at the lavenderia and face the scowl and snarl of Miguel any more. And no more fears about the return of the hyped-up meth-head returning to brutalize me. I shampooed my hair trying to wash the lingering stress out of my brain.

Later, brushing my teeth, I repeated my daily mantra, "It's going to be a good day," forcing myself to smile at my reflection.

Now every morning as I got off the bus and made my way to the gated employee entrance at BUD, I counted myself lucky. When I walked into the gardens I felt safe behind the hedge-covered walls surrounding the fifty acres and comforted by like-minded associates. I was part of a team of people I enjoyed working with.

As I retrieved my tools, the early-morning birds greeted me, flitting about and chirping. While loading my shovel into a wheelbarrow, I inhaled the rich earthy smell of the bedding soil piled around me. Walking to our site, I watched two squirrels swirling around a tree trunk and then both suddenly stopped to pause at the crunch of my approach on the path.

At our xeriscape site, I started my day with a hot cup of coffee from my thermos. Lately, I needed a thick jacket and gloves to start the day, but as it warmed up, I'd usually discard them. Our team had finally brought the huge piles of soil and sand down to two-foot-levels, so completion of the bed preparations was in sight. Plus today, everybody was scheduled except for Winkleman; so pretty much the same as being fully staffed.

Violet and Turner were already there as I arrived. Violet greeted me, then handed us each an invitation to a party.

"I hope you b-both can come. Just a little holiday p-party to gather the team together. The food should be good." I noticed her hand trembled a little as I took it.

Turner opened the card and stared at it for a few seconds. "Sorry, Vi, I may be busy that night. But you know, I'm not really an official member of the team. Just a volunteer."

Violet nodded, but I caught a look of disappointment on her pretty face. I said, "I'll come, Violet. Maybe I can bring someone with me?"

"Sure, I g-guess that would be fine."

But I had to decide, should I ask Nico or perhaps Victor? Victor had encouraged me to call him and now I had a reason. I wondered if Violet had a nice place. It would be embarrassing to take Victor to a party at a place like my apartment. But Violet had a car, she'd gone to college, was a team leader. She probably had a nice apartment. But those were silly things to worry about.

Violet had assigned me, Mark, and Linda Bell to dig holes in preparation of the arrival of our garden's first trees. It was tough work, but Mark kept us laughing most of the time.

Later that afternoon, tired and dirty, sitting on the bus, I thought about Nico and a date we had last Sunday afternoon. It was actually our first real date, not counting our library research and his lavanderia visit. I'd been looking forward to seeing him again.

Nico decided to take me to the movies. It was a show about comic book superheroes--noisy and action-packed, but I was bored and disappointed. Not my kind of movie at all. I hated all the fighting, flying around, and imaginary powers. Nothing was real. Fighting was nothing to joke about. It was scary; weapons had real consequences. This movie made light of all of that. I kept thinking that if these people in the theater had witnessed the things I'd seen in Juarez, maybe they wouldn't be so eager to see this violence as entertainment.

After the show, when I explained my thoughts to Nico, he disagreed.

"But, Rosie, it's good against evil; the super powers just put everyone on a more level playing field. The heroes have human problems too. Plus, the CGI! It's amazing what they can do on-screen now."

"Nico, sorry. It's not for me. That's all I can say."

He left the theater on such a high and I'd brought his mood down. We had eaten food in the theater, so neither of us was hungry and I didn't feel like doing anything else. I was confused about my feelings because I'd been so excited the first time we'd met, and then at the lavenderia, after the thief was arrested, he'd been so caring, even though his angry comments got me fired. Something was off and I suspected it was my run-in with Victor. When I'd seen him again, I immediately knew there was some kind of connection between us. Maybe Nico had been a pleasant distraction.

Sitting in his parked car, Nico suggested, "Well, we could go for a drink? Remember Christo's, the Greek bar I told you about?"

"I'm sorry, Nico. I've had a long week and I'm very tired. It's probably best if I go home."

I could tell he was disappointed, but he drove me home and kissed me goodnight at my door. But it wasn't the same as it had felt at the lavenderia. Both my heart and head had doubts.

This afternoon, stepping off the bus, I decided I would definitely call Victor and invite him to Violet's party. Later, I nervously punched in his number, and he picked up on the first ring.

"Hey Victor. How's your week going?"

"I was about to give up on you. Glad you called, Rosario."

"I wanted to invite you to a party. It's a small gathering. My boss is having a Christmas party and she said I could bring someone, so I thought of you."

"Uh, what's the date?"

"Friday, the seventeenth, at seven."

"Yeah, my Saturday's booked...but I can make Friday work. Can we make it at eight? I promised some friends I'd meet them after work."

"You sound popular."

"It's just that time of year. You know how it is. Cool, I'm putting you in my calendar. Text me your address and I'll pick you up about eight."

After we hung up, I thought about what Victor had said, with everyone being busy. I certainly wasn't. Violet's invitation was the only one I had ever received while living in Dallas. And Victor would have to see my sorry apartment when he picked me up. But if I wanted to hang out with him, he needed to know the real me. Would Victor be one of the good guys? I had to believe he was.

CHAPTER 25

Double-Teaming

VIOLET

My soul felt a little crushed when Turner immediately declined my party invitation. First person I hand it to, and right out of the envelope—a no. He said he was busy. I was afraid that might happen. Every time I tried to push myself out of my comfort zone, someone would slap me back into it. At least Rosario said she would come. I hadn't planned on people bringing dates, but once she asked me I decided it was probably a good thing. That way I knew at least two people would show up.

As Mark ambled on to the garden site ten-minutes late, I handed him an invitation. "Mark, you're late, but if you come to our team p-p-party, I won't be mad at you."

"Well good morning to you, Violet. Don't worry, if you're offering free booze, I'll show up. OK if I bring someone?"

Why did all these people have dates? "I guess. A g-girlfriend? That should be interesting."

Mark shrugged and gave the canned response he often used when ending our conversations. "Cool."

Later, as Mark and I talked about the size of the tree holes we needed, Linda Bell showed up pushing her wheelbarrow. As she passed, I handed her the envelope. "It's an invitation to our team party."

She immediately opened the card and read it. "Oh darn. It's on a Friday. That's my bowling night."

Mark turned and said, "Come on, Linda. It's one Friday out of the year. You can skip your fucking bowling night."

"Maybe. I'll have to think about it." Linda tucked the invitation in her back pocket and explained. "My team gets mad when I miss. I'm top scorer. Plus, we're having free nachos that night. You should join us sometime, Violet."

"You wouldn't want me. Last time I bowled I was be-bestowed the title of g-gutter-ball-girl." Then I began envisioning gooey nacho-fingers placed inside bowling ball holes, making my skin crawl.

So, another 'No.' This team-party was a stupid idea. Everybody had someplace to be or someone to be with. I had nothing going on during the month of December, unless I counted Mother's Christmas Eve open house, where her friends dropped by to knock back a few glasses of her famous holiday Champagne punch. I'd show up for that. The punch always packed a wallop and made Christmas Eve with Mother more palatable.

I began with assignments for the day. Mark, Rosario and Linda would begin digging holes for trees being delivered, while I decided to ply Turner with questions as he and I finished the beds along the downhill path.

While shoveling soil and sand into our wheelbarrows, he spoke up defensively. "Don't ask, Vi."

"Ask about what?"

"I know you want to ask about the donation requests for the longhorns. I wish I'd never suggested that. I've raised squat and I've tapped almost all my friends."

I stopped shoveling and shrugged. "At least you tried, right?"

"Gotta admit, asking friends for donations is a lot harder than selling something."

"Turner, if you still want to help, I have a b-better idea. And you won't have to b-bother your friends."

He eyed me skeptically. "What now?"

"R-Remember when I told you my m-mother was collecting donations for us from her friends?"

"Yeah, I remember. You took the easy way out." Turner smiled a little as he pushed his wheelbarrow further down.

I called out behind him, "Unfortunately, nothing is ever as easy as it s-s-seems." I caught up and kept talking. "Apparently, my m-m-mother is hosting a holiday gathering of thirty of her garden club pals next Friday and they're expecting *me* to speak to the group and b-beg for donations."

He stopped and said, "Sounds good. What's the problem?"

"Speaking to large groups of s-s-society mavens is not really my forte."

"Vi, you'll be fine. Just write it all up, and practice a few times."

I stabbed my shovel into the dirt. "No, I will not be fine. You don't understand; my stomach has been tied in knots since M-Mother explained this to me. But...*you* could be a big help to me and therefore, not r-r-renege on collecting your part of the donations."

He looked at me, frowning. "A big help doing what? Society garden parties aren't exactly in my wheelhouse either."

"We need to d-double-team them at the party. Me, as the nerdy bi-biologist and lead gardener, and you as the eager volunteer and sp-sponsor. Remember Turner, you're a valuable two-fer!"

He thought about it for a second. "I get it... Like you're the steak and I'm the sizzle. Learned that one in marketing class years ago."

As we pushed our loads down the hill, I was panting. "See... you understand this s-stuff...You can't have started your own s-successful company without talking p-people into letting go of their money...and acquiring new accounts...You must have real sk-skills in that regard."

"I'll be honest, it all seemed daunting in the beginning, but I ended up being pretty good at reeling in the clients and early investors because I believed in what I wanted to create and what I was selling. That helps a lot. So, you're saying we need to approach this like a business, and not so much as a philanthropic thing."

"I think so." I started slinging my soil into the bed. "That's why I need your help. I've never s-sold anything."

"If that's the case, you shouldn't mention the word, *donation*. The garden club ladies should feel like *investors* in this great botanical-xeriscape experience. And the payoff—they can get in on the ground floor of this new and unique teaching garden in their community." Turner snapped his fingers and turned to me. "I got it... they need to think of themselves as community garden ambassadors."

"Yes, exactly! See, you're good. And if it wasn't for their special early investment, p-parts of this garden would never happen. They need to b-believe and understand that."

Turner leaned on his shovel, thinking out loud. "Right, that sounds good... but then we should finish off the talk with plans to invite them all to a big cocktail bash for the grand opening of the garden. Nothing like free drinks and society media to draw those people in."

I nodded, encouraged by his growing enthusiasm. "P-Perfect. My mother's friends love going to openings; makes them feel like they're on the c-cutting edge. And well worth their money if they get their picture in the paper. So...you're on b-board? You'll d-do this with me?" I looked up, smiling at the prospect of his help.

Turner shoveled out the last of his sand and stepped back. "I didn't say that."

"Oh." I nodded and walked my wheelbarrow hurriedly back up to refill. I didn't want him to see how disappointed I was.

Then he laughed behind me. "Yes, Vi. I'll do it. Who can say *no* to those pretty puppy-dog eyes?"

I wheeled around with a broad smile across my face. "You will? Th-Thank you. You have no idea how re-relieved I am!"

Turner took a few long strides and caught up with me. "It's so clear to me now why I couldn't raise much in donations. I was trying to solicit unmotivated friends to donate money to something they didn't care about. But now, we'll be asking for investments from women who are already interested. We're just there to serve up the spiel, and then seal the deal."

"I couldn't have said it b-better m-myself."

"Yeah Vi, that's kind of true. So, what are we gonna do about that stutter?"

"What st-stutter?" Then I laughed nervously--a lot. "So you noticed that?"

"If my questions make you uncomfortable, just tell me to shut up, but the stutter... is it something you've had for a long while?"

"Yeah. I don't talk much about it, except to my speech therapist. Most p-people just pretend like I'm speaking normally and then slowly p-p-pull away. It seems to make them feel uncomfortable. And yes...had it as long as I can remember. But, believe it or not; it's actually b-better lately. Lexy, my therapist says when I first meet p-people, I should tell them about my impediment. You know? Kind of take the air out of the b-bag."

"I agree. For the garden talk, you should lead off with that at the outset. Don't hide from it. If you think about it, a lot of us have some kind of disability or issues. But some people's problems aren't as obvious as others."

"You think? So, what's yours Turner?"

"Hmm, that's probably a discussion for another time. Let's focus on this garden party thing. Now I'm really curious to see how much we can raise. Let's knock this out between us, do a little back and forth and hopefully have them writing big checks. How long do we have to work up our spiel?"

"We need to have it l-locked down for p-presentation by this Friday."

"Damn, not much time. Let's talk it over while we work."

"You read m-my m-mind."

Then Turner said, "And then maybe we should practice once or twice over dinner."

Dinner? Could that officially count as an unofficial date? My mind quickly added another check mark on my socialization list. Lexi would be so happy.

CHAPTER 26

Steak and Sizzle

TURNER

The day flew by as Violet and I worked together while kicking around ideas for the garden party pitch. Vi was interesting, but a conundrum. Both clever and intelligent, but at times, she was so unsure of herself when suggesting something; seemingly uncomfortable in her own skin.

As much as I had doubted diving into this volunteer work, today I felt good about my decision. I was physically immersing myself in a large garden project which I knew would make a positive impact--something good for the body, mind, and community.

Then my mind went to my dad. He'd called a few times recently and I had ignored his messages. I knew once I told him about my volunteering, he would think I had lost my mind. I could hear his voice in my head admonishing me for wasting my days working hard at BUD for no visible profit, while he felt I was needed at my own company.

If nothing else, the pure physical exertion of the work was giving me a good night's sleep, and planning the garden-party presentation with Violet would keep me away from the temptation of drowning my issues in alcohol.

As we walked to our cars that afternoon, I said, "So Vi, let's each write up our own bullet points tonight and maybe Tuesday and

Thursday we'll meet, work out the rough spots, and rehearse. What do you think?"

Looking down, she nodded in agreement. "We can meet at my place Tuesday. Around six? I'm staying in my mother's guest house, just across the lake. I can arrange for food."

"Sure. Don't go to any trouble. Grab some take-out and then I'll take care of Thursday. See you then."

A few days before, I'd decided to start back part-time, two days a week at Rapid Logistics. Initially, the thought of going back to work regularly made me almost physically ill, caused by a mix of emotions. I figured it was my guilt of all the personal time that I'd robbed from Allie and myself, and definitely now there was business stress with all the supply chain issues bombarding our business. But on top of all that, there was that look in my associates' eyes when they spoke to me. It was a blend between pity and uncomfortable which gave me the creeps.

Tuesday morning I woke early, put on the first dress shirt and tie that I'd worn since the funeral, and made myself a healthy breakfast of eggs, toast and fruit. No one knew I was coming in. I was curious to see what everybody was up to. I'd been checking in with frequent phone calls, but a personal visit was a whole different animal.

While taking the elevator up, I checked my reflection in the mirrored walls. I straightened my tie, held my head up, did a mental gut check, and walked into the reception area.

Fern, our receptionist, looked shocked and then smiled. "Surprised to see you, Turner. Welcome back."

"Thank you, Fern. Good to see you too. I'd like to schedule a ten o'clock meeting today, all the department heads and my father. Everybody in yet?"

"Hmm, some are. I'll let everybody know and make sure they're in the conference room by ten."

"Thanks. Speaking of the conference room, can you send me some website links for office chairs? Maybe everybody would be in better moods if we purchased more comfortable chairs. I know it would make me happier.

"Sure, Turner."

I sat down at my desk and stared at the opposite wall which had a western inspired oil painting featuring a sprinkling of bluebonnets in the foreground, a ram-shackle ranch house, and a windmill and water tank in the background.

I picked up the phone and buzzed my dad. "You in yet, Dad?"

"In where? If you're referring to my shower, the answer is yes and it feels damn good this morning."

I smiled hearing his ornery voice. "You take your phone to the shower?"

"Yup. Got one of those new waterproof models. I like listening to my tunes while I'm scrubbing up in here."

"Well Dad, I guess you're the one running late today."

"Son, just thought I'd take a page out of your playbook and do whatever the hell I felt like."

"Point taken. I realize you don't approve of my current work ethic but it's something I need to do for mental health. But never mind that...just had a thought. Down at the lake house, is there still that old windmill on the property?"

"Yeah, I haven't used it in years, but it's more trouble to tear down than to keep. Why?"

"It's something that might look good in the garden at BUD, where I've been volunteering. Would you be interested in donating that? By the way, I'm at the office right now and just called a ten o'clock meeting if you'd care to join us."

"First you're talking damn windmills and then you're announcing a meeting in forty-five minutes? What's got into you? Maybe you do need some mental health assistance."

"Probably. Why don't you dry off, come in and find out. See you soon, Dad."

Around five I purposely closed my laptop, while I made a quick review of my productivity before leaving. This was going to be the new, improved Turner. No more working late hours, strategizing with clients over happy-hour meetings, no taking last-minute trips to close out deals. I could still be the face behind the company, pulling the strings, but would try not to personally make every face-to-face meeting. After gathering with key personnel today I knew I had competent people who could probably take most of those meetings.

I let Siri direct me to Violet's place, suddenly realizing she lived less than a mile from my house. I pulled up into the curved driveway, recognizing an impressive home I'd passed by for years. Allie had always whined about wanting a big wrap-around porch like the one at the Hill home. I followed the driveway to the back and saw a two-level, predominantly glass guest house across from a large pool.

Violet stuck her head out of one of the French doors, smiled, and waved me in. I was hoping this meeting would go quickly. After my first full day back at work, I was ready for an evening appointment with my hot tub.

"Gr-Great, you're right on time. The cook just brought over a plate of loaded nachos and they're still hot."

"Perfect way to start a meeting. Only had a salad for lunch so nachos are sounding good." I immediately started looking around her impressive little place. "How was your day, Vi?"

"Had four dessert willows p-planted and some crepe myrtles. Thankfully, forklifts brought them over, but we had to f-fill in the holes after they were dropped. It's all starting to take shape now. It's exciting!"

I began looking around her place. "Fantastic quarters you have here. You're lucky to have your own space while staying at your mother's." I was busy glancing at the art, and then went to examine the countertops and cabinets of the kitchen area.

"Yeah, thanks. Have a s-seat. The nachos are the starter. M-Maria is bringing over tortilla soup and tamales, shortly. Her's are the best."

I sat down and looked hungrily at a platter of quartered and fried tortillas loaded down with refried beans, cheese, guac, and jalapenos. "You're ruining things for me, Vi. I was going to treat you to In-N-Out Burgers Thursday. How can I compete with this?"

"No worries. Help yourself."

I finished one off in two bites, washed it down with a cold Dos Equis beer, and reached for a second nacho. As I wiped my hands on my napkin, I said, "So, not to rush, but can we go over our talk topics while we eat. I have an appointment in a little over an hour."

Violet was still nibbling on her first nacho and looked a little upset after I announced my anticipated appointment. I didn't mention it was with my hot tub.

"Uh sure, we can do that. Let me b-bring my laptop over. Why don't you go first? And what's with the t-tie?"

"Went into work today; my first full day since September. It was such a long day, but it's only because I'm rusty. Lots of stressful things going on there right now. I used to spend at least eleven to twelve hours a day at work.

"Wow, quite the tr-transition. So...what do you have for us, Turner."

He plugged in his laptop and pulled up his notes. "I was thinking it might be great if we could have some backdrop photos up on a screen behind us as we speak. Any chance you could get a hold of some equipment? I could snap some shots tomorrow when I come into the gardens."

"Yeah, that would be cool. S-Sounds like a Magna question."

"What's a Magna?"

"Magna's a her... My m-mother's extremely competent assistant. I'll check on that."

"Great. I think *you* definitely need to open the talk. Smile, thank them for hopefully becoming a vital part in this innovative gardening project...blah, blah, blah. You know the drill. Then you introduce me."

"OK...here's what I wrote." Vi became hesitant, even shaking a little as she read from her screen. "Turner Cooper was our first sp-sponsor and volunteer and we're so l-lucky to have him here. I hope he can help inspire you to join us on this adventure into our first tr-

true xeriscape garden of the southwest at BUD." She looked up at me expectantly.

"Yeah, not bad Vi, but it needs more excitement, more punch. Just think how you've become excited about the project and put that into your introduction."

"B-But you said I was the steak, and *you* were the sizzle."

"Yeah, but a thick, juicy, exciting steak. Not an old piece of left-overs."

"See. I told you I'd be t-t-terrible at this." Vi looked down at her screen, frustrated, shaking her head.

"Hey, sorry. That comment was out of line. Honestly, you've probably got the bones of a good first attempt. Let's work on it together. But first I'll need another nacho and beer. We'll nail this down. Don't worry."

About fifteen minutes later, Maria came in with course two and three, just as we finished rewriting Vi's first opening sentences. It looked like I wouldn't be making it to my tub appointment tonight. But at least there was beer.

CHAPTER 27

Nach-yo Mama's Margaritas

ROSARIO

I was dreading going home Wednesday afternoon. Already twice this week, I'd had my recurring dream with the horrible tattooed arm grabbing at me. It was so frightening, jolting me awake with heart palpitations. I'd finally managed to push back the nightmare involving Roberto's murder to just a few times a month, but now, here I was having a scrambled version of both dreams taunting me with a vengeance.

As I grabbed my backpack out of the BUD locker, Violet came up behind me. "Hey Rosie, after we get cl-cleaned up this afternoon, why don't we go out for a drink? I could pick you up? I noticed a place with five-dollar m-m-margaritas in the neighborhood."

I was getting to know Violet pretty well by now, and knew she had probably been gathering her courage all day to ask me to join her. Sure, I'd go. It was the perfect solution to delaying the bad dreams. "*Bien*. I'd like that, Violet. I can maybe meet you there?"

"No, taking a b-bus might get complicated. What if I p-pick you up around five-thirty? Just put your address and number in my ph-phone."

"Sure. Oh...wait, VI. I'm only twenty. Is that a problem?"

She shrugged and laughed. "There's always lemonade."

I was excited. My first Dallas happy hour! I spent my bus ride home deciding what to wear.

By five-fifteen, I was showered, with hair straightened, makeup on, wearing my favorite pink jeans and a blue denim jacket. I sat on the front stoop of the apartment complex watching for Violet.

As I waited, I recognized the white Corolla that pulled up to the curb and stopped. It was Nico's. I had mixed emotions about seeing him. He was a really nice guy but I wanted to leave myself open and available for Victor, hoping things might go well at Violet's party. I didn't want to encourage Nico beyond friendship.

After he got out of the car, I waved and met him halfway down the sidewalk. "Hey Rosie, you look great."

"Thanks. So what brings you here?"

"I dropped a fare off up the block and thought I'd see if you were home. How you been?"

"Really good, but a friend from work is picking me up soon. We're going to happy hour."

He nodded, looking a little disappointed. "Where at? Maybe I'll meet you there later."

"Actually, I really don't know. All she mentioned was five-dollar-margaritas. But maybe another time?" I saw Violet's car approaching and waved as she slowed down. "That's her. Let's talk next week. I'll call you."

"Sure. Next week?"

I walked quickly to Violet's car as her red Subaru pulled up behind Nico's, and then I turned and waved goodbye. I felt bad about being so vague with him, but I thought it might be for the best. I could have invited him, but that might make Violet uncomfortable. I just wasn't sure of the rules people went by here. In Mexico, it wouldn't have been a big deal to invite a friend to join us, but maybe here it was different. Especially with Violet being so shy.

I jumped in and buckled up. "Hi *chica*. Thanks so much for picking me up. Was it very far?"

"Not too bad; I've been around this area be-before. So, who's the guy? A n-neighbor?"

"It's Nico. I think I told you about him? He was my Uber driver a while back and we really hit it off. We studied together, he visited me at the lavenderia, took me to the movies...but now, I don't know. I'm really attracted to Victor and don't want to lead Nico on." I shrugged my shoulders. "We'll see. What do you call it? Feast or famish? For a year I went out with no one and now I have two men interested."

Violet smiled and nodded. "The word's f-f-famine, but close enough. I understand. I've been in the famine category with guys for years."

"Oh, that's why you're so skinny, girl." We both laughed as I made a little jab at her flat stomach. "We just need to make you a little curvier. You're so beautiful, though. I think we both need to put ourselves out there more. And I've been meaning to ask ... Do you like Turner? I've noticed the way you look at him. Monday, the two of you were talking together all day."

"It's n-n-not what you think. I needed to beg him to help me p-p-pitch my mother's garden club for some big donations for BUD. I was too nervous to do it alone. I f-finally got him to agree. Compared to me, he's a natural salesperson. So while working the other day, we planned our pr-program for Friday. Maybe if we can bring in some big money I'll get on M-Molly's good side for a change."

"OK... whatever Vi. I still think you like him." I smiled and nudged her.

With her eyes on the road, Violet sighed and made an admission. "I guess I am attracted to him. It's his c-c-confidence, his attitude. Wish I was more like that."

"I knew it, Vi!"

"But I think he also has some issues he's hiding. Being a widower--at his age? Must be a ter-terrible thing to overcome. But it's also like he's holding something back. I can't quite figure it out. But that's enough about him. Maybe tonight we'll both m-meet some new people."

"Sounds good. So... five-dollar-Margaritas? Did you know in my area of Mexico, nobody drinks frozen margaritas? It's an American thing."

"Actually, I read they were invented in D-Dallas. You know, this happy hour idea was all my sp-sp-speech therapist's doing. She keeps encouraging me to b-build my confidence."

Vi eventually pulled up to a shopping center near the lake. I noticed several cars already parked around a small place called *Nach-yo Momma's Margaritas*. As I laughed at the brightly-colored sign, Vi started looking nervous and I noticed her hands shaking as she tried to parallel park. I wasn't sure if it was the tight parking spot or the idea of talking to strangers, but after parking, she shook her hands out, checked her lipstick in the mirror, and timidly asked, "Ready?"

"Violet, it's a bar, not a firing squad."

"Then next time I s-s-suggest this, bring a blindfold."

Walking into the noisy place, we noticed all the bar stools were full but there were a couple of high-top tables against the windows. I grabbed a table while Violet approached the busy bartender with her ID and ordered two margaritas. She walked up, standing behind two guys, looking like a nervous twelve-year-old.

The guys walked away with their frosty mugs and the bartender smiled at her. After close scrutiny of her license, he handed Vi two icy lime-green mugs. As she approached our table with drinks, I said, "Bravo! We passed inspection. I'm hungry too. Let's get burgers."

As I said this, two men walked in looking like they'd just come from work. "Oh Vi...I love men in dress shirts and ties. That tall one--he's so hot!" I leaned into Vi's ear and whispered. "Look, he has dimples too. So cute."

Violet looked their way, but their backs were now to us as they ordered at the bar. She asked, "Which one?"

"Definitely the dark-haired one. I like them tall, dark, and handsome." At that point, the bartender pointed to our table and the guys nodded. "Vi, they're coming over! *¡O mi dulce Jesús!*"

"Wait, I've seen that other guy," Vi whispered to me. "At the dog park."

As they walked up, I delivered my biggest smile, while Vi attempted a grin, but her lips were quivering. The tall guy spoke first, "Hey, mind if we borrow your extra stools. It's full-up around here."

I didn't know if it was the tequila mixing with my empty stomach, but I felt a surge of confidence, putting my foot on the rail of the stool and pushing it out. "Please, join us if you like." They looked at each other, shrugged, and sat down.

Dimples reached out his hand and shook both mine and Violet's. "Enrique Martinez and this is my buddy, Kevin. Pace yourself with those Margs; they're strong here, ladies."

Violet attempted to make a stab at conversation. Looking at the other guy, she said, "Kevin, I've s-seen you at the dog park at White Rock. Curly-haired, blonde dog, right?"

"That's me. I'm surprised I don't remember. I usually notice the pretty girls."

Her face turned red at his compliment, but she continued. "Well, it was my first day at the p-park with my dachshund, Cocoa. She was growling at several dogs and I actually sc-screamed as they got into a fight. But then a guy I knew came over and separated the dogs. It all turned out fine but I was s-so scared at the time."

"Yeah...I do remember that. A month back or so? I've met that dude. Turner Cooper, right? So, you're a good friend of his?"

"Sort of. He v-volunteers at BUD, where I work."

"I love that place. I used to volunteer at Nature's Kitchen with a friend sometimes. What do you do there?"

At that point, a waiter walked up with our chips and salsa. Vi told him, "I'm r-running a tab with the bartender. Can you also bring us two burgers?" The guys got their drinks and we all settled in for some conversation,

Thirty minutes later, I was already over dimples. I could tell he was definitely a player, trying to get me to leave with him, making forward advances, and touching my leg under the table. While he went up to the bar, I asked Vi to go to the restroom with me. In the bathroom, I said, "I think we should go. Tall, dark and handsome isn't so great. All flash and hands, but no heart. Maybe we try another place? It's still early."

"OK, b-but I think Kevin is kind of nice. He apparently lives near me...we both like dogs. W-What do you think?"

"He seems nice enough; but remember who he came with." Then I snapped my fingers. "I got it. Invite him to your little party coming up. Maybe he'll come."

"You think? I don't have any m-more invitations."

"Jesus, Violet! He doesn't need a printed invitation. Just get his number to text the details."

"You m-make it s-sound so easy."

I pulled her arm and dragged her out of the restroom. "I'll help." As we walked to our table, I saw Dimples already hitting on another girl at the bar. As far as I was concerned, he was all hers. Kevin was still sitting there looking amused by his friend's tactics. Standing up next to him, I said, "So Kevin, Violet is having a little holiday fiesta for a few people the Friday after next. You should join us."

Kevin looked at Vi, and said, "Is that right? Hmm, maybe."

Vi then took over. "Uh...F-Friday, the seventeenth? Give me your number and I'll t-text you the details. You sh-should come."

He nodded as I handed him my phone. "Sounds good. I'll try to make it. Uh, is Cooper coming?"

"No. he told me he had plans."

I reminded Violet, "You better close out your tab before we go. Kevin, we're leaving now. Nice to meet you."

As we walked to her car, I patted Violet on the back. "Good job, girlfriend. You got a guy's number! How does that feel?"

She paused in the parking lot, gathering her thoughts for a second. "L-Liberating, exciting...kind of scary. Where to next?"

CHAPTER 28

Picture Perfect

VIOLET

Magna knew a guy who'd take care of our audio-visual needs for our little garden party presentation. As the human rolodex of problem solving, my mother's personal assistant *always* knew somebody. In prepping for the slide show, Turner and I took shots of the emerging BUD xeriscape garden while at work, and then also shot photos of our plan rendering, showing what we hoped to accomplish at completion, including our proposed rock wall and longhorn sculptures.

At work, while watering recently planted trees, Turner mentioned another inspiration he had, suggesting we drag in an old windmill his father owned on some property. He thought it would look great in the garden, set up next to the longhorns.

"A windmill? You can take that one up with M-Molly. She seems to hate every idea that comes out of my m-mouth. Try your seductive charms of p-p-persuasion on her and see what happens."

"I'll ask, but you should at least come with me. You're the team leader."

"Does the windmill even work? It would make more sense if it p-p-pumped the water from the tank back up the trail, recycling it to the p-plants like a fountain. Find out from your dad. If it works, I'll push for it. R-R-Right now, I'm more concerned with getting my part of our presentation down and bringing in some big d-donations. That's the priority right now."

Thursday evening, we practiced our talk once again, using the photos we had uploaded to the large screen set up in Mother's sunroom. Earlier in the week, Magna had the room cleared of its normal furniture and plants and had the event planners set up six round tables, each sitting six. A decorating crew had come in and hung all of Mother's coordinating holiday decor and at the front of the room they'd set up a very tall, but narrow, white flocked tree with pale pink and citron green decorations. The center-piece of each table was a miniature of that same twinkling tree.

Walking into the room Thursday night, and clicking on all the sparkling lights, brought out my anxiety again. I stared at the low-lit room, almost in a trance. It looked absolutely beautiful, the white tone-on-tone porcelain china, the best silver, the alternating white and pink linen napkins, the refracted light bouncing off the stemmed crystal glasses. Everything was too perfect, but in contrast, I knew I wouldn't be.

Even at my best, there would be sputters, stutters and pops.

Turner had all the equipment plugged in. "OK Vi, remember, it's fine to look down at your notes occasionally but try not to read from them. Use them as a reference. It's important to speak extemporaneously. I've turned on the mic. Let's do a final run-through."

Turner's voice broke through my holiday decor hypnotism. I shook my head, dreading that Turner had to listen to my voice magnified through the large empty room. "Do we really need the mic on now?"

"Sure. Let's check for reverb, see how it all sounds. Go ahead. Talk to your imaginary audience of lovely, smiling ladies."

"They're not too imaginary. I've met pl-plenty of them." *And can already see their judgemental faces staring back at me.* I approached the mic, frowning at Turner. "Here goes..." I cleared my throat and flipped on my most enthusiastic tone.

"Hi ladies. I'm Violet Hill, Suzanne's daughter. My m-mother and I are so excited that you decided to join us at one of her f-f-favorite holiday traditions, hosting your annual holiday garden p-party. You are such an amazing group. Before I get too f-far into all this, I just wanted to let you know that I have a sp-speech impediment, which results in occasional stuttering, so just b-bear with me and know that I'm fine and all is normal."

I looked over at Turner to see how that had come across. He nodded and smiled, urging me to go on. "Early this fall, I had the exciting opportunity to take on a new position at the f-fabulous gardens at Botanicals United of Dallas. Known better to all of us as B-BUD. It has truly been a life-changing event for me. One that I can't wait to share with you ladies, knowing how m-much all of you care about gardening and making the community you live in a place of unique b-beauty and learning."

Turner interrupted, with a big grin across his face. "My God, Vi. You've improved so much! I'm impressed. Sorry to interrupt..."

I nodded nervously and continued. "I've b-brought a friend over to help explain our m-mission today. L-Ladies, this is Turner Cooper. He's what we at BUD call a very valuable commodity. He's a generous garden sp-sponser and also a hard-working v-v-volunteer. Turner, why don't you briefly explain the goal of the xeriscape garden we are creating at BUD."

He joined me at the front and we continued on through our scripted presentation, going back and forth, stopping occasionally to smooth out a few rough transitions, but overall, we were both pleased with the end result.

"Dang Vi, I think we got ourselves a winner." Turner put his arm around my shoulders for a second and gave me a little congratulatory hug. I thought my heart would jump out of my chest as he did that. "It's amazing--the improvements you made in just a few days. I'm serious."

"Thanks. You r-really helped me s-so much." Just then I heard Mother's infamous heels clicking down the hall like a snare drum. Shit!

Her perfectly made-up face beamed toward us through the double doors. "There you are, Violet. Thought I heard voices. So, what's going on?" She swooped in carrying a shimmering cocktail dress on a hanger and walked directly up to Turner with her other hand outstretched. "Suzanne Hill, Violet's mother."

"Hello there; Turner Cooper. Vi and I just finished running through our presentation."

Mother looked a little confused, then stared at me. "I see. I thought this was to be *Violet's* presentation."

Turner jumped in, coming to my rescue. "Well, I'm a volunteer *and* the garden's sponsor, so we both thought the two of us would make a stronger presentation to generate donations."

"Fantastic! Good point. Well, it's a pleasure to meet you, Turner. So, how's it going? Violet occasionally has a few anxiety issues, but I bet the two of you will be great. Hope you're ready to impress these women into opening up their wallets."

I plastered on my smile. "That's the goal, M-Mother."

Turning to look all about, she asked, "So, what do you think of the room?"

"Truly amazing, Mother. I think it's your b-best yet." Turner then echoed my compliments.

She did a full three-sixty, turning to smile at us again. "Thank you. Yes, I'm pleased. And I can't take all the credit. Magna helped a little too. But the colors were all my idea. Oh, speaking of colors, here's a present, Violet. I just came in from shopping." She handed me the pale pink dress on a heavy wooden hanger. "Now, I know how you hate to shop, but I wanted you to wear something special for tomorrow."

"S-Seriously? I think we're wearing our B-BUD polo shirts and khakis, right Turner? It's just a luncheon." I glanced at him for confirmation, but he remained mum.

"Only a luncheon?" Mother's eyes popped as her voice got shrill.

Ouch! My bad...lousy choice of words. "W-What I mean is...we're coming straight from work..."

"Well, you'll come straight from work thirty minutes earlier and take the time to put this fantastic Stella McCartney original on and look sharp about it. I'm sure Mr. Cooper has a handsome jacket and tie he can find to wear. Correct, Turner?"

"Happy to do it, Suzanne."

I was mortified. She'd embarrassed me and was now commandeering Turner into her ridiculous dress code.

"Actually, Violet, it's probably best to slip the dress on right now so we can check sizes. I'll call my girl there tomorrow morning to exchange it if it's not right."

"Now? Mother...

"Yes, go ahead. It'll just take a minute. Use the powder room in the hall. I'll keep Mr. Cooper company. As I gripped the hanger and began trudging through the room, she called out, "Remember, regarding tomorrow's presentation...you're representing BUD, but you're also representing me and our family. And I know you are both going to look and be fantastic!"

I shook my head and kept walking. In the powder room, I held the opalescent pink creation up in front of the mirror. The shade should look good, contrasting against my dark hair and light eyes, and of course, Mother had me coordinating with the room decor. It looked like a perfect size four.

I yanked off my clothes and carefully slipped on the light-as-whipped-cream designer dress, and pulled the zipper up the back. The simple, classic-cut princess lines nipped my waist and closely skimmed my hips, with the hem line grazing slightly above my knees. Damn it! Mother had picked a winner. How did she do that? I shook my hair out of the pony tail and walked barefoot back into the sunroom.

I held up my arms and did a little twirl. "Here it is. I think the s-size is good. What do y'all think?"

Turner's mouth dropped a little. "Wow, pretty perfect. That's a ten. Great choice, Suzanne!"

Mother nodded approvingly. "Yes, I agree. You look lovely dear. I'm so glad I thought to pick up something. Now, I'll leave you both to it. We're excited to hear your little talk. See you about twelve-thirty?"

I mumbled, "Sure," as I listened to her heels echoing down the hallway. Then I turned and whispered to Turner, "I apologize. I'm s-so embarrassed. My m-mother's a trip."

He shrugged it off. "Hey, no big deal. You gotta literally read this room, Vi. Our BUD-logo shirts in this place? Come on. I'd already decided I was going with a coat and tie, but looking at that dress, maybe I should rethink. I'll throw on my black suit. By the way, you look really stunning. Your Mother may be a little scary, but she has excellent taste."

He glanced at his watch and picked up his backpack. "I gotta run. Then he gave me a funny smirk. "Meet you here tomorrow, *as commanded*. Great working with you today, Violet."

Back in the guest house, I gingerly hung up the dress and covered it in a garment bag. I knew this dress cost more than my monthly salary. It was gorgeous, but somehow, even with its light weight, the pressure on me had just multiplied.

The following day, after my morning work at BUD, I rushed home, showered and dressed. After brushing my hair out, I pushed it back with a pale pink padded headband, and lifted my legs three-inches higher in a pair of nude strappy heels. The new additional accessories had miraculously appeared in shopping bags on my dining table while I was at work. I felt like Cinderella, after a hit by the fairy godmother's wand, making all components of my festive garb align perfectly. It was chilly outside, so I threw a long off-white pashmina across my shoulders and traipsed down the sidewalk to the backdoor of the sunroom. Mother and Magna were busy scrutinizing every aspect of the room.

Walking in, I announced, "So, M-Magna, what do you think?" I pulled the wrap off and revealed my outfit. "Tah-da!"

"Oh, there you are darling." Mother glanced down at her watch while walking towards me. "Good, right on time. Take a look, Magna."

Magna nodded approvingly. "Absolutely you, darling."

Mother added, "I totally agree. *Spot on*. I see you found the headband and shoes too."

"Yes! Thanks ladies. What can I do to help?"

"Nothing really, sweetie. Magna and I will be greeting our guests at the double doors here. Place cards are all arranged. I'll be announcing you and Mr. Cooper after lunch. Just find your seat and read over your material. That way, it'll all go off without a hitch."

"Will do." I may have looked the part, but my stomach was already acting up. I was used to this. A common anxiety issue every time I faced a crowd. And that usually only involved conversation, not giving a presentation in front of my judgemental mother and her cronies. I found my table near the front and off to the side of the microphone stand. I cleared my throat and brought the stack of small index cards out of my dress pocket, sewn in the side seams. As I was reading over my cards, I suddenly felt a hand on my shoulder.

"You're gonna be fine. Just relax." I lifted my head up and stared into the clear green eyes of Turner. "That color looks amazing on you. With those violet-blue eyes of yours...you should wear pink every day." Turner casually dropped into the chair next to me and switched his place card with someone else who would now be three chairs away.

I laughed. "Better watch it. The table p-police are pretty strict here. By the way, you look rather sm-smashing yourself."

"Thanks; so, you're feeling good? We're gonna be OK?" Turner took my hands, clapping his over mine. Probably more of a coaching technique than a romantic gesture, but it felt nice.

"Hopefully," I said and then continued to nervously chew my lip and went back to studying my cards.

As the club members arrived, several of Mother's close friends stopped by, patted my shoulder, and wished me a happy Christmas. As our table filled, I continued to smile, make occasional small talk, and took deep long breaths, trying to convince myself, *I can do this. I am ready.*

First, an arugula and raspberry salad was served, then a rich cream-potato soup. I only took a few small spoonfuls, playing it safe. Creamy things occasionally played havoc with my system. Finally, the salmon and vegetable plates arrived. I skipped dessert, already pushing down queasy feelings continuing to bubble up. I had to make Mother proud and mollify Molly from BUD. She'd been asking me daily about extra donations to complete the garden. A lot was riding on our little presentation.

Mother eventually got up, tapped the mic, and made pleasantries about the garden club business and the budget. Then she looked over at me and smiled, talking about how proud she was and pleased at what I had accomplished.

My stomach was heaving, my face got hot, then my head felt wobbly.

"So now, I'm pleased to introduce my lovely Ms. Violet Hill."

I yanked on Turner's sleeve and whispered, "I can't do this now. You have to go up there."

Keeping my head down, I quickly got up and walked out of the room.

CHAPTER 29

Dynamic Do-Over

TURNER

Crap! Violet just bolted with most of the garden club ladies noticing as she scurried past the tables to the door. How did I not see this coming? The first thing Violet had said, when roping me into this, was how uncomfortable public speaking was for her. I didn't realize she meant terrified. I got up, attempting to keep a look of confidence mixed with nonchalant chill, while I offered to take the mic from a flummoxed Suzanne Hill.

"Thanks Suzanne. No, ladies. Sorry, I'm not Violet. I'm Turner Cooper, a volunteer and a proud donor at BUD. If you will indulge us for *just* a few moments...Violet and I realized our presentation photos were not all loaded. So, please forgive us this brief delay. Suzanne...maybe this is a good time to pass out those superb bottles of wine you were telling us about?"

Still standing next to me, she looked perplexed for a second and then said. "Oh yes, great idea." Vi's mother quickly pulled it together and snapped a few fingers in the servers' direction.

I threaded through the tables, as the event staff hurried to the kitchen to open several bottles of her wine stash. Walking down the hallway, I listened for the sound of Violet's voice. Opening up the heavy wooden doors of what appeared to be an office, I saw Violet leaning over a trash can while sobbing, as her mother's assistant held her hair and patted her back.

"I'm so embarrassed, Magna. But I had to leave. Almost threw up all over the table."

"It's alright. Just get it out, dear. Just do whatever your body needs to do, but better in the can than on me, please."

"How can I help?" I walked up, startling Violet, right as she began retching into the can.

She ignored me until her stomach stopped heaving, and then wiped her mouth with the tissue Magna handed her. She finished a raspy cough and asked, "Turner...the presentation...I thought you were doing it?"

"No, because it's not near as good without your part. Remember... steak and sizzle? I need you out there with me, Vi, because you *are* the steak. But don't stress. Everybody's being served glasses of wine. All of our ladies should be in a great mood shortly. And I'm guessing you could use a cold glass of water right now? "

Magna looked at me with grateful eyes and said, "Excellent idea, Turner. By the way, I'm Magna Temple. Good to meet you."

"Been hearing great things about you, Ms. Magna. I'll go find the kitchen." It was crowded with the catering crew, but I wedged my way in and retrieved the water and filled a small plastic bag with ice. I returned to the office seeing Violet sitting at a desk with her face in her hands, as she took in long deep breaths.

"Here you go, Vi. Water, ice compress, and a few mints. The instant pick-you-up."

"Thanks." She cleared her throat and took several sips and plastered the ice bag to her forehead, with a shaking hand. "This feels so g-good. I had such a heat rush to my head, all mixed up with rapid heart pa-p-palpitations. Anxiety attack pr-probably. I get those."

Magna added, "Try the mints too. They help soothe upset stomachs."

I was counting down the minutes, wondering how long we could keep our garden crowd waiting. After another minute of Violet cooling her head, I told Magna, "Violet and I should be back soon. Please ask Suzanne to delay things just a bit longer."

"Sure, I'll let her know." Magna reached over to pat Violet's shoulder. "I know you'll do well, Violet. Just get back on the horse. Remember those first riding lessons? After a while you were amazing." Magna looked at me with a nod and left.

I sat on the edge of the desk waiting patiently while Violet drank all her water, still continuing to stare down at the desk with the ice bag pressed against her forehead. Then I softly took her one free, quivering hand. "Violet, I'm going to be standing right next to you. You wrote a great script, and it would be a shame for all our prep this week to go to waste." She was nodding, remaining silent after I spoke. "I told the garden club that we were missing a few photos for the slide show and we'd be right back. You have nothing to be embarrassed about."

In a timid, shaky voice, she said. "You're right. I need to do this. We have a lot riding on this talk." Then she looked up at me with a hint of a smile. "We need to raise money to pay for the longhorn sculptures that *you* were supposed to take care of."

"OK, don't rub it in. And don't forget your amazing dress? Ms. Stella McCartney would be furious if she heard you didn't get to show it off."

Vi rolled her eyes at me. "I'm sure she'd be devastated." She put down the ice bag, took another long deep breath and said, "OK, I guess I'm ready." As she pushed herself up from the desk, I stood up and took her arm. Walking down the long hallway, Violet said, "I appreciate you, Turner."

"Likewise. Hey, I thought you were a runner? Let's pick up the pace, kiddo."

"Kiddo? I'm not that much younger. How old are you, anyway?"

"Thirty-five. And you're what?...Twenty-two?"

"Actually, a very mature twenty-four."

I snorted. "I wouldn't go that far. Alright... you've just been promoted from kiddo to kid." We were approaching the doors to the sunroom. "OK, we're cool now? We're about to board a rollicking ship--filled with those scary garden club ladies." Violet's eyes opened wide and she almost laughed.

I pushed open the door and we sailed calmly through a sea of women busy chatting with each other. As we approached our table, I quietly asked, "How's the stomach?"

She whispered back, "Definitely better."

"Good. Let's drop anchor and walk the plank."

We both stopped briefly at our table, with Violet taking a sip of chilled Chablis, while I threw back my goblet of wine in one big unclassy gulp. "Ok, kid. Time to get up there."

Vi looked at me, gripped my arm for a second, and then stepped up to the mic stand. She confidently looked about the room, smiled, and in a clear voice, said, "S-Sorry for that delay, ladies. We just wanted an excuse for M-Mother to uncork her pr-prized wine. So, let's get this party started, shall we?"

Violet did even better than I hoped for. Sure, there were a few stutters and stops along the way, but nothing that felt uncomfortable. Guests laughed when they were supposed to, I remembered my bits and pieces, and the slide show was effective. Even better, the garden club members all played their part, writing out checks or signing up for debit card withdrawals, all to the hefty sum of thirty-five-thousand-dollars.

Even Suzanne Hill seemed to have a genuine smile on her face, as she came over to thank us for the successful presentation. Wrapping her arms around us both, she said, "Violet, Turner...excellent, motivating presentation today. I almost doubt I could have done better myself. I'm proud of you both." As back-handed a compliment as it was, Violet looked quite happy.

With the thirty-five-thousand generated, and a slew of new volunteers signed up, Violet now had great news to give Molly and hopefully get on her good side. Mark's realistic rock wall would get the thump's up, while I now needed to locate two bronze long-horn sculptures, and maybe even get a windmill trucked in from West Texas. All seemed to be coming up roses.

As I walked along the driveway to my parked car, I received a text notification from Katrina: *Holiday drinks and music, my place Friday the 17th at 8:00? Let's catch up! See address below.*

I immediately thought to reply that I was busy, but...what the hell. Why not go? An attractive, friendly, and frankly, sexy-as-hell woman, invited me to her Christmas party. Perhaps I should take a step forward. I texted back:

Sure. Should I bring ham sandwiches? See you there.

CHAPTER 30

Can't Judge a Book By Its Brown Suede Jacket

ROSARIO

Tonight...my date with Victor! I was excited about Violet's party and getting to know Victor better. He was still my dreamy prince of the lavenderia. So handsome...Swooping in very late one night at work, charming and flirty, asking me out and introducing me to Botanicals United on our first date.

But all that fell apart when he was called away abruptly after I'd barely finished my coffee and sandwich. I still had doubts about him, no matter how hard he'd tried to explain it away. But after running into him again, I knew I needed to give him a second chance. He was too smart and good looking to pass on. I was curious to really get to know the man whose dreamy face had tied me up in knots for the last several weeks.

He called to confirm on Thursday evening and said he'd come by at eight. I tried to convince him to meet me at Violet's, but he insisted on picking me up. I was tired of being embarrassed about where I lived, but when I'd recently done an online apartment search at the library, I was in sticker-shock at rent prices. A move wouldn't be possible for a while.

In preparation for the party, I straightened my hair and put on my short little black dress that hugged my curves. Not only was it my little black dress, it was my only dress. Excited and ready to go, I waited outside. From the stairs, I saw his black SUV pull up alongside the curb while I watched him step out of his car.

Victor did not disappoint. Tall, slender, and better looking than I'd remembered. I walked closer, noticing his snug-cut brown suede jacket, worn with dark denim jeans, brown boots, and an open-collared white shirt. I didn't know much about men's fashion, but this guy was definitely bringing it.

We met on the sidewalk, where he gave me a little hug, and then looked around at the apartments. "So, this is the mystery place you didn't want me to see before? Don't worry about it, Rosario. You should have seen my first place...I'm not judging."

"Thank you. You're looking very handsome tonight."

"And look at you--that dress fits you like a gorgeous glove."

Good. The dress was working its magic. I said, "We should get going; we're a little late already."

He sort of laughed and said, "Chill, Rosario. It's a party, not a work meeting." Once inside his car, he asked, "So, where are we headed?"

"It's my friend's house...well, actually her mother's place. I haven't been there, but I have the address for the GPS." I handed him Violet's invitation. "She's staying at a little place at the back of her mother's house."

He punched it in and began driving. "That's kind of lame. How old is your friend?"

"Um, twenty-four, twenty-five. Not really sure. Violet's my boss at BUD. She's pretty shy and was very nervous about nobody showing up, so I don't want to be too late."

Victor shook his head and mumbled, "Sounds like a raging party." Then he turned his electronic club music up so loud it was almost impossible to speak over the heavy vibrating beats. As we sped down a busy road, he yelled out, "So, just to be clear; we're not going to be the only people at this party, right?"

I turned down the volume to speak. "No. I think there'll be some other people from work. Not too many though. But I know she's prepared lots of good food and drinks."

"Good, didn't get a chance to eat when I met up with my friends earlier."

As Victor ran a stop sign and dodged a vehicle in the intersection, I began worrying. "So, you've been partying this evening for a while? Maybe slow down. I want to get there alive."

"Nah, a couple drinks. I'm cool, Rosario; you're in good hands." At that point he put his arm around me, pulled me in closer, and turned the volume back up. So much for sharing a good conservation. Other than his wardrobe, Victor was not scoring any points.

Within fifteen minutes we were cruising along White Rock Lake with Victor finally slowing down as we neared the address. I looked up to my right at some amazing homes built up along a small hill overlooking the lake. "Check it out. These look like modern-day castles, right?"

Victor glanced over. "Yeah, nice. I'm gonna have me one of these some day." Then GPS announced: *One hundred feet. On your right... You have arrived.*

Victor slowed to the side of the road. "Rosario. Are you sure this is the correct address?" We were stopped next to large iron ornamental gates which were open and balanced on both sides by two tall magnolia trees and a long curving driveway lit up with white twinkling lights.

"You punched the address in yourself. Double check." I handed him the invitation again and he looked it over.

"Yeah, it's correct. Cool. Guess it's party time."

He gunned his motor and pulled up the steep long drive, and then continued to follow the driveway to the back of the house. We passed by an adjoining drive that led to the front entrance of a grand two-level white home with an immense wrap-around porch graced with tall, old fashioned columns connecting the porch and upper levels. Continuing up the hill, we passed the aqua waters of a brightly-lit rectangular pool and sitting next to it was a predominantly glass, two-level mini house.

I'd been envisioning a dark spare bedroom in her mother's converted garage. How could she never have mentioned to me that she was rich? I mean this was *really* rich. Like, super wealthy. She always acted like she *had* to stay at her mom's and really didn't like it, even complaining about it. I was confused and still convinced there was a typo on the invitation. But then I saw Mark's old truck parked in one of the two spots in front of the guest house.

We got out and knocked on the door. An anxious, nervous looking Violet quickly opened the door, stuck her head out and whispered, "Thank G-God you're here. Mark's inside and you'll never believe who his date is!"

"OK?...Violet, this is my friend, Victor Morales."

Victor smiled and said, "Violet, impressive place you have here. Really attractive."

"Thanks, c-come in." Violet walked us over to a long wooden table surrounded by chairs, next to her kitchen. "Victor, this is my friend M-Mark and our b-boss, Molly." *Molly came with Mark? Really strange!*

Victor reached out his hand to shake Mark and Molly's hands. "So Violet, if you're Rosario's boss, Molly must be the really big boss."

Molly shrugged and said, "Guess so. I'm head horticulturist at BUD. Oversee all the different gardens there. Although, after seeing Violet's home, you'd never know *I* was the boss."

I was still getting over the shock of Mark and Molly dating. After absorbing that, I thought Molly's remark sounded awkward and rather resentful, and she'd said it with an ugly tone. Everyone let her comment slide and continued to chatter about the beginnings of the new rock wall we'd started at the xeriscape garden, and how tired and sore we were after our first day of working on it. BUD had hired two professional masonry guys who were guiding us, but all of our crew were assigned to speed up the project.

Violet handed Victor a beer and poured a glass of wine for me. Her table was fully loaded with several platters of appetizers, mini-sandwiches, and sweets. As we began filling our plates, two other lead gardeners, Bobby and Annalese, came in and joined the group. I'd seen Bobby around in the mornings along the garden paths, but it was my first time to speak with him. He was cute! Mark stood up and got some tunes going on Violet's speakers and we had the beginnings of a party-vibe.

Around nine, Jeff came in, bringing Linda Bell with him. She explained she had won the first two games for her bowling team but decided to forego free-nacho-night and join us.

A little later, Victor told me he was heading out to his car for a minute. After fifteen minutes, with Victor still gone, I started to get concerned and stepped out to check on him. His car was still parked there, but no one was inside. As I turned to go back in, I saw a shadow approach from the big house and realized it was Victor. I stayed to watch him as he quickly went to his car, opened and closed the door, and then realized I was standing outside.

I whispered over to him, "Victor, where have you been? You're not being very polite."

"Had to take a few phone calls and was walking the grounds. It's beautiful out here. You need to check this place out."

I pointed to the glass door. "*This* is Violet's place, not the other house."

"Whatever. Hey...all that BUD talk going on inside is pretty boring. You ready to bounce?"

"Already?"

"Yeah. We should meet up with some of my friends. Apparently, there's a big party brewing at a private club I go to. Come with me. It'll be fun."

I continued whispering, not wanting to be heard by Violet inside. "We've only been here a little while. I don't think we should go. It would hurt her feelings."

Victor wasn't convinced. "Well, I'm ready to split. I guess I can set you up with an Uber again if you have to stay. At that point he put his hands on my shoulders and pulled me closer to him. "Come on, Rosario. Let's go. You've done your duty."

I quickly pulled away, saying, "It's *not* my duty. A good friend of mine is having a party that I *want* to stay at. If you can't understand that, please leave now. I'll find my own way home."

He shrugged his shoulders, and his face told me he could care less. "Alright. Your loss. You're missing out on meeting some really dope people."

"Just leave, Victor," I said with a sigh. I was disappointed in him and mad at myself. I should have listened to that voice in my head a few months ago. It was usually right. "I'll tell Violet you had an emergency come up."

Victor nodded and reached for the car door. "Sure, tell your friends it was good to meet them."

"Yeah...And Victor... make sure you lose my number, *again*."

I stood there shaking with anger and wiped away an emotional tear. Then I remembered one of my mother's favorite sayings, 'Fool me once, shame on you. Fool me twice, shame on me.'

Apparently, Victor was not the perfect prince I'd imagined. I was looking for a special person who could fill the hole of loneliness I'd felt since Roberto's murder. Once I'd run into Victor again, I'd been floating around in an imaginary fairy tale. As depressed as I felt, maybe I should be glad that Victor showed his true colors early on...again.

As he pulled out with tires squealing, a truck came up behind him and parked along the drive behind Jeff's car. As I tried to calm down, I watched a man get out and walk towards the door. As he passed into the light from the house, I recognized him. It was Kevin from the margarita bar. The guy I'd encouraged Violet to invite.

"Hey there, it's Rosario, right? I'm Kevin... from the other night?"

"Sure. Good to see you again."

"Thanks. Uh, Violet sent me a text about this. So, she's inside?"

"Yeah. Go on in. I'm right behind you." For some reason, he made me feel a little jumpy; probably just my reaction from Victor leaving. For Violet's sake, I now hoped Kevin was one of the good guys. They seemed to be in short supply.

CHAPTER 31

The Happy Hour Hook-Up

VIOLET

Mark was trying to convince everyone to collect their drinks, go outside, and sit around the blazing fire pit. Everybody seemed into it except his date, Molly…of course. She announced she didn't want to get smoke in her hair. After a little persuasion, we all decided to move outside, just as Rosario walked in with Kevin. I couldn't believe he'd shown up.

As they came in, Rosario announced loudly to the group, "*Atención a todas.* This is Kevin. Kevin, these are all people from BUD." She then immediately went to the fridge and pulled out a beer for herself and guzzled it down. It was odd; smiling Rosie seemed suddenly upset.

Seeing Kevin, I immediately felt on-edge. A guy *I* texted had shown up…This stuff didn't happen to me. I wasn't the girl that whipped up little parties and had friends actually show up. Where was that woman now who had the nerve to get this guy's number, at a bar no less? She felt suddenly tongue-tied and no longer the carefree Violet who lived in my head. I tried to convince myself to continue the illusion.

As everyone else picked up their drinks to take outside, Kevin looked around smiling and said, "Hey, hope you guys aren't leaving on my account."

Then turning to me, he approached with a friendly grin while I felt my face freeze up. At the margarita bar he seemed pleasant enough, but maybe it was only in contrast to his jerk friend who was hitting on Rosie. I had no witty banter, no party jokes. Let's face it; I had no game.

And yet, here he was standing in front of me. Pretty good looking too, in a buttoned up way. Hair cut short, wearing a dark denim shirt tucked into denim jeans. Wait...wasn't there some fashion rule about not wearing two matching denims together? I'd have to check in later with Mother on that.

While closing the door, Mark yelled, "We're migrating to the fire pit, see you two soon."

Kevin and I were suddenly alone. "I'm s-surprised you came," I said, while nervously rubbing the long silver pendant on my necklace. "Was not ex-ex-expecting to see you."

"I told you I'd try to come." He looked around downstairs. "Love your place. I take it the owners rent out their guest house?"

"Yeah, kinda like that. What can I get you? B-Beer, wine, tequila?"

"I better stick to beer. In the fridge?"

"Yes; help yourself and fill up a p-plate." *Loosen up, Violet. He's not going to bite.*

Kevin uncapped a Modelo and took a deep drink. "It's a pretty night. Perfect for a blazing fire, but do you mind if we stay inside for a few minutes and talk. I felt like the other night we really didn't get to know each other very well."

"Sure. Uh, you go first." *Don't look down, Violet. Eyes up, stop shaking, quit acting like a weirdo.* I pulled up a chair at the table and refilled my wine glass.

He shrugged, put some chips and salsa on a plate, and sat down across from me. "Uh, I'm a neighborhood guy, don't live too far from here. Let's see...you already know I'm an engineer for Texas Instruments; been there about eight years now. Work on *top-secret* munitions; can't talk about that though. Fascinating stuff, but unfortunately off limits."

Yawn. OK, brainiac engineer.

Kevin continued on, "But trust me, I'm saving you from a half-hour of boredom. Let's see... Of course, you remembered my dog, the goldendoodle. Her name is Sandy. You know... after the play and comic strip?"

I stared ahead in a daze, concentrating too hard on what I was going to say about myself.

He looked at me with confusion. "Still not registering? Little Orphan Annie and her dog... red curly hair."

It suddenly dawned on me what he was rambling on about. "Oh sure, of course. *Annie*. I g-get it." Great, now he thinks I'm just slow. Then, as if on cue, Cocoa, my dachshund, who had been cowering from the crowd upstairs, clicked her way down. "And here's my little girl."

"I remember her. She was so fierce at the dog park."

"P-Probably more scared than fierce. It was our f-first outing together. Although, I'm sure I was more distraught than her. Cocoa's the only dog I've ever had, so it's taken us a while to get used to each other but she's s-s-super sweet." She was now winding around my legs as I reached down to pet her. "She pr-probably needs to go out. Do you m-mind walking up and down the driveway with me? It's about time for her final pee of the night."

"No problem. Let me grab a few of these cookies for the walk. So, you made all this stuff? Impressive."

"Honestly, no. A friend arranged all the pr-preparations for me. I'm not much of a cook." I got Cocoa's leash from the pantry and connected it to her collar. As we stepped outside, I heard talk and laughter from the fire pit, off to the side of the pool. I probably should be joining them. That's what a hostess was supposed to do, right?

"Yeah, I'm lame in the cooking department too. My wife did all the cooking."

"Your wife?" *Of course he's married. At least he's honest about it...kind of.*

"Yeah, no worries though. I'm not going out on her or anything. We've separated. So, cooking for myself, happy hours, showing up at parties alone--all this is new territory for me. By the way, these cookies are really good."

"If you're not cooking much, feel fr-free to take some food home. There's so much pr-prepared." As we stopped at one of Cocoa's preferred driveway hedges, I asked, "So… how long have you been s-separated? Has it been difficult?"

"Honestly, the pain from the break up is all pretty fresh for me. If you're OK with it, I'd rather talk about other stuff."

"No problem." *Great, first guy I meet at a happy hour is a wounded love warrior.* "So, you mentioned the other day you sort of know Turner Cooper. We recently worked on a f-fund-raising project together. How did you two m-meet?"

"Oh, he's only a passing acquaintance. Doubt he even remembers my name. I knew his wife. We'd run into each other at neighborhood functions. Saw her a lot at the dog park. Stuff like that."

"Oh...that was s-s-so sad about her illness. To die so young. That's why Turner started volunteering at BUD. Sort of a tribute to her."

"Yeah, it was really surprising. Hey, you're having a party. Let's move on to more upbeat topics. By the way, I hope I'm not being too forward saying this. You probably hear this all the time, but you're really beautiful."

"Actually, not very often, but th-thanks." I'm sure I was blushing brightly. Fortunately it was kind of dark.

"And I think you're a runner too, right? I have to admit, I've noticed you before, running the trail at the lake. Fast and lean. Bright green shorts?"

This made me pause for a second. "You have?" *A little creepy.* "Yeah, I generally do a five mile run, when I leave Cocoa be-behind. It's so ironic; I sp-specifically wanted to get a dog for protection while running, but her legs are so short, I can only walk her." We'd reached the end of the driveway and turned around, walking back up.

Kevin laughed and said, "Yeah, three-inch-legs will definitely slow you down. I attempt to jog, but I noticed you're super-fast."

Hmm, odd that he's noticed me running. Or did he just start stalking me after I texted him? Either way, the hair on my head started tingling a bit. "Kevin, let's walk over to the f-f-fire pit. Time for my hostess d-duties."

As we headed across the yard, I noticed the headlights of another car pull up. Perhaps it was Victor returning. I'd been wondering where he went off to but hadn't had a chance to ask Rosario. As we walked near the fire pit, I heard a voice call out across the driveway, "Hey Violet, wait up." I turned and saw the silhouette of a tall man with a precarious walk.

Surprised, I called out, "Turner, I thought you weren't coming?"

CHAPTER 32

The Gladiator Makes His Stand

TURNER

I was frowning at a three-quarter-empty bottle of bourbon. I didn't even like bourbon. What was I doing here?

Katrina had invited me to a little holiday soiree at her home to toast the Christmas season. I hadn't felt like going to any social events since Allie's funeral, but I thought maybe now I was mentally ready to attend something festive. Once there, I realized I had not understood Katrina's full intent. Instead of a neighborhood gathering of friends, it seemed I was the only invited guest. And she almost immediately mentioned her son was conveniently staying with her ex. Although feeling slightly set-up, I decided to jump into the spirit of the evening and began by pouring myself a tumbler.

On first sip, it didn't take much bourbon to notice that Katrina was looking especially hot in her red satin shirt and shiny, black high-waisted pants, much like one of Santa's tall, curvy, tempestuous elves.

But now, as time and bourbon slipped away, I was having doubts about the scene. We were sitting fairly close on a navy velvet couch in her living room. She heard the ding of her oven and told me she'd be right back. While waiting for food, the room began to take a slow spin. And it didn't help that my empty stomach was clawing away inside at the scent of bacon wafting from the kitchen. Definitely, a glass of water was required. It wasn't long before Katrina walked back in, balancing a platter of bacon-wrapped mushrooms in one hand and carrying a large stuffed gift bag in the other.

She sauntered up to me slowly singing, "Here comes Santa Claus, here comes Santa Claus, right down Santa Claus Lane." She leaned over and set the tray down in front of me. God, she looked great, smelled great, a blend of...I don't know...something like bacon-scented cinnamon, or maybe sandalwood and sin?

But something was off. All the signs were pointing me somewhere, but I couldn't make the connection.

She sat down next to me, inching closer. "Now Turner, have you been good or bad this year?"

"Let's see, if I was good would I qualify for one of the bacon things on your tray?" I smiled, looking into her brown, almond shaped eyes.

"Absolutely."

I reached for a mushroom and took a bite. "Wow! Excellent. Nothing wrong with a sauteed stuffed mushroom, but then, when you throw bacon around it, you got yourself an absolute prize-winning appetizer."

Then Katrina jiggled the gift bag at her feet. "And I got you a gift."

"You shouldn't have. Whatever it is, it's way too much." I lifted the bag, judging it's heft. "It's not another ham, is it?"

She laughed, moving even closer, and took another sip of her drink. "Go ahead, open it. It's just a little something I saw; reminded me of you."

"OK, now you've piqued my curiosity." I reached into the red and green bag and pulled out a house plant, or maybe some type of small shrub? "Well... this is unexpected, but lovely. Thank you."

Katrina reached over and fingered the tiny pink and white flowers dangling from the leaves of the plant. "Look, aren't these amazing? It's called a Bleeding Heart bush. The blooms look just like tiny little hearts, don't they?" She leaned in toward me, showering me with her fragrance and a full deep view of her decolletage.

"Wow, you're right. Exactly like a heart. So th-thoughtful of you,"

I stammered, while quickly putting the plant back in the bag. "I'm going to put it next to my coat, so I don't forget it." I stood up and felt dizzy just walking to the chair where she had slung my coat. Definitely time for that glass of water. I'd stayed away from any serious drinking for a few weeks now and seemed to be feeling the effects more quickly tonight. "Mind if I grab a glass of water?"

"Help yourself. I keep water bottles in the fridge." As I went to her kitchen, she called out, "I thought you'd like a plant since you seem so interested in your volunteer work at BUD."

I quickly opened the plastic bottle, gulping the icy-cold water down my throat, trying to collect my thoughts. Coming back from the kitchen, I said, "You're right. I have been enjoying my work there. It's a fun little bunch of people I'm working with. Been interesting and physically challenging. I like that part too."

"Yeah Turner, I can tell. You're looking really fit. More bourbon?" She poured another two fingers into my glass. "Oh, I downloaded the best music the other day. Let me put it on my speaker."

While she fiddled with the tunes on her phone, I sat back down, while my mind thought about the group at BUD. I had to laugh to myself...Mark, sneaking off, doing who knows what, but he really knew his stuff about plants. Rosario, always upbeat, who came across as grateful for every day she was at work. Linda Bell, a little strange, but efficient and pragmatic, followed around by her faithful puppy-dog, Jeff. And of course, there was the curiously intriguing Violet. Actually, I'd been ruminating about her quite a lot this week. I had actually enjoyed working with her on the fundraiser, although initially I was dreading it.

I looked up at Katrina who was now standing on the living room floor, swaying to the music and inviting me to dance to her sultry, jazzy tunes. "Come on, Turner. It's Christmas. I haven't danced in ages."

I reluctantly stood up. "Full disclosure. I'm not much of a dancer." Her eyes were almost closed as she continued to sway and then put her arms around my shoulders, bringing me in close. Her scent which had seemed alluring was now so strong it was almost cloying. My brain went to Violet's scent. Clean, simple...almost as if she sprayed the air with a hit or two, and then walked through it. Nice. Then Katrina went in for a warm nibble on my ear with her lips.

Violet...shit! It just hit me. She had invited me to her Christmas party weeks ago for this same night and I had totally dismissed it out of hand. What an asshole, and instead, here I was dancing in Katrina's living room while my brain was screaming out caution signs: *Leave now, Abort! Abort!* Even under the haze of bourbon, the full realization hit me. I wasn't ready for anything Katrina might be prepared to offer.

Violet's house--that's where I should be. The song ended and I created a distance between us. "Thanks for the dance, Katrina." I leaned over the table, grabbing another bacon-wrapped delight and downed the remains of my water bottle. "I hate to say this, but the truth is, I failed to tell you earlier. I have another party to go to. I assumed I'd just be one of several guests here tonight."

"Are you serious? You're going to leave me by myself? Already?"

"I'm so sorry, but I really should go."

She offered up her best seductive pout. "Come on, Turner. The night's still young."

"I'd stay a little longer if I hadn't promised I'd show up. Really gotta go."

She snapped out of her sexy dance mood, realizing I was really leaving. "Well, that sucks. But you'll have to leave the bleeding heart plant here. I don't think you deserve it anymore."

"Understood." I turned and walked quickly to retrieve my coat before she or I talked myself into staying. "But hey, thanks for a lovely evening and Merry Christmas, Katrina."

Reaching for the door, I felt two light whacks on the back of my head. I turned quickly and caught another flying bacon-wrapped mushroom in mid-air. "Oh yeah, these were great too, thanks." I popped the last one in my mouth, and then slammed the door, as the metal appetizer trey clanged against it.

~

I unrolled my car windows and drove. Between the guzzled water and the chilly night air, I began to feel slightly less intoxicated driving over to the Hill's stately home. It was now ten-fifteen. If there were just a couple cars left, I'd go home. Pulling into the drive, I saw six cars and parked behind them. White twinkling lights were set up along the driveway and also strung across all the tall live oaks on the property. Once out of the car, I heard a group of people gathered by the pool next to the fire pit.

Picking up my pace, I recognized Violet walking up to the group with her dog and called out to her. She smiled and waved as I got closer. "Turner, I thought you couldn't m-make it."

Under the lights, I noticed she was wearing jeans and a purple cabled turtleneck, which brought out those gorgeous eyes of hers. "Hope you don't mind me showing up after all. My other thing ended kind of early so I thought I'd take a chance and see if anybody was still here."

"Yes, s-surprisingly, everybody showed up. Turner, this is K-Kevin. I think you guys sort of know each other, right? Kevin and I recently m-met at a happy hour."

I glanced over at the guy standing next to Violet. *Kevin...*Allie's Kevin? My dead wife's cheating boyfriend, Kevin? The hypocritical asshole, Kevin, who offered me his shoulder to cry on if I needed someone to talk to? Kevin, the sender of heart-wrenching texts to Allie, and organizer of romantic weekend get-aways, Kevin?

I hadn't even noticed him, but there he was, standing next to me chugging a beer.

"Yeah, I guess I do know Kevin." *Unfortunately, I know him too well. And he'd probably heard an earful about me from Allie. That was really uncomfortable to think about.*

He looked over at me, offered his hand to shake, and said, "Hey, good to see you again, Cooper. Merry Christmas."

I slowly turned full face toward him, but instead of shaking his hand, I knocked the beer out of his left hand, and said, "And fucking Happy New Year to you." He stood there speechless, staring at me in surprise. I hated his arrogant, blank face.

Then, I couldn't stop myself. I pulled my fist back, swung it hard into the side of his jaw, and knocked Kevin off his feet, sending him sprawling into the grass.

I was in shock. I didn't do this kind of stuff. I probably hadn't been in a fight since junior high, and if recollection served, I'd lost that one.

All the party-talk around us suddenly grew quiet as Violet shrieked at the sudden unexpected violence, while her dog, Cocoa, began snapping and barking at me. "Oh my God, Turner?" Violet shouted out, "What the hell? K-Kevin is my guest. I can't b-believe this!"

She was crouching down to check on him, while I had to bite my lip to keep from yelling out in pain. I'd hit Kevin so hard my hand felt like it was broken. He continued to stare at me for a few seconds from the ground, probably afraid to get up. I pointed at him, stammering, "This...this guy, Vi. He was screwing my... my wife secretly for two years...*and* he's married! Whatever he's told you; it's probably a lie."

Kevin pushed himself back up, tenderly touching his jaw, and began walking quickly away. Then he turned and hollered, "You're absolutely crazy, man; Violet, I'm out of here."

Violet looked at me like I had lost my mind and then ran after him, asking, "K-Kevin, are you OK to drive? I'm s-s-so sorry this happened."

I continued to yell. "Keep running Kevin; that's what you do best."

He turned and shouted back. "I'm not running from anything. But I *will* be suing your ass."

"Bring it on," I yelled into the dark..

Then I felt an arm around my shoulder and heard Mark's voice in my ear, "Uh, you sure know how to make an entrance, dude. Turner, let's grab a seat. You might want to mellow out a little."

I sat down with my head swimming in a mix of embarrassment, adrenaline, alcohol, and anger. I ignored everyone and began taking in long deep breaths. The fire pit group had gone totally quiet and was staring at me. I turned and explained, "Sorry guys, but I really hate him."

Mark added, "No worries, he didn't impress me much either."

Jeff shrugged and said, "Well, I'm impressed. Awesome right hook, Coop."

Then, in a louder voice, Mark asked, "Drinks...anybody need refills?"

Mark stood up a little unsteadily, while I noticed a light coming from the back door of the main house. Suzanne Hill, dressed in spangled formal attire, walked up to the group, tottering somewhat in very high heels. She looked distraught, calling out, "Violet? Vi? There you are. What's going on out here?" She stepped towards Violet, who was walking back to the group and seemed to be in a daze. "I just got out of my Uber minutes ago and heard shouting... and who's been in the house?"

Violet looked immediately on guard. "N-Nobody that I know of, M-Mother. Maria said she'd leave the door unlocked in case I needed food b-back-ups from the kitchen. But we've all b-been out here together. What's wrong?"

Suzanne continued to look frazzled, "I know I left it by the kitchen sink...right before I left. It's your father's heirloom Rolex. It's missing!"

CHAPTER 33

Tick-Tock, the Rat Ran Away With the Clock

VIOLET

Were parties always this stressful? Fights, thefts, mothers! After a few concerned questions, I convinced Mother that she probably had too much holiday punch and simply forgot where she'd left Dad's old Rolex. It was something she enjoyed wearing around the house, but she always switched to a watch with more bling for events.

"M-Mother, first thing tomorrow, I'll help you hunt for it. It's got to be inside. We'll f-f-find it. Everything's cool here. You should go on to bed."

"You're sure no one's been inside? I was so convinced I set it there when I poured myself a cocktail before leaving. But you're probably right. We'll check tomorrow. Good night all." Her tone had come down from hysteria to resignation. She did a parade-perfect wave, turned and did a delicate trek in high stilettos back down the walkway. About halfway there, she stopped and said, "Vi, actually our watch hunt will have to wait. I just remembered, I have a big brunch benefit tomorrow at the Fairmont. Let's look when I get back."

"Sure Mother. Good night." Thank God. One minor crisis postponed. If she hadn't had a lot to drink already, she probably would have patted everyone down and then asked our little rag-tag bunch to leave.

I was still shaken up over Turner hitting Kevin. The whole altercation was so bizarre. I was obviously missing a few key parts of the story. Honestly, I was ready for everybody to go home but unsure of proper party-hostess protocol. How do you end a party? Checking my watch, I guessed it was still too early.

Conversations started up again and everybody seemed content sitting by the fire, so I offered to bring some food outside, and asked Rosario to help. As we walked back to the guest house, I said, "So Rosie, what's happened to Victor? Is he c-coming back?"

She shook her head. "I hope not. He wanted me to go to a club and I said I wanted to stay here. So he got in his car and left. *Estupido*! And I thought he was a gentleman."

"There's a s-saying here, Rosario; the clothes don't make the man. Good riddance. You deserve b-b-better."

"*Gracias*. But I better call an Uber soon. The later it gets, the more they cost."

"Don't worry about it. Sleep on my s-sofa tonight. I'll run you home in the m-morning."

"Oh, that's a good idea. I was kind of worried about Victor coming round to my apartment later tonight, now that he knows my address."

We were walking in, as Mark walked out carrying a small cooler full of beers. He stopped and asked, "So what happened to your date? Did that jerk up and leave you?"

Rosario motioned for Mark and me to come inside. "Guys, I didn't want to say anything in front of the others, but Victor was walking around the property by himself for a while before he left. Now that I know what he's really like, I think it's possible he stole your mother's watch."

Mark nodded, set down the cooler, and opened a beer. "I didn't trust that guy. He looked too slick--something about that brown suede jacket. And that certainly narrows down the suspects...if the watch is really missing."

I was surprised at Rosie's admission. "You *really* think so?"

"Well, after I went out to look for Victor, I watched him come up the walk from the house and then go to his car for a minute. He seemed surprised to see me waiting outside and then quickly wanted to leave. Is the kitchen close to that unlocked door?"

I nodded, grabbed a beer and began twisting off the bottle cap, and then stopped. "Yes, and Mom's cook left the light on in the kitchen if I needed anything. The watch would have been in plain sight if Mother left it by the sink."

Mark got interested in this bit of news; almost excited. "We need to find this dude while the trail's hot, before he hocks the damned thing. Rosario, do you know where he was headed?"

"I have no idea. But he mentioned some party at a private club. I do have his cell number though."

I turned and looked at Mark like he was crazy, shaking my head. "Wait a m-minute, you two. Are you s-s-seriously going to drive around looking for a guy with a *possibly* stolen watch? M-Maybe he's dangerous, and there are still guests outside waiting for beer and snacks. This is a p-party, remember?"

Mark checked his phone. "It's eleven now. We'll give 'em until eleven-thirty to clear out of here. Tell them this is the last of the beer. That usually clears a party pretty quick. Meanwhile Rosie, you track down Victor and tell him you've changed your mind; say you and Violet still feel like partying tonight and want to know where to meet him."

I was shocked at Mark's plotting. "Are you k-kidding me? What's c-come over you? And why am *I* getting tangled up in this?"

Rosario was busy filling a tray full of mini-tacos and spicy avocado egg rolls. "Hurry Violet, let's stop wasting time. You should go check the house. Make sure your mother didn't set the watch down somewhere else."

As we trailed back outside, I was objecting to the whole plan. Then Mark said, "Look Vi, we're doing it for your mother and your dad's memory, and, if we're lucky, maybe there's a reward involved. Besides, I hate thieving assholes like that. *And*, you need to come because you have to drive. You're the only one who seems half-way sober. So, don't finish that beer."

"Damn Mark, when did you get s-s-so bossy?"

"It's my residual angst from when I worked as a private detective...another lifetime ago. Also, we should bring Turner."

"Was that be-before or after you became a starving artist and started m-mowing lawns?" I stopped before we got to the fire pit and whispered, "And why should we b-bring Turner? He's clearly wasted."

"Didn't you notice earlier? Drunk or not, the dude can pack a punch."

I just shook my head, hoping he'd forget the whole idea in a few minutes. "Mark, you're ignoring your date, M-Molly. What role does she p-play in this caper?" But as we came up to the others, I noticed Molly was gone. "Where's M-Molly?"

Bob Rodriguez spoke up, "She said to tell you guys good night. She called a car. But she was looking kind of pissed. You know how she gets."

Mark threw up his hands and sighed, "C'est la vie. OK, guys. Guzzle it down and eat up. This is the last of the beer and food. And Turner...Vi, Rosie, and I need to speak with you for a second."

Turner got up unsteadily, came over and looked at me. "Vi, I'm really sorry I messed up your party. But that Kevin guy...I just didn't want him near you. I swear...totally untrustworthy."

"You know, I'm p-pretty much over it, and to be honest...he's kind of b-boring. We can talk about it later, b-but apparently we have bigger b-balls to bust and Mark wants you to come along as the m-muscle."

Turner laid down on the grass and closed his eyes. "Remind me never to drink a bottle of bourbon again."

While Mark explained his plan to Turner, I quietly went into the house and double-checked on the missing watch. I made a cursory search of the key rooms, without finding it. While I went inside, Rosario attempted to call Victor, but he didn't pick up. After I rejoined the group, she eventually reached him.

"Victor, it's Rosie. Yes, Rosario. Can you hear me? It's so loud there. You still at the club? Hey, I'm sorry we had that little fight. *Bien, yo también*. Things are winding down here and Vi and I feel like dancing. Yes, really! How about we join you in a little while? Yes? So where should we meet?" She repeated the address while I put it in my phone. Then she had to shout to be heard over the club music. "Can you put our names on the list so we can get in? Yeah, miss you too. See you soon."

Within thirty minutes, as Mark predicted, my guests thanked me, said they had a great time, and left. My first party...I thought it was a disaster, but everybody seemed to have fun. I was amazed.

Before the four of us piled into my Subaru, Rosario looked at me and said, "You can't wear that to a club."

"What's wrong with jeans and a turtleneck?"

"Vi, you look like you're going hiking or something."

I looked at Rosario, wearing her tight, short little black stretchy dress and heels. "I'm not going there to get p-p-picked up; I'm going to get a watch back. B-Besides, I don't own any tube-top dresses, or whatever you call that thing you're w-wearing." I sighed and said, "Let's just go if we're really doing this."

"OK, Vi, just saying..."

I punched the address into my map app. The club was located in downtown Dallas, about a fifteen-minute-drive away. Rosie and Mark were in the back and Turner was my reluctant wingman.

Mark began sounding more like a PI than a gardener as he worked out the plan. "First, we determine if the watch is on Victor, or still in his car. It'll be a lot easier if he's wearing it. And if he used the valet to park his car, he probably wouldn't leave it in the car. My bet is he put it on. Plus he's a show-off kind of dude anyway."

Rosario chimed in, "*Sí, sí.* You're so right."

"So once we're inside," I asked, "What h-h-happens?"

Mark leaned toward the front seat. "OK, I'm just spit-balling here. I suggest...Rosario finds Victor, dances with him, gets on his good side, then you, Vi, wander up to Rosie and Victor and ask if he has the time. So, dummy, Victor, casually checks the fancy Rolex and Rosie makes a big deal out of this pretty watch, right? Then Violet takes a look at it and says, that looks just like my Dad's, which went missing tonight. Turner walks up, announces he's with the Hill family's private security team and says, we know you stole that watch, but we won't press charges if you turn it over quietly. Now, Turner, at this point, you gotta look serious, and dude, keep it real low-key. Don't attract a lot of attention."

Turner turned to the back seat and asked Mark, "And what the hell are you doing? What's your role?"

"I'm the one writing the script. Besides, I'm old, dude. I sit at the bar, watch it all go down and have fun. Seriously though, I'm your backup, if there's any trouble... but I don't see that happening."

CHAPTER 34

Dancing With the Devil

ROSARIO

Violet focused on driving, not saying much. Sitting in the back, I asked Turner to switch on some music to cheer up the suddenly somber mood in the car. "Guys, remember, it's the holidays. ¡*Feliz Navidad*! Let's brighten up."

Violet responded, "It's *lighten* up...and I r-r-really don't do well with confr-frontation. Just not my thing."

I patted Vi on her shoulder, "Vi, just think how happy your mother will be when you get the watch back for her."

"That's *if* we get the watch back and honestly, how m-m-many watches does one woman n-need? Although, this one does have s-sentimental value. Just no fighting in there; p-promise?"

"Fine with me," Turner said. "I've gotten in my one hit for the decade."

Turner switched on a country song I didn't recognize. Leaning back on the headrest, I began remembering the dangerous fights that would occur at bars when I lived in Juarez. "Mark, you don't think there will be guns or anything, do you?"

"Hell yes; this is Texas, darlin'," Mark calmly answered."But everybody just needs to chill. We're talking about a dead man's old watch, not a kilo of cocaine. I've been thinking...Once we get there, maybe I should just sit in the parked car, keeping us ready for a fast get-away."

Turner screwed his head around to the back, "Bullshit. Hey, Magnum PI, this was all your idea. You're coming in."

Mark shrugged, "Whatever. I just always fancied myself as the get-away guy."

Violet pulled up next to the club's address. It was in an old brick building with no sign. Instead, there was just a tall, thick guy dressed in a dark suit standing next to a large padded double door, and a line of about thirty people waiting to get inside. Located on Elm Street, the club looked to be located on the ground floor of an older multi-storied building.

Mark suggested, "Cruise the block, Violet. See if you can grab a parking spot next to a meter. That way, we can leave quicker."

About a block up, she parallel parked, squeezing in between two other cars. As we got out, I explained to the group, "I asked Victor to put our names on the list, so we shouldn't have to wait." Checking out the people in line, I noticed the crowd looked to be young, dressed up, primarily Latino, all ready for a big night out. I looked like I would definitely fit in better than the rest of my group. Approaching the doorman, I said, "Hi, Victor Morales put our names on the list. It's Rosario Guzman and Violet Hill."

He looked down on a clipboard, checked me out and said, "You can go in. But not these others."

I was surprised my new friends were being excluded. "But we're all together." In a low voice, I told the doorman, "I know my friend looks bad tonight, but she just flew in from camping in Colorado, with no time to change."

Violet called out behind me, "You know I can hear you, r-right?"

I gave him my most pleading tone, "Can't you please make an exception? We're all in the same car. Our friends are inside."

The bouncer looked determined, shaking his head. Mark coughed and told Turner, "Give him some grease, man. Pay the guy off."

Turner stared Mark down, then shaking his head, he reluctantly pulled out his wallet and waved a hundred-dollar-bill in front of the bouncer. "Will this do it?"

The guy pocketed the bill quickly and opened the door. As Violet passed the doorman, she said, "Don't worry; I'm good at being a w-w-wallflower. No one will notice me."

The four of us trailed down a long dark hallway, lit by the occasional red bulb. The walls pulsated with the heavy rhythmic beat of Latin club music, making me want to dance.

Passing through the darkness, Turner said, "Guess we won't be doing any line-dancing here."

The hall eventually opened up to a wide, elevated, and crowded dance floor with a long, curved bar running down the length of the left wall. It was still dark, but the couples on the dance floor were hit by rotating beams of light circulating from the ceiling, allowing each dancer their few seconds to shine. It was a cool effect, but made searching for someone difficult.

Violet offered to buy the guys a first round of drinks at the bar, while I went on the hunt for Victor. I told the three of them, "I'll text you when I find him. Then give us a little time before you and Turner come over."

Mark nodded, taking a sip of his beer. "Good idea, Rosario; let's give Turner some time to put his boxing gloves on."

Above the crowded dance floor, was a raised platform supporting the DJ and all his equipment. There was a permanent spotlight on him, giving him a God-like aura, as he lorded over the dancers below. I actually liked this place and wouldn't have minded staying for a while, but I had absolutely no desire to hang with Victor.

To speed up my search, I tried texting him, letting him know I was here. I walked up to a second floor landing and looked down, but still didn't see him. Walking further upstairs, I noticed a balcony ringing the walls of the club, stuffed with little round tables and lounge chairs. This looked like an area where I'd find Victor; a place where he could hold court among his friends. In the corner, I spotted him sitting with about seven people. It was a mix of guys and girls, with an attractive, long-legged blonde in a very short skirt practically sitting on Victor's lap. He had probably just bought her a drink, trying to make me jealous.

I quickly texted Violet: *Spotted him.*

I felt nervous watching him with his gang of friends. I made my best attempt at a sultry look and sauntered over to his chair, speaking loudly over the music, "Hey Victor. Cool place; I like it."

He nodded, "Told you that you would. Join us for a drink."

I leaned down, speaking next to his ear. "Maybe later. I'm really in the mood to dance. I've been sitting around drinking all night. Join me?"

He motioned for the blonde to get up, dismissing her like a prop, while he took his time standing up. "Cool. This DJ slays; let's do it."

He put his arm around my shoulder as we headed downstairs and I felt the weight of a hefty metal watch under the wrist of his suede jacket. Pulling me closer, he said, "Wasn't sure if this place was your scene. I'm glad you like it, beautiful."

"Back home I used to go dancing a lot with friends, but in Dallas, never. So how do you know this place?"

"Oh, you know, word gets around. A lot of my people congregate here as the night goes on."

That comment made me even more anxious. I wanted to finish up this little exchange and get the hell out. A familiar song started up. I looked out among the dancers and thought I could match their moves. "You dance bachata, Victor?"

"Yeah man, let's do it." We stepped on to the lit-up dance floor and quickly began moving in sync, with gyrating hips, our feet and bodies moving sensually to the beat, while he turned and guided me across the floor. After a year and a half, I thought I'd be rusty, but the dance moves came back quickly and Victor was actually an excellent lead. A really good dancer, but a thief, a jerk, and a bad driver. One out of four stars was not a great number.

Out of the corner of my eye, I saw Violet and Turner standing discretely near the bar watching us.

One song blended into the next as we moved fast and seamlessly together. My pulse and heartbeat was going crazy. Finally, a slow song came on. I began fanning myself to cool down, as I walked toward the bar. "Wow, Victor, smooth moves! I think I'm ready for that drink now." He followed, waved down a bartender, and I told him I'd love a martini, only because I thought it sounded sophisticated.

After the busy bartender handed us our drinks, Vi came over with Turner following behind. "Hi guys, I was w-watching you dancing from the b-b-bar. Impressive!" She took a sip of her drink and then asked, "Either of you have the time? I have to get up for work s-s-super early tomorrow."

Victor might take that as an excuse to drive me home later. *Good thinking, Violet.* He pulled out his arm, bending it at the elbow, pushing up his jacket sleeve. I kept my eyes glued to his wrist as he said, "Almost twelve-thirty. Night's still young."

I acted surprised, grabbing his wrist. "Are you sure? Already? Hey...that's a beautiful watch." I squinted to read the logo. There it was: *Rolex*. "Nice Victor... Rolex, right? Is it real?"

Victor pulled back his arm quickly and said, "Of course it's real. You think I'm going to wear some back-alley knock-off shit?"

Then Violet pushed back his jacket sleeve again and glanced down. "Yeah, my Dad had one just like this. Looks real to me. What do you think, Mr. Cooper?"

Turner stepped forward, grabbed and continued to hold Victor's arm more forcefully, as Vi let go. He turned the watch face toward Violet for closer inspection. "What do you think, Violet?" She nodded back. Turner was now nose to nose with Victor and spoke in a soft but menacing tone. "Sir. I'm with the Hill Group security team. This watch was stolen tonight, with the incident recorded on our cameras."

As Turner said that, I was surprised. *Impressive spur-of-the-moment lying skills. Go Turner!*

To be heard, Turner leaned in, speaking directly into Victor's ear, still holding his wrist. "The piece has special sentimental value for Mrs. Hill, so if you hand it back immediately, with no fuss, we'll call the whole episode over and done. Mr. Morales, for your sake, we'd hate to get the police involved."

Just as Victor looked like he was about to give up the watch, four of his friends from upstairs appeared and circled our group. Their expressions looked as if they were on high alert, asking for a fight. A chubby guy in a black suit asked, “Hey Victor, everything cool? This guy bothering you?”

A smirk crept over Victor’s mouth, as he worked a nervous crick out of his neck. He was probably weighing his odds, four of his crew against one pasty-looking white guy with two women. Victor said, “No, he was just admiring my new watch.” He loosened himself from Turner’s grip. “You don't want any trouble from us, right, Mr. Cooper?”

Victor turned to take a step over to his friends, when a hand shot between me and Turner and yanked Victor back like a rubber band, causing me to drop my martini to the floor, with a crash, putting everyone on edge. I glanced at Violet and her eyes and expression told me she was about to shit her pants.

I jerked my head around and saw it was Mark holding Victor’s shoulder, with a small pistol pressed into Victor’s back. Speaking next to his ear, I heard Mark say, “Quit fucking around, Morales. Take off the watch *now,* and give Mr Cooper a hundred bucks for his trouble.”

Victor started to turn around and say something, but Mark pressed the gun harder. “Don’t say it Victor. Time to cut your losses.”

Victor laughed at his crew. “Just kidding guys. It’s his watch. I was deciding if I was going to buy it from him, but nah...I’d rather get the Rolex President--all gold, super sleek. Thanks Cooper; but not really my style.”

His boys looked at everyone menacingly for a few more seconds and then shrugged shoulders and melted back onto the dance floor, while the watch went from Victor's arm to Turner’s.

After slipping it on, Turner said, “And I’ll take that hundred now too.”

Victor jerked his chin up, “I don’t have it on me.”

“Sure you do, Morales. If you can afford a Rolex President, you can certainly reward me with a hundred bucks for keeping your ass out of jail...or maybe we need to renegotiate terms. What do you think, Mark?”

"Fine with me. I'd love to see his skinny ass in an orange jumpsuit."

Victor took out his wallet and counted out a fifty and two twenties. "That's all I got, man. Seriously."

I grabbed the cash from him and handed it to Turner before Victor's guys noticed the transaction. "Ninety works. Victor, just ask that tall blonde upstairs to buy your drinks. Time to go guys." The four of us quickly filed out, trying to keep straight faces, leaving Victor standing there looking embarrassed and mad as hell.

Mark was behind us, saying, "Keep walking... quick... move."

I pushed the door open, breathing in the chilly night air and it felt glorious. As Violet passed the bouncer, she announced, "Just not our s-scene; I think I'd rather go hiking."

Walking quickly, I allowed a smile to creep over my face the closer we got to Vi's car. Then I heard him yelling my name.

"Rosario... Hey, Ro-sa-rio! You lying bitch! Hey... turn around. Remember, I know where you live."

I turned to scream back at him, but Violet and Turner grabbed my arms and pushed me into the car. Turner said, "Let it go, Rosie. He's not worth it."

Driving back to Vi's, I was quiet for a moment but then began smiling as I realized that I may not have found the dance partner of my dreams, but I knew I'd found three good friends who had my back, which was way more than I'd had in a while.

CHAPTER 35

Hot Sauce and Sweet Dreams

VIOLET

I let Mark fulfill his get-away-driver fantasy and handed him my car keys, as I climbed in the back with Rosie. I put my arm around her shoulder. "Don't w-worry about Victor. He's just a b-bully who lost face in front of his creepy friends. You did a b-b-brave thing tonight."

Mark gunned the motor of my safe, sensible Subaru and hauled ass. Within minutes, we were all downplaying Victor's idle threat, becoming almost giddy with relief, while we laughed at the retelling of the grand Rolex retrieval.

I leaned up to the front seat, telling Mark, "I sw-swear, I almost lost it when I looked down and saw your g-g-gun in Victor's back. I came close to throwing up."

"Sorry about that, but sometimes Heidi comes in handy. She's my little German pistol, but she wouldn't hurt a fly. Hasn't been loaded in over ten years."

"That's my kind of gun," I said.

"And where do you hide Ms. Heidi?" Turner asked.

"Keep her tucked in my underwear, warm and safe."

We all laughed and Turner said, "Mark, you've got balls of steel, man."

Mark made it back to my place in record time, finally slowing down on the driveway. Once parked, he jumped out, telling us, "Gotta run. Guess I need to go apologize to Molly."

Turner looked at the Rolex he was still wearing. "It's getting close to one; a little late for that isn't it, Magnum?"

"Nah, she'll be ready and waiting."

Rosie broke out in a laugh. "You're way too sure of yourself, Mark, but you got some big *cojones*. Be careful; Molly can be pretty tough."

"Why is everybody so concerned with my private parts tonight?" Mark got in his truck, backed out and rolled down the window. "Hey, Violet--thanks for the laughs. Good times!" The three of us just shook our heads as he backed out.

The more I got to know Mark, the more surprised I became. Initially, he was my mother's part-time pot-smoking gardener. But now, besides possessing serious artistic and gardening skills, he'd become a man-of-mystery, a ladies man, and someone capable of plotting flawless watch heists while pocketing guns in provocative places.

After unlocking my door, Turner and Rosario followed me in. I knew Rosie was staying the night, but why was Turner coming in? Not that I minded.

"Violet, I'm really ready for a shower," Rosario said. "May I use yours upstairs?"

"Sure, go ahead. And you'll find clean T-shirts in my t-top drawer to sleep in."

Turner took a seat on the ottoman and was looking at me expectantly. As usual, once we were alone together, my self-confidence parked itself outside the door. Turning my attention to the kitchen, I busied myself putting away or tossing the remaining food. There were a few unclaimed Christmas cookies, guacamole turning a blackish hue, a thick and congealed queso dip, and left-over tacos. "Uh, there's still a little f-food and drinks here if you w-want anything."

Turner walked over to the table. "Nothing more to drink, but maybe I'll take some tacos. Between an early breakfast and now, I've had three stuffed mushrooms. Could have had more, but I couldn't catch them fast enough...but that's a whole other story."

He put two cold tacos on a paper plate and leaned against the counter watching me as I continued to fastidiously cover dishes with plastic wrap, keeping my eyes focused on the food. "S-sorry for how they taste. They were d-decent about four hours ago."

"Uh, a little of that hot sauce will help." Turner's hand reached over, stopping my hand from covering it with plastic. I felt a sizzle of electricity shoot through me with his touch, making my hand accidently hit the bowl. We both looked on helplessly as the container of red, chunky liquid clattered to the floor, rolling under the table.

"S-Sorry. I'm s-so clumsy," I said, while grabbing a roll of paper towels. I quickly kneeled under the table and started wiping up the mess. "I've got m-more in the fridge; I'll get it for you in a second."

Turner kneeled down next to me, taking the paper towels from my hand. "Don't worry about it. I'll get this mess. Sorry I startled you."

Both of us were on our knees under the edge of the long pine table. I forced myself to look up and stare into his eyes, as they crinkled into the most delightful smile. They were green, but circled with brown. *Very Nice.* Funny, I'd never noticed that before. Quit staring Violet, say something witty, endearing... anything!

"Well, you know what they s-say? The way to a m-man's heart is through a j-jar of great hot sauce. Sorry...that's stupid...nobody says that." I nervously began to stand up and immediately hit my head on the table above, which slammed me onto my rear, landing me back on the floor. "Crap! Oh my God, that hurts." I winced, tenderly touching the top of my head.

Turner softly touched it with his free hand that wasn't wiping up hot sauce. "Yeah, I think you're growing a baby dinosaur-egg up there. Let's forget the hot sauce. Maybe you should lie down. I bet you feel dizzy."

"Not really dizzy, just seeing stars."

He artfully dodged the table overhead, stood and gave me his hand. Again, touching his hand gave me a jolt, but thankfully, no dangerous flying bowls were in close range. Putting my hand in his, I slid out beneath the table and let him guide me to the couch. He then propped up a pillow for me to lie down on.

"Here, just relax for a minute. You have any plastic bags?"

"On the t-table. Next to the cheese sl-slices."

He quickly filled a baggie with icc and brought it over, attentively sitting on the edge of the couch, near my ballooning skull. With a delicious grin, he placed the bag on top of my head and said, "You know, Vi, this is the second time in two weeks that I've brought ice for your throbbing head. You're kind of needy, aren't you?"

My eyes were fighting sleep as I tried to answer. He was only inches from me. "Hmm. Not needy, but perhaps klutzy? It's your fault, making me so jittery..." I felt my eyes rolling back, everything going dark, but I wanted to talk more. He was so close; but after the tense evening I was exhausted, struggling to keep my eyes open.

From upstairs, I heard Rosario's voice yelling. "What's wrong with Violet? Did she faint?"

I turned to shake my head, but Turner answered for me. "I think she's OK, just hit her head on the table. Seems really tired. Why don't you throw a pillow and blanket down here for her, and you sleep upstairs. I'll stay for a few minutes and make sure she's fine before I leave."

I remember smiling to myself, eyes firmly closed as I lay there, thinking: *Now he's going to kiss me. Go ahead, let's give it a try...*

I felt the heat of warm breath speaking close to my ear, and a gentle nudge on my shoulder. I reached for his hand and pulled it across my body. Wait...did that voice have a Spanish accent?

"Violet...wake up...*por favor.* I took an extra shift today. A noon wedding at BUD. I need a ride home to change."

I turned over, looking up into the face of Rosario and then felt the squish of the plastic baggie below me as water spilled out around my back. I squinted into the morning sunlight flooding through the window sheers. "Already?" I asked. I was still wrapped up in my dream of Turner leaning in for a kiss and disappointed to see Rosario.

I sat up, staring down at the empty plastic bag and water absorbing into the sofa fabric. Then loud snoring directed my eyes to the chair and ottoman where Turner reclined in deep sleep, clutching a sofa-throw. So, he *had* decided to hang around, although he wasn't looking so hot. Then again, neither did I.

I whispered, "What's Turner still doing here?"

"He said you hit your head and wanted to wait to make sure you were OK. Guess he fell asleep too. Sorry Vi, but I need to get home."

I reluctantly nodded and stood up. Still wearing my clothes from last night, I was almost ready. "Let me br-brush my teeth and throw some water on my face. You mind waking Turner up?" I ran upstairs, pulled a brush through my hair, pulled it into a ponytail, and washed up, taking off black smudges of residual mascara.

When I came downstairs, Turner was leaning against the kitchen counter guzzling water, looking miserable. "Morning Turner, sorry to rush you out, but I need to take Rosie back to her place."

He shook his head, looking to knock his alcohol addled brain back into place. "Sure. No problem. Oh, almost forgot. Your mother's watch." He pulled it off his arm and handed it to me.

"Thanks for this, b-both of you guys. Your efforts last night really m-meant a lot."

"You're so welcome," Rosie said. "That's what friends do."

Turner added, "Well hopefully, we don't do *that* again."

As the three of us headed out, I locked the guest house behind me. Turner hesitated a moment, turning towards me. "Vi, I never got to explain the details about Kevin last night. That's why I came in."

Rosario got into my car, while I stopped and said, "I'm definitely going r-r-running in about an hour. If you want to join me then, we can talk."

He didn't look enticed by the offer. "Running? How about a walk with our dogs. I need to eat something and clear my head. How's noon?"

"That works. Call me later and we'll m-m-meet up."

I drove over to Rosie's neighborhood and dropped her near the entrance of her building. A minute later, as I was turning the corner to head back home, she called, screaming into the phone.

"That fucking *pendejo*!" This was followed by a mix between crying and yelling in Spanish.

"Hang on. I'm coming b-back."

CHAPTER 36

I Know Where You Live

ROSARIO

I walked up the steps, immediately noticing the cheap door knob dangling from my apartment door and scars around it scraped into the wood. My heart seized up as I touched the mangled door, watching it swing in. My hands were shaking as I held my breath, peeking inside, not knowing what to expect. I tiptoed in, thinking I shouldn't be in here alone. But I had to see what chaos waited inside. The few belongings I had were thrown around or broken. I quickly glanced into the bathroom, shower, and then the closet. No lurking intruders. I let out my breath.

While screaming out in anger, I called Violet. When she said she was coming back, I felt a little better. I'd faced a break-in before in Juarez, but that's when I had Roberto next to me to help pick up the pieces.

I stepped over beige chunks of plastic realizing they were what remained of my clock radio. Why break it? Not even worthy of a steal? My spool table was tossed over and rolled against the wall, along with a single plastic chair, spray painted with graffiti. All my clothing was tossed onto the carpet, and the few dishes I had lay in shards on the kitchen counter and floor.

I immediately went to my sock drawer where I always stashed my extra cash. The money was gone, apparently the only thing of value worth stealing. It was the money I scrimped out of every paycheck to send to my mother.

Sheets on my bed were shredded, my pillows, now thrown on the floor, had yellow foam hanging out. I collapsed on the bed, laying across the mattress, trying to stop the jagged crying. Ugly, spray-painted graffiti screamed back at me from the walls. I swung my arm over my eyes so I wouldn't have to look. My mind jumped to Victor, making me wonder; was this the action of an angry, pride-wounded petty thief or something more sinister? I was too tired to care and definitely didn't want to find out.

"W-What the hell! Rosie...you OK?" Violet walked through the open door and stared at me splayed out across the bed taking in deep breaths. She sat down next to me and patted me gingerly on the back, as if she was afraid to touch me. "It's g-g-gonna be alright. Stay at my place until you're resettled. This m-mess has to be Victor, right?"

"Yeah, I think so too. What an asshole! I slammed my fist against the wall. "I can't believe I was so attracted to him. I'm such an idiot."

"Don't bl-blame yourself. He's a b-b-bully and a thief." Violet got up, peeked into my bathroom and then stepped over the pile of clothes. "Man, he really trashed the place and looks like he stole a lot of your stuff too."

Her comment made me laugh through my tears. "Vi, the good thing about being poor--there's not much to steal; only the cash in my drawer. That's all gone. A hundred and twenty-two-dollars. Could have been worse, I guess." I pushed myself off the bed with a sigh. I leaned over, picking through my clothes, mentally exhausted from the simple effort. I found my white shirt and black pants. "I need to get dressed. What time is it?"

Violet had grabbed a pile of clothing and was hanging items. "It's ten. You're still going to work?"

"I *have* to Violet. What am I going to do here? Sit around and be scared all day? The only way I get out of this shithole is to keep working extra shifts and earn enough for a new deposit. I'm not like you. I have no one else to turn to."

Violet forced a happy face. "Well, you have me. I'm ha-happy to help. Hurry; go take a hot shower, clear your head. You'll feel b-better. I'll give you a lift to BUD so you won't be late."

I nodded, headed to the bathroom and glanced at the torn plastic shower curtain, dangling from the last two rusty rings on the rod. I turned the faucets to hot, and stared at my reflection. I had to shake my head as I pulled off last night's stretchy black dress, remembering I'd worn it wanting to impress Victor.

That thought now turned my stomach.

Scattered drops splashed out onto the floor as I stepped in, but I didn't care. As the hot water hit my upturned face, I wondered if it was ever going to get easier? Why did everything have to be so hard? Why me? Other women managed to meet the occasional hot guy, have a night out, and didn't end up with them turning into thieving psychos. I knew Roberto had essentially died for me, defending me and himself against the cartel. Was I a magnet for attracting bad people? Did I give off that vibe? Crazy thoughts began cycling through my brain.

I dried off quickly, telling myself to stop thinking like this. I'd already spent a year here hiding away. I couldn't hide all my life.

Violet called through the door with a forced cheerfulness. "Hey Rosie, they didn't steal your iron. I see it at the top of the closet. Want me to iron your shirt and pants?"

"*Gracias*." Her simple offer made me feel better. I did have a friend that cared. I wasn't alone. Perhaps, I'd just been unlucky.

I pulled my hair back in a tight ponytail and put on a little blush, lipstick, eyeliner, and mascara; my version of a mask to hide the fear inside. I walked out of the bathroom in my bra and panties and looked at Violet holding up the freshly pressed shirt, looking quite proud of her accomplishment. "Here you go; first thing I've ironed in months. Looks p-pretty good."

"Don't tell me... your mother still does your laundry?"

Violet then looked down at the floor. "No. It's her m-maid. But I do try to shop for wrinkle-free f-f-fabrics. Anyway...I was th-thinking...while you're at work, I'll p-pack up your clothes and stuff and contact the apartment manager and po-police. You should stay at my place for a while, at least until we get this place fixed up."

I got dressed as we talked. "You would do that for me? Gracias, Vi! The apartment manager lives in the back. I'll give you his number. But *policía*? You really think that's needed?"

"D-Definitely. If there's any more ha-ha-harassment, we need to get it on the record. Who knows; maybe Victor has a police record already and left fingerprints? That's what they do on TV."

"OK. Hope this isn't too much trouble." I looked around, shook my head, and sighed. "Guess I'm ready."

I was one of the last of the event workers to arrive, and hurried to the check-in room. While attaching my black bowtie and punching in, I couldn't shake a recurring thought. What would have happened to me last night if I'd been home when Victor broke in?

Walking into the apartment this morning brought back the recurring memories of Roberto's brutal murder. He'd thought he was strong enough to buck the gang system in Juarez. But no. I'd convinced myself things would be different here, but maybe they weren't?

Today I needed to focus on working this wedding event for the next several hours. The distraction would probably help. Since I'd started at BUD, I always felt safe behind the ivy-covered walls and decorative iron gates. But then I remembered. Victor was the person who had introduced me to BUD and he knew I worked here. Maybe the safety of those walls was only an illusion.

Compartmentalize. Fortunately, it was a gorgeous winter day for an outdoor ceremony. We had eighty chairs to set up in a hidden garden featuring a carpet-like emerald green lawn, surrounded by rock walls draped with purple and yellow pansies. Our crew of six unloaded and set up white wooden folding chairs in straight lines across the grass, leaving a center aisle.

Red cardinals darted among the vines and squirrels scattered over the walls. I watched them for a moment and felt a pang of jealousy for the lucky bride and groom who'd be celebrating in such a wonderful place. After setting up chairs, I headed back to the entrance. I was assigned to drive one of three electric visitor carts, which took the less mobile guests from the main gate to the ceremony garden. Seeing everyone dressed up, in cheerful moods, and grateful for our help, put my head in a better place.

At least I had Violet as a good friend, and could also count on Mark, and maybe even Turner; three people I was grateful for. And while I was working, Violet was packing my things and offering me a place to stay. That type of friendship was rare, especially in a new country.

After the ceremony, I carted guests over to the reception area. Then I returned to the garden to take down and stack the chairs on a truck. It was repetitive work, but for the extra money, I was happy to stay busy and I needed to refill my stolen nest egg.

By six o'clock, I'd carried the last guest to the exit, turned in my bowtie and punched out. At the employee entrance, Violet was waiting for me. I got inside her car, happy for this day to end. "Ahh, feels so good to sit. Violet, you are too generous. Thanks again for letting me stay with you."

"Yeah Rosie, about that...I need to tell you something."

CHAPTER 37

Tub Talks

TURNER

I drove home leisurely, taking the long way around the lake while contemplating the strange last twenty-four hours. It was now ten AM, a crisp, sunny Saturday morning. I physically felt like crap--tired, thirsty, hungry as hell, with a banging hang-over. But, oddly enough, I was in a great mood. Why? I should be miserable. Despite needing water and food, those needs were minimized by an unusual sense of well-being. Contentment...even happiness? How long had it been since I'd felt that? I couldn't even remember.

The sun coming through my driver's side window warmed my face and left arm, pulling a smile out across my face. I slowed my drive, eyeing the colorful parade of cyclists, walkers, and runners. Looking beyond them, I squinted at the shining glint across the surface of the lake, as a white heron glided in for a graceful landing. All this added to my rare euphoria,

Eventually, I pulled into my drive knowing Blaze would be hungry and mad at me. I unlocked the door and immediately heard him barking. "OK, boy. Sorry I'm late. I got you." His deep brown eyes stared at me impatiently as I poured out a big bowl of dry dog food. I lead Blaze through the back door and set the food bowl outside. While on the deck, I switched on the hot tub and gave my reliable red-head companion a good scratch and rub behind his silky ears. Perhaps all was forgiven.

I returned to the kitchen and opened the refrigerator, reaching for a cold beer, but quickly grabbed two, pulled out cheese, cold salami, thick bread, and took a bag of potato chips from the pantry. I stood for a minute and stared at everything on the kitchen counter. "Nope," I said, talking to the walls. I reopened the refrigerator and put everything back. "Damn it!"

Sighing, I reached for a thermos, filled it with water and ice and went hunting in my lonely vegetable bin: a half head of lettuce, a spare tomato, and a shriveled cucumber. "This'll do." I chopped up the makings of my little salad, drizzled it with Italian dressing left over from Allie's shopping days, and threw a few crackers on top. While returning the chips to the pantry, I noticed a jar of peanuts and sprinkled them liberally over the salad. "Better."

Plunking myself down outside on a deck chair, I began to take bites of salad between throwing a mangled yellow tennis ball to Blaze. The guy just couldn't get enough of it, bobbing and weaving energetically across every inch of the yard while retrieving his favorite toy. He eventually tired and laid down, while I stripped and hopped into the tub...my reward for semi-healthy eating.

Plunging into the heat and bubbles felt almost orgasmic. I leaned my head back against the tile, as spasms of pleasure shot through my brain. But then again, I had done without for several months, so my orgasmic expectations were at a pretty low bar.

But this euphoric feeling...What was it? Where was it coming from? No drugs in my system. Work and issues at Rapid Logistics were still unsettled, account growth was slightly down. My time spent at BUD had been exhausting but energizing. I really liked the idea that we were building something unique and beautiful from scratch.

Last night was pretty crazy. Starting with a near slippery slide into the cloying world of Katrina, who looked so amazingly hot. But even last night, I could already anticipate the eventual result. The flying mushrooms and bang of the platter hitting the door were my punishment for letting things get as far as they did. Thankfully,

Violet's pretty face, crooked smile, and strange little party invitation flashed across my brain, saving me from the path of Katrina destruction.

Then there was knocking out Kevin with that painful punch...I looked down into the water, noticing my knuckles were still a little swollen. But honestly, that hit had felt so incredibly satisfying, yet so oddly inappropriate. The fact that he was there as Violet's guest was incredibly bizarre, as if some just god was serving Kevin up on a platter for me to punch out. And the vigilantism of our little BUD squad was ridiculous, although we prevailed in the end, putting smarmy Victor in his place. So fitting and fair, considering how nice Rosario was.

And today, I was looking forward to an afternoon without interruption with Violet, anticipating our conversation and walk on this glorious winter day. Perhaps, that was the source of today's happy break from the gray malaise which had been stalking me lately. Whatever the source, I was overwhelmingly grateful.

Checking my phone, I saw it was getting close to 11:30. Just enough time to shower, dress, and meet Violet. Still holding the phone, it buzzed, flashing her name.

"Hey Vi, just thinking about getting dressed to meet you."

"Yeah, about that. G-Guess I'll need to cancel. B-Bad news.

Of course, bad news. "What's wrong, Violet?"

"It l-looks like Victor and his p-pals made good on his threat. After I dr-dropped Rosie off, she called me so upset."

"Fuck! What happened?"

"We don't know for sure it was them, but s-sometime last night, somebody b-busted open her door, spray-p-painted the walls, and stole her little stash of money that she s-s-sends her mother. It was a little over a hundred bucks, but that means a lot to her."

"Man, I didn't think he'd have the nerve to follow through. Victor's worse than I thought."

"Me neither, Turner. M-More than anything, Rosie's s-super scared. She told me before about how her twin b-brother was decapitated by a gang in Juarez. It was h-horrible!"

"What? I had no idea! Man, she's been through a lot."

"Anyway, after R-Rosie calmed down, she still wanted to work her special event gig at BUD, so I drove her there. I'm b-b-back at her apartment now, waiting for the police and the apartment m-m-manager's having someone fix the lock. I'm going to pack up Rosie's stuff, so she can stay with me temporarily."

"That's really kind of you. Do you need help?"

"N-No. Thanks though. It's the *least* I can do. If it hadn't been for my m-mother's stupid watch, none of this would have happened."

"Violet, your perspective is a bit off. Remember, Victor stole the watch to begin with. That's not exactly normal party etiquette. Nor is breaking into someone's apartment just because you're mad at them."

"True. You're right. And honestly, th-think about it. It could have been s-so much worse if Rosie had stayed at her apartment last night. Can you imagine? She's been w-wanting to move anyway. That's why she's working extra shifts."

I sighed, quickly starting to feel down with the turn of events. "OK... sounds like you're doing a really good thing for her; but I'm sorry about missing our walk today."

"Oh... I just thought you suggested a dog walk because you were trying to get out of going for a run."

"All true. But I was looking forward to walking with *you*. Tell you what, why don't you let me take you and Rosario out to dinner tonight?"

She hesitated a little too long. "So, it'll be kind of like a date?"

"Yes, Violet. Like a date, well...a date with two friends." *This was awkward.* "It's a damn dinner invitation, Violet. How's seven o'clock?"

"Yes, s-seven should be fine. I'll be here at least a few more hours p-packing and waiting for the police."

"I'll pick you both up at seven."

How can it be that this woman has no idea I'm attracted to her? It's like she doesn't have a clue. Well, maybe because I didn't realize it myself until maybe last night? Am I that obtuse? I needed to improve my game, but I'd been out of the dating scene for so long.

I looked over at Blaze who raised his head from the deck. "What do you think, Blaze? Am I crazy for wanting to get involved with somebody now? Too early? Not a fair question--you'll always be an Allie loyalist." Hearing me say her name, he barked appropriately.

I did understand one thing. Approach cautiously. Violet skitters like a deer. And maybe I would too.

Then my phone buzzed again. *Dad.* I got out, toweled off and picked up. "Hey Dad. What'cha got?"

"I guess you already heard, but thought I'd make sure."

"Heard what?"

Son, we got ourselves another cluster-fuck to contend with. Damn railroad people say they're going on strike. Everybody's talking about it. Need to get your ass over to the office and let's try to get ahead of all this."

I sighed and said. "Sure, Dad. I'm on my way."

Enter the gray cloud of malaise. My stalker had returned.

CHAPTER 38

Mommy Dearest

VIOLET

The police were no help at all. An officer eventually showed up at Rosie's apartment two hours after I'd called it in. He wrote up a report, while another guy dusted for fingerprints on the mangled door. I mentioned Victor's previous night's threats to Rosario, but because there were no witnesses to the break-in, there was no real evidence that connected it to Victor. Once the cop realized the only thing awry was a little over a hundred bucks, a broken lock, and some vandalism, he was ready to move on to something bigger. By his nonchalance, it appeared this case was going nowhere. By three o'clock, the lock was repaired by a maintenance guy and I headed back home.

Pulling into our drive, I noticed Mother's car parked in front so I decided to go in and update her on the missing Rolex. It was always difficult to know which way her mind would take things. I debated between telling her I'd simply found the watch in another room, or explaining how we actually retrieved it. I wasn't sure of the best way to spin the story, but I eventually opted for the truth.

I wandered about and found Mother in the library wrapping a Christmas gift. She was dressed up, wearing a fawn-colored cashmere sweater-set, heavy gold jewelry, looking like she was about to walk out the door.

"Mother, hi...You'll never guess what ha-ha-happened!"

She looked up with relief. "Oh good, you're just in time. Violet, press your finger right here on the bow while I tie it. These are so difficult. Magna was supposed to have wrapped this for me."

I leaned over and lent her my appendage. "M-Mother, have you heard of g-gift bags? No bows required. One of last century's most clever innovations."

She looked at me as if I'd suggested wrapping the gift in discarded newspaper. "Gift bags? No! They're so pedestrian, like something you'd get at a grocery store. There's nothing better than a beautifully wrapped gift. Remember Violet, it's *all* about the presentation. An important lesson, by the way."

"Sure. I'll j-jot that one down in my diary. Anyway...about your watch."

"My watch?" She looked up at me quizzically. "What about a watch?"

"Good God, Mother. Too much holiday champaign last night? The watch you basically accused everyone at my party of stealing." She continued to stare at me, looking confused.

"Dad's Rolex...you couldn't find it last night. Remember?"

"Oh, of course. I've been so busy, I'd completely forgotten. So you found it then?"

"Actually, *we* did. Turner, Ro-Rosario, Mark and I."

Instead of looking happy, she seemed concerned. "Well, I certainly hope you didn't have a bunch of strangers ransacking the house looking for it."

"No, the truth is, s-someone did take it."

Now her face looked elated, a difficult maneuver with botox injections. "I knew it! I was convinced I'd left it in the kitchen. Who was the scoundrel?"

"It's kind-kind of a long story, but Rosie brought a date, a guy she bare-barely knew, but he seemed very promising, anyway..." I went on to tell her most of the details, leaving out Hiedi-the-pistol's part, and then finished up with Rosario's apartment break-in.

Mother looked shocked as I handed her the watch. "I can't believe all that happened last night. Well, I certainly appreciate the effort your friends took to get this back. Very kind of them. You know how sentimental I am about your father's old watch. *And* I hope you've learned an important lesson." She looked over at me with the semi-smile often used when she was about to bestow one of her commandments upon me.

"A lesson?"

"Violet, you need to be *really* careful about the people you associate with. If you don't know their background, you have no idea about what trouble you might get into. Especially when hosting parties. You're much too innocent and unguarded, my dear. Stay clear of that Rosario girl. She's obviously not the type of person you should hang around with. Consider who she brought into this house."

Of course, she would prohibit me from hanging out with the *one* girlfriend I'd found since moving home. I stomped my foot on the floor, shaking my head. "If Rosie hadn't immediately told me her sus-sus-suspicions about Victor, we never would have recovered the watch. You have *her* to thank for it."

She leaned over the wrapped box, curling the ribbons on the bow. "That's one way to look at it, but she also has to share the blame."

I stared at her placid, resolute expression as I began to fume. "Mother, she's alone here in Dallas. With no family. She has nothing but a vandalized apartment to return to. I invited her to stay with me until she finds a new place."

"I hope you're joking! I forbid that, Violet."

"All the trouble we went to was for *you*...I thought you'd be happy!" I began to walk out of the library and then turned around. "Rosie is my friend; somebody I r-r-really like. I can't turn my back on her when sh-she could be in danger."

Mother stood and stared at me, her lips beginning to twitch, still holding her stupid, perfectly wrapped gift. Before she could speak, I walked out of the room and headed down the hall. Behind me I heard her shrill voice calling out, "Violet, I mean it. I forbid it. That girl is not staying here!"

I slammed the door on my way out. I was so angry I couldn't

think straight. I walked past the pool, unlocked the door to the guest house, and collapsed on the couch, not realizing until now how exhausted I was. I checked my watch: four o'clock. I set the alarm for five and closed my tired eyes.

Instead of my alarm, I woke up to Cocoa's warm, wet tongue on my face. She was standing on her short hind legs, barely able to reach me on the couch. Poor thing. I'd been so caught up with the break-in, I'd forgotten to let my dog out earlier. I attached her leash and we walked across the yard.

I glanced around at the expansive rolling lawn, the manicured garden beds, and picture-perfect glass guest house. As beautiful as everything was, it would never feel like my own place. This was all Mother, down to the smallest selected details; from color combinations of the potted mums dotting the walkway, to the exact number of twinkling holiday lights per tree in the yard. *Suzanne Hill Creations presents!* Staying here, I would always be her embarrassing only child, the girl afraid of her own shadow, the one stumbling over her words.

At that moment, I decided it was time for me to get my own place again. I was grateful for the use of the guest house, but it was only meant to be a transition spot. I was ready to move on. Obviously, it would be a large expense, but perhaps Rosie might be the perfect roommate to share the rent and apartment with, if she was interested. She needed a safe place in a better neighborhood and I needed independence from Mother. I'd never considered the idea of a roommate before. This might be a good solution. Mother didn't want Rosie here, but she could say nothing about us sharing a two-bedroom flat. That would be our own decision.

As Cocoa led me back inside to fill her food bowl, I received a text from Rosie.

Wedding reception wrapping up. I'll be clocking out at 6:00. See you at the employee entrance?

I needed to hustle. We had a date with Turner to prepare for. An actual Saturday night dinner date! Totally new territory for me. I was nervous but excited and this was something Mother would have loved to have discussed with me. A topic mothers and daughters bonded over. Right?

The last time we had a conversation about dating was back when I was in high school. Mother had set me up on a blind date with one of her friend's sons, Collin Wentworth. Total disaster! It lasted a little over an hour before Collin got a sudden stomach ache and needed to take me home. I definitely got the impression he was embarrassed to be seen with me. My prep school rep was abysmal.

Before heading back to BUD, I showered and dressed in something Mother bought me last Christmas, which I'd never worn: a soft blue knit sweater with a short navy skirt and tights. While driving, I was deciding on my approach to Rosie about the possibility of being roommates, trying to pick the right words. This was a big step for me. Once Rosie got in the car, the first words out of her mouth were about how grateful she was to stay at my place.

I immediately felt guilty about Mother's pronouncement. I stammered for a few seconds and then came out with it. "Yeah, Rosie, about that...actually, I had a b-better idea. The thought just-just came to me today." I kept staring at the steering wheel, unable to look her in the face. "Me staying at the guest house with my mother...It was only meant to be a t-t-temporary thing. Until I got a decent job. I've noticed some ni-nice looking new apartments near the lake on Garland Road. What would you think about being flatmates?"

I turned on the ignition, began to drive, keeping my eyes on the road. "We c-could get a two-bedroom and share expenses. Cheaper for both of us."

Then I heard her crying. I glanced over, as she shook her head. "Rosie. W-What's wrong? Still upset about Victor?" Concerned, I looked at her again as I turned a corner. "I understand. Some p-p-people can't handle roommates; they need solitude. I've always been that way. Haven't had a r-r-roommate since the dorms, my freshman year, but I--"

"*Si...si. Definitivamente si*!" She wiped her tearing eyes with her sleeve. "Vi, I'm so ready for company, so tired of being alone. I've been afraid for too long. Haven't been able to trust anybody."

"Oh...OK. That's g-g-good!" I let out a laugh of relief.

"Violet, until you said it, I didn't realize how much I want that... for real...trust and friendship. Yes! Yes, let's start looking tomorrow."

"Alright, cool." *That went amazingly well; now the other part.* "Actually though, there's s-something else. My mother wasn't too excited about me bring-bringing in a house guest she doesn't know. You understand, insurance risks and all that stuff. Of course, if it was *my* house, it would be no problem. So-so-so, anyway...you're welcome to stay with me this weekend, but after that, you'll need to stay at your place until we can move in together."

She was quiet for a few seconds and then shrugged. "It's OK. I understand."

"Oh, one other thing. We're both going out to dinner with Turner tonight. It's a *date*."

Rosario looked over and shook her head. "No, my friend. For one, I'm too tired. Two, Turner wants to go out with *you*, not the two of us. I'm sure he's only being polite. A very nice offer, but tell him I'm too tired. Those weddings are not easy--been on my feet since eleven."

As I pulled in the driveway, past the house, I noticed Mother's car was gone. Good. Rosie and I could unload her stuff without being seen, then she went upstairs to shower. I texted Turner letting him know Rosie was staying in for the night, but I was still available.

He simply replied: *Perfect*. Followed by a very uncharacteristic happy-face emoji.

CHAPTER 39

Mixing Business with Pleasure

TURNER

An hour after Dad called, I found myself in the conference room at Rapid Logistics organizing an impromptu Zoom meeting with my team leaders. I'm sure this last-minute Saturday afternoon meeting would guarantee me topping the list of least favorite bosses in Dallas. But hey, when you're in the supply chain business, the occasional rail strike was a very big deal. Everybody had popped up on screen except Sarah from sales.

While we were waiting, the four of them looked wary and on edge. At least my ass was finally comfortable in the padded, upholstered chairs I'd recently ordered. Unfortunately, that small comfort was one of the few contributions I'd made to the business recently. I saw Sarah pop up on the screen and detected an unhappy look on her face. Time to get started.

"Hey guys, sorry to disrupt everyone's weekend, but Dad and I thought we needed to get everyone up to speed on this possible rail strike. It's all moving way faster than I anticipated. Ed, as the lead on rail freight, why don't you update us on what you have."

Ed pushed his glasses back up his nose, glanced up from his laptop, and nodded. "Sure, uh, right now, government's doing their best to intervene or delay. Politically, the rail strike would really look bad for the administration at this point, especially with supply chain issues starting to settle down. If they don't help mediate or knock together some sort of agreement by midnight Tuesday, the iron wheels all come to a screeching halt."

Everybody was shaking their heads and murmuring doom and gloom. I asked Ed, "What's our exposure at this moment?"

Ed shrugged and sighed, clicking a tab. "As of 1:15 today, about forty percent. That's both incoming and outgoing rail deliveries. Could be worse I guess."

I looked at the rest of the team. "OK...let's talk solutions. If we divert all remaining domestic shipments from rail to trucking *today*, then sixty percent of our accounts should be alright. That's not horrendous, correct?" Everyone seemed to nod unenthusiastically. "Ed? Any possible way we can pull any in-route cargo containers off some rail lines and onto trucks?"

"Very unlikely. But I can try. I'm sure every company in the country is trying to do the same thing right now."

"Possibly, but some may just be sweating it out. Helene, see if you can line up a few more of our independent truckers to take on some cargo out of the LA port. Get together with my father and Sam on that. And Sarah, compile a list of clients from the forty percent that will probably be delayed. Call and give them all a heads up. They'll appreciate the notification, even if it's bad news.

Sarah groaned, "Why do I always have to be the bearer of bad news? This is getting old."

I looked at her sympathetically. "I know it's tough, but in sales you have to build trust with those clients. It's essential. And if Ed miraculously gets a few containers on trucks before the strike, you'll turn into their hero. Just finesse the message. That's part of the job. I'll jump on some of those calls."

We all went into emergency mode, working the phones, checking delivery routes and time lines, heading off as many customer delays as possible. By late afternoon we had diverted about twenty-five percent of the forty that would be immediately affected by a strike. Other than personally begging rail workers not to strike, we had taken all the preemptive action we possibly could. By five-thirty, everyone looked bleary-eyed and probably ready for a hefty cold beer.

Before everybody clicked off the screen, I said, "Good job today, guys. Appreciate everyone helping out, and next Friday, happy hour's on me. You guys pick the place."

My father and I walked out together. "Dad, thanks for giving me a heads up about this. I heard talk about the possible strike, but lost track of the negotiation progress. Your call probably saved us a client or two,"

"Yup. Somebody's got to watch the chicken coop, son, or those foxes will get 'em every time." He wrapped his arm around my shoulder as we neared our cars. "But hey, you did some good work in there today. Man…I'm hungry. Why don't you join me for a thick steak and a brew at KC's?"

"Sounds great, but believe it or not, I actually have a dinner date with two women. They're just friends. We made plans earlier today. Next time, OK?"

"A date? You're right. I'm really surprised, but good to hear you're getting back into the swing of things. Time for that rooster to crow a little."

I had to smile and shake my head. "Dad… that's your second chicken metaphor. See ya' soon."

Checking my watch, I figured I'd have time for a quick sunset walk with Blaze, tidy myself up, and then pick up Violet and Rosario. An hour later, Violet texted. When I saw her name on the screen I was sure she was canceling again, but instead, she let me know it was only her meeting me for dinner. I didn't mind the change in plans; I was ready to see what an actual date would feel like with a woman I was interested in. I was so rusty; and hadn't done this in what… over thirteen years?

I couldn't help but think back to my first date with Allie. A set-up in college with a fraternity brother and his girlfriend. Once I walked into the bar and saw her sitting at a table, my nerves set in. Allie was a beautiful woman. But it was time to shake off those memories. I was older, and hopefully a more confident, capable person who had wined and dined countless female clients over the years. Driving over to pick Violet up, I convinced myself everything would go smoothly.

When she opened the door, I was immediately smitten. Even working at BUD, I found her attractive in her jeans, baseball cap, and ponytail. But tonight...her long, dark glossy hair was down, hanging below her shoulders. She had on a soft, fuzzy light blue mohair sweater worn with a very short, dark-navy skirt and tights. The sweater's color was the perfect complement to her large pale eyes, but she wouldn't look at me directly and seemed fidgety while opening the door.

"Hi Vi. You look scrumptious." *Bad word choice*? "Rosario upstairs?"

"Yes, she's exhausted. Cleaned up and went to b-b-bed. Uh, let's see," she said, pulling open the refrigerator. "You want anything--water, b-beer?"

I took a few deep breaths trying to keep calm. "Actually, I'm incredibly hungry. If you're ready to go, I've got a great new place picked out--unless you have a favorite."

"No. New is good." She turned from the refrigerator and put the chain of a small bag across her shoulder. "You know, it's been a m-m-month *of new* for me. Let's keep it rolling." Then she finally glanced up with those intense eyes and smirked, while my heart lurched just a little bit.

I reopened the door for her and said, "Yeah, let's get to it."

Outside, I glanced around at the dancing lights in the trees. "It's beautiful here. Really nice."

"Yes, M-Mother certainly knows how to enhance the holidays." After I opened the passenger door of my truck, Violet slid up into the high seat with ease.

I came around, got in and started the engine. I glanced at her profile, with her eyes staring straight ahead. "I'm really glad we're finally doing this, Violet."

"You mean having *a date*?"

I turned the truck around and drove down the winding drive, trying not to laugh. "Yes, having *a date*. What is your obsession with that particular word?"

"Truth?" she said, twisting her hands in her lap.

"Of course, the truth."

"You're going to think I'm s-some kind of weir-weirdo."

"Good, I like weird." I turned on Lawther Road and headed south.

A long sigh came out. "I'm twenty-four. This is the first d-date I've been on since I was six-six-sixteen. Lexi, my speech therapist, and I made a list of things we hoped I could acco-accomplish this year. Making new friends was one. Hosting a p-party was two. And going on a date with a nice guy was three. That's three things I've done this m-month. Stupid right?"

I reached my right arm over and gave her shoulder a quick squeeze. "I think it's amazing. Hmm, so I qualified as a nice guy? I like that. Thanks for letting me know; a lot of people wouldn't be so honest. Oh, and don't forget adding public speaking at the BUD event. You were great...well...after the vomiting part."

"Thanks, I suppose we can give that p-performance an honorable mention. Honestly, none of that would have ever come off without your help."

"Vi, when you asked me to speak at that, I *really* didn't want to. But you guilted me into it and here we are tonight. Worked out pretty well, I think."

"Yes. I'm happy we're friends."

Ugh. Friends. Nothing wrong with friends, but let's face it. It was every guy's nightmare refrain: *I just like you as a friend.* Hopefully I wasn't just a check mark on Lexi's list.

We rode the elevator to the top floor of a new downtown hotel. I'd heard great things about their restaurant's Asian fusion cuisine. Walking in, Violet seemed enthralled by the wall-to-wall windows showcasing the city below. With child-like exuberance, she said, "It's gorgeous here. Let's get a good table by the windows."

We started with cocktails. I opted for Dewars and water and Violet ordered a Napa Cabernet. We clinked glasses, then Violet immediately averted her eyes and looked out the large window. To fill the awkward silence, I said, "I guess we have BUD and Blaze to thank for bringing us to this point. Remember...You were jogging up the hill as Blaze made a mad dash toward you."

"Actually, I was s-s-so scared by that. I've never been around dogs much. But that was the day I decided to get a dog. For company and pro-protection."

I had to laugh. "And what kind of guard and running partner did you get? A dachshund!"

She started laughing uncontrollably too. "I know. A guard dog who can only pr-protect me from the ankles down." She picked up her napkin and dabbed her eyes. "But she's so sweet. It's been wonderful having a pet. I can't be-believe I never had one before."

"Yeah, I get it. Blaze has gotten me through some dark times these last few months. They're so intuitive, aren't they?"

"Yes, and for me, it's such a realization that I can be re-responsible for someone else. I'd always doubted that. And, if no one else is around, Cocoa's always there to offer up that undying look of lo-lo-love." Violet finally turned and looked at me, while taking a sip of her wine. "At least that's how it feels. She's pro-probably just staring me down, hoping for one last doggy treat."

With the aid of the waiter, we decided on five small dishes, wanting to sample a variety. Vi loved the spicy and hot, while I leaned heavily on the more traditional meat dishes. I wasn't sure if it was the low-lighting, the view, the conversation, or the food, but when we finished, I thought this was one of my favorite meals in years. Everything went perfectly and I wasn't ready for it to end. I suggested, "How about coffee and dessert somewhere else?"

She nodded her head eagerly and smiled. "Yes! Sugar and caffeine. A gr-great way to end the night."

Before leaving, I leaned across the table, touching one of Violet's hands. "I hope this doesn't sound too over-the-top, but you look beautiful against this backdrop. How about a commemorative selfie for us."

"Really? I'm not big on photos."

"Don't you know how stunning you are?" I pulled the phone out of my jacket pocket and pushed my chair over to her side of the table. Within seconds of my phone appearing, our attentive waiter insisted on taking the photo and whisked the phone away. I put my arm across her shoulders, bringing our heads closer together, as the waiter snapped a few pics. I felt her body immediately tense up as I touched the soft, luxurious knit of her sweater.

If we were ever going to get close, I realized I would need to take things slowly.

CHAPTER 40

Serving Up a Slice of Heaven

VIOLET

As the waiter took our photo, Turner's strong arm wrapped around my shoulders. Was it possible to swoon in a photo? My body was shaking and I'm sure the pictures would reveal I closed my eyes during most of the shots. What I really wanted was to place my head on Turner's soft wool jacket, nestle in between the crook of his shoulder and neck, and continue to lay my head there for a blissful minute or two. *Don't do it, Violet--highly awkward and much too catlike for restaurant behavior.*

Unfortunately, my fantasy was crushed immediately when Turner had to maneuver inside his jacket pocket to retrieve his credit card for the waiter. But he'd asked me about having coffee and dessert...so I hadn't totally blown the date. At least he wasn't claiming stomach aches and the need to skedaddle. Thanks for *that* recurring memory, Collin Wentworth!

Now it was my turn; I assumed Turner was going to put the ball in my court, asking for my favorite chic place for dessert and coffee. OK, this was a perfect one to lob over to Mother, but calling her for venue advice while on a date was out of the question. Especially after deciding on my intended emancipation only this afternoon. Oh yes!...the Violet and Rosie move. It was another topic of conversation that would fill a minute or two.

While Turner waited to sign the check, I announced, "I have news. Rosie and I have decided to find a two-bedroom pl-place together. It's been almost four months since I moved into the guest house. Time to find my own place."

"I don't know... Free rent, amazing location, lux little place. Hard to beat that."

"Yeah, and I'll really mi-miss that pool, but it's time. When I mention to people that I live at my mother's house, I f-f-feel like such a kid. But, even worse, *she* makes me feel that way."

The waiter brought back the card and Turner signed off. "Makes sense. So, is this another item from your therapist's list?"

"No. This one's all m-mine. I've been considering places for a little while. There're some new apartments close to the lake which look prom-promising. Rosie and I are checking places tomorrow morning. Any re-recommendations?"

He shrugged and put away his wallet. "Not really up on the rental scene. But watching the news, I know rents have gone through the roof. So--where's our next stop?"

I knew this was coming. What to suggest? I hesitated a few seconds, thinking. "Umm, do you love pie? Particularly choc-choc-chocolate-bourbon-pecan pie?"

"Twist my arm; I might be persuaded."

"I know *the* best p-pie shop. It's my strongest addiction, hands down."

Turner stood up and took my hand. "I can think of a few worse ones. Unless maybe you're eating the whole pie by yourself."

"Oh my God, did you install a spy-cam in my k-kitchen?" I stood up laughing and continued to hold on. Is that how this worked? I'd hold his hand until he dropped it. I glanced at my watch. "We have time if we hurry. They close at ten on Saturdays."

"Alright, calm down, Vi, before you get the shakes. So, you know their weekend schedule and you're starting to sweat. You're seriously hooked." We walked to the elevator and he pressed down.

"A S-Slice of Heaven, that's the name. It's just a hole in the wall I discovered in South Dallas."

Arriving at his parked truck, Turner broke hand-to-hand contact when he opened the passenger door. *Another personal best! At least three continuous minutes holding a man's hand.*

"Slide in Ms. Violet. Heaven awaits."

By the time we arrived, it was ten minutes before closing. Their neon sign was blinking and time was ticking, but I hated to rush a good pie experience. As we walked in, I could tell the shop was clearly in lock-up mode. Their five little tables were wiped down with the chairs stacked on top, and the shelves behind the glass counter were pretty bare. Hearing the door buzz, a friendly baker walked out.

She greeted me with a smile, leaning against the counter. "Well, hi there. You're late today." *Yes, I admit, my pusher and I were becoming friends.*

Turner glanced at me with a big grin. "Man, you weren't kidding."

I leaned down looking at what was left, not seeing my favorite. "Any of that wonderful choc-chocolate bourbon pecan left?"

"Sorry, no. Oh, wait a second." She returned after a minute and said, "I do have two in the freezer, made earlier today. You could defrost it in your oven or use the microwave for about ten minutes."

Without hesitation, I looked at Turner and said, "We'll take one pie. My treat. Do you have a microwave and coffee at your place? Rosie's sleeping, so I'd hate to wake her."

He shrugged his shoulders. "Sure."

While driving over to Turner's house, I had to admit that tonight was a real highlight. We had a wonderful dinner, stutter-light conversation, my hand was held from table to car, I'd just bought the best pie ever, and soon...I'd be sharing coffee at a *date's* home. And the night was still young!

We pulled up in the drive of a nice split-level ranch with a second story. As Turner unlocked, he said, "Sorry for the mess. Sally, my housekeeper, hasn't been in since Wednesday. That's the one day I should invite guests, it goes downhill from there."

We were greeted by the sound of nails clicking down the tiled entryway. "Hey boy. How you doing?" He ruffled Blaze's ears and neck affectionately. "You remember, Violet, boy? Sorry, he'll probably give you a sniff or two. Or wants in on that pie."

"Hi Blaze." I gingerly touched his head a couple times. "Show me the way to your microwave." Turner turned on the light leading from the den to the open kitchen area. After he quickly tossed a take-out food bag, an old newspaper, and some paper cups, the kitchen counter was decently tidy. I glanced around "I like your place. It's sp-spacious."

"Thanks. We always planned to update but never got around to it. But now...I may put it on the market. It's a little big for one person."

"It looks so comfy. I'd give it some time before you decide."

"Yeah, I guess. That's what everyone says, but the vibes... my ex is everywhere here."

"Your ex? That sounds odd." I glanced at the kitchen shelves and pulled out a plate, then slid the pie onto it for the microwave.

"Lately, that's how I see Allie. More as an ex. I'll explain over coffee. Let me start a pot."

"Actually, I'll have tea, if you have any. Doesn't k-k-keep me awake like coffee does."

He walked to the pantry and began searching. "Yeah. Allie liked tea too. There's still a box of decaf green tea?"

"P-Perfect."

"You know, if you're not having coffee, I think I'll pour myself a little glass of bourbon. Sounds great with the pie, right? Want to join me?"

"I'll stick with tea."

After the boiling and beeping, we were ready for our post-dinner *piece de resistance*. We settled onto a comfy leather sectional with paper napkins, forks, and plates. I first took a sip of hot tea and then a tasty bite of pie. Initially, I tasted the lightest buttery crust, then my tongue touched over crunchy pecans congealed in a bath of alcohol-infused chocolate which blended with brown sugar and molasses gooey goodness. "I've never de-de-defrosted one of their pies before. What do you think?"

Turner put down his glass of bourbon and quickly took a bite, letting it move around slowly in his mouth before swallowing. He nodded, saying, "You picked a winner, Vi. We've got ourselves a little slice of heaven."

I took another taste, savoring it. "Oh good. So glad you like it." *Maybe this pie would bind us together? Dessert addicts secretly indulging in tandem.*

Turner looked at me, examining my face. He picked up his napkin and leaned over, dabbing my upper lip. I dodged the incoming hand for a half-second, not used to the close invasion of personal space. *Violet...just let go.*

He smiled and backed off, "Oops sorry, a bit of pie managed to escape you." And just like that... he leaned in and gave me a soft, little kiss. "Ah, there. Much better."

A kiss! All these years wondering how it would feel, how it would occur, how awkward I might make it...and boom...it happened and it was so simple, pleasant, thrilling even!

Then Turner asked, "What about me? Any pie residue that needs removing?"

"I can try." I leaned in closely, forcing myself to stare into his eyes, and nodded. "S-S-Seems like there's quite a lot; it may take awhile." I reached up and softly held his face and kissed him back, holding on a little longer than he had. This was wonderful; all I'd read about, studied, and then some. Sharing something intimate with someone special. Lips touching, teeth somewhat involved, and then some warm tongue interaction. "All good now," I said while dabbing his lips with my napkin. "Th-that was nice."

I picked up my tea cup and my eyes linked with Turner's. He softly said, "You're mesmerizing, Violet. You're just sucking me in."

Then I reached over and tried out another kiss. This one became more exploratory. In fact, it was exhilarating. The scientist in me came out. I wanted to investigate all available territory with my mouth. His lips were soft and warm but I moved on. I brushed my lips on his cheeks, feeling a slight bristle from his shave of several hours ago. I liked that and I felt my stomach lurch about, or perhaps that sensation came from somewhere a little lower.

Then Turner reciprocated, kissing my neck and clavicle. It was intense, with my pleasure meter inching toward red. All those dumb love stories and romance books...I suddenly got it. But looking down at my crew-neck mohair sweater, I had to laugh, thinking, *Nope, no bodice ripping tonight. And, what was a bodice anyway*?

Turner softly brought my hair over my shoulder and touched it. "It's beautiful, your hair. So shiny. He then dove in for another neck kiss, nuzzling my skin, as his hands began to explore further down. He whispered, "You smell so good too."

Then Blaze walked in and nosed his way between us, batting his tail back and forth. We both reached over to pet him, our heads bumping together as we laughed. Turner softly said, "Hey guy, don't be jealous. Honestly...Blaze misses Allie so much. You probably remind him of her. She was the one who spent the most time with him. Both he and I went through weeks of depression after she died. Quite a tailspin."

He sighed and looked up again. "Sorry, don't mean to dwell on that. Look, I may as well fill you in so you know what you might be getting into. That is...if you're interested."

"Sure. I feel like I re-really don't know you that well." He put his arm around my shoulder and pulled me closer, while Blaze relented and sat down by our feet.

"Yeah, I guess we've never discussed Allie." He stared across the room, as if lost in his own thoughts. "She died in early September. I was just numb; lost, confused, and feeling incredibly guilty. Guilty for not paying enough attention to her, for not making the most of our relationship these past few years, for spending so much time with work, maybe for putting off having a kid for as long as we did."

Turning back to me and looking down, he continued. "I don't know; when someone close to you dies, your mind goes through so many *what-ifs* or *I-should'ves*. Kind of drives you crazy."

"I understand. After my dad died, I always regretted not spending more time with him. Still bothers me a lot, after ten years."

Turner nodded back. "Violet, I haven't told anybody about this, but I got a big wake-up call that first month after her death. I received a voice message from an attorney Allie had hired. A reminder about a payment owed. Before she died, maybe before she realized her cancer was back, she had decided to divorce me, but never said anything. I was totally blown away when I read the divorce packet, which I'd apparently signed for at some point, and then stacked it on my desk along with a hundred other items I was ignoring at the time. I can't begin to describe the emotion and amount of Scotch I went through."

"Wow, what a shocker!"

"And it only got worse after I discovered she'd been having an affair for a couple years."

My hands flew up to my face in surprise. "Oh! S-So that was Kevin?"

"Yes, and I was clueless when I'd met him a few months back. And then to see him at your party last night, acting like nothing had happened... I guess all my anger, disappointment, frustration--everything just poured out of me in one big punch."

"I'm s-s-sorry. Guess I over-reacted about that. The coincidence of him being there is so crazy."

He nodded and was silent for a moment. "So, not to dwell on this, but as much as I felt guilty and sad about Allie's death, after realizing the truth about her deceit and subterfuge--I've now come to think about her as an *ex*. I know, it's all very confusing. It's still coming together for me."

I shrugged, knowing I was without experience or perspective. "Hmm. R-Relationships; they're so daunting, aren't they?"

Suddenly, I heard my phone playing *Bad to the Bone*, my ringtone for Mother's calls. "Sorry, that's my phone in the kitchen, but I'm going to ignore it. Shall we try again?" I asked, turning slightly, while putting my arms around his shoulders. Our faces were drawn together. Soft lips, breathing in heady after shave, intriguing tongue, my hands were now running through his trimmed hair, pulling him even closer. I couldn't believe this was me, on the advance, and loving every second. I couldn't help but think of my freshman year fencing class--parry and thrust, advance, advance, step back. Fantastic, what a dance!

Then, a few minutes later, *Bad to the Bone* started up again. Followed by a ping, as a text came through.

Exasperated, I pulled back. "Sorry, guess I should check that."

"Whoever *Bad to the Bone* is, they sound ominous."

"Yeah, she is."

I went to the kitchen and listened to Mother's ranting message:

"Violet...I can't believe this! Saw your light on and your car parked out front so I came by to ask about some gift ideas. Anyway, I glanced in and who do I see? That Mexican girl, Rosie or Rosarita or whoever...sitting on your couch in her pajamas all by herself, right after I had forbidden you to have her stay with you. How could you? And where are you? No telling what she may have stolen already! I asked her...

I had to click off her voice mail. I couldn't listen to it any more. Then I checked the text. It was from Rosario.

So sorry to interrupt your date, but your Mother just came into the guesthouse and asked what I was doing here and then left, slamming the door. I didn't know what to say, but she seems very mad. Please call!!!

I wanted to scream in frustration. What terrible timing! Why now? My big chance at romance dashed by Mother. My second thought was to ignore the call and text and do what I wanted to do for a change--go back to making out with Turner. But I couldn't leave Rosie dangling with Mother hyperventilating and making threats.

I walked into the den and threw my phone on the couch in anger. "Turner. I need to go. Trouble brew-brewing back at the homestead."

He nodded with a smirk, "*Bad to the Bone* acting up?"

"Afraid so."

"You didn't even get to finish your slice."

I asked, "Can you save the rest of the pie? I pr-promise our next dessert will be drama-free. I de-definitely liked where this was going."

"Well, a little drama is good, but I'd say we already had a full weekend of it. Let's get you home, and we'll reschedule a re-do soon."

We both stood up and he embraced me with both arms, as I laid my head on the soft jacket, in the crook of his neck and shoulder, for real this time. It was the warmest, safest spot I'd felt in a long while. I was almost purring.

CHAPTER 41

The Good, the Bad, and the Crazy

ROSARIO

One quick glance from Violet's mother let me know she was not happy. There was no warm welcome, not even an attempt at faked civility, only anger and fear in her eyes. I was the new Mexican immigrant invading her territory. If I was planting pansies in her countless pots, or cleaning up in her big fancy kitchen--¡*No hay problema*. But spending the night with her daughter in the precious glass box--out of the question! It wasn't so much what she said, but how she said it.

Before she came in, I hadn't been able to sleep and went downstairs to watch television and turned on a lamp. The door opened slightly, and she poked her head in. She glanced about anxiously, stepped inside, then demanded, "Where's Violet and who are you?"

I tried to remain calm, explaining. "Rosario Guzman, ma'am. A friend of Violet's. We work together...at BUD." Then there were no words from Mrs. Hill, as I watched the color of her face turn from white to red to purple.

"Uh, she invited me to stay over. But later, she went out."

"Out? With *you* here? Leaving you with the run of the house? I don't understand." She looked panicked, calling Violet on the phone and yelling, and then slammed the door behind her.

I could hear her ranting on the phone as she crossed the yard to the big house. Within minutes of me texting Violet, she replied, letting me know she was returning soon and not to worry. I turned off the TV and went back upstairs. Would her mother now not allow Violet to get an apartment with me? I was sure she would hate that idea.

Just this afternoon, everything had sounded so promising. A chance at renting a nice fresh place, maybe meeting some new friends, and leaving behind loneliness and fear of Victor. Now these plans were probably broken because of Violet's mother. I'm sure she thought I wasn't good enough or smart enough for her daughter.

Back in bed, I heard Roberto's voice laughing at me. *Come on Rosario, are you letting some old, rich bitch defeat you? That was nothing. Less than nothing! Forget about it. You're going to work hard at that garden job you got, get a promotion, find a decent place to live, smile and show your best self. You'll see--the world will come to you. Endurance, beauty, brains--you always had that in spades. Man, you gotta live for the both of us; I'm with you, mi hermanita.* I loved it when my brother spoke to me. I wished I could see his face, feel him nudging my shoulder, pushing me along. I missed him so much, and he was right. As usual.

Violet's mother had the wrong impression of me. So what? I only needed to change that impression or, better yet, quit worrying about what she thought of me. Who cares? Things would work out. I sat up in the king-size bed and waited for Violet's return. Too hyped up to sleep, I began looking through the only reading material on the nightstand, Vi's exciting collection of gardening magazines.

Around midnight, I heard the door open as Violet called out to me. I replied, "I'm still awake. Up stairs." Violet came up and sat on the edge of the bed. I immediately began apologizing. "I'm so sorry I texted you. I hated ruining your date. I just needed to tell you about your mother. She seemed very angry."

"No worries. I already st-stopped in and talked it out with her. It'll all blow over. She'll find something new to occupy her mind within twenty-four hours. She's k-kind of like CNN."

"What are you saying...CNN?"

"Oh, n-nothing. I think she's nervous because she's starting to lose control. Of me. You think she'd be re-relieved. What a joke--I'm twenty-four and still f-falling in line and marching to her drum."

I was sitting up, my knees raised under the covers, my head against the padded headboard. "Hey Vi--no matter how old we get, we're still our mother's little girls. They want to protect us. My mother is the same. Believe me."

After saying that though, I realized our roles were almost reversed. Although both our mothers were now widows, my mother really counted on me for her meager income and had been almost absent from my life once I turned seventeen. Violet, on the other hand, was trying hard to extract herself from the flypaper of her mother's control and all the fancy stuff that came with it. I realized that nothing was ever as easy and wonderful as it appeared.

Violet nodded back. "I guess you're right. So--still ex-excited about looking for an apartment together?"

"*Si*! And your mother? What did she say?"

"I'll tell her after we sign a lease. One issue p-per day is all I can handle. With Mother, you have to know when to pick your b-b-battles."

A sense of relief flooded over me. "Now, tell me all about your date. I'm excited for you, girl!"

"All went sur-surprisingly well. Hold on a minute." Violet grabbed her PJ's, cleaned up in the bathroom, and came in and looked down at me. "There's p-plenty of room in this bed. Scoot over. One night on the couch was enough."

I rolled over and patted the spot on the other side. Violet got in and leaned back with her knees scrunched up. She looked over at me excitedly, like a little kid, and said, "Turner and I had the b-best kiss *ever*. Actually several." Then she laughed. "That sounds stupid, right? How w-would I even know what a good kiss is? It was my *f-first* kiss. But so magical, Rosie! I can't believe it."

I had to laugh at her exuberance. "For real? Oh Vi--you've got it bad. Tell me every detail. And start at the beginning."

~

Sunday morning, we reheated the last of the tacos from Friday's party, while coffee got us motivated early to check out apartment complexes. Once we drove up and parked in the garage of a complex Vi liked, I could tell the rent here would be too high. And once inside, I wanted to move in so badly it hurt. The two bedroom apartment had big bedrooms on either side of the living area and a really large kitchen. Each bedroom had its own bath, and the closets were almost as large as my current apartment. From the living room we could look down to a pretty aqua pool and the lake view was just beyond that. In addition, the complex was located on the bus line and less than a mile from BUD.

Violet immediately asked the property manager about costs: rent, monthly bills, deposit. Even split between us, the rent was way more than I was currently paying, but I might be able to swing it if I continued working at least two extra event shifts every week. My mind quickly calculated the cash flow.

But the downside came when the apartment manager announced that the contract required a first full month's rent, and a last month's rent up front, *with* a hefty deposit. And it required renters insurance, which I'd never had before. In addition, if we didn't sign today, she said the rates fluctuated and could go up as early as tomorrow. This was crazy--I had no savings or even a bank account. Any extra I made always went to my mother. I picked up the brochure, thanked the agent, and told Violet we needed to keep looking.

Walking back to her car, Vi said, "I loved that place. It's wonderful."

"Violet, I have *no* extra money. When I moved to my current place, I paid the guy the first month's rent--that was it, *and* the bills are all paid. But of course, look where I live. That's how they keep the place filled and they rarely make repairs. They know everybody there is living payday to payday and no one can afford to move."

Violet said, "We can look a little more, but my guess is that most pl-places of this caliber are going to be priced similarly."

"Well, Ms. Violet, we just have to lower our caliber."

"Look, I have a trust fund I can dip into occasionally to cover the upfront costs and insurance. If I cover that, can you make the monthly rent?"

This was a very generous offer. I realized Violet was short on friends and really wanted out of her mother's too-perfect home, but I felt guilty about having her pay all the extra costs. I considered this for a few seconds. "Yes. *If* I can work extra shifts, I can afford the rent with a little left to send to my mother. But hopefully, when my review comes up, I could start paying you back. My goal is to open a savings account."

"Good plan. OK. Let's check out at least a few more pla-pla-places. Unless they're substantially cheaper, I really love this place."

At our third stop, we found *the one*. It was more reasonable, a little older and less expensive, but the floor plan was similar and the view was still great. One bedroom was substantially bigger than the other. We opted for the lower rent, the less shiny fixtures, and I insisted on taking the smaller bedroom. But it was heaven compared to my old place. We left with smiles plastered across our faces, even though I had to return to my old apartment and stay there another month. That would be the hardest part. I was on a month-to-month lease with my landlord, so I needed to give him notice as soon as our contracts and references were approved.

Back at my place, Violet helped me carry back the belongings she'd packed yesterday. I insisted on leaving her house today. I wanted no further run-ins with her mother. She was too scary. As Vi got ready to leave, I assured her, "It'll be fine. I've managed to live here over a year without problems."

"Well, if anything comes up, call me and that p-police officer's card is on your bed. See you at work tomorrow, roomie."

"What is roomie?" Violet just rolled her eyes at me and waved goodbye.

Once inside, I couldn't stand to look at the graffiti. I had to repaint, immediately. The place was so little, it wouldn't take too long. There was a small hardware store about four blocks away. I grabbed my purse and left. As I walked down the busy main road, a familiar white car honked and then pulled over. It was Nico, again. I had dismissed him after Victor and I had hooked back up, foolishly thinking Victor was the better choice. Nico was nice, but I'd decided he was definitely not the one. But he seemed to keep popping up.

I leaned into his open window. "Hello Nico, it's been a little while. How are you?"

He ran his hand through his thick curls, looking nervous. "I'm OK. Can I give you a lift?"

Something about his mood or tone seemed off. "You know, Nico, I really need the exercise. I'm only going a few blocks, but thanks."

"Well, can we talk? I need to speak to you. Actually, I stopped by your place this morning. You weren't there."

Still leaning in the car window, I said, "Yes... I stayed with a friend. What is it?"

Nico looked around at the busy traffic. "Can we go somewhere and talk?"

"No. Look, there's a bus bench on the corner. Park your car and we can talk there, but hurry. I've got things I need to do." It wasn't just my imagination, he *was* acting strange. And he'd always been so calm and playful. I walked over to the bus bench, and waited impatiently. I felt I owed him at least a conversation since he had come to my rescue after the robbery attempt at the lavanderia.

He turned into a parking lot and walked over. When he sat down, he looked at the pavement and kept punching his fist into his hand. "OK Nico, start talking now or I'm leaving. I don't like the way you're acting."

"It's because I feel so bad."

I was shaking my head, exasperated with him. "What the hell, Nico. What did you do?"

CHAPTER 42

Take Me Out to the Ball Game

TURNER

Sunday, normally my day for drinking, wandering about the house aimlessly, and binge-watching old movies. This Sunday, though, I was finding it hard not to let my mind drift back to last night and wallow in the pleasant afterglow of my time with Violet. It was such a long time since I'd felt excited about someone.

Was it only sexual arousal...curiosity? Or maybe that thing about her eyes, once I finally got her to look at me. She was so different, surprising and bright about so many things, but totally out of touch in other fairly common spheres. But I enjoyed her odd and almost innocent enthusiasm; and caught myself smiling thinking about her.

I was sitting at the kitchen counter, staring at the front page of the Wall Street Journal, reading the latest about the impending rail workers strike. And I was smiling? Very strange. Even this potential economic pile-up wasn't letting my gray cloud of doom rain over my current happiness.

Mondays were normally one of my volunteer days at BUD, but I knew tomorrow I needed to follow-up with all departments at Rapid Logistics regarding the rail strike. I'd have to let Violet know I wouldn't be able to come in. Or maybe I was just looking for an excuse to call her.

While I was contemplating our conversation, Blaze wandered into the kitchen for his afternoon treat. I tore open a new box of synthesized bacon-wrapped chews and threw one up and over to him. Blaze calculated the distance and snapped it up like a major league first baseman.

"Good job, boy." He looked up at me hoping for more, but I decided to engage him in conversation. "So, what do you think? Is it too soon for me to call her? I'm falling way too quickly, right? I could text ...but I'd rather call."

He barked twice in response. "Yeah, you're probably right. Let's take a walk and think about it. We both need the exercise." I bundled up in a lined zip sweater, baseball cap, and gloves. It was down to the low-forties but the sun was still out. I grabbed Blaze's favorite ball and we headed to the lake.

I decided to purposely circumvent the dog park for a while, wanting to avoid another run-in with Kevin. His deceptive long-term affair with Allie broke my heart *and* angered me, but at this point, it wasn't worth further escalation. I'd made my feelings known clearly Friday night. For me, it was done and in the past.

We headed over to a wide swath of grass along the jog and bike trail for a game of repetitive toss-and-retrieve, with Blaze scoring all the points. I watched him running, dodging, and fetching, thinking that I'd be in a lot better shape if I was a dog.

About twenty minutes in, I couldn't help but notice a pair of shapely, long, muscular legs running past me in a pair of fitted black running shorts, topped with a loose gray sweatshirt and a knit cap pulled over a long dark ponytail. *Wait, I know those legs!* My heart skipped a beat or two, as I called out, "Violet! Wait up. Violet!" This was strange; somehow the universe kept throwing us together. Violet turned, smiled, waved at me, and then continued running. Well, maybe not.

I could chase after her, but there was no way I was keeping up with that pace. She looked happy to see me, but apparently, not happy enough for a conversation.

About fifteen minutes later, I put the leash back on Blaze and we headed down the sidewalk, before crossing the road to walk back through my neighborhood. As we were about to cross, I saw Vi and her forward stride heading back our way. I stopped and waited. This time she'd have to stop; there would be no drive-by wave. As she approached, Blaze began barking and pulling against his leash, but I yanked him back, keeping him close.

Stopping, in a halting, breathy voice she asked, "Turner. Hello. Are you guys following me?" Then her face broke into a grin while laughing. Vi's face was scrubbed clean with a natural glow, her cheeks bright pink from exertion, with a dewy sheen of sweat above her lip, and all I could think about was kissing that exact spot.

"We're not following you. We're headed home. Blaze and I were just getting in some exercise."

"Looked like Blaze was running harder than you." Ouch, a direct hit, but she said it with an endearing smile.

"Hey, we can't all be racehorses like you. Are you done for the day?"

She checked her watch for distance and said, "I still have a mile to go, but I could be persuaded. I have hot chocolate and cookies at my place." I gave her a non-committal look. "Or maybe beer and chips?"

I nodded. "Blaze loves chips." I put my arm around her shoulder and we crossed the street and headed up the hill over to her place. At the gate entrance, Vi pressed her electronic key and the two iron gates slowly opened. Glancing up the driveway, I noticed Suzanne's black Range Rover parked in front. "Looks like *Bad-to-the-Bone* is home," I said with a laugh. "You OK with her after last night?"

"I guess. Mother had stopped by to talk to me and found Ro-Rosario alone at my place. She was so upset. She had ex-explicitly told me earlier that Rosie could not stay with me. Of course, I ignored her and that dr-drives her nuts."

"Yeah, parents are like that. My dad still calls every few days to remind me of everything I'm doing wrong with my own company. You gotta love it though."

"I don't know...I can't imagine what she'll sp-spout out when I tell her Rosie and I just si-signed a lease together. We found a great apartment this morning. M-Mother has no idea, but I'll have to let her know soon."

As we walked past the big house with its massive columns, we both started talking softer as if Suzanne Hill had her ear pressed to a window and was listening in.

"Hope she gives me a thumbs-up," Turner whispered. "Did you tell her we went out last night?"

"Yes. She seems to approve. That's what eventually c-calmed her down last night. I told her I had to leave R-Rosie at my place because you'd asked me to dinner and I didn't want to cancel."

"I wonder if she thinks I'm too old for you?"

"My Dad was fif-fifteen years older than her." Then she paused for a second and added, "Although currently, she seems to be dating younger. Testing out her c-cougar moves, I guess. Anyway, I don't really care much what she thinks. I'm d-done trying to do things to make her happy. I'm just gonna be me and stop trying to twist myself into a pretzel to please her."

Walking through Vi's door, I said, "Good for you. I like this sense of independence."

The yapping of Cocoa immediately greeted us. I held tight to Blaze's leash as the two pets sniffed each other out and eventually decided on a territory truce. Violet went to the fridge and pulled out a bottled beer for me and poured herself a glass of wine. She glanced at her watch and announced, "I suppose we're well into happy hour now. Cheers!"

I followed her to the kitchen and clinked my bottle against her stemmed glass. After a long draught, I looked down into her face. "I'm glad we ran into each other. I'm about to make an uncharacteristic admission. I spent most of the day thinking about you, and then, out of the blue, you ran right past me. There's got to be a reason we keep coming together, right?"

Vi appeared to think this over for a few seconds. "Well, we b-both live less than a mile from each other, like to r-run or walk, and you volunteer where I work. Seems pretty l-logical that we would."

"Man...way to take the serendipity out of it, Violet. Mind if I kiss you before you totally suck the magic from this moment?"

Her eyes immediately looked down as she said, "No, I wouldn't mind."

I lightly lifted her chin with my finger and tilted her face towards mine. Hints of Cabernet and Dos Equis mingled together in an enjoyable taste as her warm lips melted with mine. Explosions of pleasure released in my brain as my free hand pulled off her knit cap and my fingers ran through her thick hair.

We eventually broke apart and Violet said, "I guess our date was a s-s-success. I thought about you too. Most of the night. Lexy will be pleased."

"That's certainly my goal; pleasing speech therapists. I hope you don't share *everything* with her."

"No, not everything. Let's move to the couch, I'm sure you're *exhausted* after your dog walk."

"Now you're just being mean," I said with a grin. "I did end up chasing a couple of his balls."

"Doesn't count."

We both took sips of our drinks and then tried out more comfortable positions on the couch. It was a modern looking, low armed sofa, loaded with numerous decorative pillows, looking like something from *Architectural Digest*. It was definitely selected more for style than comfort. As I batted away extraneous cushions, I leaned against the arm of the sofa and Violet turned and scooted onto my lap, putting her arms around my neck, kissing me again deeply.

I was all in. There was nothing else that mattered at that exact moment. No lingering thoughts of Allie, no guilt, no recriminations, no thoughts of work. Only the simple pleasure of her lips on mine and her arms wrapping around my neck, as I held her. I needed to freeze this moment...it was only about me and this delightful woman who was now breathing warmly into my ear.

Wait... awkward. I felt my cock definitely moving and on the rise.

Then she innocently asked, "You're my first l-lap kiss. How was it?"

"Home run, for sure! But lap kisses? I don't think those are really a thing." I moved my upper thighs a bit trying to make an adjustment.

"I'm pretty sure they are."

I gave her a doubtful look, then the ding of a text interrupted a double play. Violet scooted off me, and reached in her back-pocket for her phone, as I grabbed a handy accent pillow and placed it casually on my lap.

"Sorry. Molly said she might call about work." She quickly scanned the message and shrugged. "No. It's just Bad-to-the-Bone." Vi held up her screen, smiled and read it back to me. "She says: 'Violet, if you're still speak-speaking to Turner by Christmas Eve, you should invite him to my Holiday P-Punch Bowl Soiree.' She looked up at me and said, "Guess that means you're in, Turner. She only invites p-p-people that matter."

I nodded back. "So, you're saying if I want to go to *the* party of the season, I have to keep this *talking* thing going with you for another week?"

"That's the deal," she said, setting her phone on the sofa.

I sighed loudly. "OK, I'm a team player. I'll make the sacrifice play." I patted my pillow. "Now let's get back to more of those kisses. I believe you were about to lap those bases."

CHAPTER 43

The Devil Made Him Do It

ROSARIO

I was about to get up and leave the bus stop. Nico was definitely not acting like himself and I wasn't in the mood to tangle with another strange guy. He was so tense and his mind was somewhere else. This was my life...a magnet for weirdos.

"Tell me right now, or I'm walking, Nico."

He looked up and grabbed my hands, while looking into my eyes. "Look, just promise you'll hear me out. I want to explain."

I jerked my hands back from his, grasping my backpack, holding it on my lap like armor. "Go on."

"Remember a few months back, when Bright White got robbed and I came in right after it happened?"

"Of course. Being held at knifepoint by some strung-out addict--not easy to forget. I was grateful you were there."

"That time--after the police left and before your boss came--that was pretty amazing. It was like all the barriers were down between us. We really connected."

"Yes...that part was nice." Where was he going with this? We kissed, made out in the office, and it felt pretty great. But did he forget that his big mouth also got me fired after he and Miguel argued? I would never remember it as a wonderful night.

"Rosie, I just wanted to recapture that feeling. You trusted me, needed me...That night was special. But then, after you started working at BUD, you ghosted me, man. What happened? I tried calling a few times, texting--and then nothing. So Friday night, after dropping off a ride near your place, I knocked on your door."

"I went out Friday night."

"Right, no answer. So anyway, I picked up a few more fares and then met my cousin for drinks. Actually, a *lot* of drinks." He shrugged and sighed. "OK...I got shitfaced. Anyway, around midnight, I got the stupid idea to try and see you again and when you weren't at your place, I just broke in. That lock you had was crap."

After he said that, I thought I'd heard him wrong. I was stunned. It was *Nico* who'd trashed my apartment? Not Victor? I jumped up, shaking with anger and confusion. What could possibly push him to do that? A few unanswered phone calls?

"Why would you *ever* do that, Nico! Are you crazy?"

"It sounds so moronic now. I feel like shit."

"So you were drunk; that's your stupid excuse?"

"Hear me out. Friday night, I got it in my head that when you came home and saw the break-in, maybe you'd call me. You'd feel scared and I'd come in and make you feel safe again, help you put everything back together. But you never called... and by the next morning, waking up in my car with a really bad hangover, I felt so guilty, so incredibly stupid, and honestly, everything sucks right now. I had to tell you."

"This is one of the craziest stories I've heard!" I was standing, gesturing, wanting to leave but also needing to yell at him to release all my frustration.

As my rant winded down, he took a roll of cash out of his shirt pocket. "Here, this is yours. I wanted to make it look like a break-in, so I stole this. It's all there. You can count it. All I can say is I'm truly sorry."

I grabbed the roll of hard-earned cash and stuffed it in my backpack. "Do you know how scared I've been? Walking in on that mess Saturday morning and having to go to work the same day, freaking out about some creep inside my place. Saying you're sorry will *never* be enough!"

The city bus pulled up and its doors opened. Nico waved the bus on, but the driver looked over from his steering wheel and asked me, "You alright, ma'am? Need me to call anybody?"

"*Gracias*. I'm OK." As the bus drove away, I continued, "I don't want your sorry-ass apology. You're going to buy me paint, get me a decent new radio, dishes, new sheets, and a good deadbolt lock. And I want it all *today*."

He stood up, nodding, almost eager. "I already bought the paint stuff. First thing I did when I woke up and remembered what I'd done. I can start painting now; I want to."

"No. I'll do the painting. I don't want you in my place again. You can go to the store and get the radio, sheets and deadbolt." Having him in my place while helping me, would only give him the satisfaction he wanted--becoming the boyfriend coming to my rescue again. I didn't like the way his mind worked.

From his car, Nico brought over a gallon of primer and another of white paint, with a roller and brushes. He almost begged me, "Please. At least let me take these to your apartment."

I picked up both cans with each hand. "I can handle it. Just bring the other stuff back before tonight. Call me when you arrive and I'll pick it up at the curb."

While walking back home, I couldn't decide if I felt better or worse knowing Nico instigated the break-in. It was such a disappointment. In two days, two guys I liked had ended up as vandals or thieves. Was I such a bad judge of character? I saw another side of each of them that I never expected, but at least Nico had the decency to tell me the truth. Victor only came clean once a gun was pressed to his back. But, for Nico to do what he did, told me he also had drinking issues and was hiding a violent temper. I definitely needed to stay clear of that. At the very least, I had my money back, and Victor had hopefully only made idle threats.

Once back inside, I put on an old tee-shirt and began covering the walls with wide white strokes with the roller. With every few strokes of paint, I began to feel better and stronger, as if I was erasing all the negativity still clinging to me. Instead, I kept my mind focused on the modern place I'd be moving to, thinking of it as a new chapter, out of the shadows, living with a good friend in a place I could be proud of. And the best part... I'd soon have a new address that neither Nico or Victor would ever know about.

CHAPTER 44

A Holiday Punch

VIOLET

It was a chilly, damp Monday morning at BUD. Mark's remote speaker blasted out eighties-era rock anthems, while Rosario and I worked alongside Linda Bell, Mark, and Jeffrey. The five of us were crouched down, wearing heavy jackets and thick work gloves with cold drizzle misting our faces while singing along to AC/DC's *Back in Black.* Mark was unsuccessfully doing a reach for the high raspy lead, while we backed him up on the chorus. It was a good thing no one else was around.

We were continuing to build up the rock wall along the path of our garden. The professional wall builders had laid the foundation and now we were following behind them mortaring on layers of limestone rocks over their cement. This was all new to me, but I was enjoying the learning process, much like putting together a massive jigsaw puzzle.

Rosie decided to stop singing and interrogate Mark, "So, not to be all in your business, but how did it go with Molly Friday night when you showed up so late? I bet she was mad, right?"

Mark carefully applied wet mortar across the back of a rock, then pressed it firmly in place. He quit singing and said, "If you're not going to be all in my business, why you asking me about it?"

Rosie stood, stretched and in a teasing voice said. "Come on Mark, I know you want to tell me. I'll tell you how my night ended if you tell me about yours. Promise, it will be our secret."

Linda and Jeff scooted closer, with Jeff nodding, "Don't worry bro, we won't say a word."

Mark rolled his eyes at us as he bobbed his head up and down to a new tune. "First of all, I didn't ignore Molly. I was just fraternizing with other people which is what you're supposed to do at parties. There were some big issues to discuss that didn't involve her. Secondly, she felt tired and left early. Although, I gotta say, she woke up pretty quickly when I knocked on her door. And...I'll leave it at that, but just so you know, she welcomed me with open arms."

I could only chuckle, thinking of head horticulturist Molly in her lacy nightgown getting it on with Mark. Before Mark decided to offer up any more details, I broke in and said, "OK crew, as leader of this mer-merry band, I say that's enough p-personal talk about our supervisor. Anyway Mark...glad your evening ended well. Have you been dating M-Molly for a while?"

"I guess since right after my interview. Seems like we just sort of clicked. But we're keeping it on the down-low." Linda Bell turned an imaginary key to her lips, then threw it away, sealing the door on Mark's secret romance about as securely as the door on Rosie's vandalized apartment.

Rosie proceeded to fill us in on the latest news of her break-in and the surprising admission by Nico, the Uber driver, as the burglar. So, evil Victor hadn't been the culprit after all! My date with Turner couldn't begin to top that story, so I didn't bring it up. Plus, I didn't want anyone making comments about us when Turner volunteered at BUD.

Besides, I didn't know how to define what we were doing. Was it a relationship? Did one dinner date and several kisses mean I had a boyfriend? Was I jumping to conclusions? I had no idea how any of this worked and I didn't want to make assumptions. Best to keep quiet about it so nobody would feel sorry for me when it all fizzled out.

Close to lunch time, Molly came by to check on the wall and

evaluate our work. She walked up and down the path in her black rubber boots, much like a military commander examining the ranks, checking the wall's current status and the tree plantings we'd completed earlier. She stood back with her hands on her hips with a pronouncement. "Looking good, Team Xeriscape! I'm glad I decided on this plan. It's all coming together. Violet, may I have a word please."

Interesting. She wanted nothing to do with my original drawings of this garden and now it's become *her* plan. She turned and walked up the hill as I followed along. "I understand Turner is still lining up the buy on the longhorn sculptures? Try to get an update from him soon."

"Sure, Molly. And the windmill? He thought that would look great at the bottom of the hill and it can be used to pump the water back into the rainwater receptacles at the top. He has the windmill, but only needs BUD to pay for transport."

"Yeah, he mentioned that to me earlier. I don't know...maybe it'll look too busy? Get me a delivery price and I'll get back to you. Now, keep in mind, we're going to schedule a big reveal party for this garden at the end of February. Just about eight weeks away. I've already decided on the date. With the extra money your mother raised, we have the budget for a big society blow-out to introduce the garden. So we need everything on target for completion."

"Got it. Actually, Turner and I r-r-raised that extra money. We came up with the pro-program and pitch."

"Sure, Violet. Whatever."

And you're so welcome, bitch. Oops, these things pop into my head, but rarely make it to my tongue.

"Violet, in addition to this, I'm tied up with two other projects so I'll need you to check on all plant deliveries and schedule everything for completion by mid-February. I'll order all the garden signage details, but I'm counting on you to do the rest."

I nodded, offering up my most competent business face. "We'll be r-ready. We've got a great team here. Everyone's ex-excited to see the end result."

Saturday afternoon was Christmas Eve, commencing with Mother's Holiday Punch Bowl Soiree. It was her annual ritual which included old friends, philanthropic acquaintances, mutual board members, and whoever happened to be on the elusive and exclusive hot-list within Dallas society. It was a four-hour open house event, allowing for guests to come and go, keeping the crew of valet parkers sprinting.

Attending the party as a child, I was generally ignored, except for the occasional pat on the head. I'd eat and drink anything I wanted as I wandered about. But later, into my teen years, I became more wary as guests felt obligated to ask questions and delve into my future plans. I would stammer my way through vague college goals until the guest would nod and make a quick turn, away from the corners where I preferred to hide.

But this year was different. I had a date with a handsome, professional business owner any mother would approve of. And I also had new shoes and a stunning little black velvet strapless number left on my bed, which I had to assume Mother had purchased for me as appropriate party attire. As I tried on the dress, I couldn't help but notice it was once again a perfect fit. She had amazing skills in that arena. Once I moved, I was going to miss these shopping surprises. But, honestly, I was a fully grown adult now...although still a lousy shopper.

I was upstairs anxiously deciding whether to wear my hair up or down. I went for easy and left it down. Turner pulled up to the guest house a little after three, wearing a dark suit and red tie. As I walked downstairs, I gave him a whistle when he walked in the door. "M-Mistletoe-perfect Mister Cooper. Love the red tie."

"Thanks." Then Turner's eyes lit up as he looked me down and then up, from red ankle-strap heels, past the fitted black sheath, to the little diamond studs in my ears. I felt him literally drink me in. "You know...the other day you looked pretty hot in your running shorts and ski cap, but I gotta say, you and that dress are amazing together."

I looked down, embarrassed to meet his admiring eyes, twisting my hands together in front of me. "Give thanks to the shopping pr-prowess of Suzanne Hill. So, are we ready? I'm *really* ner-nervous."

"Why? Isn't this just a bunch of your mother's friends dropping in?"

"Exactly."

Turner held the door open for me and then took my hand, while we walked down the driveway. "No worries, Vi. I'll stay close and we'll drink our way through the evening. It'll be great."

"And there's lots of g-good desserts. I took a sneak peek after the caterers set up."

He lightly kissed my cheek. "See, things are looking up already."

Now for the question that I'd been considering all week...*just blurt it out, Violet.* "So Turner, should I introduce you as my boy-boyfriend?"

He took a second, cleared his throat, and said, "Honestly, this is all coming so soon on the heels of Allie's passing; it might be better to introduce me as your friend or coworker. Do we really need a label? You understand, right? Four months since her death might be rushing it."

"Sure." Why did I ask? I felt so stupid, and of course he was right, or was he? It *wasn't* too soon for dinner and foreplay, but it *was* too soon to have a new girlfriend? I began to feel hot and dizzy. I knew that feeling--often getting a rush to my head after excruciating embarrassment. A few glasses of wine would help.

Turner suggested we enter through the front door, going through the gauntlet of well wishers at the long entrance hall. In the past, I always arrived through the kitchen, went straight to the bar, and found a comfy corner chair to sink into. As we entered, Mother was near the front, with Magna hovering nearby with her headset on. Mother immediately took my shoulders and brushed both cheeks with a faux kiss and whispered in my ear that she was pleased her dress selection looked absolutely wonderful on me.

Then, after guiding my elbow, she turned me toward an elderly couple. "Tom, Whitney... you remember my little daughter, Violet? Isn't she all grown up? Darling, tell them about your amazing work at BUD. They're dying to hear all about it." Then she took Turner's arm, and began walking him toward the bar saying, "And you, my friend, have *got* to try my punch. It's absolutely famous you know..." As he was pulled away, Turner glanced at me and shrugged as I turned and smiled weakly at Whitney and Tom, who couldn't wait to hear the latest on xeriscape gardening. But first, I'd have to explain to them what it was.

I began babbling on, but after my brief garden intro, I noticed Whitney's eyes wandering about looking for a familiar face to move on to. "So, we're very excited about the garden's pro-progress and our grand opening in late February."

Tom nodded, touched my arm and said, "Best of luck to you my dear. I know we've taken up too much of your time. Merry Christmas."

Behind me, I heard Magna speaking into her headset. "Catering...bring on the cranberry and goat cheese canopies, along with the chicken and spinach. High alert... Banquet table being quickly devoured." Then I felt her hand on my shoulder. Magna leaned down and whispered, "Better check on Mr. Cooper before your mother inebriates him with that damn punch."

"I'm on it." I glanced into the dining room as a herd cycled around the massively long mahogany table, picking up fancy hors d'oeuvres on tiny Versace china plates. I remember Mother reminding me once, 'Violet, when hosting cocktail parties, make sure your kitchen staff only uses the bread-and-butter plates. Easy to handle with a drink in hand *and* it will keep your guests from eating all the food too quickly.' Just one more life-affirming lesson Mother had passed on to me.

Not seeing Turner, I moved on. At the far end of the living room near the fireplace, a temporary bar had been set up. With punch glasses in hand, Mother was integrating a circle of men with her arm still wrapped through Turner's. I walked quickly over to rescue him, as I heard her say, "Gentleman, let me introduce you to my handsome new friend, Turner Cooper."

Hmm, was she being kind and friendly to her daughter's possible new boyfriend, or being *overly* kind and friendly. I continued to listen in as she made her introductions. Oh my God; I saw it! She was looking up and giving Turner the Suzanne Hill infamous twinkling *blue-eyed-wink-with-a-half-smile*. I knew that look so well, reserved only for the fortunate few. Did her hand just give his arm a squeeze? Oh...she wouldn't! Or would she?

CHAPTER 45

A Dance and a Glance

VIOLET

There was no other way to put it; my mother was putting the moves on my date. Maybe she just couldn't help herself. It came to her so naturally--feminine wiles she'd been honing for decades. But what did Turner think? Did he like the attention, think she was being overly charming, or bizarrely strange? Would she scare him away? I sensed potential flight risk with my maybe-future boyfriend.

And what could I do about it? This was something new and oddly insidious. With Mother, there was a fine line between being friendly and coming on to a man.

Instead of injecting myself into the group, I retreated to my favorite corner, skirting past my mother's group of men, and sat down on a butter-soft leather armchair. It was located to the left of the bar, next to a set of oak bookcases, a former favorite reading spot. I sat down, holding my spiked punch, with my legs stretched across an ottoman, and decided to see if Turner would soon untangle arms with Mother and come looking for me.

Introductions within their small circle seemed to be complete. Now, it was time for everyone to brag about their latest trip or update the group on recent business exploits. Eventually, Mother chimed in. "Now if any of you gentlemen have major shipping concerns, Turner has his own supply chain company, which I hear is doing quite well."

How did she even know that? She and I had never discussed his business. She only knew he was a donor and volunteer at BUD. Did Mother have Magna do a dossier on him?

Eventually, three of the men broke off and merged with another couple passing by, and the fourth moved on to a woman across the room. It was all like a choreographed dance of social party etiquette--the coming together, the charming small talk, the elusive smooth exit, and then moving on to the next person, which left Mother and Turner temporarily alone with arms still entwined.

I leaned forward, attempting to eavesdrop and catch every word. I distinctly heard Mother say something rather odd. "Now Turner, I know how tough it is getting businesses up and running for entrepreneurs, so if you're *ever* looking for an investor, let's talk more. I love diving into new things with people who have strong skills. I think you'd be a good bet." On a surface level, I guess this sounded somewhat legit, but then again, you could read a lot of *wrong* into those comments. *Mother, what are you doing?* My stomach was doing twists and flips which I was trying to ignore.

Turner looked a little taken aback and then nodded. "Suzanne, I'm honored. Thank you, but I begged and borrowed my way into Rapid Logistics twelve years ago when I was getting started, and frankly, I'm now enjoying being free and clear of that debt." *Oops, sorry Mother, no takers for now.*

She nodded, smiled, broke arm contact, and gave him a shoulder pat. "Certainly. Good for you! But of course, expansion and finding the next big thing is always exciting. Think about it."

"Absolutely." Turner looked about and added, "Well, great party you have going here. Guess I should hunt Violet down. We'll talk again soon, hopefully."

Then she was off, calling out to Bebe Wentworth, who I recognized as Mother's crony and the mother of the dreaded Collin Wentworth. Ugh. I could make a dash to the restroom or continue sitting to see how much longer it would take Turner to find me. We were only six feet away from each other as he returned to the bar for a refill. While waiting his turn, he glanced over, saw me in the dark corner, and walked over.

He crouched down to my level, "There you are. Life of the party, I see. What are you doing here?"

"Just wa-waiting for you. This was always my favorite spot at these parties. Inches away from everybody, but miles away from interaction. By the way, it's a really com-comfortable chair."

Turner grabbed my hand and tugged playfully. "Come on. Get up, little Miss Wallflower. You're way too pretty to sit here by yourself. Besides, there are desserts to devour, remember?"

We both refilled our punch glasses and I made a quick detour. I took a trip to Mother's bathroom, threw up, gargled mouth-wash and returned to Turner, as if everything was normal. I led him into the dining room, explaining the set-up. "Ap-Appetizers, canapes, mini sandwiches, and sliders in here; and desserts are set up in the sunroom. What's your pl-pleasure?" We joined the crowd at the table and picked up our tiny plates.

"I'm really hungry, Vi. Why are these plates so small?"

"One of Mother's par-party philosophies. Yum, you need to try one of these goat cheese things. They're delish." Turner loaded up his plate and mine and then we moved on to the sunroom. I picked up a fruit custard tart and suggested, "We can eat outside. They set up heaters next to the t-t-tables."

On the patio, a few other guests I didn't recognize were sitting amongst the dozen small circular tables placed around four gas heaters. The flagstone deck was lit up with criss-crossing strings of lights, and the holiday music of classic Mariah Carey sang out from speakers placed in the trees.

Stepping to the edge of the patio, Turner took a deep breath. "Love it out here. I know you've grown up with all this, but I hope you appreciate the beauty of this amazing backyard."

"Yeah, I really do." I began to shiver a bit, even with the heaters close by.

"Here, try this." He took off his suit jacket and placed it over my bare shoulders.

It felt warm and oddly comforting. I brought the lapels close to my face and inhaled. "Your jacket smells like you, or a mix of you and your cologne. I like it."

He was halfway through his miniature slider, swallowed the bite, and said, "Glad you approve." After wiping his hands on a napkin, Turner put his arm around my shoulders, gently pulling the two of us closer together, and then he lightly nuzzled my neck. "You smell pretty great too."

I brought up a fork full of fruit tart right as he leaned over for a kiss, and his mouth ran into the creamy custard instead of my lips.

We both laughed as I grabbed my napkin and dabbed the custard from his mouth and cheek. Then I whispered in his ear, "I believe you owe me some dessert."

He leaned in for a quick but intoxicating kiss and grabbed my hand as he stood up. "Dance with me, Violet."

I looked around. Nobody else was dancing and I was terrible at it. I'd taken ballroom dancing in junior high, prepping for a cotillion--a disaster I'd never quite forgotten. A mish-mash of memories involving white cotton gloves, clutching my arms across my chest, and waiting two hours for anybody to ask me to waltz.

"Thanks, but I r-really don't dance."

"It's OK. I'm only looking for an excuse to hold you close while we move around somewhat rhythmically." He tugged at my hand again. "Come on. You'll do fine. Think of it as your Christmas gift to me."

"Alright." I finally gave in and smiled. "Guess that's a fair trade." I stood up in his overly-large suit jacket and wrapped my arms around his neck while he encircled his hands around my waist. Madonna's version of *Santa Baby* floated through the trees as we slowly held each other close, swaying back and forth. After we started dancing, two more couples got up and did the same.

"Look Vi, we're trendsetters." He softly kissed my cheek and said, "I could do this all night."

I closed my eyes thinking, I could do this *and more* all night.

Madonna finished and Nat King Cole was crooning as the sunroom door opened, allowing the loud flow of inside conversations to invade our quiet, magic space. Then I heard Mother's voice,

"Violet, Turner...There you are!" She reopened the door and called inside to guests. "Come on, everyone. There's dancing outside. It's beautiful out here!"

I looked up at Turner with a smirk. "Here we go... M-Mother's holiday punch has officially kicked in. Pre-Prepare for the conga line soon." Bad-to-the-Bone moved onto the patio shimmying her shoulders to *Rockin' Around the Christmas Tree,* followed, like the pied piper, by a string of guests coming through the door. Everyone was picking up the dance pace, while I was still enjoying my up-close-and-personal dance moves while pressing my body against Turner's.

Still clutching him tightly, I heard, "Vi darling, mind if I cut in for just one quick dance. This old song is my favorite."

Really Mother? Find your own partner. Turner looked helplessly down at me and smiled, as I stepped back to our table. She took both of his hands, shifting her weight back and forth as they did a push and pull to the music and smoothly executed an under-the-arm twirl. She was glowing, smiling from ear to ear, as her tawny, perfectly streaked hair flew around her shoulders. Damn, she still had it at fifty...Or was it fifty-two? I was never quite sure, it varied with her stories.

After two more songs, Turner begged off and he was quickly replaced by another willing partner. As he sat down, he said "Man, your mother loves to dance. Guess she didn't pass on that gene."

"No...another item to add to her list of disappointments." I was sitting with my chin in my hand, watching all the activity. "Maybe that's why I took up running, the solitary sport. Anyway...I enjoyed *our* dance. So, if you want, it would pro-probably be acceptable if we crept out of here. We can grab some more food and drinks on our way out the front door."

Turner nodded. "I like that idea."

We both got up to go as I watched Mother do a double twirl under her partner's arm without blinking an eye. Inside, I stacked a few blocks of fudge and cookies on a plate and, before passing the bar, I stepped behind it and pulled out one of several bottles of Veuve Clicquot Champagne stacked inside a bar refrigerator. The bartender started to say something to me, but I put up my hand and said, "It's OK, she's my mother."

As Turner and I exited the front door, we giggled together like two kids sneaking out of the house at midnight. Relief flooded through me as I held up our bottle and smiled, saying, "I'm about ready to pop this cork. How about you?"

CHAPTER 46

Popping the Cork

TURNER

We continued laughing all the way to Vi's door. Probably a mixture of relief after leaving the party, and nervous anticipation for what might lay ahead.

But I was now understanding some of Violet's resentment toward her mother. To me, Suzanne had been playful and friendly in a touchy-feely kind of way, but once she mentioned investing, it began to feel like a bribe. Was she offering to invest for the sake of her daughter, or was she interested in me? Suzanne was an attractive, engaging woman, but surely not? That part was still a little foggy, but the whole scene made me wary. Now, on top of that, was I really ready to take things further with Violet? I felt conflicted.

My arm was still around Vi's shoulder as she unlocked the door of the guest house and we both tumbled onto the sofa in the dark. I landed on my back and Vi followed on top, as we both kissed hungrily for several minutes, exploring with our mouths and tongues, every inch of each other's face and neck. I felt her warm breath in my ear and almost lost it as her hand inched underneath my belted trousers. I hadn't felt arousal like this in a long time.

Maybe there *was* some magic in Suzanne's holiday punch. Vi's hand went tentatively lower to my groin, and began rubbing my penis through my boxers.

I whispered to her, "You sure you want to go there?"

In a breathy, excited voice, she said, "Yes...but let's go upstairs." We unhooked ourselves from each other and Vi got off the couch, locked the door, and grabbed the Champagne bottle. I sat up in a foreplay-daze and squinted as she turned on a light at the kitchen counter. She asked me, "Can you open this b-b-bottle? Somehow, the cork hits me every time."

Vi pulled some flutes from the overhead shelves, while I opened the bottle with a gentle pop and watched a small jet of white foam curl over the edge. At that moment, I knew all my driveway doubts were now being easily overruled. This was going to happen. With the bottle in one hand, I used my other to grab Vi's hand and led her upstairs without conversation.

She flipped on a small lamp next to her bed, while I took the flutes she'd carried and filled one for each of us. We both stood, taking a few sips, while Violet's eyes darted nervously around the room. I turned Vi's body around, placing her back to me. Taking her shoulders and bringing her in close, I leaned down gently, kissing her neck, shoulders, clavicle, and then slowly unzipped her strapless velvet dress, letting it drop to the floor. Vi stepped over it, and then I turned her to face me again. She had on an unexpected and tantalizing matching red lace bra and thong, which left me speechless, as I stared in admiration at her long, slender body, thinking she looked absolutely perfect.

Her eyes immediately dropped to her feet, embarrassed to look up at me. Pointing to the strapless bra, VI said, "M-Mother bought the dress, but this other stuff was all my doing."

I slowly put my finger under her chin and lifted her face. "I'm in awe, honestly. A second excellent gift choice."

She offered up her little smile, while she sat down on the edge of the bed and removed the strappy red heels. "So, you really like it?"

I shook my head and laughed. "Yeah, quite a bit."

Vi scooted back on the bed, leaning against several pillows placed along the headboard, and covered herself with the comforter. Then she pointed at me. saying, "Your turn, Mr. Cooper."

"OK. Just wish I jogged and worked out more lately." All those weeks of binge drinking and laying in bed had left me with a softer and fluffier physique than usual. First my trousers dropped, then I unbuttoned the shirt, pulled off the t-shirt and stood there in my reindeer boxers. "As you can see, I came promoting full holiday spirit tonight."

"Bring Rudolf a little clo-closer pl-please."

I hurried things along, yanking off my socks and taking a final gulp of Champaign. The rubber! I fumbled through the inside pocket of my jacket, and then laid down next to her. As we embraced, I felt the light touch of fingertips moving slowly and softly up and down my back, giving me chills, while I pulled my fingers through her soft hair. We continued exploring, skin against skin, caressing and kissing, extending our expectations, building anticipation.

Eventually, Vi stopped cold, pulled up and said, "I'm ready. You're my f-f-first."

I let out a little nervous chuckle. I wasn't really surprised, but the sudden announcement caught me off guard. "Thanks, no pressure, Vi. You're absolutely sure about this? It's early days with us, I just don't want you regretting anything later."

"No doubts... whatever happens, I st-st-still want this. More than ever."

I felt pressure on me to get this right. To please and excite her, while remaining gentle and caring. A delicate dance. I cleared my throat and said softly, "Not to dampen the mood, but rumor has it that it's not always great the first time."

"Quit tr-trying to lower my expectations. Don't worry, I've been st-studying up on this."

"Why does that not surprise me?"

This was it. The culmination of a slow sexual burn that had been building between us. I really had no idea when the attraction began. Initially, she was the tall, pretty woman with the stammer, who barely glanced at me. A little awkward, with no finesse. But maybe it was her brutal honesty, the quirky sense of humor, the intelligence, and absolutely...the physical attraction. But frankly, it was the total unique package which had drawn me in and landed me right here at this pivotal moment. A switch was flipped and I was ready to proceed.

I started with her lacy thong, inching it down her smooth legs. Then I focused my attention where the red strip of fabric had been. She squirmed initially and then fell into a pleasurable rhythm as I tasted her completely. I felt her body shudder as she whimpered a moan, eventually reaching orgasm, as I pulled up and stared down at her beautiful face and asked, “Happy?”

“You have no idea,” she whispered. “Your turn now?”

“Catching on fast for a novice, Vi.”

“I told you bi-biology was always my thing.”

I easily slipped inside her wet vagina, feeling immediate excitement, as my brain disappeared for a few trance-like moments, followed by a sense of euphoria which enveloped me, as our excitement built. Over and over I plunged in, looking down at her face, looking for cues. She stared back at me with mesmerizing eyes, emitting groans of pleasure as I eventually came in gratifying bliss.

I softly said, “I promise, next time it’ll be better. Give me ten minutes.”

She nodded eagerly. “OK, tell me when.”

After a few more attempts, she was satiated and I was exhausted. I got up and filled our flutes with the bubbles, got back in bed and we clinked our crystal glasses together. “Merry Christmas, Violet.”

“Merry Christmas. You g-gave me way more than I expected.”

An incredible sense of calm came over me. It seemed we were both in the most perfect melding spot in mind and body. I wrapped my arms around her again. “Pretty excellent, Vi. You sure this was all new to you?”

“I would have re-remembered.” She cuddled up next to me, placing her head on my chest. “We missed you at BUD this week. Wasn’t quite the s-s-same without you.”

I nodded, leaned over, kissed her and laid my head against the pillows. “I actually missed being out there too. Unfortunately, I had to calm the waters on several issues at work. Needed to get rid of a couple people and started to do some interviewing.” I sighed and continued, while Violet pulled me in even closer. “I don’t know…

some days my heart's just not in it anymore. Something's happened. Used to be, Rapid Logistics was all I thought about. But now, something feels different."

Vi said, "I'm sure you'll straighten everything out."

"Hope so." I glanced at my watch. It was now almost nine o'clock. "Damn, Vi. Where did the time go? Are you and your Mom doing anything special tonight?"

"No, but we always have breakfast together Christmas morning." She got up and looked through the blinds. "I'm sure everybody's gone by now. The p-party's supposed to go from three to seven, but it's usually at least eight before everybody cl-clears out."

I stood up and pulled on my boxers. "Sorry. I'd love to stay if you'd have me, but I promised my parents I'd be at their place by nine. Somebody distracted me."

Vi got back in bed and pulled the covers up to her chest. "S-Sorry about that. So, are you an only kid too?"

"Yeah, they'd be heartbroken if I didn't show up on Christmas Eve, especially with Allie gone. I'll make it up to you soon; I promise. I'll check in tomorrow." I pulled on my shirt and trousers, and then texted my parents, letting them know I was on my way. I turned and gave Violet a hug. "I really don't want to leave. This has been more than great. We'll talk soon, OK? "

She sighed from the bed, looking like a wide-eyed disappointed child. "Alright...I guess it's time for me to check in with Bad-to-the-Bone."

And right on cue, Vi's phone began playing the infamous ringtone, and I suddenly had the urge to race out.

CHAPTER 47

Dinner and a Date With the Methodists

ROSARIO

BUD closed early on Christmas Eve, allowing the crew to leave at two o'clock. Unfortunately, our pay was docked the extra hour, but in its place we received a baggy filled with three decorated Christmas cookies--probably the remains from this morning's volunteers-only appreciation banquet.

I took the crosswalk to the bus stop. The day had grown chillier and a cold mist was drifting down and freezing into place across the metal bench I waited on. I pulled my thick jacket tighter over the sweatshirt I'd layered underneath and grabbed a black knit cap out of my pocket to cover my ears. Was it the weather or what? I felt a dark mood come on, even though Christmas Eve was always my favorite holiday.

Traffic was light and the bus arrived a little early. I climbed on board, grateful for the warm air inside. There were three other people on the yellow DART bus, one sleeping and two scrolling through their phones. I sat down and stared out at the street I'd been riding down daily for the last few months.

Christmas Eve--with no plans. I pulled out one of the cookies and took a bite, snapping off Santa's head. At least last year, I'd been invited to the home of my former boss and cousin, Miguel. But I'd burned that bridge when he fired me. Didn't matter anyway. He was a terrible boss and the tamales he served weren't even homemade. I was looking forward to calling my mother this afternoon, but that was about it.

Four blocks before my stop I noticed the marquee sign of a Methodist church welcoming all visitors to their seven o'clock candlelight service. It wasn't a big fancy church like the Catholic one I attended in Mexico. But the little sign spoke to me. I decided right then that I'd go home, clean up, and walk back to that church this evening. Why not take comfort and joy with others in celebrating El Nino's birth? I wondered if it was alright for a Catholic to slip in amongst the Methodists?

At my stop, I got off and walked another two blocks to my apartment. Now each time I unlocked my door, I counted down the days until I'd be moving into my new place with Violet. She really was my only true friend in Dallas. This afternoon, she'd left work earlier with plans to attend a big party with Turner at her Mother's home. It hurt my feelings that she hadn't included me, but she explained it was her mother's party, not hers. I bet the food and decorations were beautiful inside that grand house. Although she complained about her mother, I think she had no idea how lucky she was. Unlike me, she'd be surrounded by cheerful, fun people, with her mother close at hand.

I dropped my work clothes on the floor and stepped into the hot shower. That was one thing to be grateful for. This crappy apartment always had a strong surge of hot water pouring out and today it felt especially needed. Later, I pulled on my black stretchy tube dress, brushed out my hair and put on a new black velvet headband I'd bought recently at the Dollar Store. I outlined my lips and applied a bright red lipstick, mascara, and smiled back at myself in the mirror. "Happy holidays, Rosario!"

Back home, even the poorest of families came together with friends and neighbors and feasted on homemade *tamales*, hot *menudo, ensalada de noche buena*, and always a few glasses of *ponche navideno*. Instead, I heated up a left-over burger in the microwave while humming *Feliz Navidad*. Sitting down to call my mom, I forced myself to speak in a more enthusiastic tone than I was feeling.

Hearing her voice, I let the comforting, warm sound of Spanish flow over me, "Ah, *mija*...my darling girl. I was hoping you'd call. How are you?"

"Really great, Mama! Work is going well; they let us leave early today and gave us cookies to take home."

"Oh, that's nice. So happy you have a wonderful place to work. And your new friend, Violet? Is she with you?"

"No. Not tonight. Her family had a party she had to go to. But I think I'll go to church this evening. There's a Methodist church near me that's having a special service. Close enough to walk to."

"Meth-o-dist? Ahh, so not the *true* church. I guess, this one time, Jesus will not mind. Listen Rosario, I've been wanting to talk to you about something important. It's pretty wonderful, really."

I was in the middle of taking a bite of the microwaved burger encased in a soggy bun. "I could use some good news."

"Well, you know the garage on the corner of Avenue North, the white building with the green trim."

"Oh sure." I had to laugh remembering the old geezer that used to work there, always staring at the girls as we walked by. "I remember. On our way home from school, a mechanic there used to stand outside and whistle at the pretty girls."

"Oh, he's just friendly. By the way, he's not that old, and he asked me out to dinner a few months back."

"Wait... the old guy with the white hair and beard--always wearing blue overalls?"

"Yes, yes; that one. He's sixty, so not too much older than me. *Anyway*, we've been going out a little each week since then. He's so nice; always bringing me candy or flowers. And last night, *mija*, he asked me to marry him! His name is Jorge Espinoza." Her voice sounded so happy, but I couldn't believe her words.

"Marry him, Mama? It sounds like you barely know him! So, what did you say?"

"I said yes, yes, a hundred times yes! Rosario, what do I have to lose? I have no one here, money is so tight, you can't come home, and I miss the companionship of a man. I think Jorge will be a good man."

I started feeling anxious. "Is it too soon? It's just that it doesn't seem very long ago since Papa died."

"My darling, I thought you might feel that way, but it's been over a year and I'm not getting any younger--almost forty-five! Be happy for me. I feel like it's a Christmas miracle!"

I began softly crying, somehow feeling like I was now losing my mother, after already losing my father and brother. I wiped my eyes with my sleeve as I lied to her. "I'm happy for you and I hope it's for the best. I'll look forward to meeting him at the wedding. Uh... I get vacation after my first six months, so maybe in April or May? We should plan a nice wedding around that time." *And maybe the whole idea will blow over by then.*

"Oh, that would be wonderful! But we're not waiting, Rosario. We're planning a New Year's Eve wedding. Next week. We thought that might be fun with all the fireworks celebrations. But when you come, we'll have a little party."

I stood up, ran my hands through my hair, as my caution turned to panic. "Mama, why so fast? Take your time; enjoy your engagement."

She laughed a bit. "Engagements are for the young, Rosario. We don't want to waste any more time. This way, by April, when you come to visit, we'll be all settled in his house. It's a small place, but very nice and there's a space for you in the garage, a nice separate space. You'll see; you'll like it."

"So, you're selling our house?" I was in shock. The last constants in my life were disappearing. Our little white home and garden outside of Juarez would be gone and my relationship with my mother would be totally altered by this new, strange man in her life. It all seemed so wrong.

"I might as well sell it, Rosario. The extra money will be nice and there's no need for two houses now. Be happy for me."

This was devastating, but she sounded so excited and overjoyed. "I am, Mama. I'm happy, but please, be very sure. Check his history, his records, previous family, whatever...just be careful."

"He's a good man. I understand these things. Sorry to cut this short but I have to go. I'm meeting him after he closes the shop.

We're joining several of his friends for a big Christmas feast. I love you so much, *mija*. Call me soon. Merry Christmas!"

I sat back down, stunned, not knowing what to think. It was not the warm, loving call I'd been planning all day to help cheer me up. But I understood her loneliness and fear of financial instability. I'd had those same fears. Hopefully, this Jorge Espinoza would treat her well. He better! Roberto, what do you think? I sat and listened to my head for a full minute, but my brother's voice didn't come to me as it usually did. I guess he was busy too.

Here I was, my second Christmas living in a large city filled with lots of people my age, and I was alone. My old school friends wouldn't think this was possible... *Rosario, the outgoing one, the girl with the bright future.* What a joke.

I looked down at my now cold--again--hamburger and threw it in the trash. It was Christmas Eve. At least, I deserved to treat myself to a decent meal. But where to go? Some place different, not the usual little taco and breakfast places I occasionally stopped at. The first time I'd met Nico, he'd mentioned going to a Greek bar and restaurant near my apartment. Greek? That might be good. Mediterranean food sounded exotic. Time to try new things.

But I couldn't remember the restaurant's name... Christopher's, Christine's, *Christo's*, that was it. I checked my phone and saw a place called Christo's about a mile away, too far to walk in this cold. But I could schedule an Uber, a rare treat. I called the restaurant to make sure they were open. A woman with a rough voice answered over the sounds of a loud crowd. "Yes, we're open now, but closing early, at eight. You want a reservation?"

I made one for five-thirty, allowing myself time to get to the church later. I opened the envelope of extra cash Nico had returned to me--after stealing it. I pulled out fifty dollars hoping I wouldn't need to spend all of it, but better restaurants in Dallas were expensive. Anyway, it was a gift to myself. Even though I'd be sitting alone, I would hopefully be surrounded by happy people.

My Uber came quickly and dropped me in front of Christo's in minutes. It was located in a simple building with a large blue neon sign on Greenville Avenue, a section that had a combination of old-

and-rundown businesses competing with new-and-hip. Christo's seemed like a blend of both. I walked into a loud, raucous crowd, and waited near the door, noticing a busy bar and about twenty occupied dining tables. It was dark, with blue twinkling lights decorating the bar and walls.

An older woman with heavy eye makeup and a tight dress let me know I had a twenty-minute wait but there was an empty stool at the bar if I wanted to sit down. Sure, why not? A pre-Christmas drink couldn't hurt, and hopefully the Methodists wouldn't object. I climbed up on the unclaimed stool and looked around, enjoying the warmth of the crowd, reminding me of some places back home.

"Hey beautiful, what can I get you?"

I swiveled on my stool and stared at a young man behind the bar with slicked-back dark hair and a wide smile. I had no idea what I wanted. "Uh, what's popular?"

The busy bartender swung his arm back, indicating a large, fully-stocked bar. "The world's your oyster, babe. You want something that packs a punch, something to sip on, or a good yeasty beer...?"

I noticed two guys and a girl next to me clinking glasses filled with a white frothy-looking drink. I pointed to theirs. "I'll try that... good choice?"

He nodded and yanked down a long slender blue bottle from the shelf. "You picked pack-a-punch; it's called ouzo. If you like licorice, you'll love it. Trying sipping it slowly at first. You're a newbie." Then he leaned over and whispered, "Hey, it's Christmas Eve--first glass on the house, babe."

"Thank you!" He dashed off quickly to wait on another patron. I swiveled half way around again and watched the threesome next to me drinking their ouzo, as I attempted my first sip of the unusual drink. Hmm, different, but good in a strange way.

The girl drinking between the two guys eyed me and shook her head. "Not like that. You gotta bang that drink down! Guys, show her how it's done." The two guys picked up two more of the small glasses from a row lined up in front of them. They clinked, swallowed the shot at once, and yelled, "Opa!"

I laughed and leaned towards them so they could hear me. "It's my first try. The bartender told me to go slow and sip. But I appreciate the lesson. My name's Rosario."

They introduced themselves, told me the bartender didn't know shit, and explained they were cousins, trying to get slammed before facing an evening at their grandmother's house. We chatted for a while and then the hostess found me and said my table was ready. I asked the cousins, "Have you eaten already?"

One of the guys, Marcus, explained, "Yeah, dinner's at Granny's tonight. We need to be heading over now. But we should all go out soon. Let me get your number."

I nodded eagerly and thought, *why not*? We exchanged numbers and they left as the hostess led me to a back corner table for two, which was great for viewing the crowd and checking out the delicious smells coming from everyone's dishes. I pondered the long list on the menu and decided to wait for the waiter's recommendation, eventually picking grilled white fish, rice, baked squash with tomatoes, and stuffed grape leaves. I took my first bite of the seasoned fish and it melted in my mouth. I was so glad I'd tossed my microwave burger. The waiter was attentive, brought me another ouzo, and I took my time eating one of the most delicious meals I'd had since arriving in Dallas.

I was surrounded by the buzz of happy, contented couples and noisy families and didn't mind that I was eating alone. About twenty minutes before seven, I scheduled another Uber to take me to the church. After my restaurant choice, I was looking forward to the candlelight service.

I pushed open the restaurant door to wait outside and suddenly found myself face to face with Nico. Both of our eyes opened wide and we were caught with nothing to say to each other. I stepped out as he went in. I waited in the cold, holding my black thrift-store coat closely around my short dress, facing the parking lot. I heard the door open again, letting out the noise of happy chatter inside.

Feeling a gentle touch on my shoulder, I turned around and watched the brisk wind blow through Nico's hair. "Hey Rosie, just wanted to tell you Merry Christmas. I still hope you'll forgive me someday. Sorry I'm such a fuck-up."

I nodded and shrugged. "You know, Nico...you suggested this place to me once. I really liked the food here tonight. And the ouzo."

He laughed, shaking his head. "Can't believe you tried that on your own. Hey, my cousin's inside. Why don't you join us for another drink?"

I actually thought about it for a second and then my Uber pulled up to the front door. I checked the plate number against my notification. "Thanks, but this is my ride. Have a nice Christmas, Nico."

"Sure, you too."

By the time I got in the car, he was already back inside. Emotions were surging through me. Was it the two glasses of ouzo? My face suddenly felt hot and I began sweating. Could I ever forgive Nico? How could someone that seemed so fun and genuine do something so cruel and frightening? Then my mind began swirling with doubt. How could my mother marry the old goat that whistled at teen-age girls? Would I feel left out, with no sense of belonging? Just a space in a garage? Would Mama be safe and loved; or abused? Our house was small, and compared to American standards, worth little, but in Mexico it might tempt someone unscrupulous to take advantage of a lonely woman. I was worried about her.

And what about Violet? We were from such different backgrounds. Would my lack of education embarrass her? Would her stutter and shyness keep us from doing things together? Why didn't she invite me to their party tonight? She had to know I'd be alone.

And where was Roberto when I needed him most? Talk to me, *hermano!...por favor.*

I leaned my head back, allowing the competing worries to build, completely erasing the warm, happy ambiance from the restaurant.

"Ma'am, we're here... Ms. Guzman?... East Rock Methodist Church."

I opened my eyes, surprised we were already at the church. "Oh... sorry." I grabbed my bag, got out and said, "*Feliz Navidad.*" I looked up the steps, watching a couple walking toward the chapel doors. Checking my watch, it showed seven o'clock. Now, I was suddenly unsure of my decision to come. Maybe I should walk back home. As they opened the door, I saw soft yellow light peek out and heard lively music coming from inside. I sighed and headed toward the chapel doors.

Inside, I noticed there were no candles to light for the loved ones who had passed. I was hoping to light one for my father and Roberto tonight. Also, underneath two stained-glass windows near the altar, there was a band playing a rock version of *Oh Holy Night* on a stage. The band included two guitarists, a keyboard player, and a drummer. Was this a late mass or a rock concert? I was confused. The chapel was about half full and so different from the crowded midnight Christmas mass in Juarez, which was always led by a somber male priest at the altar. I timidly chose a half-filled middle pew.

Bright red poinsettias circled the stage. When the song ended, a woman dressed in a sparkling holiday sweater approached the altar. She had a beaming face and greeted us with such a joyful glow and excitement that her spirit caught me completely off guard. She was perhaps in her mid-twenties. Could this young woman be the head of a church?

She spoke so convincingly, while keeping a broad smile across her face, totally commanding my attention. "With love in our hearts, excitement in our minds, and pure joy to be shared amongst friends and strangers, let us join together for the most magnificent celebration of the year; one where we can all come together in one belief--in celebration of the birth and return of our lord, Jesus. Can you feel the wonder of it all? Can you feel the exultation tonight?"

Her eyes were wide, her voice pulsed with excitement, and I was ready to follow where she led.

She directed us in prayer and then the band broke into another song, with the lyrics of the song displayed on an overhead screen allowing the whole congregation to sing along. Then the young woman, who introduced herself as an associate pastor, gave a short, inspiring sermon about faith, strength, and belief.

At mass in Mexico, we all took turns kissing a doll representing Jesus and received a bag of candy, but there was no baby kissing here. Only a quick and simple communion with bread and wine, much more singing, and some prayers.

Then candles were passed to the congregation and we were asked to form a circle inside the sanctuary, and clasp hands. It seemed that I'd somehow come between a young husband, his wife, and their child. The wife grasped my hand and said, "Welcome! Haven't seen you before."

"Thank you. Yes, I'm new...Rosario."

"I'm Robin. Great to meet you. We love having new people!" Then her little girl began whining, wanting to clutch her father's hand, so we switched places. The church lights dimmed while a lit candle passed from hand to hand throughout the circle and everyone raised hands together holding up their burning candles. In the darkened sanctuary, as the circle of candlelight began to glow, we joined in singing multiple verses of Silent Night without the band. It was so simple, quiet, and beautiful.

I felt the love the pastor was radiating. I felt community with the hands I clasped on either side of me. There was a strength shooting through that circle that flowed through me. I truly felt renewed with my head and heart lightened.

Stepping outside later, I noticed the mist and wind had stopped and the night air had warmed slightly. Robin and family came out behind me and she called out, "Hope to see you again, Merry Christmas!"

I waved back, pulled on my cap and began walking home, grateful for the sense of companionship the service had given me. Stars were popping out in the black sky as the dark clouds and my head began to clear. Then I finally heard him.

Feliz Navidad, baby sister--still seven minutes younger, but who's counting? Hey, why are you doubting yourself or Mama? She deserves to move on and so do you. You still hanging on to those nightmares? No joke, it's going to be scary and lonely at times, but you're one of the strongest people I know. Hermanita, you're gonna be fine without me. Believe in yourself...make smart choices...

My phone began buzzing. I told my brother, *Don't leave me just yet; hold on.* I pulled my cell out, surprised to see it was Marcus, one of the three cousins I'd just met at Christo's. "*Hola*?"

"Rosario!...We're wrapping things up over here around ten... wanna come out and play later? I can pick you up."

He'd probably been drinking for hours. "Thanks for calling Marcus, but no. I'm good for the night. Maybe another time."

"Come on. I've still got a half bottle of ouzo to share."

"Merry Christmas, Marcus." I clicked off and then said to my brother, *I promise, Roberto. Smart choices.*

CHAPTER 48

You Put The Wait On Me

VIOLET

Christmas day brunch--our mother-daughter tradition. I walked down the drive to the house and looked at the full display set up on the table: eggs benedict, English muffins, sliced ham, fried potatoes, mixed fruit, a few desserts... far more food than either of us could consume. Maria, Mother's cook, had gone all out. We were eating in the sunroom at the round glass table usually reserved for playing bridge. In the background, I heard the hum of vacuum cleaners traveling through the rest of the house, cleaning up after last night's party.

I sat down sipping hot coffee while waiting for Mother, and noticed there was not the usual stack of perfectly wrapped gifts waiting for me to open. That was fine. I really was in need of nothing, and no one could derail me today. I looked out the glass doors and smiled. Last night's cold and misty weather had transformed into a chilly but beautifully clear day.

As Mother sat down to join me, I couldn't help but feel my face was all a-glow with the thrill of my own transformational night--my deflowering, my first complete sexual encounter, my hitting a home run and touching all four bases. And Turner said he would call this afternoon. Something special to look forward to, as my mind kept our evening aerobics on replay.

"You look happy today, darling. That was some party last night, wasn't it? Where did you and your Mr. Cooper go? I remember us all dancing and then...poof. Oh, pass the melon please, Violet."

I handed over the bowl and then continued to butter my muffin while thinking how best to respond, always cautious of accidently landing on an explosive topic. "Yes, fun-fun party! Loved the conga line. M-Mother, you are such a great dancer!" *Compliment and redirect.*

"Well, you know I took all kinds of dance lessons for years. Can't credit it all to sheer talent."

I nodded, biting into the crunchy muffin. "Everything tastes so good. Big thanks to M-M-Maria. It's always amazing that you get her to whi-whip all this up on Christmas morning."

Mother waved her hand in dismissal. "She slept in, didn't have to get here until nine, *and* got to leave early yesterday after the catering crew arrived."

"Nice." *Suzanne Hill-- always the benevolent overlord.* I sweetly smiled back.

Then Mother jumped in. "So Turner...he seems quite pleasant. Good looking, intelligent. I thought he seemed promising at the garden club fundraiser. I'm glad I asked you to invite him."

"Yeah, he's a great guy. We really s-s-seem to be hitting it off."

"Just be careful, Violet. I don't want you getting hurt. Don't go too far, too fast. These older men...you never know their agenda or what they really want."

Good, she obviously had no idea what happened between us last night, although I'd felt sure my face was broadcasting the momentous event. "He's not *that* much older, about ten years."

"Hmm, so twelve years younger than me." She said this slowly, as if counting on her fingers.

I gently nudged, "Wouldn't that be fifteen years younger than you?"

She shook her head, saying, "Whatever. Math was never my strong suit. Anyway, *my point is* that he seems to be a busy man with many contacts and may not be able to offer you the attention you're seeking. That's all I'm saying. So be careful."

"Got it. So... I brought you a few gifts. S-sorry to say, they're in *gift bags*."

"Didn't I recently go over the gift presentation talk? All our little chats obviously mean little to you. Anyway... it was thoughtful of you, and gift bag or not, I *do* appreciate them."

While leaving work a few days before, I'd conveniently purchased my mother's gifts at the BUD gift shop: a hand painted bird house, a colorful silk-screened scarf, and a book about native Texas plants. It was always tough buying for the woman who had everything, and then some. She opened each one with glee and appeared to love everything. Even going so far as to actually put the scarf on over her robe. "They're all beautiful, Violet! I'll have the gardener hang the birdhouse this week."

I was thrilled to get a rare good gift review. I decided the convenient BUD gift shop would now replace Target as a primary shopping spot.

"Now Vi, for your gift. I kept it simple. I know that you never planned to stay at the guest house forever, and you appear to be settling into your job. So, whenever you're ready, I set aside a ten-thousand-dollar account with my decorator, to furnish your new place. Now, with only ten-thousand, you'll really have to rein in her tastes to get enough bang for your buck, but that should get you all the basics. I know how you hate to shop, and this woman is amazing."

It was an extremely generous gift with perfect timing. Almost too perfect? Did she know I'd signed a lease already? Anyway, I would take all the decorating help I could get. Mother was right. Furniture stores always overwhelmed and intimidated me. While we resumed the brunch, I thanked Mother profusely and mentioned that I had actually been checking out some places recently. At this point, I would leave the topic of Rosario as my roommate out of the conversation. No need to start a ruckus on Christmas morning.

As she added more pepper to her Bloody Mary, Mother said, "I'm excited about cruise season starting up again. Imagine, canceling three years in a row. I had not missed a January cruise in twenty years prior to all this pandemic nonsense. I believe it's safe now, don't you?" Then she turned and threw out the offer, fairly safe in the knowledge I would never accept. "I don't suppose you'd like to accompany me, Violet?"

"No, thanks. You know--b-b-busy at work. We have the garden's big opening at the end of February."

"Oh yes, be sure to have Magna put that on my calendar, darling."

After brunch, we decided to watch our favorite Christmas movie, *Love Actually*. When it ended, Mother was ready to nap and I returned to the guest house to wait for Turner's call. This was difficult. The waiting part. I tried to recall his parting words. Something about his parents missing Allie, needing him there, checking back with me. I'd been so keyed up about my fabulous sexual awakening, that the details were vague.

I passed the time reading up on the best xeriscape planting product for Southwestern climates. Surely, that would calm my libido. Two hours later, I switched to looking up sculptural plant design ideas. I'd already signed up to take on-line classes in landscape architecture through Cornell University for the spring and I was anxious to get started. I missed academia and studying in general. With my work schedule, I could easily handle the evening class load.

Three hours had passed and Turner hadn't called. I'd give him time. He was with his family.

Five hours of waiting. This was miserable. Maybe having a *maybe-boyfriend* was all about waiting? Should I call him? No, wait a little longer.

It was now eight o'clock. I was tired, edgy, thinking I'd done something wrong, I botched the sex thing? I'd acted odd, wasn't sexy enough, too eager? I gave in and texted him:

Hi there, Happy Christmas. Thinking of you!

Then I deleted the exclamation mark, thinking it perhaps too aggressive. But was a simple period too somber? Definitely overthinking this, I pressed send.

Again, I waited. I gave up around eleven, showered, and went to bed. Just as my eyes closed, finally...the ding of a text. I yanked my phone off the nightstand. It was Turner.

Sorry things got derailed today. Major issues at home. I'll explain all later.

Hmm, not good. And I'd thought nothing could make me unhappy today. What was the major issue? I'd have to discuss all this with Rosie tomorrow. She usually had good advice. We had *so* much to talk about. I attempted to sleep but spent most of the night thinking about what I'd probably done wrong.

The team was all back on the job at BUD Monday morning, with the exception of our volunteer, Turner, whose attendance record was becoming rather spotty. Today we were blending soil for our cactus garden which would be planted a little later. In wheel barrows, we created a special mixture including crushed brick, carpenter's sand and decomposed granite which all worked well for drainage. Jeff, Linda, and Mark were each bringing loads of the mixture down to the bottom of the hill, as Rosario and I shoveled and blended it in with our existing bedding soil.

Mark was the first down the hill to join us. I had to ask, "So Mark, just curious, did you and M-Molly spend Christmas together?"

"None of your business, is it?" He shoveled a large load into the cactus bed, but then, as usual, he continued. "Actually, no, we didn't. And since you'll probably pester me about it, I'm letting you both know, we ended it. No hard feelings with Molly, just not the person I thought she was, and that's all I'm gonna say."

"Oh, sorry to hear that." Although I was thinking, *Good! Those two were definitely a miss-match.*

"Don't be, Vi. There's one thing I'm sure of; there's always another woman out there just waiting for a good man."

Rosie giggled and asked, "And I suppose that good man is you?"

"Yup. I don't mean to brag but..."

I jumped in and said, "Well good luck Mark. Please try to find someone new by February 28th."

"Why then?" he asked.

"It's the ki-kick off to Bud's spring events *and* the bi-big opening for our xeriscape garden. Don't forget! I want the whole team there."

Rosie excitedly clapped her hands. "Oh yes, and Violet told me it's a big dress-up deal and we can bring dates. Do you suppose there will be dancing?"

I shook my head, "Doubtful; it'll just be donors, BUD members and the directors. Not a d-d-dancing type crowd. At least, not the kind of dancing *you* do. Remember all that money Turner and I raised? Some of that is paying for this p-party. Actually, Molly's been p-pretty antsy about everything. S-Seems very up-tight lately. We'll be ready, though. I have everything planned out for the garden's completion."

Mark shook the remaining soil out of his wheelbarrow. "OK, cool. Sounds like I may have to get my brocade smoking jacket out of mothballs then. 'Scuse me ladies. I'll be taking a break. Have a little business to attend to."

We both laughed behind his back, knowing Mark was going to a favorite secret spot for his morning joint.

Once we were alone, Rosario asked, "So Vi, tell me all about your Christmas Eve party. Bet you had fun."

"Honestly, it was all my M-Mother's friends, so for me, it was kind of boring. Of course, Turner was there and the food and drinks were good. But Rosie, after we left the p-party, things got *very* good!"

"Really--for real, Violet! With Turner?"

"Yes." I whispered, not wanting Jeff and Linda to hear. "I can't st-stop thinking about everything we did, and about him. Turner was wonderful and so g-g-gentle, yet firm. Well, you get it, right?"

Rosie leaned over wide-eyed and whispered, "So, you did it? All the way?"

I nodded excitedly. "The only problem is, he never called me yesterday and he said he would. He only texted very late and s-s-said there were family issues. What do you think? Should I be w-worried?"

Rosario had a skeptical look on her face. "Hmm, family issues? Sounds kind of fakey, right? I guess maybe something could have happened--a doctor-type emergency? But why wouldn't he tell you?" She patted my shoulder. "Don't start worrying yet. I bet he'll call and explain, but *don't* call him, girl. Makes you look desperate."

I kept my eyes to the ground, already embarrassed. "T-Too late. I was the one that fi-finally texted him first."

"Ohh..." Rosie nodded and just kept quiet while blending dirt.

"Was that really so ba-ba-bad? I was tired of waiting."

She stopped, leaned on her rake and said, "My friend, that is what we do. Especially early in the game. We women *always* end up waiting."

"Well that's a st-stupid rule."

She shrugged her shoulders and gave me a smile. "Don't worry. He'll call--maybe. Now, forget all that and tell me *every* detail after you left the party."

CHAPTER 49

Changes of Heart

TURNER

Mom nudged me awake, as I tried desperately to hang on to sleep while sitting on the vinyl recliner in the cold hospital room.

Whispering, she said, "Turner, I brought you hot coffee." I turned my head and squinted up at my mother's face in the brightly lit room.

I reached out for the styrofoam cup. "Anything hot is gratefully accepted. This place is a friggin' meat locker. I'd been tempted to steal Dad's blanket, but I thought his nurse would frown on that.

Mom dropped a large brown paper bag in my lap. "I just checked in with his doctor. He said your father had a better night, seems to be responding to the medications."

"Good to hear." We both glanced toward my father, still deeply sleeping while hooked up to several machines. Then I looked back at the bag of documents she had dropped in my lap, and shook my head.

"Turner, it's all the related insurance paperwork I could find. Sorry it's so disorganized. Your dad took over all this stuff a while back, and I just don't have a clue. I'm sure you'll sort it all out."

"Yeah...No problem, Mom. You deal with the doctors and I'll try to get through this mess."

Dad had suffered a heart attack Christmas morning around eight. He came into the kitchen looking white as a ghost, poured himself a shaky cup of coffee, announced his left arm was hurting like hell, and then leaned over the kitchen sink and threw up. I couldn't even remember the last time my dad had been sick. We'd always shared a dark joke about him being way too stubborn to die and too ornery to be let into heaven.

But all the symptoms were there: nausea, sweating, difficulty breathing. I called 911 and the medics arrived within fifteen minutes, tested his vitals, strapped him on a gurney, and quickly wheeled him out. After throwing our clothes on, my mother and I were panic-stricken and followed behind in separate cars. We were distraught most of the day, nervously wandering the hospital halls, asking annoying questions to random health care workers, hoping for positive signs. First it was the emergency docs, then we progressed upstairs to the cardiac ICU for surgery, followed by a move to a recovery room. It had been a long and dreadful day and night.

I paused from pulling documents from the bag to glance over at Dad. At least he had a tranquil look on his face right now. The triple bypass surgery seemed to have gone well. We would just have to wait and see how he would respond after waking up.

It was at the ER registration desk when I discovered that my parents had not opted into any additional coverage plan besides the basic Medicare, which would probably *not* cover much of what he needed. I found it hard to believe that my father didn't have a supplemental plan for himself and my mother. Before Mom went home last night, I'd asked her to bring all policy-related documents from Dad's files. I didn't think it would arrive jumbled up in a brown bag.

Mother offered to go to the cafeteria to bring us some breakfast, while I allowed my mind a few minutes of reprieve, wandering back to Christmas Eve with Violet. Was that less than two days ago? I wished I could crawl into her warm bed right now and spoon, feeling her back side right up against me, holding her close, and then fall into a deep long sleep. Quite a contrast to the solitary deep-freeze recliner I was sitting in next to my father's beeping bed.

Violet and I had shared a great evening, but I had to leave way too quickly. Then yesterday, I'd been so consumed with Dad's emergency that I failed to call her. I eventually sent a brief late-night text, but I was too exhausted and stressed to go through any details of the day. I pulled out my phone to call her but then realized she would be busy now at work. I'd check in later, and called Rapid Logistics instead, letting them know Dad's condition.

I was beginning to realize it was time for Dad to step back from the business. Although he often came up with off-color and annoying comments at work, he really was everybody's cheerleader and would be sorely missed. But I could only wonder if the recent business climate had pushed his stress level over the brink. And lately, in my absence, he'd been doing a lot of the worrying for me.

After my mother and I finished off our cafeteria trays of semi-cold eggs and bacon, I wheeled an empty dinner tray over to the recliner to use as a desk and started going through a plethora of medical paperwork that initially made my head spin and then doze off. Later, for the second time, Mother shook me awake, telling me Dad had finally opened his eyes.

The two of us stood up on either side of his bed. In a raspy, familiar voice he said, "Why are you two making googly eyes at me? I'm hungry and ready to get the hell outta here. Son, help me unplug all this nonsense hanging off of me." There was a barrage of stickers on his skin attached to cardiac monitor wires, along with IV drips.

Still blurry eyed from my nap, I shook my head. "Dad, slow down. You've had a massive heart attack. You're not going anywhere. Just lie still and rest."

Then he looked up at my mom. "Well at least get me some food! Myrna, can you rustle up something from the cafeteria? I'm feeling a tad puny. A big steak would be just the ticket."

Mom rolled her eyes and shook her head. "You'll be lucky to get Jello. All that red meat is probably the reason you ended up here. You'll have to follow the doctor's diet."

"Hogwash!"

He went on and on, continuing to complain, threatening to walk out. I loved my Dad but I couldn't take the crazy comments this morning. I grabbed my bag of documents, put my mother in charge, and went home to shower and switch out of the sweats I'd thrown on yesterday morning. After a hot shower, a normal indoor temperature, and some soft jazz in the background, I felt revitalized.

I decided it was time to call Violet. I wanted to, yet I was now actually hesitant to make the call.

After sex on Christmas Eve, I knew expectations had changed, even though Violet claimed it wouldn't matter. I knew for both Violet and myself, we had crossed over into something different in the relationship. It hadn't been just a playful romp. The sex became way more than I had expected, with me guiding the way, and Vi--a very fast student.

To put it simply, I just wasn't sure if I was ready again for a full-blown, new relationship. I was beginning to feel I was over Allie and her betrayal, but was I ready to jump through new hoops right now, just as I was getting stronger? Violet had some issues; it wouldn't be easy-breezy.

I thought I'd been honest with Violet about all that. I'd explained myself when she asked me about the *boyfriend* thing on Christmas Eve, explaining it was probably too early to put a label on us. But when I left, I'd promised her I would call. I made the call with some hesitancy.

She answered immediately. "Turner, hi. I read your text. W-What's wrong?"

"Well, nothing's wrong with me, but my father had a massive heart attack early yesterday. It was touch and go most of the day but he seems stable now and was demanding steak and fries when I left earlier."

"Oh wow. I'm so s-s-sorry. Sounds like he's doing b-better if he has his appetite."

"Yeah, hopefully. He'll probably be there for a week or so. I'm home now, but I'll be heading back to the hospital to stay the night--need to give my mother a break. We're doing a tag-team thing."

"Oh...That's good. I was hoping to se-see you soon. Bu-But I understand."

"Yeah, me too. Thought about you a lot today. But between Dad's health, their insurance mess, and stuff at work, it might be hard to see much of each other for a while. Hopefully, we can squeeze in some time."

"I see. Yeah, sounds like you're b-b-busy. Well, that'll give me m-more time to study. I'm taking la-landscaping classes online through Cornell this semester. I'm excited about that."

"Oh, you didn't tell me...great idea. Well, hate to rush, but I need to get to the hospital. I'll be in touch soon."

"Yes, hopefully soon."

Man, that conversation sucked! I sounded like a wooden puppet. I could hear the disappointment in her voice. Flowers! I should at least send her flowers. No. She might read too much into that. I'd call tomorrow. Tomorrow would be better.

Back at the hospital, Mom explained that things were chaotic after I'd left. Dad became so irrational and irritable that he kept pulling off his fluid and med connections and they had to put his arms in restraints to keep him safe. Mother was exhausted from putting up with him, and left me to take over the night-time vigil. In the middle of the night, Dad woke up and wanted to talk business until early morning, going over issues from old trucking services we hadn't used in years to non-existent problems with account receivables.

After leaving the hospital the next morning, I forced myself to go into work. I checked in with each department head, interviewed two candidates on Zoom for a sales replacement, and looked over Dad's existing paperwork, trying to make heads or tails of what he was working on, without much success.

Before leaving, I received an interesting call from a business acquaintance of Vi's mother. Tim Dawcett and Suzanne both served on an investment board. Through their work together, she knew Dawcett was involved with a major league company in the Supply Chain business, and he'd called me to ask for a meeting. I thought it was a bit odd, but we agreed to meet Friday for lunch.

Later that afternoon, on my way to the hospital, I kept thinking about Violet. I was headed to that cold, antiseptic hospital room, but all I really wanted to do was crawl into bed with her, talk over our last few days while apart, and then begin exploring each other's bodies. But then that doubt crept in again. Don't do this if you're not ready. Give it some distance. I kept driving.

A few minutes later, at a red light, I sighed and said. "Shit, who am I kidding? Siri, call Violet Hill."

She picked up quickly. "Violet? Hi, I'm on my way to visit my father for at least a few hours tonight, but if you want company, I'd like to come over later, maybe nine or ten? If that's too late, I totally understand."

"No. I'd l-l-like you to come over. Nine is fine."

"Warning though. I'm pretty wiped out. If I fall asleep in the middle of a sentence, just remember, it's not you."

"Turner... I'll do my b-best to keep you entertained."

"Like the sound of that. See you around nine."

CHAPTER 50

Looking For Mr. Maybe

VIOLET

I was excited after Turner's call. I immediately showered, added a touch of eye makeup, and stood in front of my mirror considering a wardrobe change. I decided to stick with jeans and the sweater, but did elect to take my hair down and curl the ends. Then I read up on various blooming cacti gardens. That last bit was just to keep my heart from racing.

At nine o'clock, I tried arranging myself in alluring poses on the sofa, testing out a couple different positions. But after ten minutes I realized the idea was stupid. Let's face it; I wasn't pin-up material.

By nine-thirty, I nervously thought he'd be a no-show. I took Cocoa out for a final walk, came back and turned on the TV, catching the end of a bad sitcom--why did they add annoying laugh tracks? I checked my phone for messages--nothing. The news--depressing. Where was he? My enthusiasm had popped and was beginning to evaporate. By ten-thirty, I was pissed off and fading fast.

Turner knew I had to be at work at six-thirty AM. We said nine, right? I recalled our phone conversation. I'd said, 'Nine is fine,' and Turner ended with, 'See you at nine.' Not ten, not ten-fifteen, and certainly not ten-thirty! I was about to stomp upstairs when I heard a soft knock. I pulled aside the sheer curtain hanging over the door, and stared at Turner standing under the outside light. I shook my head, while slowly opening the door a crack.

He spoke softly. "Hey, I'm sorry I'm a little late. Dad got wrapped up in a big phone conversation with a friend. You're going to love hearing about it. He pushed on the door slightly. "You're not letting me in?"

I was still holding the door firmly, and hadn't really decided. This was not cool. Ten-thirty-five was beyond a little late. "You said nine. It's *way* past nine. Tar-Tardiness is rude."

Still whispering, he said, "I'm truly sorry. But where are we; back in elementary school?"

"Prom-Promptness is important to me. It means you care."

He reached out, nudging his hand through the slightly open door, and touched the side of my face, as I pressed the door tighter on his arm. "Hey! That hurts. Vi, I do care. A lot. But things have been crazy lately. I'm trying to keep my business going, and didn't want to leave the hospital until Dad went down, and I've been running on about four hours of sleep over the past forty-eight hours. So please...forgive me. I thought I said ten."

"No, we d-decided on nine."

Then his tone turned somewhat angry. "OK, I guess my schedule doesn't run quite as efficiently as yours." Then he whispered, "Vi... May I *please* come in? The security cameras around here are probably now on high alert."

I sighed and opened the door. He had presented a decent defense. I headed over to the fridge. "What can I get you...b-b-beer, wine?"

He followed behind me, sounding relieved. "Just you and a glass of water. That's all I need."

I turned and looked at him. "Wow. That's quite a line."

"Yeah. Not bad." He smiled, looked down at me while holding onto my shoulders, and kissed me.

Pulling him in closer, my hands ran through his hair, then I linked my fingers behind his head. We stumbled over to the chair and ottoman in a wet and hungry lip-lock and fell on top of the chair, with me landing in his lap. After a couple days of waiting, I realized how much I'd missed him. My anger at his tardiness flew out the door. The sensation of his body under mine felt so good. Was it the sex, was it him, or the whole package? Right now, it didn't matter.

When we finally came up for air, I said, "You taste interesting." I kissed him again quickly and licked my lips with the tip of my tongue and laughed, saying. "But why am I tasting Cheetos?"

He smiled, making his eyes crinkle at the corners. "You have strong deductive powers. My dinner was catered by the hospital vending machine."

I looked down and began tugging at the top button of his jeans. "Sorry, just curious."

He pulled my face toward him again and we kissed several more minutes as I melted inside, growing hotter by the second. Our hands began exploring below waist bands and underneath our shirts. I wanted him so badly. I knew I'd be kicking myself tomorrow at five-thirty AM, but this was going to be worth it.

Turner suddenly began coughing. "Sorry, I never got that water." He scooted out from underneath me, heading over to the refrigerator. "Can I pour you a glass too?"

"Sure."

He handed me my glass and remained standing, "Uh...would you like me to head home or shall we continue this upstairs? As good as you look right now, I need to tell you...I'm beat."

I stood up, grabbed his hand and led him upstairs. Standing in front of my bed, Turner took a big gulp of water and stared at me as I pulled off my black turtleneck and jeans, and stood in front of him in a basic white bra and hip grazing white cotton undies. "Sorry, not quite as t-t-tantalizing as my lacy red thong."

His eyes opened wide as he said, "Honestly, it's even better. So simple. Either way, I love your body." He reached out and glided his hand down my side, skimming my waist and hips. As his hand gently touched me, I felt a quiver run from my scalp to my toes. "Vi, I can't begin to tell you what a turn-on you are." He reached over, unhooked my bra, dropping it on the end of the bed. "And your breasts are perfection." He cupped a breast with each hand, and then bent over, kissing the top of each one delicately, making me shudder with excitement.

I was surprised by his comment and said,"Maybe they're a b-b-bit too small?"

"Never. I can't see you any other way."

As I got in bed, sitting up under the covers, I recalled my days of being bullied. "I used to be so thin; the guys in high school called me the st-stuttering stick."

He shook his head, unbuttoning his striped shirt. "Fuck high school. Those guys would be tripping over themselves to ask you out now."

"Th-Thanks, but doubtful." Pulling my knees up, I leaned against the headboard watching him take off his shirt and step out of his jeans. I had absolutely no complaints as I enjoyed watching him undress. I gently pulled him over on top of me. "I love f-feeling your body on mine."

He reached over to turn off the lamp, but stopped midway and looked down at my face. "You're amazing."

I felt uncomfortable, unused to all the compliments, and turned my face away, cuddling close as he whispered to me, "I envisioned this exact scene two days ago. It feels better than I imagined." I moved even closer in, allowing his arms to encircle me, making me feel so safe and complete. I wanted to hang onto this forever.

He began kissing my neck as I turned slightly, my hand reaching out to rub his firm penis. He flipped me over on my back and slipped easily inside me, pushing in over and over, moaning with excitement, while I wrapped my legs around his hips, bringing him in tighter. hearing my uncontrolled breath come out in short, fast gasps.

This was better than the first time. I released my brain from thinking and just felt the closeness, the hot sensations of touch and breath, the rush of pleasure and pain.

Unfortunately, it all ended pretty abruptly, with Turner crying out, while my heart was still racing and wanting more. I laid my head on his chest and began rubbing him again.

In a very sleepy voice, he said "Sorry, Vi."

"That's OK. I loved it." He was here with me right now. That's all I really wanted.

"You sure? Hey...before I doze off...I finally found your bronze longhorns, for the garden."

"That's w-wonderful. You came through!"

"My dad knows a guy, some eccentric rancher with more money than God."

I had to laugh. "Only your d-dad would know that guy."

"True. So we called him tonight from the hospital. Dad says he has this bronze display with thirty head of longhorns loping across the giant front lawn of his house. But now the wife wants to move back into Fort Worth and he's selling off the land, the real cattle, *and* the bronze ones. I got him down to a real good price for two of them. I'll send you photos soon."

I smiled, charmed that he was still on the hunt for those darn longhorns. "That's wonderful. Can't w-w-wait to see them."

I waited for his response, but only heard snoring.

The next morning we had the longer lucious sex I'd missed the night before, but there was no lingering after-glow. I jumped up, shocked at the time. Almost seven and beyond late for work! I'd never been absent or late. Turner got up, dressed, and said his goodbyes, as I jumped in the shower for a quick rinse. I threw on yesterday's work clothes only because they were still laying on the bath mat from last night's shower. Thankfully, my coffee pot was on a timer and the coffee was still hot, ready for my thermos.

Putting on my hat and jacket, I stared out the open window and saw Turner in the backyard speaking to Mother in her robe, while Mark walked across the lawn with a tall ladder. Turner and Mother looked to be having a friendly conversation, with Mother laughing and talking. Then I watched her go inside through the back door, as Turner drove off and I dashed to my car.

On my drive to work I was stressing out about three things: One--my lateness--just one more thing Molly might find fault with. *Two*--

what Mother might have to say to me now that she knew Turner had stayed over. *Three*--What would the two of them be talking about?

I tried to calm myself down, noticing I'd just blown right through a blinking-light school zone at regular speed. *OK Violet, what would Lexi remind you to do?* Just breathe, slow things down, deep breaths, count it out. Yes... that helps. What else?

In the big scheme of things, nothing terrible had happened. It was a nice day. I would still have a job and survive. Perhaps a little white lie was in order for Molly? And if Mother demands an explanation about Turner? I tell her I'm a grown woman and may occasionally have a sleep-over guest. Easier thought than said, but maybe? And Turner and Mother's conversation? I'd simply call Turner later and find out what was discussed--easy enough.

And one more thing...Why was Mark climbing a tree in the backyard at seven-forty-five AM when he never arrived for gardening duties before ten? Sidebar--non issue, and no time for that.

I was nearing the BUD gate; well over an hour late for work! Deep breaths, You'll be fine. Thanks Lexi.

CHAPTER 51

New Place, Happy Face

ROSARIO

The day finally arrived and I couldn't have been more excited. Violet and I were moving into the most beautiful apartment I had ever seen; although, to be honest, while living in Dallas I'd been inside very few apartments. But the best part was, Violet and I had become like sisters at work, helping each other out, working as a team, sharing secrets. I think we were both thankful we'd found each other and would become good roommates.

All I was bringing for the move was my mattress, clothing, and a few boxes of essentials; all of it fitting easily into Violet's car, with the mattress tied to the roof.

Almost everything else inside the place was shiny and new, and the decorating lady had the guys from IKEA set everything up. Walking in, I saw two small matching navy-blue sofas facing each other, set between a rug patterned with colorful wild animals. A planked wooden table sat near the kitchen with a matching bench and two chairs with print cushions. Long dark navy curtains covered the windows and were pushed back on either side of the sliding glass doors which looked down on the pool. Knowing I had little furniture, Vi had even bought a bed frame, nightstand, lamp, and chair for my room.

As we both looked around the new furnishings, I said, "Vi, for real--I feel like I'm in a movie." I stood and stared at every detail, and couldn't believe her generosity.

"G-G-Glad you like everything. It's homey, right? All I did was tell the d-decorator what we needed, told her the colors I liked, and said don't go over bu-budget."

"It's perfect, and a TV! That will help with my English even more." On either side of the flat screen were two large bookcases filled with all of Vi's books. But my personal favorite items were the washer and dryer in a hall closet. "This has to be the best part of all. No more trips to the laundry."

"Yeah, Rosie--you're own personal Bright White Lavanderia."

"¡*Dios mio*! Don't remind me."

The next day at work, while eating lunch together, Vi brought up something I hadn't considered. Speaking softly, she said, "Rosie, don't take this the wrong way, but at least for a while, let's keep this ro-roommate situation to ourselves at work. I'm not sure there's a p-problem with it, but I don't want to give Molly any ammunition.

"Why would it be a problem?"

"Because, I'm officially your boss and have to write bi-annual re-reviews for team members. Those are coming up s-soon."

I whispered back, "I see. OK...I won't say anything."

Violet shrugged her shoulders. "Who knows, m-maybe after our garden opens they'll have us working on different teams or maybe you'll get pro-promoted."

"You think?" My eyes opened wide. "I'd never considered that."

"I think we always need to be working toward new goals. That's funny--sounds like s-something my mother would say. But, R-Rosie you would make a g-great team leader."

As we spoke, I saw another team leader come in. I leaned over and whispered to Violet, "Bobby Rodriguez is heading our way. He's so handsome!"

"You think so?" Violet turned and looked up. "Oh, hi Bob, join us."

He looked down at me and smiled. "Always happy to sit next to you two. Best looking gals in the garden."

Violet was taking a chug of water during his comment and laughed, spewing it on the table. "Bob, you never m-mentioned that when you trained me. I think you mean Rosario."

He shrugged and sat down. "Maybe. So, how is life over in Land Xeriscape? Everything coming together for the big reveal?"

I jumped in saying, "It's so beautiful! We planted so many cyclamens along the path today. They should be blooming red and pink by the end of February. Can't wait... and the cactuses arrive next week."

Bobby nodded in agreement. "Yeah, those cyclamens are nice. Great color during the cooler climate. Hey, if you guys need help when the cactus shipment arrives, let me know and I'll check it out with Molly. I've never worked much with cacti and succulents before. I'd like to learn more."

Violet put down her sandwich. "We would l-love your help. Turner was a strong v-v-volunteer for us but he's tied up with his regular job now. He's not coming in as often."

He nodded at her and then turned his attention back to me, "So Rosario, what days do you work?"

I laughed at his question. "Monday through Friday and any other day or time they want me. I need the money. If your gardens need extra help, I can use the overtime."

"Hmm, maybe? I'll look into it."

Violet stood up and gathered her backpack. "I need to m-make a few calls. See you guys later."

Bobby and I had never sat alone together and he seemed a little nervous as Vi left. I suddenly had a great idea. "So, Bobby, have you heard about the special party BUD is having for our garden opening? Violet says it should be fun. Why don't you come with me?"

"Really? I haven't heard anything about it. The gardening crews don't usually attend the donors' events. But I guess it helps if the team leader's mother is loaded--that house at Violet's little Christmas party...that was something else. But sure, I'd love to go with you. Let me know more about it when you have the details."

"So far, all I know is the date. It's February 28th."

He pulled out his phone, and put the date in his calendar. "Hey, if you're not busy this afternoon I was meeting some friends from school after work at Mesquite Mike's, across the street. You should join us,"

"I don't know... I only have my work clothes here."

He shrugged. "Me too. It's OK. Half of my friends are in the same business. We all met in school at A&M." I had to smile at the comment. Violet had mentioned that Bobby seemed to work his A&M degree into every conversation, but I didn't mind. If I had a college degree, I'd be proud too.

"Anyway, the place is super casual. And the bar-b-que is great."

"So, is it close enough for me to walk? I take the bus."

"Really?" That comment surprised him, as if he'd never been on a bus before. "Tell you what. Just meet me at the employee entrance at three-thirty. We'll go over together."

"Sounds good." I got up, clearing my trash. "See you then."

I headed over to the supply shed and met Vi, who was pulling equipment for the afternoon. I sang out to her, "Guess who has a date for the BUD reveal party?"

"You're k-kidding? You asked Bob?"

"Yes, why not? He said yes and then asked me to go to Mesquite Mike's today! I think that's what you guys call a two-for-one. Right?"

Violet smiled and nodded. "I'd never have the nerve to ask out a guy like that. Good for you, roomie."

"Why not? If he'd said no, he's either not interested or has a girlfriend, right? Why wait? Sometimes you have to jump right in."

I followed Violet back to our garden. Even though I was pushing a wheelbarrow full of smelly manure, I had a fast-beating heart, a spring in my step, and a smile plastered across my face. Everything had gone so well since I discovered that church on Christmas Eve. God must really like the rock-n-roll Methodists. I'd been attending each week since then and had met several families and new friends.

Talk about counting my blessings! I was now finally out of my depressing apartment, I had a best friend, and now a nice guy asked me to meet his friends and eat barbacoa. It was like a dream. No longer a total outsider, I was becoming part of a community and that made me happy.

Two weeks later a deep freeze, called *Stormageddon* by the TV people, was projected to hit Dallas with heavy ice and temperatures dropping around zero for a week. Apparently, this was highly unusual for our area. Giant rolls of white cotton tarp were placed over every bed throughout the acres of gardens. Everyone was on high alert, scrambling to get the tender new shoots and trunks covered before damage could occur.

The worst part was, the annual garden's spring event was scheduled in three weeks. Brochures had gone out, signs were printed. Everything was a go.

Once the deep freeze hit, pipes burst across Dallas, power was out in many areas, and the garden shut down, which, according to Molly, had rarely happened. All the BUD associates were told to take the week off, unpaid, with the exception of a few workers who stayed on to maintain the grounds. I was one of those workers that volunteered to stay because I needed the money.

Mark had asked earlier for that week off for a fishing trip in south Texas. Linda Bell claimed she would spend most of her time in a warm bowling alley perfecting her strikes, while Jeffrey was happy to sleep his mornings away. Unfortunately for Vi, Turner announced he was going to LA for an important business trip. He hadn't been working at the garden much and she seemed to really miss him when he wasn't around.

But I was clocking in with a dozen other brave associates that were desperate for a paycheck. We bundled up in our puffer coats, hats, and thick gloves, with only our eyes exposed, looking like a pack of rolling Michelin Men. We kept a check on all water lines and faucets, made sure tarps stayed tight over the beds, assured management that all numerous fountains were secure, and the de-icing units were working in the koi ponds. We called ourselves the dirty dozen, bonding over our frozen acres of white tarp. Only time would tell if the bulbs and buds would make it through this unbearable cold.

CHAPTER 52

I've Got a Secret

VIOLET

I was reclining on my sofa, with a thick navy throw pulled up to my chin, while staring down at my laptop. My Cornell online professor was droning on about optimal garden soil conditions in the Southwestern quadrant, but my mind was elsewhere. Mother had left three days before on her Caribbean cruise, which I had declined. As agonizing as seven days with Mother and continuous Mai-Tais might have been, thoughts of warm gentle breezes and sandy beaches were distracting me. I glanced out my window, looking down at frozen ice and bare, broken tree branches. Maybe I should have gone.

At the time of Mother's cruise invitation, I figured I might be spending my time staying warm in front of my new fireplace, wrapped in the arms of my new maybe-boyfriend. Unfortunately, that wasn't happening either. I'd only seen him a few times since his late-night visit. And he seemed distracted.

A few days ago, Turner called saying he was being pulled away for some important business meetings in L.A. He sounded excited, but out-of-sorts, and said he'd explain things when he returned, after everything was worked out. It all seemed quite mysterious and unsettling, but perhaps I felt that way because I was restless, not being able to work due to the ice storm.

Rosie was working, holding down the fort with the dirty dozen, but the rest of us were told to stay home and I was bored. I closed out my lecture video and decided to call Magna, wanting to speak to an actual person. Since my move, I'd missed our daily conversations together.

"M-Magna, hello. Staying warm, I hope."

"Actually no! My power's been down for twenty-four-hours. I tried to stay at your mother's place while she's gone, but hers is out too."

"My God, M-Magna, why didn't you call earlier? St-Stay with me!"

"Oh, I couldn't impose. I just keep thinking this can't last forever."

"Well, you can't sit alone in a dark fre-freezing condo. I insi-si-st. Please come. I'll let you watch all the Downton Abbey episodes in a row while s-s-sipping hot chocolate. That's an offer I know you can't refuse."

"You do drive a hard bargain...Alright. I accept. What can I bring?"

"Your fav-favorite pillow, a blanket, and snacks? I have everything else. And you can meet my roommate, Rosario, tonight."

"Ah, yes. The one with the thieving boyfriend? Suzanne may have mentioned her."

"You're mi-missing a few pertinent details. I'll f-fill you in when you come over."

"Good, and I have a few concerning thoughts for you too, Violet... on other matters. If I can get my car started, I'll see you soon."

"Great, I'm te-texting you my address now. Once you're parked, take the elevator to the third floor."

I immediately jumped up and started straightening things around the apartment. Then, checking on ingredients in the pantry and refrigerator, I decided a big pot of spicy chili was in order. The perfect choice for someone who'd been sitting in the cold and dark for two days. I turned the thermostat up a few notches and put the gas fireplace on, hoping to defrost Magna.

A few hours later, we were sitting at the table, both on our second bowl of chili, laughing at some of my childhood recollections of my father. Magna, being initially hired as *his* personal assistant, always had good memories of Dad to share with me.

Magna took a deep gulp from her mug of heated mulled wine--her contribution to the meal. "Those were great days back then. I'm so sorry we lost him while you were so young. But Violet, on other matters, I do have a slight concern I wanted to bring up with you. Perhaps I shouldn't, but I know you'll keep it to yourself."

"W-What is it?" I was intrigued and smiled. "Will I need more w-wine for this?"

"Oh, it's probably nothing, but I'll pour you another glass anyway." Magna reached over to the heated pot and filled my mug.

"You know your mother originally had me book her cruise for January with her girlfriends, but then she canceled and had me rebook it for this week, saying a few of the girls had scheduling conflicts."

"Yes. She m-mentioned that to me a couple weeks back."

"Well, she had me book a suite for two."

"And?"

She looked back at me as if I was stupid. "Violet...Suzanne Hill *never* shares a room with girlfriends, even if it's a suite." Then Magna spoke in a whisper. "I think she invited a man. Someone new. It's really none of our business, I guess."

While she continued to explain, her voice went back to a normal level now that the secret was out. "She's usually so transparent with me, letting me in on all her intrigues. I'm just a little concerned because she's keeping things so hush-hush. I honestly really care for your mother. We've been through a lot together. I'd hate for someone to take advantage."

I didn't know what to think. Should I be concerned? Or maybe I should be happy for Mother. It was high time she fell in love again. "Hmm, I'm not sure, Magna. Perhaps she and her friend, Bebe, just decided to economize and share a suite."

"Highly doubtful. I usually assist Suzanne in packing for her trips, but on this one she said she'd do it herself. Earlier in the week her suitcase was out and I saw her quickly fold a sheer leopard-print teddy and toss it in her carry-on. Now Violet, you know that your mother has always been a pajama person."

"True. She does love her Ralph Lauren PJs. But I don't know if that's real sm-smoking-gun evidence, although I can see why you'd be sus-suspicious. Maybe she packed it in hopes of meeting someone on the cruise. You know--like that terrible TV show, *Escape to Love Island.* "

"Not familiar with that, but I remember *Love Boat.* A cruise ship with new romances every week."

I stood up, drinking the last from my mug. "Hey, if Mother can find love on a cruise ship, more power to her. I say we just clear our heads, turn on Downton Abbey reruns, and watch some highbrow *fictional* intrigue."

"Great idea."

We moved over to the sofas, each of us with a blanket. I flipped on the TV to the PBS streaming channel. The opening credits began with the sweeping overview of the Grantham mansion, the charming music playing in the background, with the tinkling of the bells summoning the servants...when suddenly, I bolted upright, inhaled deeply, began coughing, and then pressed the mute button.

"Oh--my--God--Magna! She w-wouldn't have. Would she?"

"She wouldn't have what? What are you asking about?"

"M-M-Mother! You don't think she would have invited *Turner* to go with her, would she?"

"Turner? The young man you invited to the Christmas party? Surely not. Why him?"

"I know it s-sounds crazy. Maybe I have it all wrong." I knew I was going to start hyperventilating, as my wheezing began. "It's just that...Turner's been kind of...distant lately...then he left for a trip to LA on the same day... that Mother left." I wheezed again as my air passages continued to constrict. "It came up abruptly... and he was mysterious about it." I couldn't get the words out fast enough. "Like he didn't want to tell me the details."

"But he's way too young for Suzanne. Besides, he's *your* boyfriend."

I got up, ran to the kitchen, and poured a glass of water, drinking it down, hoping to make the wheezing stop. Instead, I coughed up water all over my face. I shook my head at her comment. "No... he actually hasn't c-c-committed. At the Christmas party, he told me it was too early for a relationship. His wife died several months back." I had to stop speaking as I leaned against the dining table.

Magna got up and grabbed a paper sack from under the kitchen sink. "Here Vi. Try the bag; calm down." Bent over, the wheezing continued as I walked to the sofa. She stood and rubbed my back as she had numerous times in the past. I slowly got my breathing under control, while watching the bag inflate and deflate dozens of times.

I whispered, "Thanks Magna, I think I'm feeling b-b-better." I leaned over, pressing my forehead to my hands and stared at the floor for a minute. Reining in my emotions, I continued with more deliberation, speaking slowly. "To your point--Turner's only twelve years younger than M-Mother. She actually brought it up to me on Christmas day. Although, I think her math is fa-faulty. But the w-w-worst part was the way she was flirting with him at her p-party. It was *embarrassing* for me."

Magna shook her head in disbelief. "Violet, Suzanne can be somewhat insensitive at times, but I don't think she'd be *that* cruel. Do you?"

I looked back at her with a deadpan expression. "I didn't think so either. B-But I do know this. Whatever Suzanne w-wants, Suzanne gets." But I had to wonder, could Turner be that cruel too?

CHAPTER 53

The Blur of the Blue Kimono

VIOLET

The next morning, the temperature began inching above zero, hovering in the teens and then finally, the sun broke through. The sunshine helped lessen the sense of doom I'd created in my mind last night, while tossing on the sofa-bed with images of Turner and Mother swirling through my mind. By morning, some of my murderous thoughts had tempered and I decided perhaps it was all a matter of coincidental timing.

That anxiety was also lessened when I saw a text that morning from Turner. I read his words over three times:

Miss you! Lots of balls in the air. I'll explain everything when I get back. Stay safe and warm.

There wasn't too much to glean from those four very short sentences, but my take-away was this: *One*-- He'd thought enough of me to send a ten-second text. Obviously, that's not saying much. *Two*--'Lots of balls in the air' sounded more like a business reference than a weird juggling gigolo thing, although now I had an image of flying balls and penises burned into my brain. *Three*--Turner intended to see me to explain something important on his return, whether that was announcing he and my mother were retiring together in the Bahamas or he was going for global domination in the supply chain business--all this was still in question. *Four*--He wished me warmth and safety which was endearing in a grandfatherly sort of way. Maybe that wasn't so good.

I did my best to try and shake off last night's discussion with Magna. Yesterday's rumors were behind me. But occasional bad thoughts kept coming out to play, so I kept myself fully occupied with other matters. The plan for today was to refresh, plow into my studies, and put Turner Cooper and Mother on the back-burner until I could have an actual one-on-one conversation with the maybe-boyfriend.

Rosie had already left for BUD, but I missed our daily camaraderie and couldn't wait to get called back to work. I was anxious to see what the ice and freezing temps had done to the garden, hoping that most of our new plants survived. The good thing was that most of the shrubs, bushes, and trees we'd planted were hardy native stock, conditioned for North Texas weather. But this week's cold weather was unprecedented.

Finally, after the seven longest days of my life, temperatures shot up to the upper thirties, normal for Dallas winter weather. I put on thick leggings and a zip jacket and went to the lake for a run. It felt amazing. Looking around, it seemed as if everybody had crept out of their homes and was now wandering about in daze on the jogging trails after surviving power outages, burst pipes, and binge-watching TV.

While running, I got a call from Turner. I stopped quickly and took the call with trepidation. "Hello?"

"Hi Vi. I'm back! Just now leaving the airport. Why don't we meet for dinner tonight?"

"Dinner? Yes, I'm available. S-S-So what's your big news?"

"Let's talk about it later. It can wait. I'm on my way to pick up Blaze at the kennel, drop my bags at the house, and then go see my parents. I need to check on Dad's rehab. Hey... I missed seeing you."

"Yes, me too. S-S-So where do you want to go tonight?"

"I heard about a great Turkish restaurant, Cafe Izmir. You game for that?"

Interesting; it was the same restaurant Mother had taken me to when I first moved back to Dallas. "Sure. I've be-been there. The food's good. How'd you hear of that pl-place?"

"No idea, maybe somebody from work? OK Vi, see you around seven."

An hour later, I'd completed my run and was heading up the sidewalk to my apartment when Mother called. "Darling, just wanted to let you know I'm back. And I'm brown as a beetle and feel so invigorated and refreshed!"

"Good to hear, Mother. Hope your power is back. Magna said it was off a few days ago."

"Seems to be fine now. Drop by soon--we need to chat."

"Sure; some day soon."

Now I was even more conflicted. The timing of Turner's and Mother's arrivals was as suspicious as their departures. Mother sounded downright jubilant, rather rare for her, except when she scored major deals at Neiman's semi-annual sale. But Turner sounded more worn out. Perhaps I was letting my imagination run wild...again.

After I showered, I checked my closet for possible dinner outfits, oddly feeling like I was competing with Mother, which was impossible. I would always be simple Violet, the quiet, unassuming flower near the bottom of the bouquet, shadowed by the large, bright-orange, attention-grabbing Tiger Lily. I looked through, shuffling the hangers of my dull wardrobe. After all the dark days, I was tired of wearing black. I opted for simple, choosing an off-white pull-over sweater with light-colored jeans.

While dressing, I received a text from Molly at BUD:

*Forecasts appear normal for BUD to reopen. Monday, the day after tomorrow, we are reverting back to regular hours. All lead gardeners and crews need to be on hand **tomorrow** to ready the gardens for reopening. All lead gardeners must contact their teams immediately for tomorrow's work. Thank you, Molly*

I called my team, reaching Rosario first, who already heard the news. I reached Mark, who said he was on his way back from his South Padre fishing trip. I left a message for Jeff who was probably napping, and I interrupted Linda Bell right after her seventh strike on the front ten. Not sure what that meant, but she seemed quite excited about it and I heard thunder in the background.

Thinking my dinner with Turner might run late, I pulled out my work clothes for tomorrow and noticed I was missing my rubber boots which I definitely needed. I assumed I left them at the guest house while moving, perhaps under the bed? I still had plenty of time before Turner arrived so I drove over to find them.

My plan was to drive up, grab my boots and go. I wasn't in the mood to hear about Mother's fabulous cruise and afraid of the details. I quickly went up the drive, parked in front of the guest house and went in. Sure enough, they were under the bed. As I headed back to my car, I couldn't help but notice a man sprinting across the backyard from the tool shed. A man wearing a blue floral kimono, which looked like something my mother occasionally wore. I stepped a little closer, squinted, and sucked in my breath in surprise.

"M-Mark? Mark! It's Violet."

He turned and looked at me as I continued walking towards him. For once, Mark seemed to be at a loss for words. He stopped in his tracks, looking quite tanned, with the tight blue kimono tied at the waist, reaching above his knees.

As I approached, the strong scent of pot wafted through the air. "Mark?... w-what are you doing here? And... is that my m-m-mother's robe?"

In a low voice, he held up his hands and said, "What can I say, Vi? Suzanne loves me in blue."

I just nodded, shook my head, and then began laughing uncontrollably as tension and relief flowed through me. "W-Wow...are you kidding me? You and my mother? Oh my God!" I was busy considering the when and how of it. Then I recalled seeing him here very early several weeks ago, and then there was his sudden request off for a fishing trip.

"Hey Vi, let's keep this whole thing between the three of us. Uh,

I'm getting a little chilly; nothing here but my privates hanging out in this flimsy robe. I'll fill you in later."

"My pl-pleasure. By the way, how was your *fishing* trip?"

He smiled, nodding as he walked away. "Really good. Caught myself a real wild one."

"Mark, you have no idea w-what you have on the line. I wish you luck."

On my way home, I couldn't help but keep laughing. Humoring myself at Mark's ability to continuously surprise me, and the total cliche of the whole scene--the rich lady schlepping the gardener, although, I think the story usually involved a shirtless pool boy. I had to wonder; would Mother keep Mark a secret? Or would she slowly introduce him into her circle after she cleaned him up and reinvented him? Then again, it may have been a spontaneous short fling.

The thing that really kept the smile across my face was the disappearance of the image of Turner and Mother together in my mind. I shivered again thinking about it and felt guilty believing Turner would ever do something like that.

When I returned to the apartment, Rosie was there and said Bob had called and asked her out for this evening. I was happy for her. He was a nice guy and seemed really attracted to her. Then I decided to call Cafe Izmir to ask for delivery. I requested the same dishes my mother and I had enjoyed months ago. I realized that Turner would probably get here exhausted after a three hour flight from LA, a trip to his house, the kennel, his parents place and then back over here. The last thing he would probably feel like doing was drive to a restaurant.

I turned down the lights, had the fireplace going, lit a few aromatic candles, and set the table for two. Rosie came out of her room looking gorgeous and smelling even better than the candles.

"Vi, it looks so beautiful. Turner will love it. Look at us...two girls with Saturday-night dates. I can't believe it." She reached over, giving me a big hug, although I still turned rigid every time she got too close. Rosie was definitely a hugger; something I needed to work on giving and receiving.

A few minutes after Bob came to pick her up, Turner arrived looking as tired as I thought he'd be. Opening the door, I reached up, put my arms around his neck and kissed him hard. "Come in and relax." I walked over to the kitchen counter. "I've opened a re-really good Cab. You're going to l-love it."

He looked down at his watch. "Sounds perfect, but I made a reservation for seven-thirty."

Walking back with two glasses, I said, "Call and cancel. I ordered de-delivery from Cafe Izmir. It should be here any time now."

He sat on the sofa, let out a big sigh, and smiled. "Thank you! Did I tell you you're wonderful yet?"

I joined him on the sofa. "I'm happy to see you. This p-p-past week felt so long."

"Didn't it? For me too. Good news though. I don't think I'll be traveling that much anymore, for business that is."

"Why's that?"

"That's my big news. I sold Rapid Logistics this week. All gone--after twelve years of building it from almost nothing."

I was shocked. It was like his baby. "What? W-W-Why?"

"You've probably noticed; the work just wasn't inspiring me much any more. I thought it was all tied up with Allie and guilt of never being available for her. I'm really not sure; I think I'm just done with it. I figured something out during the last month or two." He reached for his glass and took a slow sip of wine.

I waited for a few seconds. ..."And?"

"I think I'm better at building up a business and developing clients than I am at *running* a business. Either that, or I need a good partner who is more detail oriented. Anyway... now with this sale, I've got a big stack of cash and can investigate other business ventures for a while. And the crazy thing is, I owe it all to your mother."

At that moment the doorbell rang. I opened up to the DoorDash guy, while the delicious smells of dinner invaded the apartment. I tipped him, and put the food from boxes into serving bowls. "I hope you're going to l-love this Turner. B-Bring the wine and come to the table."

We sat across from each other and he sighed again, offering up a contented smile. "You're making me very happy. This looks fantastic." Turner pulled off a piece of flatbread and popped it into his mouth. "I'm sorry if I've been distant lately, but my mind has been jumping all over the place. I'm seriously thinking about going to therapy."

"Really? I'm s-surprised. You usually seem so together."

"Maybe I've put up a good front, but scratch the surface and I'm a mess. You know I had the guilt trip going for a while, and obviously a big heap of grief after losing Allie, and then I got walloped by her betrayal. I tried hiding or burying it all, but finally I realized, I'm just kind of messed up, Vi."

I looked down at my hands. "I think th-therapy is a healthy idea. You've been through a lot. L-L-Lexi is not a clinical psychologist, but she's helped me so m-much this year. Without the talks and goals she set, there's no way I'd b-be sitting here across from you. When I lived in Austin, I would literally go w-weeks without sp-speaking to another person. I was afraid of everything."

I picked up one of the bowls. "Here, try this meat, it goes over the pita, and then p-pour this butter and sauce over everything. Tell me what you think?"

He took a bite, closed his eyes, savoring it, and nodded. "*Almost* as good as kissing you."

My face blushed as I changed the subject. "S-S-So what did my mother have to do with the sale of your b-business?"

"She put me together with the guy who offered to buy me out. They're both on the board of an investment firm. Your Mother truly seems to know everyone."

"More than you can even imagine," I said, thinking of Mark darting across the lawn today.

"I wasn't really interested in taking on an investor or an equity partner, but the more we talked, the more intrigued Tim was with Rapid Logistics and particularly several of my clients. He already has a large stake in another supply chain business and was wanting to get a toe-hold in the Texas market. I met with him and his team in LA and after everyone looked through our books, they eventually made me an offer that I jumped at."

"That's fantastic. But won't you m-miss it?"

Turner looked up at the ceiling considering my question. "It'll feel strange no longer being a part of it. But, you know...something will bubble up and interest me soon. I've had a few thoughts already."

"So how did your father take the news? "

"Dear Dad." Turner smiled and shook his head. "He was really pissed for about thirty minutes today while I was explaining everything to him. Then I handed him a check for his founder's portion which Dawcett signed off on, and he quieted down real quick. It's all for the best. He was in way over his head on the technology end of the business. And Mom is thrilled. She'd been trying to get him to retire for the last ten years."

"Then it's truly gr-great news. You m-must be so happy."

"Very happy, except for one thing." Turner took another bite of the meat, and looked into my eyes. "I hated being away from you. I purposely haven't been around much, testing myself, trying to clear my head, and I'm sorry about doing that to you. But it was like I had to take a step back and look at everything from the outside in, to decide what I really needed. I know it sounds bizarre."

"No, I think I understand. S-Sometimes we have to cl-clear all the clutter before we can see what's important."

"Vi, I was thinking about you every night. And then you even started invading my day dreams at some of the meetings I had to sit through. Instead of looking at spreadsheets, I'd see you walking down the hill at BUD in your cap, pushing your wheelbarrow, or running past me on the trail at White Rock. And of course, I had a few visions of you standing in front of me in your underwear too; but anyway, I decided that this *thing* between us might be the real deal." He cleared his throat waiting for my response. "I mean...I hope I haven't messed things up and you feel the same way."

I forced my eyes to stare into his. What a day! Earlier, I'd almost convinced myself he'd been cruising the Caribbean with Mother, and now he was facing me, saying he wanted a relationship. My heart was singing. I smiled and nodded. "Yes, I'd really like that. S-So, does this mean I can tell Lexi I have a b-boyfriend?"

He grabbed my hand and kissed it while laughing. "Yes, please Vi. Tell Lexi, Rosie, the crew at BUD, your mother and Magna, the DoorDash guy, and whoever the hell else you want. I am the *official,* committed boyfriend."

CHAPTER 54

The Fixer and Mixer

VIOLET

It felt so good to get back to work. Fifty degrees, the sky--a deep blue, with my heart and mind feeling happy and clear. I was carefully examining all of our plants but noticed the blooming cyclamen had not survived and hundreds would need replanting before the reveal party. The cactus garden at the bottom of the hill was fine, but their flowering buds were stunted and none of the succulents would be blooming for the event. If the sun continued strong for the next two weeks, a few of our flowering trees might begin to blossom. Our xeriscape garden wouldn't be filled with the gorgeous beds of blooming color that many of BUD's visitors clamored for, but that wasn't what this garden was about anyway.

The bronze longhorns looked ideal; one was sculpted as if he was heading down the trail at a trot, and the second one at the bottom of the hill, had its head down as if taking a deep drink from the windmill water tank. Both the longhorns and the windmill had been Turner's ideas and they made a great compliment to the southwestern look we wanted to achieve.

Later today, I would test the power source from solar panels placed on the shade coverings over the tables and check the rainwater storage tanks for dispersal through our water lines. Mark was busy painting the wall we'd all helped build, blending the paint in a light wash of golden rust, which blended to tan, and then brown, much like the Big Bend rock formations we were simulating.

All the elements were coming together and it was exciting to watch the final pieces fall into place.

Then, I heard Molly's voice from a distance. "So, how'd it fare in your part of the gardens, Violet?"

I turned around and squinted, looking up into the morning sun and saw her at the top of the hill. My rubber boots crunched up the caliche trail to get closer. "Hi M-Molly. I think we're going to be OK. Need to re-replant the cyclamens, and clear out a lot of dead leaves and some plantings, but it l-looks like we'll be ready."

She scanned the beds and glanced around. "Yeah, not too bad. I think your area fared better than most." With her hands on her hips, she gave me a nod. "I'm pleased we decided to add the longhorns and windmill. Looks good. Glad we stuck with that idea."

Yeah, the idea you hated until it got set up. "Yes, that was all Turner's doing. He bought the statues off a rancher west of Abilene. Turned out g-great."

She nodded and then gave me a concerned look. "Certainly hope he's not running the show here, Violet. He's only a volunteer."

"Oh, not at all. Actually, he hasn't been able to v-v-volunteer much lately. But the wi-windmill and bronzes were his pet projects from the beginning."

"Good, because I expect capable leadership from my lead gardeners."

I forced a smile at her backhanded slap. "Understood. B-By the way...the team is excited about the re-reveal party for the garden opening. They're all coming, some with guests. Should I give the event organizer a head count from our gr-group--for food and all?"

Molly looked at me with a confused expression across her face. "What are you talking about?"

"The p-party for the opening. Remember...some of that money we raised was going towards that. You told me the date a while ago."

"Violet, that party will *not* include your team. Are you serious? It's for gold-status garden members and big donors. The grounds people *never* attend these events. I barely get invited, but I'll *have* to attend to introduce and explain this project to guests."

My face turned red from embarrassment. Of course I had assumed our team would attend. We had designed and created this project. We'd been working for months on this. I'd told everyone to attend and had them all excited about it. "S-S-Sorry. I just assumed. It's a celebration for the opening. I thought the p-people who did the work would be invited."

She shook her head and began walking away, and then turned back. "No Violet. It doesn't work that way. Do the caterers and decorators attend the party--no, of course not. This is the same thing--no matter who your *mother* is."

I yelled back at her, my voice getting shrill. "Since Turner and I raised the money, I think my team should attend the celebration."

"Sorry. That's a *firm* no. I have other areas to examine. Have a good day."

I was devastated. I normally hated parties, so it was odd for me to be so passionate about attending. But I'd been building up this opening in my mind. It was a goal to work toward and the party was the reward. I was proud of everyone and we had all worked so hard. This wasn't right! For now, I'd keep this conversation to myself.

I tried to calm down as I walked down the hill to compliment Mark on his painting skills. "The w-w-wash that you're doing on the limestone looks amazingly real. Great job, Mark."

"Thanks; it's all about the brush stroke and the amount of water mixed in with the paint. I've used this technique before. So, what did Molly want? She say anything about me?"

"No, nothing. Just checking the st-status of the garden."

"She's mad because I broke it off with her. Molly expected me to take her to the opening party--but no way. She's a real ball-buster."

"Interesting; so you were supposed to be her date?"

Mark shrugged. "Maybe in her mind. Hey Vi, have you and your mom had a talk yet about...you know...me in her kimono the other day?"

"Not yet, but may-maybe it's time. So, give me a little background. How did this *thing* b-between you two happen?"

Mark stopped painting, giving me his full attention. "Let's see... It all started with that birdhouse you gave her. A while back, while I was raking the yard, Suzanne asked me to hang the birdhouse in the big live oak shading the patio. After I finished, she brought out a couple of Bloody Mary's for us and we got to talking about birds. I'm an amateur ornithologist, so I guess we sort of bonded over that. She even had me get some additional bird houses, and you know...how one thing leads to another?"

"Yeah, especially when m-morning Bloody Mary's are involved." I shook my head while laughing. "And *of course,* you're an or-or-ornithologist. So, you think this thing between you and Suzanne is the real deal?"

Mark looked up into the sky and raised his arms. "Who knows where the heart leads, darlin'. But we'll have some fun following it around."

"Right. Just don't let her sap your s-s-soul."

~

The following day, I decided to schedule an evening chat with Mother. I called, checking in with Magna first. "So, are you in the office alone?"

"Yes. What can I do for you today, Violet?"

"Have you heard about M-Mother's L-Love Boat connection?"

She lowered her voice and spoke in a conspiratorial tone, "Yes, I'm appalled. Mark and Suzanne are canoodling all over this house in the middle of the afternoons. I'm a little worried. I've never seen her like this."

"I agree; pretty b-bizarre. Just keep the credit cards and checkbooks under lock and key. Although, I think Mark is probably harmless and they're just enjoying each other."

"Oh, I can assure you. They are!"

"Anyway... I need some M-Mother-time. What time slot can you give me?"

"Tuesday nights are generally good. Maria usually does Taco Tuesdays for dinner."

"G-Great; put me down for six o'clock and t-t-text me back if Mother agrees."

"Will do."

I chuckled to myself, picturing Magna freaking out, while spying on Mark and Mother *canoodling*, whatever that entailed.

Tuesday evening I was sitting across the dining table from Mother, munching on crunchy, meat-filled tacos, black beans, rice, and plenty of guacamole. Mother jumped into her new relationship discussion with zest.

"Now Vi, I know you and Mark have talked and you now understand we are dating."

I coughed up a bit of taco. "Seems like it m-moved *beyond* dating a while back, but M-Mother...do whatever makes you happy. Just be careful. Much to my amazement, M-Mark seems to get around. Uh, with women, I mean."

"Well, he's hard to resist, honestly." I shook my head at the comment, still not clear on that vibe. "But I understand what you're saying, dear. No worries, we're both benefiting from the relationship."

Yikes! Time to move on. I scooped up some guac with a chip and took a bite. "I had a question for you, Mother. Are you still p-planning on attending the reveal party at BUD? It's next week, S-Saturday evening."

"It's definitely on the calendar and I was thinking of inviting Mark, seeing that he's a master gardener. It might be a perfect time to introduce him to some of my friends who adore gardening. He'll fit right in."

I was a little taken aback. "So you're not keeping this whole thing with him a s-secret?"

"Well, I'll start with a few friends and see how it goes."

"The reason I'm asking is that I was pl-planning on my entire BUD team attending, but M-Molly said we can't go. Apparently, all garden crew are off l-limits for these events."

Mother stopped eating and looked shocked. "That is absurd and I can tell you this--my daughter *is* coming to her own reveal party! It's utterly ridiculous. Of course...you could go as a guest with

Turner. He must have been sent an invitation since he was the first garden sponsor."

"I've c-considered that, but what about the others? Besides M-Mark, there's Rosie, her date, B-Bobby, Linda Bell, and Jeffrey."

Mother held her fork in the air while in deep thought. "Hmm, I reserved a ten-top, and paid handsomely for the privilege, so I can invite whoever the hell I want. Let's check in with Magna for a minute. She shouldn't mind."

Mother picked up her cell and buzzed Magna, putting her on speaker.

"Magna, I'm here with Vi. Have we already sent out e-vites for my guests attending Violet's BUD reveal party?"

"Hi ladies. No, those are scheduled to release tomorrow. Do you need to make changes?"

"Looks like it. I want to include some of Vi's team. She and I are discussing this now and we'll have a new list for you tomorrow."

"I'll wait on your instructions, Suzanne. Good night."

So, high drama and intrigue within the garden party scene--who would have thought? I hated having to bring Mother in to help me with this problem, but occasionally you had to use your trump card. My sway was minimal.

Becoming energized with her own manipulation skills, Mother dropped her taco back on the plate. "OK Vi, write this down in your phone notes. Let's see...You and Turner can sit at another table together. I can't honestly see the director throwing out the date of the key garden sponsor, can you? Now then...At my table, Rosie-the-roommate can sit next to Collin Wentworth. He should be pleased; from my recollection she's kind of like a miniature Sophia Viguarro, isn't she?"

Rolling my eyes, I said, "I have no idea who you're t-talking about."

She ignored my comment and continued. "Then Collin's mother, Bebe, will sit next to Rosie's date, Bobby? If he's attractive, Bebe will love that--very Mrs. Robinson! That should work."

I responded with, "If she likes fresh Texas A&M graduates, she'll be pleased."

She stopped to count on her fingers. "So that's six with me and Mark. Now, who's this Jeffrey person?"

I ate another chip and then described him. "A young twenty-something, who doesn't know what he wants to do in life and hangs around with Linda Bell, who's in her forties."

She nodded. "I see...Possibly gay?"

I shook my head at her interpretation. "Not that I've noticed."

"Why not this...Let's invite Johnnie Jones, that hot-shot realtor. You remember him, Vi? Blonde highlights, cute and gay as a bunny; maybe he would pair well with Jeffrey? Even if Jeffrey's straight, Johnnie's a lively raconteur. And you mentioned...a Linda Bell?" Mother's mind was clicking through her friend and acquaintance roster like a high-speed computer. "What's she like?"

"All I know is she likes b-bowling and seems very good at it."

"Let's see, we need a real beer and pretzel kind of guy then, right?" I shrugged as she snapped her fingers. "Perfect. Remember your soccer coach from junior high?"

"Vaguely. Uh, Coach Little?"

"That's it; we all call him Little Bill. He's still around at all the school benefit functions, and loves to show up at events. We'll put those two together. Now, no one else needs to know about this. I'll simply put all their names down as guests for my table. And your little worker bees will mix it up with my friends. It will be fun! No one would *dare* stop my guests from attending. Not even *Molly*--who ever the hell she is."

"She's my b-boss, and Mark's previous girlfriend."

"Really? *Perfect!* That will make this even more fun. I'll get Magna on the changes first thing tomorrow."

It was amazing. Someone had taken over the brain of Suzanne Hill who, a month ago, would never even conceive of sitting down to a special-event dinner with a landscaping crew. I had to wonder, was it all stemming from Mark's weird magic, or maybe the afternoon canoodling?

I was genuinely overwhelmed with gratitude, with my eyes tearing up. "M-Mother, this m-means a lot to me. I can't thank you enough. I was s-so worried about disappointing everyone." I got up, rounded the table, stooped down and hugged her hard, perhaps for the first time in my memory.

Mother started to cry and held me tighter. The embrace was becoming too much, but I remained still, scrunching my eyes shut, and hung in there.

"Violet, I've waited for this moment for so long. Don't pull away dear. Let me just hold on for a moment longer." Silently, I counted to ten, just as she released me and said, "Fantastic. I think that's enough; don't you? Pass the tacos please."

CHAPTER 55

So Happy Together

TURNER

My head was in a much better place after the sale of Rapid Logistics. I'd selected a psychologist to work with while plowing through my issues, trying to make sense of life after Allie. And I was excited about the prospect of new business challenges on the horizon. I was still contractually obligated to be at my company for another month to help the buyout transition go smoothly, but in reality, I'd already checked out and was ready to move on.

But the one thing in my life that felt right and helped center me was the time I spent with Violet.

It felt like we were both shedding old skins and revealing something fresh and new underneath. I saw her gaining in self confidence almost each time we came together, as she revealed more of her true personality. Her shyness might always be a hurdle, but her transformation was amazing to witness.

And it went both ways. Vi challenged me to be better, more caring and more transparent. I attempted to take note of the small things that were important when building a relationship: honesty, daily involvement, enthusiasm, punctuality, and taking an interest. Things both Allie and I had completely stopped doing for each other.

On Wednesday, Vi called me while on her lunch break. "Hey there; is our top v-volunteer ever coming back to us? All the gang says hi and we m-miss you."

"Miss you guys too, but I'm digging into potential business ideas I've been considering. It's exciting actually. I'd love to pick your brain about some plans soon. How's everything there?"

"Still working on lots of re-replantings, but it's coming together. I c-called to make sure we're on for next Saturday evening. You re-received an invitation to our BUD reveal party, right?"

"Yeah, I saw something in my email. So, you want me to RSVP for two?"

"Yes, please. I'm officially *not* allowed to attend. None of our crew is per M-Molly's vehement instructions. But M-Mother says if we all come as guests of people who received invitations, it shouldn't be a pr-problem."

"Wow, hard to believe they wouldn't want you there after all you've done. I'll confirm right now. Actually...I'm pulling up the invitation in my email, as we speak, and there's a note from the BUD director. She's asking me to say a few words during dinner to the attendees about the project. I'm glad I'm checking this now."

"That is so ridiculous. They want a d-donor to speak to everyone, but they don't want to see or hear from the people who cr-created the garden."

"Way of the world, Vi. Even in our little peaceful garden, money talks. They're just wanting to encourage more donors, volunteers and get some free society press. That's pretty much the point of this shindig."

"I guess," she said despondently.

On the evening of the BUD party, I picked up Violet. She was dressed in the gorgeous pink McCartney dress she'd worn to the holiday garden party, but when she opened her door, I could see she was visibly shaking.

"Violet, what's wrong? Everything's going to be fine. This is your big night."

"I know, but I'm afraid s-somebody will throw me and my team out."

I held her tight by the front door trying to calm her down, but it only seemed to make things worse. "I promise; that won't happen. This isn't some high-security event. It's a party for garden fans. Nobody's getting thrown out. Shake it off, beautiful."

Violet pulled away, and literally shook her head, shoulders, body and hands. trying to rid herself of anxiety. She looked up with a hint of a smile. "You're right. I feel b-better now."

I couldn't help but laugh. "You know, shaking-it-off is just an expression, but glad that worked."

I helped her into her black dress coat and said, "Besides, you're almost in disguise. In that dress, with make up on, and your hair down, I'll wager most of the people from BUD won't even recognize you without the green polo and baseball cap."

"G-Good point. I guess I'm ready."

Arriving at BUD's indoor event center, a hostess greeted us at the door with a clipboard. "Yes, Mr. Turner and Ms. Hill, you are at table one. Before dinner, we're offering our guests ten-minute tram tours out to the new xeriscape garden. Please join the others if you like. Have a lovely evening."

We stepped into the large room filled with several ten-top round dining tables, which were covered in long white table cloths with dark green overlays. There were low-slung twinkling lights above, and hundreds of potted shrubs covered with pink and orange roses surrounding the interior walls of the room. It smelled as if we were in the midst of a spring garden.

"Oh, there's R-Rosie and Bob." Vi pointed to a full table near the front. We walked over and she introduced me to the people I had not met yet, but Vi had prepped me with intel on her Mother's friends.

First up--the rude and haunting high school date from Violet's past, Collin Wentworth, who appeared to be going to seed early with a bloated face and receding hairline. Vi would be pleased about that. His haughty mother, Bebe, looked quite happy talking the ear off of handsome Bob Rodriguez, another BUD gardener who was now dating Rosie. She was wedged between Bob and a realtor named Johnny, who sized me up head-to-toe and handed me his card. Next to the bored looking Jeffrey, was Violet's former soccer coach, John Little, who was talking gutter-ball strategies with Linda Bell. She looked pleased and was taking notes. And then there was Vi's mother, holding court with Mark, smiling and laughing, while they occasionally touched hands and stole sideway glances at each other.

I spoke up over the table chatter and asked, "So, who's up for taking a tram ride over to the xeriscape garden? Can't wait to see the completed project!"

Jeffrey said, "Y'all go ahead. I see it everyday."

Collin also chimed in, "Yeah, gardens...not really my thing."

Everybody else stood up eagerly, put on their coats and lined up outside for the next trams. Once we arrived, I was impressed. The garden was lit with strategically placed golden lights in the trees and on the ground, spotlighting key items. From the top of the hill, it all looked amazing. Molly was at the site, filling in as tour guide with each tram-load of guests. As we huddled together, she looked over at us and her mouth dropped, recognizing her uninvited employees.

Molly pulled herself back together and greeted us. "Hi there, welcome! I see some familiar faces here. Actually, Violet, this is my fifth tour of the night. I'm a little talked out. Why don't you step in for me. I see now how badly you wanted to be here."

"I only came for T-Turner's dinner talk."

"No. I insist. Go ahead." Molly said, beginning to remove the pleasant tone from her voice.

"Alright." Vi took over explaining all the technical innovations, including the solar panels and rain storage tanks at the top and then led us down the caliche path, pointing out all the native Texas drought tolerant plants and trees, explaining the significance of the longhorns, the inspiration of the rock wall, and the windmill. You could tell she loved her garden in a very personal way. When we reached the cactus garden at the bottom, everyone clapped, and she looked overwhelmed. Violet began to blush and almost took my breath away.

Then we climbed back into the tram now waiting at the bottom of the hill. As we bounced along in the back seat, I whispered, "That went really well. Good job,Vi."

"Thanks. M-Molly seems OK, right? I don't know why I was so worried."

I pulled her in tight and snuck a warm kiss on her cold cheek. I was happy for her and couldn't wait for us to get back to her apartment. But we still had the dinner, my talk, and the donors' pledges to contend with.

CHAPTER 56

It's My Party (and I'll Cry if I Want To)

VIOLET

As the dinner progressed, Turner stood up to give his donor's speech. I was in awe at his ease of speaking to the large group and so proud of him. His talk seemed spontaneous and fun, and he added an unexpected twist at the end.

"...So, I'm sure y'all are tired of listening to me and want to move on to your dessert, but before you dip into that cheesecake, I'd be remiss not to end with these thoughts. You know...I came to the Botanicals United offices back in September when I was in a pretty dark space. Seems like a lifetime ago. My wife, Allie, had passed away weeks before. I knew she'd enjoyed her time volunteering here. I thought maybe she'd appreciate a memorial bench in her honor. But instead, I ended up donating a sponsorship to this amazing new garden for her *and* I found a home here myself. I began volunteering three days a week working with a fun and diverse group of hard-working friends."

At this point, Turner's eyes appeared to mist up a bit. Something I'd never seen him do before, but he continued, his voice remaining strong.

"I've learned new planting techniques and developed skills I hadn't used in a while--like crouching, kneeling, and standing up again. And I always came away from my work at BUD feeling exhausted, but satisfied and happy. Happy about the crew I worked with and the sense that I was contributing to something *larger* than myself. "

Turner cleared his throat and pointed towards me and then Mark. "There's Violet Hill here, our team leader, who has an amazing knowledge of sustainable gardening. Mark Hopkins, sitting at this next table, who has a broad swath of garden know-how and always makes the work more interesting. Also sitting over there, we have our clever worker bees, Linda Bell Dinkins and Jeffrey Green. They've been essential, always there whenever they were needed. And I'd be remiss not to mention Rosario Guzman who showed up every day with a smile on her face and an unmatched work ethic. Rosie, could you stand up please."

She nervously stood, looking around as Turner continued. "Here's a young woman who came to Dallas not long ago with nothing but a backpack and a load of fear and threats from a gang who had brutally murdered her twin brother, Roberto. Tonight, I would like to dedicate the one bench being placed in this garden to Roberto Guzman, who was a brave, supportive brother and deserves recognition and a place of remembrance for his sister, Rosie."

As applause broke out, Rosie began crying as she walked over and hugged Turner. After he sat down, I grabbed his hand and whispered, "That was amazing. Thank you s-so much."

Dessert came and went, glasses of Champagne were poured for a toast and the BUD director concluded with a brief film highlighting the most recent updates for the entire garden.

When the video ended, I got up to visit the restroom. Passing Mother's table, she gently tugged on my hand. "Fantastic job, baby. So proud of you, and thanks for letting me help."

I was choked up, squeezing back on her hand. There was no gloating, no recriminations, just a genuine thank you from her. "Thank you, Mother. I-I love you." I couldn't believe I'd just said that. A bridge had been crossed. This was truly a perfect evening.

I continued on to the restroom. As I came out of the stall, Molly walked in. She glanced past the empty stalls and frowned at me. I broke the silence first, as I washed my hands. "What a gr-great event! I think everything went well, don't you, M-Molly?"

She ignored my comment and spoke in a low but angry tone. "Did I or did I *not* expressly tell you that none of the gardening team should attend this event?"

"You did, but M-Molly, all of us were invited by guests that re-received invitations. I don't think we broke any rules."

"Yes, you did. I told you not to pull rank using your mother and you did just the opposite. All these seats were supposed to be for potential donors, who bring in important dollars. Your little group brings in zero value."

I was being verbally attacked and felt like running out the door, but I forced myself to stand my ground. "W-What about the value of employee retention? Associates should feel rewarded for their efforts. I g-guarantee you, attending this meant so much to them."

"Violet, you have no sense of protocol and refuse to follow rules, and I'm exhausted by it. Whatever this *is* between us, it's definitely *not* working. You are officially fired. And I warn you; don't try to bring your mother and her attorneys into all this. It won't be worth it. You'd be fighting against someone with sixteen years experience as head of Horticulture Hiring. Just walk away."

I was in shock with no response, as three women walked in together, chatting and laughing. I quickly passed Molly, going out the door with my head buzzing, feeling numb, not seeing or hearing anything but the scene which had just transpired.

Walking by Mother's table, I felt someone grab my arm. I looked over. Mark had hold of my elbow as everyone was standing up and saying their goodbyes. "Hey, fearless leader, we're all headed to a musty, dark tavern I frequent. You and Turner should join us."

I shook my head and looked away. "Thanks M-Mark. I just can't."

Mark leaned over and said softly, "Hey there, you OK? "

I shook my head and forced a smile, "Just a little t-t-tired."

Turner came over, handed me my bag and coat, and asked, "Ready to go?"

I nodded, keeping my head down, not speaking to anyone else. I only wanted to disappear quickly and find a hole to climb into. *Two job firings within seven months. What a loser!* Turner held my arm as he guided me through the parking lot and into his truck.

Once inside, he finally broke the silence. "Vi, out with it. I can tell; something's wrong. Was it something I said during my talk?"

I kept my face turned to the window. "No. Your talk was p-perfect. The b-bench for Rosie's brother--that was so generous."

"Then, something must have happened when you left. What is it?"

"I c-can't talk about it. M-Maybe later."

"Alright. Happy to listen whenever you're ready. So, I'm assuming you're not interested in joining up with the others?"

"No. Let's go to your house... please?" Tears began running down my face as the reality of the firing sank in.

"Sure. I'm ready to listen when you need to talk."

Driving over, I kept Mollie's conversation on replay, wondering what I could have said differently. I had to wonder...was it really a fireable offense? I recalled her words: 'officially fired...using my mother's influence... not following rules and protocol.' Except for attending this party, I felt like I'd followed every direction she'd ever given me, always deferring to her recommendations. Yes, I'd come up with some of my own ideas. But we weren't robots. We were supposed to be creative, right?

My thoughts were interrupted by the whirring of the garage door. Turner touched my arm, speaking softly. "Hey, we're here. And I've got the perfect solution to whatever it is that's ailing you." He got out of the truck, opened my door, and helped me down. We walked out to the deck and heard the sound of the hot tub melodically bubbling away. Turner reached down and hugged me as he unzipped my dress. "Come on Vi, nothing relieves stress or problems like this tub. I promise you."

It wasn't the solution I was needing but I sighed, pulled off everything else and stepped down into the splashing hot water and took a seat, submerging myself up to my ears. Against the chilly night air, the hot water felt comforting. Bubbles percolated all around me, as strong jets shot out, relaxing my tense muscles.

Turner stepped inside and brought out two cold beers. "Maybe these'll help too. He tossed off his clothes and stepped in, handing me a bottle."

I took a big gulp, laid my head back on the edge of the tub, slowly letting out a long deep breath, a Lexie technique. A few minutes later, I said, "You're right...after a cold beer and a brew of hot water...p-problems don't feel quite as bad." I tried to let go of all my tension and closed my eyes. "I could sit here all night."

Turner was next to me doing much the same and looked over. "Well, that wasn't part of my plan, but I'm glad you're feeling better." He reached over and pulled me closer. "Ready to talk?"

Still with my eyes closed, I mumbled, "Tonight, in the bathroom--M-Molly fired me. Said I wasn't enough of a r-rule follower, and some other stuff about my mother."

"What? What a bitch!" After a long pause, Turner responded. "I think a touch of your rebel streak is a good thing. Shows creativity. Certainly not reason enough to fire you. But, if she resented your mother before, I'm sure she does now after seeing Suzanne and Mark together. That probably has more to do with this firing than anything else. I'm sure those two together surprised the hell out of her and she took it out on you."

I turned and looked at him. "I hadn't thought of that. M-M-Maybe you're right." Then I shrugged, saying, "Doesn't m-matter now...My days at BUD are over."

CHAPTER 57

Two's Company, Three's a Business

VIOLET

Shakira's *Hips Don't Lie* ringtone began playing on my phone. I stumbled over to Turner's dresser and picked up Rosie's call.

"*Hola*, roomy. Am I calling too early? You still with Turner?"

Between yawns, I answered. "You caught me. W-What's up?"

"I'm making a great big breakfast as a thank you to Turner. He was so incredible to say that about Roberto last night. Can you both come over?"

"Sounds good, let me check."

Turner was still sleeping. I shook his shoulder and whispered, "R-Rosie wants to make us breakfast at our apartment. To thank you."

He turned a sleepy face toward me, stretched and nodded. "Sure, always ready for some breakfast."

I responded back, "Thanks, R-Rosie, we'll be over within the hour. S-See you then."

Putting back on my pink dress reminded me of last night, but I felt a lot of my anger had fizzled out. Instead, I was just sad at no longer having a job I enjoyed. That garden had become my happy place. Turner had convinced me the firing probably had a lot more to do with Molly's issues than with my shortcomings. I hoped he was right, but I didn't have it in me to fight for the job. Molly was no longer a supervisor I had any desire to work for. Perhaps I should try going back to research work.

On the drive to my apartment, I tried to shake off the gloomy mood. Rosie wanted us there this morning as a celebration. I didn't want to be the one to bring things down.

Walking in, Rosie welcomed us with her usual morning enthusiasm and a dining table loaded with platters of food. "So glad you guys came over. I woke up with such an appetite and started cooking. I've had so much fun. Sit. Sit!"

Turner rubbed his hands together, smiling. "Looks fantastic. What a great invitation to wake up with."

Rosie leaned over taking the lids off her platters "So guys, we have *huevos de ranchero, antojitos, menudo, empanadas* with fruit filling, juice and coffee. All my morning favorites."

"Yum! Looks like you bought out the grocery store." I sat down and opened my napkin.

"Well, with Mama married now, she told me to keep my extra money, so I have a little more to spend on food."

I added, "So, judging from all this, you've been up for a while."

"Oh Vi, I couldn't sleep. I kept thinking about Roberto's bench and how happy he'll be. A special place for us to connect. Just imagine, guys; we can even eat our lunches out there. It's very special. Thank you again, Turner."

"From what Vi's told me about you and your brother, it's totally deserved." He took a big bite of the empanada, with the pineapple filling breaking through the flaky crust. "I don't know Rosie, maybe your future should be in baking. These are so good."

While we ate, Rosie filled us in on what we'd missed after the party regrouped at Mark's favorite tavern. I wondered how Mother felt being there, totally out of her element. Not good, I'd bet. She wasn't really a musty tavern type.

I asked, "And things with Bob? Everything still going well, Rosie?"

"Really good and he's such a gentleman too. We're taking it slow. I promised my brother I was making smart choices from now on."

Turner nodded and smiled. "Good for you. Seems like a nice guy."

After we finished, I got up and started filling the dishwasher. Still at the table, Rosie asked. "So Vi, when you left last night, you didn't look so happy. You both left so fast."

"Yeah, about that... sorry. I didn't feel like t-talking to anybody. I ran into M-Molly in the ladies room." I hesitated, looking down at the sink. "R-Rosie, keep this to yourself, but Molly fi-f-fired me last night." She stared at me in shocked silence. "A few weeks ago she told me that none of our gar-gardening team was supposed to attend the party. That p-p-pissed me off so I asked my mother to include all of you at her table as guests. That's why M-Molly let me go. She was so angry."

Rosie sucked in her breath in surprise. "*O Dios mio*. I can't believe it! But you can't leave; we need you!"

I shook my head and sat back down next to Turner. "There are other jobs, Rosie. I c-can't work for somebody like her. From day one, I felt like M-Molly resented me. There was something off from the st-start, but I just ignored it. I'll find other work."

Rosie pounded her fist on the table in anger. "No, Violet. You need to fight this! Who fires someone in a bathroom? And what about all your computer garden studies? Was all that for nothing? You love this work."

Turner stood up, refilling his coffee cup. "Vi, Rosie...hear me out for a minute. I know this is all a little premature, but I may have a solution. Rosie, I don't know how much Violet told you, but I recently sold Rapid Logistics."

"Yes, she told me."

Turner sat back down, clasping his coffee cup, looking calm and thoughtful. "The last three weeks I've been considering several future business options, and spent hours researching the market. One idea that kept popping back into my head was starting a landscaping company specializing in xeriscape gardening. I've checked the DFW market. There's not much niche competition and it's definitely the wave of the future, so I like the growth potential. Commercial or residential, my bets are on everybody eventually going to a sustainable landscaping option. We might as well start one of the first in the area."

I looked up, eyes open wide in surprise. "Turner, were you ser-seriously considering this before last night?"

"Among other things; yeah, I have been. You both know how much I liked volunteering at BUD, and I see the value and beauty of the work. There's definitely a need for this. Vi, you're only scratching the surface now with your landscaping design classes, but it's all stuff we could build on. It would take a while to scale up, but I've got the cash now to purchase basic equipment, build a website, lease warehouse space, and eventually hire labor."

Rosie smiled. "This sounds very exciting."

I was stunned by his revelation and was soaking up everything he said, thinking of the possibilities.

Turner took a sip of coffee and continued. "Look, I could handle sales and marketing. Vi, you're great with design, not to mention sustainable plant and bio knowledge. And Rosie, you're fantastic with people. If you were interested, you could head up the installation aspect with a team. Initially, we'd probably *all* be working on installation. Believe me... this is gonna take awhile to build up, but I've created a company from nothing before. I think we could make this work. I definitely need to crunch the numbers first, so Rosie, don't quit your day job just yet."

I was warming to the idea, and actually laughed. "What about me? I've already left the day job."

"Get scrappy, Violet. Why not get on with another landscaping group to get some hands-on commercial experience. After your BUD position, someone's going to want you as part of their design staff. Once I get some bigger accounts lined up, you'll be more prepared to design and present to clients."

Rosie asked, "So, does this mean I would get a truck to drive around to businesses and homes? I can't be taking the bus to everywhere."

"That's the cart before the horse, Rosie, but who knows...maybe?"

"I didn't ask about a horse, I said a truck, but if there will be a vehicle for me in this future job, sign me up."

I was excited but had so many questions. "I'm a little on the fence about this, but I'm leaning in your direction, Turner."

He chuckled, "Honestly, right now it's baby steps. We'd build this thing one account at a time. And we'll need a catchy name. Any ideas?"

I quickly offered, "How about *Scrappy, Sappy, and Dopey's*?"

"Am I to assume I'm Dopey?" Turner asked with a smirk.

Rosey giggled. "No, we'd have to bring in Mark for that. Wait, I have one...*No Violets or Roses Landscaping.*"

Turner laughed and said, "Clever but confusing. What about *North Texas Sustainable Landscaping?"*

I immediately shook my head. "B-Boring!

Turner shrugged and said, "I say we all seriously think about this whole idea for a couple days, write down expectations, what you could best contribute, and what your work values are. Then we gather again for a talk. Sound good?"

Rosie and I nodded in agreement as Turner stood up. "Rosie... thanks again. Breakfast was *muy deliciosa*. And no pressure on this landscaping idea. If you're happy at BUD, you should stay there."

Rosie quickly responded. "I'll be thinking about it. I very much like the truck part that you mentioned."

He laughed again. "Uh, I believe you brought that up, but we'll see."

As I stood, I said, "Th-This is an exciting idea, but I need a good, long run to clear my head. That's when I do my b-b-best thinking."

Turner asked me, "Hey, before you change for a run, do you mind walking me down to my truck?"

We took the elevator downstairs to the parking garage. Turner leaned against his truck door and wrapped his arms around my shoulders. "I'm seriously jazzed about this plan. I haven't had this feeling in so long. What do you honestly think about working together?"

I studied the cement flooring for a few seconds. "Honestly, I'm not sure. P-Partners at work--while in a relationship? How w-would that work? Will we drive each other b-bonkers?"

"Violet, I gotta say, I kind of love the idea. We both have unique skill sets, we get along pretty great, and we're capable of telling each other we're full of shit when necessary. Look, building a business... It'll be hard, challenging, frustrating, exhausting..."

I looked back up, laughing, "Whoa! I thought you said you were *g-good* at selling?"

Turner continued, "Well, in addition to those things, I think it'll be exhilarating, collaborative, and hopefully profitable. I feel good about our chances...I really do."

I shook my head. "Hmm, I don't know. For two people who b-both knew absolutely nothing about landscaping last September, I think it's p-pretty damn dicey."

Turner responded confidently. "And I'm actually pretty damn good at craps."

"G-Great! Another handy skill set I didn't realize you excelled at. But ser-seriously, there's one more thing to consider. Wasn't it your all-consuming b-business drive that b-broke up your marriage? That's kind of what you've told me."

Turner looked out across the parking garage for several seconds. "Fair question. Hopefully, I've learned from that. But I truly think having you as a business partner would make this so different than before. Allie was never really interested in my business. So we quit talking about it and we stopped being involved in each other's lives."

At that point, I couldn't resist any longer. I reached up and kissed him and he pulled me into a strong embrace and returned mine with a longer kiss. When we parted, I literally felt a rush to my head followed by a shuddering sensation below. "Wow...you know, I think I'm l-liking dicey. Let's roll 'em."

CHAPTER 58

Eye of the Tiger

VIOLET

I was oblivious to how long I'd been running. My mind was busy contemplating my firing, the new business proposition, the lovers-to-partners dilemma, all the pros and cons. I couldn't see much downside to the plan, as long as I landed another job temporarily to tide me over. And Turner made a good point; working for a commercial landscape company would give me a fresh perspective for our own possible business. Of course, getting hired was a hurdle, and I'd have to do it myself this time.

Yes, there'd be challenges ahead. Our relationship could eventually fall apart, but I was determined not to let that happen. Truth was though, people broke up all the time for all kinds of reasons. And yes, the business was probably more difficult than Turner imagined, but he was used to facing challenges and rejection. He said he'd done the research and he had working capital to invest. And I had a trust fund. Nothing about this would be a slam-dunk, but I was willing to work harder than I ever had, and I believed Turner would as well.

My thoughts were suddenly broken up by *Bad to the Bone*. I stopped to catch my breath on the trail, heaving into the phone. "Hello…Mother."

"Gracious! Are you OK, Violet? You're so out of breath."

"Yes... I'm f-finishing...a run."

"I'll never understand all this need for running. It's not good for your asthma."

"Mother... I've never had... asthma."

"Well, it sounds like you do. Anyway, Mark mentioned you looked a little strange last night. But everything's fine then?"

"I'm b-better today, but...unfortunately, last night M-Molly fired me. Didn't approve of me and my team attending the reveal party. I was really upset when I left the party, b-but I'm getting used to the idea."

Mother responded angrily, taking it all quite personally. "You have *got* to be joking. Violet, this will not stand! This Molly person has no idea who she's tangleing with, and I promise you, I'll have her out of her job before she can put her big ass in her desk chair tomorrow."

"C-Calm down Mother. Just breathe." I gave her a minute. "So, I appreciate your interest, anger and support, but T-Turner and I have been talking up an idea which I'll discuss with you soon."

"Well, I hope it doesn't include murder, but yes, I'm ready for the details. This is our family's name we're talking about. Nobody fires my daughter! Let's plan a dinner soon and bring Turner. We need to talk."

"M-Mother please...deep breaths. Keep all this to yourself and I pr-promise you, I'll sort this out in my own way. I appreciate you, but I can handle this."

"Are you sure?"

"Yes."

"All right, Violet. Against my better judgment, I'll leave it to you until I hear otherwise, but don't hesitate to check in for advice."

"Got it, Mother." I walked over to a picnic table by the edge of the lake, and sat down. "Now, on a totally different topic, how was Mark's tavern last night?"

"Horrendous. Dark, dirty, and not a decent glass of wine in the entire bar. And, of course, the people hanging out there...not my type of crowd at all."

"S-So, I guess I didn't miss much."

"Actually Violet, to be honest, it was kind of fun. We played darts and shuffleboard. Haven't played those in years. You know how Mark is, making it all so interesting. I just need to figure out how to sneak a decent bottle of wine inside."

She was more than smitten. This was getting beyond serious. "W-Wow! That's a surprise. Alright, I need to fi-finish this run but I'll t-text you later for dinner details."

"I'd love that Violet. Soon!"

I was sitting on the table top, my feet on the bench below, and staring out at the lake. The sky was partly-cloudy and the wind was beginning to pick up. I became determined to resolve this firing issue on my own. I channeled my Mother's indignation, strategized all my talking points, pulled up Molly's number, and called. I felt like my heart was beating through the phone line, but I had to speak to her clearly, without hesitation or weakness.

Molly picked up. "Violet?"

"Hello M-Molly."

"Glad you called. I've been thinking...Things got a little heated and rushed last night."

I was still certain about leaving BUD, but I wanted to leave on *my* terms, not Molly's. The more I'd thought about the firing, the more I believed Molly's boss would not allow it if she knew the truth behind my dismissal, and now, as cooler heads prevailed, Molly probably realized that herself.

I steeled my nerves and steadied my voice. "Molly, I don't re-recall feeling rushed or heated last night until you told me I was fired. Now, *I* know and *you* know, I was an invited plus-one of our garden sponsor, Turner Cooper. In addition, my team members were invited guests of my mother. Having purchased the table, she had every right to invite whoever she wanted. In addition, you recently gave me a good evaluation, nor have I been issued any write-ups on my performance. On top of that, you f-fired me without documentation in a public bathroom! I'd say you're the one who might be getting fired."

"Well, you deliberately defied my instruct---"

"I m-may have gone around your instructions, but I did it legally, for a good p-purpose. Now Molly, this is what I demand from you. I will resign my position--but *only* if I receive a *glowing* written re-recommendation from you, which I will pick up tomorrow. I will also need that letter to be put in BUD's p-permanent personnel file with no mention of the bathroom discussion. Everything clear?"

"Let's reconsider...I've decided to let you back into the fold. We need you, Violet."

"No. You made your feelings quite cl-clear to me. And frankly, I don't c-care for your attitude. I'll be out of your hair f-first thing tomorrow morning, unless you prefer I work out a two-week notice, which I'll be happy to do."

"What about your mother? She's not getting into any of this, correct?"

"As you may have sur-surmised, *no one* controls Suzanne Hill. I have no idea what she has in mind. But I've told you what I require. I'll be there for my paperwork tomorrow morning. Th-Thank you, Molly."

I clicked off and couldn't believe what I'd just said. I was shaking. Who was that person on the phone? Where had she come from and why had it taken so many years for her to emerge? Whoever she was, I liked her! She was confident. She was bold. And there was barely a hint of stutter or pop of a 'P'. But if I'd stuttered a little, did it really matter? It was a part of who I was, and I was suddenly OK with the whole package.

Mother and I would never be alike...there was way too much of my father within me. And that was a good thing. But somehow, finally, I think Mother and I were both going to accept each other for who we were. I felt like I'd just moved up a few levels on the confidence elevator. It was such a surprising revelation. Swirling through the tumult of all our mother-daughter issues, I'd found myself and reclaimed my inner voice which had been hiding for so long. I suddenly leaped down from the bench of the picnic table and began running again, cheering myself on like a crazed Rocky impersonator with a broad grin across my face.

I had a guy I was crazy about, a true, first-time best friend with Rosie, and two potential business partners! Thinking back to my dread of leaving my lonely life and secluded job in Austin, I realized I'd climbed a massive hill and I'd never felt better in my life. Suddenly, everything felt different.

Instead of my eyes looking straight forward, running at top speed, I slowed down a bit and glanced around. A sail boat regatta was in full swing; with some boats beginning to make the turn in the middle of the lake. Ahead of me, a lady was pushing a carriage. Rather than calling out my usual runner's warning, 'On your left,' I glanced over and noticed the woman was pushing the cutest pomeranian dog riding happily in her pet stroller. I actually stopped and chatted with the stranger, thinking Cocoa might enjoy something similar. I ran further, and called out to a biking father and son, "Enjoy your day!" I passed a wheezing older man who was walking, and slowed to ask if he wanted my extra bottle of water. It wasn't that I was never empathetic before, it was that I'd never had the confidence to start a conversation.

It was as if a roller shade had been snapped in front of me and I was now seeing a brighter, more vivid and inviting world, a world I'd been excluding myself from for twenty-four years. All that time I'd spent running alone, never speaking to a soul; I might as well have been running in place in my bedroom. There was so much to make up for, so many fascinating people out there, so many intriguing places to investigate.

I laughed, grinning as I continued to run, shaking off the shadow of my old self, not caring what people thought as I passed them, while I called out to no one in particular, "*Forget that shrinking Violet; she has bl-bloomed!*"

About the Author

Bobbie Candas lives in Dallas, Texas with her husband, Mehmet Candas, a stray gray cat, and a jealous tabby who does not enjoy sharing affection with the interloper. Bobbie attended The University of Texas in Austin, earning her degree in journalism. She took a detour with a career in retail management, and found her happy place when she returned to writing fiction about nine years ago.

Your reviews and ratings on Amazon and Good Reads are appreciated. If you enjoyed this novel, please take a moment to post a review. They are so important to the success of novels written by independent authors.

FOLLOW BOBBIE CANDAS ON:

Amazon Author Page:
https://www.amazon.com/stores/author/BooMNS6KVo
Facebook: facebook.com/bobbiecandasauthor
Good Reads: https:// www. goodreads. com/ author/ show/ 8292457. Bobbie. Candas
Instagram: https://www.instagram.com/bobbiecandas/

ALSO BY BOBBIE CANDAS:

The Lost and Found of Green Tree
Imperfect Timing
Luck, Love, and a Lifetime

About this novel

When at home or traveling, I love to seek out botanical gardens, arboretums, city gardens--unique places where exotic plants, blooming flowers, colorful trees, fruits, pollinators and water elements all come together in imaginative, whimsical landscape designs that offer us a feast for all our senses. A few years back, while walking through the Dallas Arboretum, I was inspired by the fall colors and thought it might make a wonderful and unique setting for a novel. I finally got around to writing this story and loved the way the characters unfolded from where the setting took me. The gardens in *Welcome to Wonderland* borrow from my wanderings through many of these city gardens, but the characters described, the garden policies and associates, and storyline revolving around the fictional Botanicals United of Dallas (BUD) are all derived from plot twists of my own imagination and do not reflect any personal knowledge of garden-related associates, business practices or policies. I hope you enjoy reading this as much as I enjoyed writing it.

Acknowledgments

I appreciate the kickstart given to me by several beta readers who volunteered to read an early draft of this novel. Your encouragement, comments, and suggestions were incredibly helpful. Many thanks to Liz Brammer, Vicki Brumby, Katy Clayton. Susie Criswell, Julie Flo, Jeanne McCaffrey, Michael Poehl, Nancy Putnam, and Bird Thomas. Thanks for pushing me forward!

Also, a huge shout out to all the online members of the Dallas Creative Writers group who workshopped most of the chapters in this novel and offered up numerous edit suggestions, fresh perspectives, and inspiration. Of special note is our group coordinator, John Archer. Our weekly sessions were always a big help to keep me pushing forward.

I so appreciate the time, assistance, and feedback of Dr. Beth Lonergan regarding psychological issues experienced by my central characters. Your comments and references were invaluable and insightful. Also, the expertise of professional landscape engineer, Mckenzie Chris, was very helpful early on. She answered numerous questions for me regarding xeriscape gardening and information about specific plants.

In addition, I'd be remiss not to give a big thanks to my husband, Mehmet, my very own Johnny Appleseed and biologist, for his love and interest in plants, his biology expertise, and his patience and support. And I have to add my appreciation for my two clever children, Cari and Demir. Thank you always for your suggestions and confirmations of the work and your technical advice and patience.

And I'm so grateful for the help and creative artistry of cover designer Betty Martinez. You are such a joy to work with.

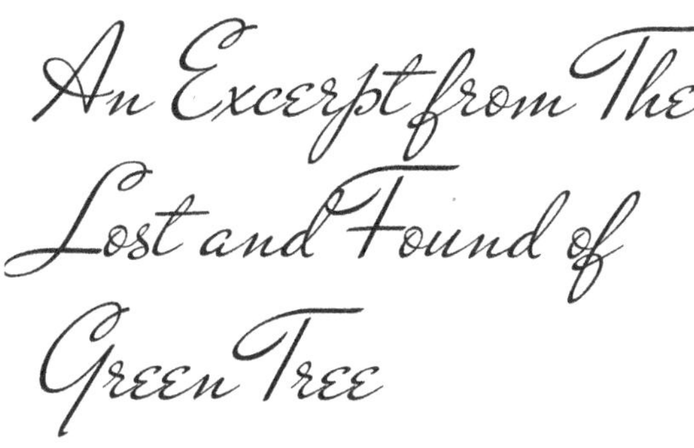

PROLOGUE

My latest issue of Silver Screen calls this decade a time of great progress for the modern woman and they're calling it, 'The Roaring Twenties.' Well, I can assure you, the only roaring going on in Green Tree, Iowa, is the occasional motorized tractor chugging down Main Street.

The name of Green Tree probably has you conjuring up images of a lovely hamlet, with winding hilly streets, surrounded by a thick forest of evergreens, populated by lots of interesting people.

No. There's just the one tree. A big, unshapely elm, growing off to the side of the brick county court house which is the center of a grid of straight, organized streets servicing the surrounding farming community, populated by, well...mostly farmers.

Of course, there's a few of us town-folk too, running the integral businesses supporting the area. But there's no movie theater, or community stage. No elegant restaurants, and only the one clothing store. There's a popular hardware store—for my needs, useless. And I'd have to say the same for the Farm and Implement Store. Although, I should add that we do have a coffee shop which sells cherry-flavored soda-pop, a personal favorite, a pool hall selling ice cream, and the drug store which just added a modern pay phone to the wall.

Also, I'd be remiss not to mention a fabric store run by my grim auntie who is assisted, under forced labor, by me, Nanette Jorgenson.

Amongst all this, I can absolutely assure you that in Green Tree I saw no possible future employment for dynamically inspired women, such as myself. By my teen years I already knew I was meant for bigger things.

CHAPTER 1

Nanette Jorgeson

I stood confidently on the makeshift plywood stage in front of the courthouse, lined up next to nine other hopeful girls, each of us praying to hear our name called. It was August, a warm late afternoon. My face muscles were beginning to ache after showing off my glistening smile for at least forty-five minutes. The Green Tree judges of the 1927 Harvest Celebration were about to decide the winning candidates for the Corn Queen's Court. Whoever was selected as queen would be the envy of every girl in town and had the honor of presiding over the Harvest Celebration parade, the corn-eating contest, the fall fruit-pie competition, and the Harvest Celebration dance.

We were judged on poise, beauty, ability to communicate, posture, and popularity; all attributes many friends have told me I excel at.

Our Green Tree mayor, dressed in a dark plaid suit, bow tie and straw boater, was droning on about all the upcoming festivities which were essentially the same ones we had every year. Just get on with it...announce my name. I was born for this. If my name wasn't announced as queen, I might not accept the role of princess or duchess. I didn't like playing second fiddle and certainly hated third.

With a crowd of next year's potential voters in front of him, the mayor couldn't simply get to the point, feeling compelled to remind us of all the good things the funds generated by the festival would do for the village. While he talked, I looked about, nodding to a few friends standing in the crowd. I saw my best friend, Catherine Anderson, and her cute younger brother, Sam, with that girlfriend of his, Mariah. What did he see in her? I then waved at Melinda Perkins. She wasn't really a friend, but was strong competition and I was happy she'd decided not to run for queen this year, so I was being nicer to her.

Then finally... "Alright. So now folks, here's what we all came to see. Our beautiful line-up of Corn Harvest Court hopefuls. Gosh, I wish we had room for all of them in the parade. Have you ever seen such a lovely group of young women?"

The mayor's pandering was followed by a light smattering of applause and a few whistles. The sun was about to set, the mayor was losing his audience, and my feet were beginning to hurt standing tall in Auntie's borrowed high heels with my hands on my hips, continuing to flash my broadest smile.

The mayor raised his hands as if he was stopping a tidal wave of applause. "OK... Alright. Let's quiet down. The judges have given me their decisions. Ladies, if I call your name, just step over here next to me. So—without further ado—for our Corn Harvest Duchess, we have... Miss Amy Shulwater."

Amy Shulwater? With the chipped tooth and frizzy hair? I guess there were perks when your father owned the implement dealership. Light applause rose from the crowd, as a young boy rushed over from the side of the makeshift stage with a dozen ears of corn tied together with a green ribbon, handing them to the new duchess. Some towns offered rose bouquets, but in Green Tree, you got corn.

The mayor jumped in with a handshake and then read from his card, "Congratulations Amy! Next, for the title of Princess, we have another town-beauty... Miss Miranda Plum." Miranda stepped forward, gushing, accepting her gift of corn.

This was it; my big moment, or utter defeat.

"And now... good people of Green Tree, the recipient of our tiara, the satin banner, and *two* dozen ears of corn goes to our 1927 Queen of Corn... the lovely Miss Nanette Jorgenson."

Was it my imagination, or had the crowd erupted in massive applause? Forget the produce, just put that crown on my head and pin the banner across my chest. I stepped over to receive my handshake and congratulatory hug. Queen Nanette was crowned!

That week was magical for me and transformative. I cut my long blonde hair into a permed and crimped bob, almost giving Auntie a heart attack when she saw my thick eight-inch braid cut off and sitting on my vanity. I led the parade while waving from the back of a decorated, spanking-new red truck, borrowed from a dealership in Clear Lake. Auntie provided me with a silver sparkling fabric which I sewed into a draping drop-waist dress, hemming it rakishly short, exposing my knees. I felt special; little girls pointed at me when I walked down Main Street, while friends from school would stop and congratulate me. Topping that, I danced with every young man in town at the festival celebration. But most importantly, at the dance I met James Iverson.

He was from neighboring East Point. Four years older, and the most handsome man I'd ever seen; a tall, strapping guy with a manicured dark mustache, whose father happened to own a bank. I'd given him a wink on the dance floor and he'd eventually made his way over to me. When he asked me to dance, that was it. I'd found my man.

At the Hot Cup, sitting next to a table of grizzled farmers, I was gossiping with my friend, Catherine Anderson. We both took long sips of our colas, gearing up for our weekly gab exchange. "So, how are all your brothers doing, Catherine? I still think young Sam is the cutest."

"Forget it Nanette, you're too old for him. Besides, he's crazy about Mariah. They've been dating over a year now."

"Don't be silly. He's cute but not my type. I'm ready for someone more mature in the business field. Speaking of which, at the dance, did you notice a tall handsome gentleman? Mustache, suspenders? We danced together at least five times."

"Gosh, yes… I think every girl at the dance was ogling him."

I lowered my voice, saying, "Name is James Iverson. Son of a banker, great dancer, and even better *kisser*."

"You've kissed him already! Nanette, be careful."

"Oh, don't be such a bluenose. It was only a little kiss. He drove me home from the dance, and guess what?" I pounded my hand lightly on the café table. "We have a date for next weekend. I'm over the moon! *Never* felt this way about a guy before."

"Nanette, you're so lucky. Why can't I ever meet someone like him?"

"You will, Catherine. Just get your brothers to introduce you to their friends. You're bound to meet a great guy."

She nodded, playing with the straw in her drink. "I suppose, but all their friends are farmers too."

I glanced around, making sure nobody was eavesdropping. "True. James seems different, not like all these boys we grew up with. A college man…. and a banker."

"Yes, you mentioned that."

I checked my watch; I was running late as usual. "Darn. Auntie is watching the clock; I'm supposed to be getting the groceries. I'll let you know how the date goes."

"OK. Please keep me posted, Nanette. I'm dying to hear how it goes." As I walked out, two more girls from school walked into the Hot Cup, waving at Catherine. I knew she'd spread the gossip about my date with James.

James Iverson. I couldn't get his face out of my mind. When I told Auntie about him, she approved of my Saturday night date. Although, at eighteen, I was officially an adult. No permission should have been necessary. But when I was twelve, my dad passed away, and his Aunt Edwina had been clucking over me like her prized hen ever since.

I checked my *Silver Screen* and *Photoplay* magazines religiously and had cut out photos of several styles of dresses I wanted to copy and sew for myself. Auntie owned a small fabric and yarn store in

Green Tree, so I'd always had access to my own creations. That week, I made a light green cotton dress with white piping, with the green fabric perfectly matching my eyes, and I accessorized it with a long string of pearls. Fake ones, but who could really tell?

Now that I had the crimped hair, the dress, and the right makeup, I found it hard to tell the difference between myself and motion picture star, Marion Davies. I wanted to stun James Iverson. I stared at my reflection and then back again at the magazine photos of Marion. The comparison was pretty darn close. If Marion could attract the attention of publishing tycoon William Randolph Hearst, I could certainly hold the eye of James Iverson from No-Where, Iowa.

Peeking out the window, I watched James drive up in his shiny dark-blue Chrysler Roadster. So stylish, I had to pinch myself. I took a minute to ask him into our small home and introduce him to Auntie. She'd made me promise to do this and immediately began grilling him. "So, James, Nanette tells me you're an East Point resident. Have a cousin still living there. Would you know Bonnie and Steven Billows?"

"Why, yes ma'am. The Billows... a fine family. I believe they've held accounts with our family for years. Miss Jorgenson, if it's alright with you, I'd like to take Nanette to see a new film in Clear Lake. It starts at eight-thirty, so we'll need to head out."

"Certainly, of course. You two enjoy this lovely evening." I could tell Auntie approved. She wasn't giving him her usual squint-eye.

He'd decided that we should see *Phantom of the Opera,* starring Lon Chaney. Clear Lake was a thirty-minute drive from Green Tree, allowing us a little time to get to know each other better. When we sat down near the back of the dark theater, he immediately put his arm around me, and the movie became so scary I had to hide my eyes against his jacket a few times. Before the film was over, we'd kissed twice and my heart was almost jumping outside my chest. Leaving the theater, James placed his hand around mine and I felt like we melted together.

He suggested we take a drive by the lake. "It's beautiful this time of year, Nanette. Only us, the water, stars, and the moon. You'll love it."

"Sure, sounds magical. Just as long as I'm home around midnight." Auntie was a stickler on the curfew, but perhaps tonight she'd allow me a little leniency with James being such a promising beau.

We drove past some cottages built along the water and cruised a bit further, parking in a grove of overhanging willows near the lake's edge. It was dark, with a background sound of frogs croaking melodically. We drove across freshly cropped grass which invaded my senses, a salute to summer's final hurrah. And as promised, a big bright moon danced across ripples on the black lake. I felt like I was on a film set. He pulled a silver flask from his inside jacket pocket, took a long swig and handed it to me.

"Maybe I'll try a sip. I really don't drink." It was strong whiskey, too bitter for me. I handed it back quickly. "It's gorgeous here, let's walk a bit."

"In a little while." He stretched out his arms above his head. "I'm feeling really comfortable, but it's even better in the back seat. Let me show you." Always the gentleman, he got out, opened my door and let me slide across the spacious, padded back seat. It was lovely. He leaned over and kissed me, but this time he inserted his tongue. It was one of those French kisses the girls at school were always giggling about.

He looked down at me. "You're so beautiful, but you know that, don't you?" His hands moved slowly lower to my breasts, gently rubbing them, as he groaned in anticipation. I pushed his hands away, surprised he'd try such liberties already.

Nervously, I asked, "Maybe we should get out and walk? It's so nice by the lake."

"It's nicer here." He pushed me back, pressing my head down on the arm rest. "You're going to love this. Pretend you're my very own little movie star."

Before I could sit up, his weight was on top of me and his hand was pushing up my dress and snaking into my panties. I wedged my elbow out on the open side and tried to stop him, but his right hand knocked my arm away and then jerked more aggressively on my panties, ripping one side as he yanked them down. "Come on Nanette, you want this as much as I do." I heard his belt unbuckle and the sound of his zipper.

"No, I'm not ready. It's too soon. Not like this." I struggled to keep my legs together, grasping the skirt of my dress tightly.

But he roughly batted my hand away again, then thrusted his fist between my thighs, pushing my legs apart. He began pushing hard, but nothing was happening. James asked me hoarsely, "Your first time?"

I nodded, repeating myself, "James, no! Get off. I'm not ready." This was all going terribly wrong.

He ignored my pleas, continuing to ram his penis into me, eventually sliding inside, as he grunted on top in jerking motions for what seemed agonizingly long. He finally stopped, got off, went out to his trunk, and handed me a small white towel. "Here, you might need this," and then he walked over to the lake's edge, turning his back to the car.

I quickly removed the remains of my panties, putting them in my handbag and then wiped the blood and wet stickiness from the seat and between my legs. I was in shock as I watched James outside the car. I was so afraid he'd come back and want to do it again. As the shock began to wear off and the reality of what had just happened hit me, I began to cry. I felt dirty and disgusted with myself.

James was now leaning against the hood of the car, puffing on a lit cigar and continuing to take leisurely swigs from his flask. He eventually came back, opened the door, then looked at his watch. "Well, it's getting late. Probably don't have time for that walk. Guess I better get you back home."

"I'm staying back here," I said in a defiant voice.

"Suit yourself."

There was no discussion of what had just happened.

I no longer cared about James Iverson. I hated James Iverson. I sat next to the window and stared out at the dark farm roads, and rode home in silence. Could I have kicked him, bucked him off, screamed? Nothing about what had happened was how I'd dreamed it would be; it was dirty, painful and felt all wrong. How did he go from fairytale prince to, to... that? Arriving at my house, I opened the car door myself, slamming it abruptly on James and never heard from him again. That, at least, was a relief.

Although my thoughts and nightmares often trailed back to that terrible night, I put on a show to others, pretending my life was absolutely normal. All that continued until October, when I realized I'd missed my period--twice. How could that be possible? Some of the girls at school who'd whispered about 'doing it,' said you never got pregnant on your first time. I couldn't tell anybody. Like I'd tried to tell James, I wasn't ready for any of this. This could not be how my life was supposed to play out. I became sick to my stomach. Often.

Then, I quickly developed a plan.

CHAPTER 2

Mariah Anderson

I'd never forget that day back in September 1924. Gosh, that seems so long ago. I'd been at Green Tree High School for only a few days, coming from a country school with a total of twelve students, grades first through eighth. Now at Green Tree High, there were thirty-two students in just my freshman class. One of my first assignments was an oral presentation on Germany for world geography class.

The night before, upstairs in our small crowded bedroom, I practiced my report out loud so many times that my two sisters, Arlene and Janeen, were throwing their shoes at me to make me stop.

"Mariah, if we have to hear about that darn Danube River one more time, Arlene and I will beat you with these shoes instead of just throwing them. We have studies of our own. Shut up, please!"

"Sorry, I'm so nervous. Imagine, standing in front of over thirty students. I want everything perfect."

In preparation for the task, I'd done three days of library research and created a poster from butcher paper. The morning of my big report, I'd borrowed my older sister's new light-pink lipstick and curled my shoulder-length dark hair. I wore a knitted pull-over sweater over a starched white collared blouse, and a pleated skirt

Mother had recently sewn for me. All of this preparation, just to give a five-minute report.

Standing in front of the class, most kids looked back at me with bored expressions. I cleared my throat, nervously pulling on my sweater, and began, attempting to exude a sense of confidence.

At lunch, I joined a table of girls I'd recently met at band practice. While unwrapping my cheese sandwich, I watched a handsome blonde boy, dressed in overalls and plaid shirt, walk over to our table. Sitting down next to me, he introduced himself and offered me his hand to shake, as my new girlfriends giggled and rolled their eyes. I grasped his rough calloused hand and shook it while he announced, "Mariah, I'm Samuel Anderson. Don't know if you've noticed me, but I'm in your geography class. Four rows over, two chairs back. Just wanted to stop by and say I liked your report. Seems like you really did your homework."

I was suspect that any boy from Green Tree would really be interested in a report on Germany. I nervously strung a few random sentences together. "Uh... thanks? I enjoy reading about new places. I plan on traveling a lot someday."

"Why?" He blinked, looking suddenly surprised.

"Why not? There's certainly something more interesting in this life besides cows and corn. That's about all I ever see around here." I took a few bites of my sandwich, and watched all the girls at my table turning their curious heads toward us.

"Nothing wrong with cows and corn. Kept my family fed for years. And I tell you, Mariah, farming's changing."

"Maybe... Send me a letter all about it when I'm up in New York working in a skyscraper office."

"And of all places, why would you want to go there?"

"Because it's not here." Our banter had the girls' heads switching back and forth, not wanting to miss whatever was about to happen.

"Just so you know... there are so many new planting techniques coming out. I been reading up on it. Farming's exciting." Sam slapped his hand on the lunch table, signifying he'd won the discussion.

I shook my head and laughed. "Challenging maybe, but I don't know about exciting. My parents have farmed for years." I shrugged my shoulders, looking around the table. "I just know I want more. Someplace where I'm not always side-stepping cow-pies, or worrying about rain and drought. But I like your passion about farming, Sam." I started wrapping up the remainder of my lunch. "I guess we all need to be inspired by something."

Sally Neilson, sitting on my other side, nudged my elbow. "Seems like farming isn't the only thing Sam's excited about."

Ignoring her comment, he lowered his voice and said, "Mariah, I'd like to buy you a slice of cake at the Hot Cup this Saturday. Let's talk more about this."

"This may sound strange but I really don't like cake." I picked up my books for class and stood up. "But I do love pie."

"They got that too."

"All right, farmer Sam. I'll meet you for pie, but don't plan on changing my mind about farming."

Initially, I was a little leery of this over-confident, tall, fair-haired boy. He seemed too sure of himself, to the point of being cocky. But honestly, I was flattered that Sam seemed to like me, a little nobody farm-girl with straight brown hair and hand-made clothes. But eventually his steady persistence and laughing blue eyes won me over and we began seeing each other regularly outside of school a few times a week.

I told my two sisters that I'd never met a boy my age who already knew what he wanted and was hell-bent on getting it. Those plans included having his own farm, marriage, and a family. In his mind, everything was all laid out. But I knew there was plenty of time for things to change; we were young, with years ahead of us, and that first love was so intoxicating.

At fourteen, with Sam in my life, the simplest of things felt fresh and new; the thrill of holding hands walking down Main Street, or sitting on a blanket together at outdoor movies on the courthouse lawn. We'd share a bag of popcorn, and watch the silent movies of my favorite actress, Mary Pickford, while Sam loved laughing through the Buster Keaton and Chaplin films.

There was one early date I'd never forget. A company passing through town set up a temporary roller-rink in our village park, and all our gang from school decided to give it a try. Sam sprung for the forty cents on our rentals as we both clamped the metal skates onto our shoes and had them keyed tightly to the soles. I'd only tried skating once before and Sam was a total novice, so we gingerly clung to the rails spaced around the rink which was set up on a platform. A large amplified Victrola played all the popular songs from the radio. When they put on my favorite, *Five-Foot-Two, Eyes-of-Blue*, I forced myself to push off from the sides and courageously skate to the tune of the music. As I gained more confidence, I pulled Sam along and soon we found ourselves skating hand in hand. We went round and round the platform, gaining in speed. It was exhilarating. When the song ended, everyone else dashed to the sides, waiting for the next record. But Sam pulled me to him and in the middle of the rink, wrapped his arms around me, and gave me a long kiss. I knew people were watching, but I had to kiss him back. If I'd been alone, I would have kissed him all night. I adored feeling Sam's strength wrapping around me and his hot breath in my ear, whispering, "You're the one."

I felt a deep shudder go through me as we broke apart, and then began skating to the next tune. That first passionate kiss resonated, making me realize Sam might be more than a passing romance.

CHAPTER 3

Nanette

I'd always wanted to get out of Green Tree, move to a larger town, and find an exciting job. With a possible pregnancy, there was now more urgency for my move. Nobody I knew could find out about this. I looked at a map and chose Mankato, Minnesota, about eighty miles north of Green Tree; not too far, but large enough to allow me some anonymity for a while. I wasn't sure what I was going to do *if* I was pregnant, but at least I could figure it out privately, on my own.

Aunt Edwina had one part-time assistant at the fabric store and me; but she could easily run it without my help. Besides, she'd never paid me for working there, but instead, gave me a meager weekly allowance. After dinner, I announced we needed to have an important conversation.

I started by serving tea and her favorite dessert, pineapple-upside-down cake. I'd actually paid a neighbor down the street to bake it. Sitting across from her at our dining table, I moved aside the bowl of waxed fruit and picked nervously at our lacy white table cloth.

"I've been contemplating this for a while now, Auntie. You know I've always wanted to get out on my own eventually." She raised her eyebrows and stared at me, saying nothing. "Well, I think it's time.

Ever since graduation I've been thinking about it....time for me to fly my wings and try new things." *Exceptionally good title for a future movie; I should write that down later.* I took a deep breath, and just told her. "I've decided I'm applying for jobs in Mankato."

"Mankato? That's Minnesota!" She said it as if I'd just announced I was moving to the North Pole. She shook her head, looking resolute. "No, Nanette. And besides, what if that nice gentleman, Mr. Iverson, comes round again."

"I told you already, he wasn't the man I thought he was. I have *no* interest in dating him... ever."

"You were always too picky. He was a good catch."

I rolled my eyes and ignored her comment and put a large slice of cake in front of her. "Take a bite, you'll love it. Besides, Auntie, a girl needs to see a few places before she settles down. I have skills. I type, good at selling, and I sew. I'm certain I'll find a good job there. There's just the issue of some seed money to find myself a little place to get settled. Will you help me, Auntie? Please?"

She took a big fork full of cake with sweet pineapple, laced with brown sugar crumbles. She savored it, took a sip of tea, and licked her lips. "I don't think so. Here's an idea. What if I start paying you at the store? I hate the idea of you being out there in the world all alone. There's too many unscrupulous people out and about these days. It's wild in the cities and Mankato's just too far."

Her comment immediately had me thinking of the predatory James Iverson. "Auntie, danger can lurk anywhere, but we can't let it consume us. And I've already checked. Mankato's only a two-hour train ride." It was actually closer to three hours, but who was counting? "And I could come back to visit some weekends." Auntie took another bite, listening and nodding. "This is actually a perfect time to apply. Most businesses are going gangbusters right now. If I hate it there, I can always come back, run your store and let you retire."

"Retire? Me? I don't know what I'd do with myself if I wasn't working. I don't need to retire!"

"How's the cake? I know it's your favorite."

"Delicious; your best yet, Nanette."

"You think so? Thanks. So then... if you're fine without me at the store, and based on your advice and business savvy, how much money do you think I'll need to find an apartment and maybe get a proper working wardrobe?"

"Hmm. Let me think on that. Oh, speaking of work clothes, we received the most adorable patterns for suits today. You'll need a smart suit, perhaps in a tweed."

"I agree. Let's discuss the money later. First, we'll need to pull a new wardrobe together. I appreciate your advice and style tips, Auntie, and I'll make you proud. There're so many details we need to consider." I jumped up, leaned over, and gave her a big hug. "Thanks so much. You're the berries! Got to go; I'm meeting Catherine."

As I walked out the door, she suddenly got up and yelled after me, "I didn't say yes. You're not going anywhere. There's more to talk about... Nanette?"

I squeezed an official 'yes' out of her within two days. Phase one of my evolving plan was coming together.

During my final week in Green Tree, my morning sickness began in earnest, confirming my pregnancy fears. I wasn't showing at all but I was having trouble hiding my nausea, making quick runs to the outhouse throughout the day.

By early November, I was on a train to Mankato with three suitcases of clothing, shoes, and hats. Auntie had given me enough cash to cover a few nights in a hotel and two months' funds for food and rent for a small apartment. If I didn't find a job during that time, I had promised to return home. In addition, she'd given me strict instructions to write her one letter every week, or she threatened to come there herself and drag me home.

The train trip to Mankato was a nightmare, with the rocking car motion making my vomiting bouts even more intense. I arrived green and exhausted; my face covered in a sheen of nervous sweat. Standing on the depot platform in my new travel suit with three large suitcases, I had no idea on how to get to the Front Street Hotel, where I'd reserved my first two-night's stay. The town looked larger and busier than I'd imagined, but apparently not large enough to have taxis.

In front of me, I watched a workman unloading wooden crates of produce from a freight car onto his dray wagon. Perhaps he could help. Dragging my three suitcases over one at a time, I walked up to the tired looking man. "Hello sir, any chance I could get directions for the Front Street Hotel? Would it be far?"

He stacked another wooden crate of cabbage in the wagon, while glancing up at me. "Nope, not too far. A little less than a mile west." He jerked his thumb in the hotel's direction.

"I see." I looked to my left, sighed, and stood there staring despondently, considering my options.

"Is all them cases yours?"

"All mine."

He stepped over, put them in the back with the cabbage crates and said, "OK, then. We best go now. I've got a delivery to make. You can get up front." He settled on the springy front bench and grabbed my hand, helping me step up.

"Why, thank you. My goodness, is everyone in Mankato as nice as you?"

"Nope, I just have a weakness for pretty girls with lots of suitcases."

"Well, you're very sweet. I'm Nanette Jorgensen and you're the first person I've met in Mankato."

The man nodded, touching the bill of his ragged cap. "Pleasure to meet you, Miss Jorgensen. I'm Obidiah Dawson, lived here all my life, and know lots of people. So, Front Street Hotel?" He snapped the reins on his two broad-backed black horses, turning them around. "What brings you to town?"

"Work. Just moved here from Green Tree, Iowa and decided to branch out a bit." The breeze picked up as I held on to my cloche hat with my hand. "Actually, I'm looking for a job and an apartment."

"A lady on a mission. I like that. This here is Front Street, main business street of Mankato. Not a bad spot to start your job search." Obidiah pointed out local landmarks as we made our way down to my hotel. Along with horses and wagons, there were numerous cars zipping up and down the asphalt road and several two, three, and four-level red-brick buildings on both sides of the street. It was impressive. We passed all of the larger buildings and eventually arrived at a dreary looking two-story wooden establishment with peeling paint and a sagging front porch. A creaking sign swung from the top level, *Front Street Hotel*. The place looked run-down and far from exclusive.

Noticing my unenthusiastic expression, Obidiah said, "Yeah, not exactly what you kids would call the bees' knees. You sure this is where you're staying?"

I took a deep breath and smiled. "I'm sure it'll be just fine. Wish me luck, Mr. Dawson." I climbed down, thanked him, shook his hand, and yanked my bags out of the back. "Do you suppose they'll come out to get my bags?"

He laughed at me as he began moving his horses. "No, Miss Nanette. I doubt any bellhops will come scampering out here. Good luck to you."

Here I was, arriving at a flea-bag hotel in a horse-drawn cabbage wagon. Not an auspicious beginning to my new life and definitely *not* movie star material.

CHAPTER 4

Mariah

By the middle of my junior year in high school, Sam was still the only boy I'd ever dated. Everyone knew we were a couple. Forgoing all his extra-curricular activities, including basketball and track, Sam began attending only a half-day of school. Instead, he focused his efforts on farming a new piece of land his father had rented from a retiring farmer, Lars Stevenson.

One late afternoon, after band practice, I walked out the school's side door and was surprised to see Sam sitting on the hood of his dad's old Model A.

He opened the door for me and we both got in. "Thought I'd give you a ride home today, but I've got a few things I need to get off my chest." He turned away from me and stared out the front window. "Been thinking about it a lot. There's something I need to say. Something important."

"You seem nervous. What's wrong?"

Clearing his throat and still looking straight ahead, he said, "Mariah, I love you more than I can express. You told me a long time ago you wanted to move to a big city, experience the world, travel to far-flung places. But I can't give you that. I'm committing full-out on this new land Dad's rented. I promised my father I'd give it everything I had. It's a chance to be on my own and try out all the new methods I been researching. Dad believes I'm ready."

I nodded and smiled. "I know. You told me already. And you're lucky to get the opportunity, especially at your age. He must really believe in you."

"He does. But I can't do it alone. I don't want to do it alone. It has to be with you. That's the only way I can see it. The two of us together, Mariah. A partnership. Maybe down the line, some years from now, I'll take you to Paris or that Germany you know so much about." He turned to look at me and took both of my hands. "What I'm trying to say is...will you marry me, Mariah? I love you so much and I'll do my darndest to make you happy."

I sat quiet for a moment, thinking, then looked down at the school books on my lap. I did want more from life than living out on an isolated Iowa farm. What about a career of my own in New York or Chicago, or taking a trip to Europe? But, if I was honest with myself, could I imagine a life without Sam? My days began and ended with me thinking about him, imagining his grinning face, entwining our arms around each other, passionately kissing him. If I left Green Tree, wherever I traveled or worked, I'd be thinking about him, longing to be with Sam. So, what was the point of moving elsewhere? As much as I hated to admit it, he'd changed my mind about being part of a farming family. If Sam was with me, I was on board.

I looked up, smiled, and threw my arms around his neck and kissed him hard, not caring who noticed. "Yes....yes! I'll definitely marry you. I love you so much. But not until I graduate. I must graduate high school."

"Whatever you want. I'll wait. But I've decided this is my last year. Work on the property is nonstop. I can't spend any more time doing class work. Several of the guys are dropping out after this year."

"I hate to hear that, but I understand. My Dad never went beyond eighth grade and did fine."

"You're going to love the house, Maraih. In the evenings, I'm going to work on fixing it up, just for you. It's old and needs updates, but I'll make us a good home. Can you see it...a place of our own?"

"Yes. It may be rented but we'll make it ours, a special place."

That afternoon, the drive back to my house was a turning point. I'd committed to a new life, separate from my parents, older brothers, and sisters. It was scary but also thrilling to think about. As long as I had Sam, I knew I'd be fine. He made me feel safe, beautiful, and desired; important requirements for a sixteen-year-old girl. I convinced myself I was ready to make this journey with him as Mrs. Mariah Anderson, while my dreams of travel and a life off the farm became a wistful memory.

CHAPTER 5

Nanette

Dragging my first two bags to the hotel's porch, I critically eyed the worn and cracked leather armchairs spaced across the front, under a torn awning. I retrieved my third bag from the street, and held one of the large double doors open with my foot, while grabbing my other two bags and dumping everything inside. Checking out the interior, a damp musty smell mixed with the scent of tobacco greeted me and then gnawed at the yellow bile bubbling up again in my stomach.

I was nervous, having never stayed in a hotel, and unsure of the protocol. Auntie had insisted I stay at an all-women's place, but actually this was the only hotel the phone operator could locate for me when I called to make an inquiry. And anyway, what difference did it make? In the small lobby, there were two men in suits and bowler hats, both reading newspapers. As I walked in, feeling queasy, one of them glanced up, folded his paper, and left it on the arm of the lobby chair.

Walking out the door, he smiled at me. "Good day, miss. You look a little lost, may I help?"

I took out my embroidered handkerchief and wiped my brow. "Thank you. Just a little overheated. Uh, registration?"

He pointed to a small counter in the corner. "You have a lovely day."

While walking to the registration counter, I grabbed his abandoned newspaper, and stepped up to the counter. A balding man with glasses looked up from his desk.

"Yes, madam?"

"Hello, you're holding a room for *N. Jorgenson* for two nights."

He paged through a ledger. "Hmm, I see that, but is the room for you?"

"Yes."

"Well, if that's the case, it's quite impossible."

I was nauseous and agitated. I needed a room immediately. "Impossible? Why, for heaven's sake?"

"Because you're a woman. A lovely woman, no doubt. But... we do not allow unescorted women here. It's simply not proper."

I was surprised and confused, but tried my best to remain calm. "So... you do take women, just not unescorted women?"

"We take *married* women who are traveling with their husbands or families."

"Oh, I see. Yes, of course. Understandable. My husband, uh... Nathan Jorgenson, will be along. He's coming from Chicago and meeting me here. We have business in Mankato--real estate. I'll need to check in now though, freshen up and meet him at the station later. Let me get the room prepared for him. He likes things just so; you know how husbands can be. What room are we in?"

The clerk looked uncertain. "Well... if you're sure he'll be here later, I suppose you can register for the two of you; sign here, names and address please." He handed me a large metal key. "Room 2 F, upstairs, to the left. Bathroom's at the end of the hall."

"And I'll need someone to bring my bags to the room please." Ridiculous... needing to have a man tag along merely to rent a dive hotel room. I was fuming, although I kept my face calm and my smile glued. "Thank you, and what's your name, sir."

"Harold White, hotel manager."

"Well, Mr. White, I appreciate your understanding." It looked like Nathan Jorgenson's train would be running very late today or might not arrive at all.

I quickly walked upstairs, then dashed to the communal bathroom, as a bout of morning sickness erupted. I dry heaved into the toilet. By now, there was little left to throw up except a disgusting yellow liquid. I wet my handkerchief in the sink, located my room, and fell across the squeaking narrow bed, placing the wet cloth over my forehead. I suddenly missed the comfort of my own familiar room, the stocked kitchen, the path leading up to our flower-laden front porch, even Auntie's nosey and concerned questions seemed endearing at the moment.

I closed my eyes, dying for a nap, but was interrupted by a voice and rapping on the door. "Your bags, Mrs. Jorgenson."

I jumped off the bed and opened the door. "Oh, thank you, Mr. White. Very kind of you."

Placing the three cases on the printed linoleum floor, he smiled and stood there, waiting.

"I guess I better get to unpacking a few things."

"Yes, lots to unpack. Would you like me to open the window?"

"Certainly, thanks."

"Will that be it, madam?"

"Yes, thanks again."

What was he waiting for? Money, a tip? I'd never tipped before. What was appropriate? I fumbled for my pocketbook. "Here you go." I handed him a quarter, which he looked at with disdain. I anxiously searched through my coin purse, handing him another coin, plastering on my best smile. "Mr. White, your service is simply impeccable. Good day."

Back on the bed, I leaned against the rickety headboard, put my damp handkerchief across my forehead, sighed and decided to open the newspaper I'd swiped downstairs. Hmm, where to look for a job? Flipping through the pages, I was distracted as my eye spotted an ad for a movie playing downtown: *The Gold Rush*, starring Charles Chaplin. Well, why not? For an aspiring actress needing to study acting skills, a movie theater might be the ideal place to apply for work; something to tide me over until I was discovered. Job-search completed, it was time for my nap.

CHAPTER 6

Mariah

Unlike his brothers, Sam's love of farming was more than a job; it was all he ever wanted to do. From an early age, he'd always been curious about crop rotations, more effective seed hybrids, and unique plowing techniques. He'd told me about experimenting on his dad's farm, and tinkering with machinery was his child's play. In this regard, he and his father, Alfred Anderson, shared a common passion.

With three-hundred and twenty acres, my future father-in-law owned one of the largest farms in the county, managing it with the help of Sam's three older brothers, all still living at home with their mother, Gerta, and sister, Catherine. Although he was the youngest, Sam was eager to be independent and strike out on his own. With the aid of his father, they convinced a retiring farmer to lease his farm to Sam. Once settling into it, he had managed two successful harvests, and now he only needed his recently graduated wife to join him. Together, we convinced ourselves we'd make a formidable team.

It was late May, 1928. Our wedding was a small, modest affair. For something old, I wore an antique gold locket my mother gave me. For something new, I purchased an impractical but beautiful pair of white satin pumps. For the borrowed, I wore my older sister's wedding dress; the price was right and I loved the simple bias-cut style. And for something blue, I selected a simple blue ribbon to wear around my neck adorned with the gold locket. I thought the bride's good-luck mantra was silly but I wasn't willing to test my luck on this marriage.

I walked down the aisle beaming, staring ahead to Samuel who stood confidently at the altar. I was proud of him looking so handsome in his new and only suit. As I stepped across from him, Sam, in silence, mouthed, "I love you." At that point, any nerves or doubts I was holding on to flew out the church doors. I knew I was making the right choice.

My family attended a country church surrounded by rich green fields of knee-hi corn stalks and the gravestones of family and friends who had passed. We were blessed with a dazzling, crisp, blue-skied day with a slight breeze. Between my family, the Anderson crew, a few of our closest school friends, and essential relatives, our wedding guests filled most of the pews in our Lutheran church.

After the service, everyone filled their stomachs with plates of food contributed by many of those attending, while my uncle took a few photographs of Sam and me, and our families. These formal family photos were rare, and weddings often provided the few times everybody could gather together in front of someone who owned a camera. Sam's parents, Alfred and Gerta, seemed a bit in shock after the ceremony, keeping to themselves. Their youngest and seemingly favorite son was flying from their tightly woven nest.

His mother, Gerta, gathered her brood. "Sam, get your brothers. Alfred, gather round. You too, Catherine. Let's get a family photo." She pulled her husband, crew of four sons and daughter together, but seemed to purposely exclude the new bride, while I stood off to the side waiting.

After my uncle shot the picture, his parents began walking away, as Sam spoke up. "Ma, Dad...we didn't get one including Mariah. Come on, let's do one more." Sam pulled me close; we were front and center. His mother, to our left, remained rigid and curt. Later,

Sam quietly said, "Sorry. Mother is kinda like our general; thinks she's the commanding officer. But, thank God, I've gone AWOL."

Luckily, the Anderson farm was eight miles away from our place, so I wouldn't have to look at her disappointed face daily.

As a wedding gift, Sam's parents gave us their old Model A, an exchange which seemed to miff his older brothers. My parents gave us a few dairy cows, not terribly exciting or romantic, but my dad was always the practical one. For our honeymoon, we drove the Ford thirty-five miles to the larger Minnesota town of Albert Lea where we checked into a downtown hotel for two days.

It was a weekend I'd never forget. It was the first time either of us had stayed at a hotel. It was just a simple room, with a springy double bed, a desk and chair, and a bathroom down the hall. But it was our room and our bed. We had made love before, a few rushed and secretive times in the backseat of the car, but it always felt off, like something special was missing. Now we had the luxury of lying in a comfortable double bed in private, exploring each other's bodies for hours.

As the sun came up through our hotel window, I looked over at Sam who was awake and smiling, his head propped up above two pillows. I asked, "So, after almost four years of waiting, was it worth it?"

He grabbed and kissed my hand, "So worth it. You're perfect. All I ever wanted."

From my calendar calculations, our family was started that day, and the twins came tumbling out nine months later.

CHAPTER 7

Nanette

The sound of traffic woke me with a start. A breeze blew through the short dingy curtains hanging at my hotel window. I stretched, feeling exhausted, not wanting to move. Pushing myself out of bed, I stared through the window looking out onto Front Street. The commotion seemed to be caused by cars honking at an ice-delivery wagon blocking their way. I checked my watch; it was already three o'clock and my stomach was shooting out hunger pains.

I passed a tiny round mirror hung above the dresser, and my reflection caught me by surprise. Disaster; my hair and face looked terrible. Makeup smudged, with more lipstick on my pillow than lips, and my waved bob in disarray. I opened one of my bags, pulling out a hairbrush, lipstick, powder and rouge. I needed to impress for my first possible job interview. Having slept in it, my suit was wrinkled, but it would have to do.

Walking quickly down the stairs in my new heels, I saw Mr. White checking in another guest, and hoped to exit before he noticed me. As I grabbed the front door, I heard his annoying voice. "Mrs. Jorgenson, just *now* leaving to meet your husband?

"Yes, I fell asleep. He's going to be upset; need to hurry. Will we see you this evening?"

"No, I get off at five. Good day to you." That was convenient, no elaborate lie needed for Mr. White until tomorrow.

The honking cars were now slowly going around the large ice wagon, and I saw a young delivery man walking back carrying empty ice tongs. I scurried up the sidewalk to ask him directions. It had worked for me this morning, maybe I'd get lucky again.

"Sir... sir? Any chance you know how to get to the Mankato Movie House?"

Ignoring me, he climbed onto the bench of the wagon, then pulled off a kerchief tied around his neck and wiped his tanned face. I stepped directly across from him, and asked again more loudly. "Mankato Movie House? Do you know how far?"

He stared at my face, smiled and leaned over, reaching for my hand. In a strong accent, he said. "I take." Was that an Italian accent? Whatever it was, I liked the sound.

"Well, thank you. Is it close?"

He nodded, clicked his team of four horses forward and we continued down Front Street. One block down, he stopped in front of a restaurant. Smiling again, he said, "Ice."

He went to the back of the wagon and pulled out a massive block, carrying it through the back door of the restaurant. Then he climbed up again. This continued with three more stops as the ice-man made his deliveries. He said only "ice" as he got down, but then smiled at me each time he came back. I kept sneaking side glances at him as he managed the team of horses. Strong chiseled chin, long nose, with dark curling hair showing below his hat, and biceps that bulged under a rough and soiled cotton shirt. But at the rate of his deliveries, I figured I'd be better off walking to the theater than hitching a ride with my handsome ice-man. The view was good but the conversation was limited.

After his third delivery, I explained, "I'll walk to the theater. In a bit of a hurry." As I turned to step down from the bench, he reached for my arm and said, "I take." Attractive as he was, trying to explain my needs to someone with a vocabulary of 'ice' and 'I take' was frustrating. He continued, making two more stops, finally we arrived at a building with a marque and he said, "Movie" and then pointed at me saying, "Movie star," grinning with a broad smile, as if he'd made a joke. Well, maybe there was more to this delivery man than just big biceps. His vocabulary was expanding.

I looked bashful, casting my eyes down, then pointed to myself. "Me? No, not a movie star. But maybe someday. Thanks for the ride."

As I jumped off the step, I heard, "Tomorrow, I take?"

"Maybe?" I shrugged my shoulders demurely and said, "I'm Nanette. What's your name?"

He pointed to his chest. "Romero."

Romero... it did sound Italian. We didn't have any of those in Green Tree. Dark, mysterious, strong. Very Rudolf-Valentino-like, my favorite exotic movie star.

I waved goodbye and turned toward the glass cubicle in front of the theater. An older gentleman in a burgundy uniform with gold braid was sitting inside selling tickets. I leaned into the opening. "Hello sir. I'm Nanette Jorgenson and I'd like to speak with the manager, please."

"He's inside; but I can't let you inside unless you buy a ticket."

"But I'm here on business. I want to inquire about a position."

"Far as I know, there ain't no jobs here. If you wanna to go inside, you need to buy a ticket."

I was so hungry and I'd already wasted fifty-cents on my tip to Mr. White. I certainly didn't want to pay to see a man about the mere possibility of a job.

"What's the ticket cost?"

"Twenty-five cents, miss."

"So, if I pay twenty-five cents, will the manager see me?"

"Don't know. He might be busy."

"Oh, for heaven's sake. You're running quite a racket here, sir." I dug in my purse and gave him a quarter, and walked through the lobby. Seeing an usher, I used my most authoritative tone and said, "Sir, I need to speak with the manager. It's quite urgent."

"Sure, miss." He pointed to a hallway beyond the concession stand. "Name's Mr. Grant. Just knock on the door. He should be in there."

I took a deep breath, knocked with exUberance, and heard a

high-pitched nasal voice say, "What is it now, Daniel?" I opened the door a few inches, poking my head through.

"Hello, Mr. Grant, it's not Daniel. I'm Nanette Jorgenson. Do you have a couple minutes?"

He looked at his watch as if there was a massive line of people demanding his time. "I suppose. What can I do for you?"

I sat down on a small wooden chair in front of his desk. The office was tiny, not much more than a closet, with a few movie posters tacked on the walls. Grant was a small man with pale skin and reddish thinning hair. Someone who looked like he'd stayed in a dark theater too long.

I punched up my enthusiasm level and began. "My goodness, how lucky you are to work in this fine theater surrounded by all these movie memories."

He was now flipping through the newspaper. "Uh-huh... well, let's get to it. I've got a lot on my plate today."

"It's just that the movies...they're all I dream about, really. And that's why I'm here today, Mr. Grant. I wanted to inquire about a job. I'm new to the city and this was the first place I wanted to apply. Now, some of my best skills include handling money and giving change; I'm also trustworthy, prompt, and *excellent* with customers."

"Well, you're certainly not shy; I'll give you that. Unfortunately, I have no openings. All my staff have been here a while now."

"I see." I sat for a second gathering my thoughts. "But, Mr. Grant, are they *good* at their job? Really good?"

He closed his paper, and ran his hand through his thinning hair. "I believe so, my dear."

"Does your ticket seller get customers excited about the movies you're presenting? The man selling tickets today certainly didn't seem to do that. Does the person at your concession counter always sell a drink *with* your popcorn? Does your usher keep your lobby and theater sparkling clean? If you hire me, Mr. Grant, I promise I will increase your ticket and concession sales. I'm assuming your salary is based on overall business performance?"

"That's certainly none of your business. Anyway, it's *not possible* to hire you. All of our uniforms are designed for men."

I laughed at the minor obstacle. "That's no problem. I can easily make a skirt to go with your jackets. I suggest you try me out at least part-time; you'll be impressed. If you don't see improvements and increases on the days I work, I'll turn in my uniform."

He pulled a clipboard off the wall and studied it. "I do spread myself pretty thin during some of my employees' days off, and then again, people get sick, have emergencies."

"I'm your girl, Mr. Grant; you obviously need some help here with your spotty schedule. What does the position pay?"

He looked around his desk flustered, seemingly confused at the turn the conversation was taking. "Well, I don't rightly know. Let's see... the men make forty-five-cents an hour, so, as a part-time woman, I suppose thirty-five cents?"

"I'll take the job for forty-five cents an hour and not a penny less. Remember, Mr. Grant, that will still be a bargain because I'm going to make *you* more money. Now, let's discuss my schedule."

I left fifteen minutes later, with a burgundy and gold jacket tossed over my shoulder and a job paying a fiercely negotiated forty-cents an hour, which included all the movies I cared to watch and free popcorn. I'd allowed Mr. Grant to bargain me down a nickel just to let him keep his pride. The job started in two days.

Now, time to find some inexpensive food. I was so hungry, and pie sounded especially good if my unsettled stomach would allow me to hold it down. I noticed a small café across the street. Traffic was clear at the moment. I walked quickly across with my eyes on the prize—the café showcased three different pies on a stacked pedestal. With my hungry eyes glued to the window, I accidently stepped into a massive warm pile of horse shit. The nasty scent bloomed around me as I pulled my sticky brown foot and new shoe out of the mess. Continuing across the street, I tried to scrape the excrement off my shoe onto the curb before entering, but the smell grew only stronger. I attempted to step inside, but customers at the front tables turned suddenly towards me, wrinkling their noses, looking disgusted. Backing out, I decided to return to my hotel, clean my shoe and foot, and then try a restaurant closer to where I was staying.

By the time I arrived, it was well past five o'clock so I had no fear of Mr. White being there. The smell of the shoe wasn't as bad as it had been earlier but the scent still lingered. On the front porch, I wrapped the shoe in my handkerchief and hobbled in, walking upstairs, ignoring the registration desk. A minute after I locked my door, there was loud knocking outside.

"Mrs. Jorgenson?"

Now what? I opened the door a crack. "Yes?"

A young man in white shirt sleeves stood there, clearing his throat, looking nervous. "Mrs. Jorgenson, Mr. White wanted to make sure I checked on you."

"I'm perfectly fine. Thank you for checking." I closed the door, but the knocking resumed. "What is it?" I asked through the closed door.

"Has Mr. Jorgenson arrived?" I opened the door again.

Putting on a sad face, I said, "He's been delayed, unfortunately. Long delays along the line from Chicago, apparently. Hopefully tomorrow. Thanks for asking, though." As I began to close the door, his foot crossed the threshold.

"Well, madam, in that case, I'm going to have to ask you to leave. Mr. White was quite explicit with me that you could only stay here *with* your husband."

Maybe tears? They were usually effective. "I can't believe this. It's just that I'm so exhausted, waiting at that train station for over two hours, and now you're throwing me out?" I collapsed on the bed starting to wail. "Sir, surely you can see this is not my fault and you're tossing me to the street?"

"Sorry ma'am. Rules is rules. Mr. White's the boss."

"This is absurd." I wiped my tears with my jacket sleeve. He wasn't budging, leaning against the door with his arms crossed. "Alright, it's a tacky little room anyway. Excuse me while I visit the powder room; I expect a full refund and I'll need my bags carried downstairs."

I hobbled to the bathroom taking my shitty shoe with me. Where to now? I'd suddenly hit an impasse.

CHAPTER 8

Mariah

They arrived, almost together, in our small drafty farm house.

Jo's wail broke through the tension, quiet, and cold as I envisioned Sam downstairs nervously stubbing out a cigarette, with a long stem of ash clinging to it in the bowl. He only smoked when he was nervous and I could smell the smoke snaking up the stairs. I'm sure he was glancing up the narrow wooden staircase, pensive, waiting for confirmation. Then my baby's wails were replaced by my own as I screamed out in agony once again. The waiting had been going on for hours. Samuel had chores to finish and a barn to close up, but I knew he wouldn't leave while I was upstairs in our bedroom going through this agony.

Then the room turned silent, no shrieking from me for at least a few minutes. I heard his heavy boots climbing the steep stairway to the two bedrooms at the top. He softly rapped on the door and asked, "For God's sake, how are things going in there? I'm at my wit's end waiting."

His sister, Catherine, called out, "All Good. Very busy here. Go tend to your darn cows, why don't you? It may be a while."

After hitting the door in frustration, I heard him sigh and then trudge downstairs. As I counted breaths between the next contractions, I envisioned him in the mud room, putting on his heavy belted coat, wool cap, and thick work gloves. Our cows would be ornery tonight. They didn't like to be kept waiting.

Lying back against the black iron bed, I smiled for a few brief seconds of relief, but that was broken by several waves of excruciating pain. It was hard to focus. I was hot and sticky but the bedroom air was so cold I could see Catherine's and my mother's breath coming out in small puffs. I tried panting away the sharp pains of labor, as my mom instructed. My mother, Renalda, held her new granddaughter, Jo, in a corner wooden chair, while Catherine held my hand and whispered encouragement for one more hard push.

"You can do this, Mariah. You're almost there. Remember, the pain is temporary."

It may have been temporary, but so is life. "I don't know if I can do it again. I've pushed all I can. It's more than I can bear." In anguish I called out, "My God, Ma, how could you ever do this time and again? I never realized...." Then I grabbed a damp cloth on the nightstand, putting it in my mouth as I gritted my teeth. Holding fast to Catherine's hand, I pressed down with one final, excruciating shriek as my second baby, Sarah, made her delayed entrance into the world, joining her eager twin. Even in those first few minutes, Sarah was always a few steps behind Jo.

I shuddered in relief after hours of struggle. We were truly a family now, with two daughters, both perfect to my eye. Jo, towheaded with a light sprinkling of down-like hair, and Sarah, with a thick dark shock of hair. As my mother cut and tied Sarah's cord and then bundled her up, she said, "You rest now, Mariah. You'll soon have double the work, but twice as much to love."

At that moment, an overwhelming sense of maternal duty overruled the fear that had dogged me these last few months. I'd doubted I was up for this herculean task of nurturing and raising a family, but now I felt content, amazed, fatigued, but excited by the challenge. Mother laid the twins on my chest for a moment of exhausted bliss before their weak crying commenced.

Only after cows were milked, pigs fed, and tools put away, did Sam return to the house. After removing rubber boots and washing in a pan of cold water in the kitchen sink, he walked into the small front parlor. I was lying on the short sofa, covered in a quilt, while my mother and Catherine talked softly, sitting in chairs across from the bright burning embers in the fireplace, each holding one of our beautiful daughters.

Seeing me on the sofa, Sam came directly over and knelt down. "What are you doing down here? Should you be moving so soon?"

"Shhh, you'll wake the babies. I'm fine. Catherine and Ma practically carried me down. It's just too cold upstairs. I was afraid for the babies."

"I'll bring our mattress downstairs."

"So go look!" I whispered. "Go see what we created. They're amazing."

My mother had suspected and suggested twins, but the actual confirmation was still remarkable to Sam.

He grinned widely, "So, two for the price of one! You were right, Renalda. And who do we have here?" Samuel peeked into the blanketed bundle she was holding and scooped up Sarah.

Catherine whispered, "That little dark beauty is Sarah, and I have Jo. Quiet now, Sam. They just went to sleep."

He gingerly picked up Jo as well, holding them both, and grinned down at their tiny sleeping faces. He softly spoke to us, saying, "I'm one lucky man with three beautiful girls to take care of now." It was a lot of responsibility for a young man of nineteen, but Samuel seemed to have been planning for this his entire life.

CHAPTER 9

Mariah

In late-summer, with the stove heated up, the hot still air in the small kitchen made me yearn for cold winter days. I twisted my long dark hair up in a bun, pulling it off my neck, while sweat dripped down my back. Then I scoffed, knowing in the winter we had to layer up four garments thick just to keep warm inside. Now here I was, wishing for bone-chilling winds to come blowing through. I reminded myself, count your blessings and enjoy the moment.

I checked the clock. It was 2:30, which allowed me about an hour for dinner preparation before my napping twins would wake for their feeding. Because I was still nursing, all tasks needed checking off before Jo and Sarah woke with hungry cries. I quickly rolled out a mound of lefse dough; the potato flatbread helped fill Sam's stomach that was never quite satisfied. Samuel worked so physically hard that he burned through calories like a work-horse. Between meal preparation for him, breastfeeding two demanding babies, and keeping up with my large vegetable garden, I had to squeeze in chores of laundry, dish washing, collecting eggs, and keeping an ever-growing sounder of pigs satisfied. As a fine dust blew through my screens, sweeping often ended up last on my endless to-do list.

I slid my circle of flattened lefse onto a pan on the stove top, and glanced around at my simple life. As tough and demanding as some days were, I knew we were lucky. We had a solid non-leaking roof over our heads, a round pine table with four sturdy chairs surrounding it, and a linoleum floor in a pretty floral pattern which Sam had installed as an early wedding gift. As a young married couple, we understood there was time down the road to accumulate better furniture, maybe a heating system, and in time, hire some household help. Perhaps it wasn't the life I'd dreamed of, but I was with a man I loved fiercely. We had two thriving daughters, and a rented home we thought of as ours.

As the lefse baked, Samuel surprised me, poking his head in the window, as beads of sweat streaked through a layer of dust across his face. "Hey there, how you doing, beautiful?"

I smiled back, pushing strands of hair out of my face. "Not feeling very beautiful; just rushing to get some dinner started."

"Good, and set a few extra places. David and Billy-Boy, from the Thomas farm, are helping me with the pump. OK if I invited them?"

"Don't know what I have to feed the three of you, but I'll find something."

Then, from upstairs, the crying commenced.

That evening around seven, our neighbors had left and the twins' final feeding was done. Samuel was in his usual spot, sitting in the brown upholstered chair reading his newspaper from the light of an overhead oil lamp. I was bone-tired, sitting in my rocker, and leaned over to set Sarah down on a blanket.

"Well, that's done for the night. These two are wearing me out, Sam."

He looked at me, peeking over his paper. "Well, I hope you're eating enough. I honestly don't know how you do it."

I shrugged at his concern. "I'll be fine, but just look at these two. I sat back and watched, amazed at their eight-month growth. After a few minutes I announced, "Well, I'm putting these little ladies to bed. Want to say good night with me?" I glanced at Sam but his head was already beginning to nod, dozing off after his tiring day. "Never mind," I whispered to the girls, as I climbed up the steep stairway. "Your Daddy worked hard today. I'll say good night for both of us."

I would have to supplement their feeding soon. Like Sam said, I needed to keep up my strength to hold the house together. We were a two-person company, committed to keeping our fragile and fickle business functioning and profitable. Our farm was one-hundred-and-sixty acres of rich blue-black Iowa soil. Lars rented both the acreage and house to us. We planted and harvested the crops, with fifty percent of the profits going back to Lars. Any improvements we added to outlying buildings and livestock were our responsibility, but we also got to keep those profits. The few dollars our egg and dairy money earned each week was precious and used as credit toward other needed staples. The occasional slaughtered swine or cow was also a big boost to our monthly earnings, and kept us fed with a steady supply of smoked meat.

I assumed, one day, we'd buy the farm, but for now we scrimped by. Married for less than two years, Sam and I had already worked through several challenges. After learning how to balance our books, I'd learned so much about the perils and success of a farmer's tenuous budget.

Although we both had extended family throughout the county, there were some days I felt so alone, as if it were Sam and I against the world and all it could throw at us. With no phone and miles between family members, it could feel isolating. I still thought about what it might be like living in a bigger city, working independently, but I knew those thoughts were now only silly dreams. I was a fully committed wife and mother and there was no going back.

After putting the girls down for the night, I came downstairs and saw Sam awake again, checking the sports page. "They went right to sleep, thank goodness. Let's see if I can find some music."

Sam nodded. "Sounds good."

Like most farms in the area, we had no electricity, but Sam had recently purchased a large battery-operated radio for fifty-five dollars on credit. I admonished him for his reckless spending but reveled in this connection to the world. Both he and I would dial through the static most evenings, eventually tuning into programs broadcast primarily from Des Moines or Minneapolis. Our new prized possession was placed on a square table between my wooden rocker and the armchair. Samuel often dialed into baseball games and I loved listening to the comedy shows like *Fibber Magee and Molly*. In the evening, as the darkness of the surrounding acreage closed in around us, we'd put tasks to the side briefly, as we tuned in, imagining the faces of entertainers we listened to each night.

After an hour, Samuel stood up and stretched, picked up a lantern and said, "Well, that bathroom isn't going to build itself. I'll get a little more framing done before I go to bed." The indoor bathroom, a rarity among farms, was going to be another of his generous gifts for me. We were building it as an extension off the mud room in the back. I got up reluctantly and sighed. "I'll help. It'll be so worth it in the end." We joined in together for one more hour of labor.

By October, the last of the preserves had been squirreled away in the cellar, our corn harvest had been excellent, and my garden was sputtering out the last of the fall produce. Our newest joy was our completed bathroom, with water piped in from our windmill tank. The simple room, with tub and toilet, was glorious and the envy of most of our neighbors, still using outhouses. Sam had purchased the needed tools, lumber and supplies from his uncle's hardware store and was paying him back in small monthly installments. I allowed myself a weekly guilty pleasure, luxuriating in a hot Friday evening bath, as Samuel looked after the girls.

Tuesday evening, while I was shutting windows in the front room, Sam said, "Special news, Mariah. Best listen for a minute." A news report was interrupting the *Amos 'n Andy* show. Static crackled through the room, followed by beeps, then the deep and serious voice of a newscaster came through clearly.

"We interrupt this program to report today's dramatic market sell-off on Wall Street in New York, with stock prices tumbling to record lows after several years of unprecedented highs with frenzied trading.Thousands of

Americans, from wealthy tycoons to poor widows, have lost their savings, and today, eleven high-flying financiers committed suicide, reacting to the downward spiral of the market." The announcer went on for several more minutes relaying the shocking news, calling it, 'Black Tuesday.'

"Oh my God, Sam. That's devastating. I had no idea the stock markets were so unstable. And those poor men...jumping out of windows. Can you imagine feeling so desperate? And to think, I used to dream about moving to Manhattan."

He shook his head, remaining silent for a few seconds. "Sounds terrible. Shocking news. But keep in mind, Mariah, we're in farming. It's necessary, steady work. Be thankful we'll be safe from all that big-city banking business."

I naively nodded my head in agreement.

Made in the USA
Coppell, TX
26 December 2023

26856263R00223